Sam Pfiester's strong sense of geology and the oil business, and his love of Mexico and its history, weave a magnificent story that captures the events and the real-life characters of the 1910 Tampico Oil Boom. *The Golden Lane Faja de Oro* portrays the essence of the developing oil field, the Mexican Revolution, and the need for oil as it affected the United States, England, and Germany prior to World War I. I couldn't put the book down.

Clayton W. "Claytie" Williams
Oilman/Wildcatter

THE
GOLDEN
LANE
Faja de Oro

SAM L. PFIESTER

Published by Chengalera Press
ISBN-13 9781503387799
ISBN-10 1503387798

Library of Congress Catalog Card Number
United States Copyright Office registration No. TXu 1-712-037

Cover design by Lynn Rohm

Photographs and maps courtesy of DeGolyer Library,
Southern Methodist University, Dallas, Texas Mss 60

Additional books by the author:
    The Perfect War (by Sam Lee)

To order books: write
    Chengalera Press
    P.O. Box 688
    Georgetown, Texas 78627
    or
    see webpage: **www.thegoldenlane.com**

ACKNOWLEDGEMENTS

Although not a geologist himself, the author has spent much of his career working with petroleum geologists, an exceptional group of men and women who believe, really believe, that they can visualize the subsurface, that they can comprehend what has been long buried, and not just as the sedimentary section is today, but as it was deposited millions upon millions of years ago and how, in the subsequent millennia, it has been buried, transported, warped, eroded, re-deposited, altered by pressure, high temperatures, hot water and all the forces of nature that in geologic time have affected the rocks through which they send the drill bit in search of…in search of what? The short answer is in search of oil and natural gas, preferably in commercial quantities, an answer that is somewhat disingenuous. A more complete explanation might be in search of the satisfaction that comes from unraveling a four-dimensional geologic puzzle as proof that they have indeed comprehended the subsurface.

Many geologists contributed to the geologic understanding upon which this book is based. Among those, in no order of eminence, are my particular friends Eugene Brumbaugh, Steve Walkinshaw, Doug Middleton, Dave Gruber, Lars Johnson, John Kullman, and Tom Swinbank. I thank them for the many patient lessons they have tendered over the years. Another observation about geologists in general, and about the above-mentioned specifically, is that they are individualistic, creative, self-confident, opinionated, quirky, at times cantankerous, and unfailingly humorous. Perhaps a sense of humor is essential when much of your life's work ends as a dry hole.

In researching the book, the assistance of the following persons was helpful and much appreciated: Dr. Russell L. Martin III and the staff of the DeGolyer Library at Southern Methodist University; research assistants at the Benson Latin American Collection at the University of Texas Austin; and research assistants at the American Heritage Center at the University of Wyoming. Highest kudos are extended to Dr. Jonathan C. Brown of the University of Texas, whose book *Oil and Revolution* was the most important source for an overview of the era. For those readers interested in pursuing the topic in greater depth, Dr. Brown's book is essential. I also wish to thank Josephine Engels, who assisted with the research.

Additionally I thank those who reviewed the manuscript with an eye for accuracy and recommendations for improvement. Deep appreciation is extended to Dr. Walter Herbert, retired chairman of the Department of English at Southwestern University; to Suzanne O'Bryan, author of four books and friend for four decades; and to Peter Maxson, grandson of Everette DeGolyer. Most of all I wish to thank Steven L. Davis, whose guiding hand shaped the book into a novel instead of a research paper. And finally, I thank my bride, Rebecca Kauffman Pfiester, for her forbearance and encouragement, and for forty years of good times.

A few years ago the author attended a geological field trip sponsored by the American Association of Petroleum Geologists to an area south of Tampico where the book takes place, with the purpose of examining the sedimentation and diagenesis of middle-Cretaceous platform margins. It was then that I was introduced to the highly productive oil fields known as *The Golden Lane*. Sitting in an outdoor bar in the city of Valles, I first learned of Everette DeGolyer's involvement in the Golden Lane and made the decision to research DeGolyer's early career as one of the pioneers of the oil industry.

Today our industry is blessed with, and sometimes overwrought by, a vast profusion of subsurface data. Hundreds of thousands of electric logs are available to map the subsurface. Three dimensional seismic data, core studies, research papers, and technological advancements of many kinds have multiplied our understanding of the subsurface in ways unimaginable to the early pioneers.

Which raises the question: with such a paucity of data, how did those early pioneers map the subsurface? How did they unravel the geologic puzzle of source, trap, reservoir rock, and timing? I hope this book will at least partially answer the question.

Sam L. Pfiester

The Golden Lane is written in the genre of historical fiction, but is more historical than fictional. All of the characters were real people. Except for minor grammatical or spelling corrections, all of the letters, reports, poems, cablegrams, and Reports to Congress are actual and unedited. If a paragraph is indented, it is authentic. Most of the events actually happened.

Beds of rock are the successive pages of a book that record ancient time: a stone diary that tells of life vanished, of the endless cycles of climate change, and of the hidden poetry of our mutable earth.

Richard Fortey
Life: A Natural History of the First Four Billion Years

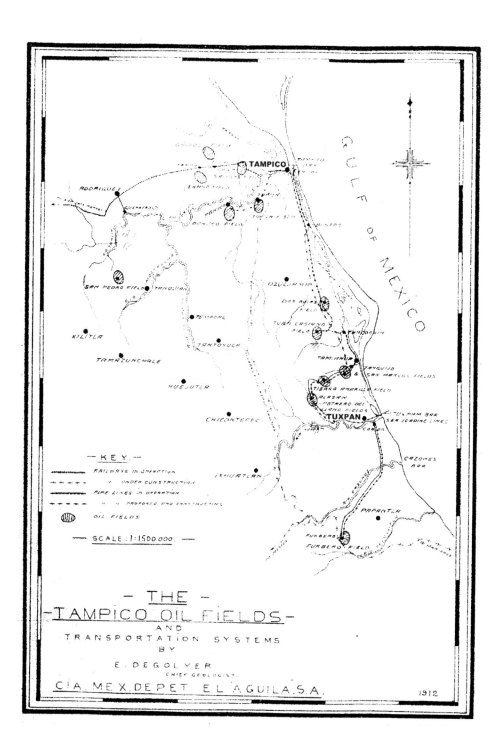

- THE -
-TAMPICO OIL FIELDS-
AND
TRANSPORTATION SYSTEMS
BY
E. DEGOLYER
CHIEF GEOLOGIST
CIA. MEX. DE PET. EL AGUILA. S.A.

1912

February 1971

"Yep, he found oil and lots of it."

The man asking the questions said he was writing a biography of Everette DeGolyer, gone these fifteen years. "You're talking more than sixty years ago," Jim Hall said. *"Sic tempus fugit."*

"When I first met DeGolyer? In 1909 I think it was, in the train station in Nuevo Laredo, Mexico. He looked like he hadn't been weaned, wore a bow tie and knickers, dressed like he was going on a picnic."

"His personality? He was likeable. He enjoyed a good cigar. Is that a personality trait? Mainly he was curious. There wasn't a thing living or dead, buried, moving, or sitting still that he wasn't curious about. It's contagious, you know, kind of like the flu. You hang around a man as curious as him, and it'll rub off. Pretty soon you'll be asking questions yourself."

"Mexico in the oil boom, oh yes, it was rough times and a rough crowd. You never saw so many men scrambling for a buck, throwing money around like it was cow poop, fighting, swearing, whoring."

"The Mexican Revolution? They called it a social revolution. Wasn't a thing social about it. Mexicans killing Mexicans by the thousands. You had to be careful of stray bullets, too."

"Can you imagine a world before cars? Well, there weren't any when De and I got to Tampico. Henry Ford had just invented the Model T."

"Yes, oil put Mexico on the map, it sure enough did. We found so much oil other countries sent their battleships to Tampico."

"Why send battleships to a third world fishing village? American, British, Dutch, German -- they all had battleships anchored right there three miles from shore in water that wasn't forty feet deep."

"To keep the oil flowing, that's why. Ever since the Tampico oil boom, countries have been dependent on foreign crude. It all started at Tampico."

Chapter One

October — November 1909

Washington, D.C.
October 29, 1909

Sweetheart Woman:
A very wonderful thing has happened. I am to go to Mexico in three weeks. Having now delivered the most burdensome part of my message, I'll tell you all about it. Dr. Hayes, head of the United States Geological Survey, is also in charge of the exploratory work for an English syndicate which is prospecting for oil in Mexico. There are two men whom I worked with in Montana for the U.S.G.S who are in Mexico now. One is Hop and the other is Mr. Washburne. I am to be the third. My salary is to be $1800 per year in gold and all field expenses. I do not know what the length of the contract is to be. Hop's is for a year and I rather think that mine is to be for a year, too.

This plays sad havoc with our plans but new ones can be made and after all, this offers the one big thing I would desire to have come quickly in my work; that is, a chance to do private work. Also I will report directly to one of the leading geologists in the United States. It's one chance in a thousand for a youngster. What means more though dear, it's giving a financial chance for you and me. It's giving us a dandy start in life. Eighteen hundred is quite an advance from one thousand and eighty. I am also to receive a two year furlough from the U.S.G.S. so that I can return to it as soon as the Mexican work is finished.

Now for the thing of immediate interest: I do not know how Dr. Hayes is going to want to send me but I do know this. I'm coming through Norman or there will be lots of trouble. I hope to be with you Thanksgiving for a week or less. I hope for a week but I fear it will be less for Dr. Hayes is impatient for me to take to the field. I am finishing my work here mapping what we looked at in the field last summer near Crested Butte.

This cooks my chances of finishing college this year but, dear, this is a chance of a lifetime. You told me once that you were going to have to have hope for the DeGolyer family, and maybe the college degree, too. But my dear, I'm going to do the work for that family. Dear, if I can only be in Norman two days, I must have every moment of your time. You won't even be allowed to sleep or teach because this is to be an awfully long trip into an awfully strange land.

Now dear, about the picture I asked you to have made, I'll bet fourteen dollars you have been putting it off. Please have it done soon for I expect to see you in about three weeks. Just think of that. Isn't three weeks wonderfully short?

Girl, girl, woman love, we are going to have to decide some very, very important things just as soon as I see you. In view of the fact that it is to be so soon, I'm going to wait until I see you to tell you about the rose kiss memories.

Dearest woman, I'm so excited and glad: glad because it is for you, glad because I am finally reaching a point in my work where asking you to quit yours for me is not such an injustice to you.

You are my white rose love and I send you a warm red rose kiss. It will have to suffice until my lips and love can reach you.

Your man, Everette

"Tamaulipas," repeated the young man. "Tam-Au-Lee-Pus. *¿Sabe?*"

The clerk behind the iron grill shook his head. "Mexico. *De aquí, solo a Mexico. No puede ir a Tamaulipas de aquí*".

"Do you speak English?" sighed the young man. The train station was packed with people shuffling and milling. Above the crowd's rumble he could hear the train's exhalation of steam through doorways leading to the onload ramps. A long line of people stood behind him.

"I need to go to Tampico, Tamaulipas."

"No to Tampico. Here to Mexico."

"This is Mexico. *Aquí* Mexico. I'm *in* Nuevo Laredo, Mexico, yes?"

"*Sí*," said the clerk.

De looked over his shoulder at the waiting line. "Okay. Mexico. Give me a ticket to Mexico. How much for a ticket to Mexico?" He held up his money clip. "How much?"

The clerk wrote on a slip of paper the number of pesos. De took off his rucksack, removed a small book, thumbed to the currency exchange scale, calculated the fare and the exchange rate, and passed the dollars under the grill. The clerk rubbed the money between his thumb and forefinger, looked at a chart, and dipped his head in agreement. He passed a ticket back under the grill: *Noviembre* 19,1909, *llega a Mexico*.

"To Mexico, yes?"

"*Sí.*"

De took the ticket and placed it in his shirt pocket. As he pulled on the rucksack, he glanced above the clerk at the portrait of Porfirio Díaz, president of Mexico, towering over the crowded waiting room in uniformed splendor, his chest adorned with campaign medals. De picked up the suitcase and the heavy duffle bag, and began steering his way through the crowd. When he rounded a bench his duffle bag bumped into a pair of scuffed cowboy boots extending into the pathway. De looked up at an unshaved face under a soiled Stetson.

"Looks to me like you need some help," said the man. "I'm getting a hernia just watching you lug that thing around. What do you got in there, rocks?"

"I'm sorry. I can get it, though. Thanks, anyway," said De.

"I know you can get it. Here, put her under this bench and take a seat. The train ain't leaving for another two or three hours."

"The schedule says we will board in twenty minutes."

"Yep, that's what the schedule says."

They shoved the duffle bag under the bench. The young cowboy pushed his sweat-stained hat back on his head, revealing red curls, and extended a hand.

"My name's Jim Hall," he said. "Just call me Jim."

De shook the hand. "Everette DeGolyer. Just call me De."

"My pleasure, De. What brings a fellow like you to Mexico?"

"I'm trying to get to Tampico, Tamaulipas."

"To the oil fields?"

"Yes."

"Fancy that. Me, too."

De looked at Jim's freckled, sunburned face. He figured Jim couldn't be much older than himself. "Are you headed to a job?" De asked.

"I've been cowboying in South Texas. When I heard about money pouring out of the ground down there in the oil fields, chasing cattle through chaparral lost its flavor."

"I thought cowboys wouldn't do anything else."

"Not this one, no sir," replied Jim. "The only folks that make money in the cow business are the ones that own the land. How do you think a dollar-a-day cowboy can ever own land? To make money you got to go where the money flows, which ain't chasing the south end of a steer headed north."

"You think the oil field is the place?" De asked as he removed his rucksack and sat down beside Jim.

"*¿Quién sabe?* Who knows? But I do know you got to go where the money flows. A lot of fellows had rather sit in a saddle the rest of their life rather than stand on the ground and pick up dollar bills, but not me. Now, what is a fellow like you doing headed to the oil fields? In this crowd, those knickers you're wearing stand out like a run-over rooster."

De looked down at his leather leggings. "Do you speak Spanish?" he asked.

"I sure do. You learn to *habla español* if you grow up in South Texas."

"Let me ask you something," said De. "When I bought my ticket, I tried to purchase one to Tamaulipas, but the clerk said I could only buy a ticket to Mexico. This *is* Mexico. What was he saying?"

"Ha! Sure, this is Mexico. But down here they call the capital city 'Mexico.' This train is the Montezuma Express that ends up in Mexico City. You have to switch trains in Monterrey to go to Tamaulipas."

"I see," said De, noting that he had purchased a ticket all the way to Mexico City.

"De, it sounds to me like you could use a good interpreter," said Jim. "If you don't speak the lingo, these folks will skin you alive. One look at those knickers and that bow tie and they'll be crossing themselves and saying *gracias* to God and *adios* to poverty."

"Thanks for the offer, but all I need is to get to Tampico, Tamaulipas. I've got a job there."

"If you had stayed aboard the train until it rolled into Mexico City, you'd think twice about needing an interpreter. What kind of job do you have lined up?"

De looked closer at Jim. He wore a faded Levi jacket. His only luggage was a small handbag. "Geologist," answered De.

"I thought geologists prospected for gold."

"For oil, too."

"Well, geologists need interpreters, not to mention somebody to lug that duffle bag around. It's more than a one-man job."

De smiled. "What do *you* intend to do when you get to Tamaulipas?"

"*¿Quien sabe?* I don't have anything *specifically* in mind. Maybe work on the rigs. I'm serious about being an interpreter. I speak Spanish *poco bueno*. Maybe some geologist will want to find his way across town without getting robbed. Or I could go into security. With money rolling around, somebody will need a payroll guard. I'll do nearly anything this side of legal."

"I'll introduce you to the people I'm working with," offered De. "They may need some hands."

"I'd be grateful," Jim said appreciatively. "Who is it you'll be working for?"

"I've been hired by El Aguila, an English oil company."

"How in the world did an English oil company get into the Mexican oil play?" asked Jim.

"The owner of El Aguila was right here in the Nuevo Laredo train station eight years ago when he heard about the Spindletop strike. At the time he was building a railroad across the Isthmus of Tehuantepec. He was hoping to find fuel for the locomotives, so he hired a team of English scientists and started drilling. Good idea, but not much luck."

"And what got him to Tampico? Is he building a railroad there?"

"He was following the lead of a fellow from California by the name of Edward Doheny, who was drilling near oil seeps west of Tampico."

"Drilling near oil seeps? Who needs a geologist if you just drill near a seep?"

"That's exactly what El Aguila did, but the wells were all dry holes or poor producers. Nobody found much until The Pennsylvania Company drilled the Dos Bocas well last year."

"Is that the well that made all the newspapers?" asked Jim.

"That's the one. It blew out and caught fire and burned for weeks. I wouldn't be here without Dos Bocas."

"I heard about the Dos Bocas well. It must have whetted your Englishman's appetite."

"Whetted his appetite for results. This past summer he let go all his English scientists and hired an American team."

"Sounds to me like the American team had better find him some oil *pronto*."

De nodded in concurrence.

"How old are you?" asked Jim. "You look to be about twelve."

"I turned twenty-three last month."

"Lordy, I'm only twenty-four," said Jim. He grinned, turned up his palms and spread his arms, showing off his dusty and threadbare clothes. "Is it my clean living that makes me look so much older?"

De laughed. "Maybe it's your pants. Have you thought about buying some knickers?"

Jim slapped his jeans and laughed. "No knickers for me. Well, it's a pleasure to meet you, De. I'll take you up on the offer to meet your *jefes* in Tampico. Now give me your train ticket. I'll straighten it out so you don't have to detour through Mexico City."

Chapter Two

November 1909

Four hours later the whistle blew, the train exhaled a huge cloud of steam and the steel wheels screeched forward in slow motion. De looked out the window at the milling crowd. Off to Tampico. He smiled to himself and wondered where the journey would lead. Who knows? *¿Quien sabe?* He liked Jim's expression.

De wished Nell was with him. He had signed on with El Aguila for only one year. After twelve months he intended to return to the Geological Survey or maybe to work for himself, but wherever he was, he was determined to ask Nell to marry him, even though she told him last month he must first complete his university degree.

The trip to Tampico took two days. The train stopped every few hours to take on water or coal and passengers or cargo. As he observed the passing desert landscape and the people at every siding, nothing about Mexico reminded De of Oklahoma. It was a poorer country, the grass was short, the cattle thin, the dogs wormy. Most peasants were short like himself, but were squatty and dark-complexioned. Many draped blankets over their shoulders and wore handmade sandals. Some of the women wore dresses stitched with colorful geometric patterns and swaddled babies tightly on their backs to free their hands for offering food or wood-carved toys for the passengers to buy. None laughed or even smiled. De wondered if their seriousness reflected their poverty. At larger towns men attired in suits and ties and bowler hats boarded the train, their western dress in sharp contrast to the peasants.

Jim had taken up a seat across from De for the long journey and told him it was a class society. In Mexico, Jim explained, the upper crust owned the land, and everyone else scratched for a living.

"Does Mexico have free public education?" asked De.

"Some towns have schools, but most of the peasants and their kids work.

They can't read or write."

De reflected on the consequences. Without an education he would probably be breaking sod in Kansas, or still working at his father's restaurant.

"How in the world did you connect up with an Englishman?" Jim asked. "Did you meet him in Oklahoma?"

"His name is Weetman Pearson, but he goes by Lord Cowdray. It was an odd connection. When Dos Bocas blew out, Dr. Williard Hayes, the head of the United States Geological Survey, went to Tampico to check out the well. While he was there, Dr. Hayes met Lord Cowdray."

"So you know Dr. Hayes?"

"I met Dr. Hayes in Montana."

"What were you doing in Montana? That's cow country."

"I was working for the Geological Survey." De explained how he and two other geological assistants had traveled by covered wagon and horseback up in the mountains of Colorado, Wyoming, and Montana, mapping the surface outcrops as a way to understand the geology.

"How did you find a job with the Geological Survey?"

"I was the short-order cook at my dad's restaurant in Norman, Oklahoma, home of the University of Oklahoma. Professor Charles Gould, who runs the geology department at the university, ate lunch at my dad's restaurant. Professor Gould liked my biscuits, so he recommended me to cook for one of the Geological Survey summer field trips."

"You got hired because you cook good biscuits?"

"The first year I was the cook, but the last three summers I was a geological field assistant. I met Dr. Hayes when he visited our camp in Montana."

"And when your Lord Cowdray asked Dr. Hayes to put an American team together, you were part of it."

"Me and two other fellows who are already in Tampico."

"Have you drilled any oil wells?" Jim asked.

"Never in my life. Dr. Hayes recommended me to Lord Cowdray to map the geology, and here I am, headed to Tamaulipas."

"You mean headed to Mexico City," teased Jim with a smile.

"I like traipsing around on rock outcrops trying to figure out how the geology fits together. Petroleum geology hasn't been around too many years. There's a lot left to learn. So the door opened, and I walked through."

"A door opened and you walked through. And it all started because you cook good biscuits."

"That's my story," said De. "What about yours?"

"Not quite as entertaining," replied Jim. "I was born in Missouri and raised on a small spread in South Texas. When I was eleven, my father took me to Mexico City for a few months where I picked up the language. When we got back to Texas I quit school and started cowboying, which ain't as romantic as the books say."

"The oil business may not be romantic either."

"I'm not chasing romance. I'm chasing fame and fortune."

Approaching the mountains near Monterrey, De observed overturned bedding in the carbonates. He wondered if the forces that caused the folding were the same that had warped and folded similarly-aged rocks he had mapped in Wyoming and Montana. He speculated both were caused by the same event, which must have been continental in scale to create the Rocky Mountains and its southern extension here in the Sierra Madre Occidental.

In the early light of dawn he and Jim switched trains in the mountain-shadowed town of Monterrey. From there the track skirted the eastern foot of the Sierra Madre Oriental until it reached Victoria, the capital of the state of Tamaulipas, where the track struck boldly across the great semi-arid plain lying between the Sierra Madre and Sierra de Tamaulipas. During the train trip Jim kept De entertained with tales of ranching in South Texas. De asked Jim questions about the Mexican culture and history. He was curious about this strange new land.

"Jim, this country doesn't grow much grass," De said as he gazed out the passenger window. The train had traversed miles of parched ranchland broken only by a few stone fences that followed straight lines to distant horizons, testaments to thousands of hours of back-breaking labor.

"It ain't all that different from South Texas," said Jim. "Mesquite country. You need cattle that don't mind a long walk between water and grass."

Gradually the landscape transitioned from Chihuahuan desert cactus and creosote scrubland to open grasslands. On the afternoon of the second day the train traversed a shrub-covered plateau, which gave way to a flat coastal plain where muddy rivers and swamps interspersed a dense jungle.

Just before sunset the train arrived at the Tampico rail station, a covered platform adjacent to a canal. Half the town turned out to witness the train's arrival. People milled and shouted and waved at passengers as it rolled to a stop, blowing its whistle and expelling steam through the crowded landing. De looked across a trestle bridge that spanned the canal to a large plaza. When he stepped out of the passenger car, several *cargadores* offered to carry his bags.

Among the milling people De recognized a familiar face standing above the crowd. De waved to the man, looked back at Jim and motioned for him to follow.

"Hop!" De shouted to his friend. "Hop, over here." The tall young man waved in recognition, and pushed through the crowd to greet De. The two friends shook hands warmly.

"Hop, only four months ago we were in Colorado and now here we are in Mexico," De said above the din. "Quite a change, isn't it?"

De introduced Jim. "Jim and I rode on the train together. He's looking for fame and fortune in the oil fields. Jim, this is Ed Hopkins." Seeing another familiar face in the crowd, De shouted, "Hey, Chester!" A second young man elbowed his way to the group of Americans. "And Jim," De said, "this is Chester Washburne."

"Nice meeting you boys," said Jim, extending his hand and smiling broadly. "It feels like homecoming."

"We all worked together with the USGS in the Rockies," explained Hop. "Come on, De, you and Jim follow us. We have a carriage waiting on the bridge. Let those fellows grab your bags."

"What in the world is in the duffle bag?" asked Chester when he saw two cargadores struggling to load it in the carriage.

"It's all my field gear," answered De. "I was worried El Aguila wouldn't provide us with surveying equipment so I brought my own tripod and plane table. By the looks of the jungle, I might be using it for a picnic table. Jim, come along and join us for supper. Tomorrow we'll line you up for an interview."

"Sounds good to me, De. I've never had an interview in my life, but I do know how to chow down the chili peppers."

The four young men jostled through the crowd to a horse-drawn cart on the bridge. From there it was only a short distance across the canal to the plaza, the Plaza de la Independencia. Two and three-story white-plastered buildings with cast iron balconies lined the plaza. The air smelled to De of the nearby lagoon and of unfamiliar tropical scents.

"There are only a few foreigners here," explained Hop as the horse lumbered toward the plaza, "mainly Americans with Huasteca Petroleum and a few English and Scotsmen with El Aguila. When Dos Bocas blew out last year, they said lease hounds from the States showed up like mushrooms after a fire. When the well went to salt water the boom went bust before it got off to a good start. Since then Tampico has reverted back to a fishing village. At least we offer a couple of good hotels."

"Have you looked at the surface geology?" asked De. "How can we map rock outcrops if they're covered by a jungle?"

"Good question and there's no easy answer," replied Hop. "The Brits stuck close to oil seeps, but without much success. You're right about mapping outcrops and bedding, though. They're hard to come by in a jungle. Too bad the play isn't near Monterrey. Did you see the beautiful folding in the carbonates?"

"It reminded me of Wyoming," acknowledged De. "Has any significant oil production been found except for Dos Bocas?"

"Huasteca Petroleum has been drilling wells for several years west of here at El Ebano, all poor wells, maybe a barrel or two per day, and one good well."

"Is Huasteca Edward Doheny's company?" asked De.

"Yes," said Hop. "Doheny came down here eight years ago and nearly went broke before one decent well finally came in. Huasteca wells at El Ebano are low gravity, high sulfur crude. It's so viscous it won't flow through a pipeline. They use it for asphalt to pave streets in Mexico City and Guadalajara."

While his newfound friends were discussing geology, Jim watched the activity around the plaza. It reminded him of other plazas in Mexico. He liked the feel of Tampico.

"Has El Aguila found anything worthwhile?" asked De.

"El Aguila has had even less success than Huasteca," said Hop. "We had an interest in Dos Bocas, but that was a costly disaster. We bought a field from an Englishman, Percy Furber, about a hundred miles south of here, but so far the best well makes maybe 200 barrels a day. Except for the Dos Bocas blowout last year, there have been no high flow rates in the entire region. Mostly El Aguila has drilled dry holes."

"Dos Bocas was probably a fluke," said Chester. "After ten years of drilling in this country, one well blows out and they think it's another Spindletop."

"Dr. Hayes convinced Lord Cowdray that geologists trained in the U.S. understand better than Brits how, why, and where oil is trapped," continued Hop. "After twenty or so wildcats and not much to show for it, the Englishmen are out and we're in."

"Well, we'll see," said De, "maybe Dos Bocas *wasn't* a fluke."

"If any significant oil was here, somebody would have stumbled into something better than what has been found so far," repeated Chester. "This barnyard has been scratched. We'll have a year to give it a try and then we'll all be headed back to the States."

"Chester," said Jim, "You're raising my hopes of finding fame and fortune down here in the oil fields. What makes you such an optimist?"

De laughed. He and Hop had spent two summers in the Rockies with Chester and they were accustomed to Chester's negative streak. De looked around at the activity in the plaza. Vendors held up packets of candies, chewing gum, leather wallets, and purses to the newly-arrived passengers. The horse pulling their carriage must have been half blind and stone deaf because it did not shy when a Mexican youth ran underneath its belly to cross the street.

"What's that smell?" asked De. "Is it perfume?"

Jim spotted a vendor carrying a bouquet of flowers. "Gardenias," he said, pointing to the white flowers.

"What a wonderful scent!" exclaimed De as the carriage pulled to a stop in front of the Southern Hotel. An American flag waved gently from a pole on its roof. Hop explained that the hotel was the gathering place for foreigners traveling to Tampico.

"Glad you joined us, De," said Hop after he and Jim were checked in. "Chester is right. We need to find Lord Cowdray some good production pronto, or else Tampico will be a short tour."

"We'll know soon enough if Dos Bocas was a fluke," responded De confidently. "*¿Quien sabe?*" He liked Jim's phrase. "*¿Quien sabe?*" he repeated.

The next morning Hop and Chester introduced De and Jim to John Body, El Aguila's Scottish general manager from the company headquarters in Mexico City. Mr. Body agreed to hire Jim Hall on a trial basis as an interpreter. El Aguila offered no accommodations, he told De and Jim, so they were quartered in the Southern Hotel. Mr. Body gave them a day to settle in and look over the town.

"I can't tell you how grateful I am for the job," Jim told De. They were sitting on the porch of the hotel sipping dark, pungent coffee while watching the swarm of activity around them.

"If Mr. Body didn't need a hand, he wouldn't have hired you," replied De. "Would you look at this scene?" and he pointed across the plaza.

Three sides of the plaza housed businesses, stores, and offices. On the south side of the plaza toward the Gulf, the Chijol Canal separated the plaza and market from the customs house, wharves and railway station.

Launches from the oil camps, boats from nearby towns, sailboats and power barges from villages along the Tamiahua Lagoon filled the congested canal. Canoes laden with bananas, oranges, corn, charcoal, and garden truck were poled by dark-skinned *indios* to the docking steps on the plaza. Dugouts brought fresh fish and oysters from La Barra, dried shrimp from the lagoons, clay pots and cloth from the *serrania* of Puebla that had been transferred from mule trains to canoes on the Panuco and Tamesi Rivers.

Vendors grouped together on the plaza by products and wares, one aisle chiefly occupied by dealers of cloth, clothing and accessories. Another aisle had grocers peddling fish, fruits, and vegetables. In one corner of the market pottery vendors hawked their wares; in another, corn merchants sold white corn from great square bins, measured in cedar boxes. Poultry dealers were relegated to the back of the market where their chickens, turkeys, and guineas squawked in raucous cacophony.

It looked to De that marketing was a business of much pawing and prodding. Housewives, each with her servant or boy carrying empty baskets, walked from booth to booth, picking over the piles of food. Vegetables and fruits were tested for firmness. Meat, fish, and eggs were lifted and held to the nose.

Chester and Hop joined De and Jim as they strolled through the market.

When asked about the bargaining, Hop explained that in Mexico *caveat emptor* ruled in all transactions, a fact recognized by the buyers as well as the sellers, who, on their part suspiciously bounced coins they received on the counter to see if they rang true.

"What's *caveat emptor?*" asked Jim. "Is that what we call horse trading?"

"It means 'buyer beware,'" said Hop.

"Hop was educated at Cornell," Chester told Jim. "Don't mind his Latin."

"I don't mind it," said Jim. "You boss men don't speak Spanish. I don't speak Latin. We'll see who can buy the bananas."

An overflow market on Calle Ribera just around the corner from the main market was also lively with merchandising. Vendors sold women's wares, hand-woven lace, perfumes, and powders spread on mats under the arcade. Mats piled with nails, staples, hinges, and screws provided sundry new and used hardware. When they walked past the aisles of spice vendors, De smelled garlic and ginger, and delighted in seeing the colorful peppers, bright-yellow chili spices, and various poultices for any ailment.

Across the street under a great open shed stood rows of tables, each comanded by a proprietress who was cooking in pots over glowing charcoal. This was the market's food court, which smelled of spicy aromas and hummed with business.

"Hop, are they selling tobacco there?" asked De, pointing to a booth where full-size tobacco leaves were draped over stretched cotton lines and several varieties of leaves rolled into cigars or crushed and in small boxes were displayed in bins. The smell of cured tobacco was pleasing.

"It sure is," answered Hop. "Shall we buy some?"

"Remember when you got me chewing tobacco at the summer field camp in Wyoming?" asked De. "Now it's my turn to pay you back." He entered the booth. "Let's give these cigars a try." He asked Jim to negotiate the purchase for two dozen. Jim wrangled with the vendor a few minutes, made the deal and told De how many pesos. De paid, picked up a cigar, rolled it under his nose, licked one end, lit the other, and inhaled with satisfaction.

"Great cigar! Hop, Chester, Jim?" De offered the other three young friends a cigar. They all lit up, puffed appreciatively and continued strolling through the market.

Hop explained that its daily rhythm harkened back to Tampico's early days. "Unlike cities founded by Spain in the colonial period when church and state built towns centered around cathedrals for the glory of God, *ad majorem Dei gloriam*, Tampico is a fairly new town of 25,000 founded in 1823 at the petition of merchants from Altimira who needed a seaport to facilitate trade. Commerce was its primary purpose."

"Commerce is still its main purpose," added Chester. "In Tampico you can buy about anything you want except Hershey bars."

Hop continued with the guided tour. "Tampico's social life centers on a second plaza not far from here, Plaza Union."

"Just like the Zócalo," added Jim, "the big plaza in Mexico City."

Plaza Union lay a block north and west of the Plaza Independencia. On one side stood the parish church, *La Parroquia*. A sundial on the church tower bore the motto *Sic Tempus Fugit*.

"Time flies," interpreted Hop. De said the clock's message was a reminder to them for the task at hand. The other sides of the plaza housed businesses, the Hotel Imperial and the Colonial Club, where mostly foreigners dined, cafes, the jail, and the municipal offices. The Plaza Union was shaded by tall palm and poinciana trees, which bloomed into brilliant red flowers every June.

Hop explained that concerts in the Plaza Union were held three times a week and on fiesta days. On concert nights the upper crust, the *criolles*, dressed in their finest and sat at their accustomed places. Men of the professional classes, *mestizos* of mixed Indian and Spanish blood, dressed in suits and tie, and their ladies in fine taffeta dresses, kept to their class on one end of the plaza. Swarms of peasants also crowded the plaza, their dress indistinguishable from what they wore every day.

"It's the same all over Mexico," said Jim. He pointed out how women, girls, and children walked around the plaza in one direction, and men and boys walked in the opposite direction. Elders of both sexes held down the benches, closely monitoring the younger generations' interactions.

"It doesn't seem that a handful of foreigners in Tampico have affected life here very much," observed De. He enjoyed this brief glimpse into Mexican culture and figured not much had changed since Tampicos' founding.

The next morning well before dawn, amidst the frenzied activities of the market, De, Jim, and Hop loaded their gear into *La Luna*, the company's launch tied up at the canal near the foot of Plaza Independencia. Mr. Body had directed Hop to drop Jim and De at Tuxpan. De was to start mapping Tierra Amarilla, a hacienda which El Aguila had under lease. Hop was to proceed to Furbero, El Aguila's oil field farther south of Tuxpan.

The launch driver backed cautiously from the plaza and wove the boat upstream through the flow of approaching boats, barges, and canoes. De asked Hop what their boat was powered by.

"Naphthalene, an extract of coal," explained Hop. The motor left a trail of black smoke. "It's slow but it beats poling our way to Tuxpan."

After a few miles the narrow canal opened onto the broad, shallow, muddy Tamiahua Lagoon. As the grey light of early morning lit the sky, De could see the horizon open expansively, emphasizing the flat landscape in all directions. Clouds tinted orange with the day's first sunrays backlit the low-lying offshore bar that separated the lagoon from the Gulf of Mexico. Shorebirds flew in swarms and the air smelled salty.

De had never experienced a coastal lagoon. He felt thousands of miles from home and was exhilarated by his new surroundings.

Boat traffic moving in the opposite direction transported goods to Tampico. Their launch kept to the deeper water, avoiding shoals and mudflats, which only an experienced hand could distinguish. The gulf wind blew fair and clean, kicking high cirrus clouds into horsetail patterns against a sky that changed tint with the rising sun from a pale opalescence to faint cerulean and by mid-morning to a dazzling azure.

By late afternoon they reached the village of Tamiahua. The town perched on a narrow sandy peninsula between the lagoon and a swamp. De was struck by the great number of tall coconut palms, whose frond-plumed tops were silhouetted against the blue sky.

They disembarked and walked along the single, narrow, sandy street to the house of an American merchant, Don Luis Kenyon, who led them to his bachelor's quarters, which served as a general store and inn. Don Luis wore shorts and was unshaven but had a friendly smile made conspicuous by his gold tooth.

They dined at his table under a tile-roofed veranda on one side of the courtyard. The menu included shrimp and rice, fried *frijoles*, eggs with chili sauces, tortillas, and coffee. It was served by two young native girls, whose eyes were wide-set under prominent brows. Their profiles reminded De of Mayan art. Both were attractive and very attentive to the guests. The food was so highly spiced that sweat soon formed on De's brow. He rolled the flat tortillas and dipped them in the sauces, savoring the spicy, unfamiliar tastes.

"How's the meal, *jefe?*" asked Jim, who was plainly enjoying the chili sauce.

"I always liked the word 'tortilla' but imagined it might be pronounced, with four syllables," replied De, holding one up. "Wouldn't it sound better if we pronounced it *tor-ti-li-a*. Doesn't that have a better ring? They sure taste good."

"They sure do," responded Jim. "These are the best *tortilias* I've had in many a moon."

The serving of tortillas was the chief concern of one of the young Mexican women. During the meal she traveled between guests, bringing each time a single tortilla hot from the piece of flat iron heated over glowing coals. De noticed her slim figure beneath a tight-fitting garment. After dinner when the dishes had been cleared, De offered cigars to his host and friends. They smoked and chatted with Don Luis until bedtime, when they retired to canvas cots beneath mosquito netting.

After breakfast the next morning their host showed them the town. There was little to see. Tamiahua's only street was narrow and covered with white sand and bits of shell, and was inhabited principally by gamecocks tethered for their morning exercise. Houses were for the most part palm-thatched with mud walls. Naked brown babies stared at them from open doorways. The only substantial structures were the church and the jail or *juzgado*, which Jim said Americans call the hoosegow.

"Down here you want to avoid the hoosegow at all costs," explained Jim. "Mexican justice ain't exactly swift unless you have enough pocket change to pay off the jailer. Once after a night at a friendly cantina I had a little run-in with the owner over the price of merchandise and was thrown in one of these *mexicano* hoosegows. It's not a place you'd pay to visit," Jim said, raising his eyebrows and grinning.

"What was the merchandise?" asked De.

"It's been a long time past, but as I recall she was real pretty."

"I see," said De. "How did you get out?"

"I spent two days and nights in the hoosegow fighting cockroaches, scorpions, and foot-long centipedes. Finally some of my buddies broke me out."

"Broke you out of jail?" asked De.

"You should have seen it," laughed Jim. "One of my compadres tied his rope to the iron bars of my jail cell window, dallied it around his saddle horn and rode off like he had roped a longhorn steer. Instead of opening the window, his horse pulled the whole wall down. I was nearly killed when the roof caved in."

De and Hop laughed. "I guess you never returned to the village?"

"Not yet, not yet. But if I make it big down here in Tampico, I may go back and build them a new jail. That would be a fine monument, don't you think, Mr. De?"

"A fitting one, it sounds to me like."

When it came time to depart, Don Luis hitched a ride with them to Tuxpan. He filled their launch with cages of chickens and half a dozen shoats to sell at the market.

As the boat approached a nondescript thatched hut on the mainland side of the lagoon, Hop pointed it out and told De the Dos Bocas well was only a mile or so beyond and asked if he would like to see it.

"That's what brought us here. Sure, let's take a look!"

Jim negotiated a ride for them on small burros from the owner of the hut. When they approached the wellsite, De couldn't believe his eyes. The landscape was completely devoid of vegetation. Dead tree trunks still covered with burnt tar stood stark like gaunt, blackened skeletons. In front of them a huge lake boiled muddy salt water and belched vapors that stung their eyes and smelled of sulfur. De jumped from his burro to take a closer look.

"They tried to control the well after it blew out," explained Hop, "but weren't able to approach the wellhead due to the fire. Ships at sea could see the flames more than a hundred miles away. It's a good thing the well started producing salt water and extinguished itself."

"I've never seen anything like this," exclaimed De, awed by the scale of devastation. "What a force!" He walked to the edge of the huge roiling mud pit, touched his finger to the liquid mud and quickly withdrew his hand. "It's hot!"

"Salt water is still swelling up from the subsurface," replied Hop. "I thought you'd enjoy the site. They drilled two more wells nearby, but neither was any good. Quite a scene, isn't it?"

Dos Bocas crater

De was appropriately impressed. He told Hop he hoped El Aguila never experienced such a blow out. "I can't fathom such a force of nature! Can you imagine the heat and the roar? Where did the salt water come from?"

"My understanding of oil wells," explained Hop, "is that salt water is produced with the oil. Salt water increases the longer an oil well produces. Maybe Dos Bocas produced so much oil in such a short time, the salt water hit when there was no more oil."

De thought about Hop's comment. "Maybe we need to learn about salt water, too."

"First, let's find Lord Cowdray some oil," said Hop. "We can figure out the salt water later."

They returned to the launch and boated two more hours to the south end of the lagoon, where they entered another canal, this one even narrower than Chijol. After a few miles the canal emptied into the Tuxpan River at its mouth on the Gulf of Mexico.

Brown waves rolled onto shore and sent large undulations up the river. Gulls and terns soared on the stiff breeze. Their boat started pitching in the waves. De, who had never seen the ocean before, was impressed.

"Tuxpan is about five miles from here," explained Hop. "They call this place Tuxpan Bar. The small edifice there with a Mexican flag is customs. We haul Furbero oil in lighters from here to offshore barges."

The driver pointed the boat up the Tuxpan River. Along the riverbank dense jungle alternated with huge cultivated fields.

"Don Luis," asked De, "why are the fields here so large? They aren't like the small farms we saw near Tampico."

"After the Civil War many plantation owners fled the South and moved to Tuxpan to grow cotton," explained Don Luis.

"What an odd place for a bunch of expatriate Americans, don't you think?" asked De.

"Farming conditions are similar here to the Mississippi Delta," said Don Luis. "The soil is rich. Indian labor to work the cotton fields was cheap. But a few years ago the boll weevil showed up and wiped out all the cotton. The boll weevil is headed north."

"Boll weevils migrate? I wonder if farmers in Texas know about the boll weevil," said De.

"If they don't now they will soon enough," remarked Don Luis. "It'll wipe out the Texas crop just like it did those here."

"What are they growing now?" De asked, pointing to a field where long rows of green vines ran in cultivated fields from the river bank to distant turnrows.

"Vanilla. A very hard plant to grow."

"Vanilla? How in the world did the farmers switch from cotton to vanilla?" asked De.

"The Indians taught them," said Don Luis. "It's a money-making crop."

"Why is it difficult to cultivate?" De asked.

"Vanilla is extracted from an orchid. The flowers last only one day. Each flower has to be pollinated by hand in the early morning."

De reflected on this and was fascinated that native Indians had salvaged the American immigrants' livelihood. "Hand pollinated?" he asked.

"A moth might pollinate one in a hundred flowers. An Indian can pollinate a thousand flowers a day," explained Don Luis. "After the fruit forms, in about five months the beans mature, are picked, cured, and fermented. Oil is extracted by percolating water through the beans."

"Who are the Indians?" asked De. "Are they *mestizo?*"

"Oh, no, they're *puro indio,*" replied Don Luis. "Like the two girls who help me at the store. Huastecan Indians. They call this land the *huasteca.* They speak their own lingo and mainly keep to themselves. They don't care much for foreigners or Mexicans either."

"Why not?"

"Probably because they were here first," answered Don Luis. "The Spaniards made them slaves. Mexicans don't treat them much better."

"Do they resent it?"

"Maybe. They seem fine unless they're drunk. Mainly they scratch a living however they can."

"Do the Indians own land?" asked De.

"Some own small plots, but most live on the land without title. A few tribes own larger tracts as tribal property. They call it *condueñzago* land. Back in the seventies and eighties under Díaz, all the unclaimed land was surveyed and then purchased by people with money. The Indians resent it."

"The same as our native Indians," replied De. "Who owns the minerals?"

Don Luis shrugged. He didn't know but Hop answered the question. "In Mexico the minerals are owned by the surface owner. Private mineral ownership is guaranteed by the 1884 Constitution. When Lord Cowdray first came to the *huasteca*, he bought half a million acres. On those lands he owns both the surface and the minerals, the same as our fee simple."

"What happens where El Aguila doesn't own the surface?" asked De.

"We take a lease on the minerals from the surface owner for a cash payment and occasionally a percent of the production, just like we do in the States. Several of the larger haciendas have leased to El Aguila or to Huasteca Petroleum."

Don Luis spoke up again. "There are lots of *rancheros*, or small farms like the ones along the Panuco, which are mainly owned by mestizos. Here in the huasteca we have three classes: the Indians, the small ranchers or *mestizos*, and the hacienda owners or *hacendados*. The hacienda owners are always of Spanish descent. We call them *criollos*."

As the boat nosed toward shore at the village of Tuxpan, Hop concluded the discussion. "Tierra Amarilla, the hacienda you're going to map, is owned by one *criollo* family, the Pelaez brothers. We have a lease on their minerals so you have to work with them on use of the surface if we decide to drill a well."

Their boat slowed as it approached Tuxpan's flimsy wooden docks. De noted the stains on the piers supporting the dock, suggesting that the river was tidal. Don Luis warned them not to swim in the river because sharks came this far up from the Gulf. Two huge trees dwarfed a scattering of wooden housing on the river bank. Standing under the trees were three saddled horses and two mules. Across the river on the south bank De saw a train siding and steel tanks.

"That's the terminal of the narrow-gauge railroad from Furbero Field," explained Hop, pointing across the river. "El Aguila built the railroad to haul the oil by train to the terminal, where it's offloaded to shallow-draft barges that lighter it to tankers beyond the Tuxpan Bar."

"Is Furbero the only oil field south of Tampico?" asked De.

"Yes, if you don't count Dos Bocas. Huasteca Petroleum is drilling a well now not far from Dos Bocas at Hacienda Casiano."

"Furbero to Tampico is nearly a hundred miles. Surely another oil field is around here somewhere," said De.

"You'd think so," said Hop.

A middle-aged Indian was standing on the dock. "There's your *mozo*," said Hop. The Indian wore a white cotton shirt and baggy pants tied at the ankles. A cone-shaped sombrero cast a shadow over his face. "Hippolito is his name. Jim, you'll like interpreting what he says."

"Hippolito speaks Spanish, I hope," said Jim.

"He speaks the *huastecan* languages. In Spanish he talks in *dichos*," explained Hop.

"In *dichos*?" repeated Jim. "You're telling me our man only speaks in proverbs?"

"Jim, toss him the line there," directed De. Jim cast the line to the *mozo*. The Indian caught it and wrapped it to a cleat. After the Americans jumped to the dock, Hop introduced De and Jim to Hippolito, who nodded slightly. His face was expressionless.

De and Jim helped Don Luis offload his pigs and chickens. When Don Luis had stacked the cages high on the river bank, he returned to the dock, shook hands all around and asked that they stop at his store anytime they were near Tamiahua. "My emporium is yours," he said. "Drop by anytime." His front tooth flashed gold in the morning sun.

De and Jim unloaded their baggage and carried it to the pack mules, which stood placidly on the muddy river bank, watchful as the *mozo* arranged and loaded their luggage evenly by weight on the pack frames, wrapped it with canvas, and expertly tied the double diamond over the tarp. De could tell he knew what he was doing.

"De, I'm leaving you and Jim here," said Hop when the mules were packed. "I'll be headed south to Furbero. Hippolito will take you north to Hacienda Tierra Amarilla. Our instructions are fairly broad. Dr. Hayes said to map the topography, to note any beds of rock, to measure their strike and dip, and to pay

*see Glossary

24

special attention to oil seeps. He wants us to look for evidence of anticlines."

De eyed the flat expanse of the coastal plain. No topographic feature broke the horizon. He wondered again how in the world he might comprehend and predict the subsurface when any bedding was buried beneath an impenetrable wall of jungle.

Anticipating his concern, Hop said, "Look for dry streambeds or *quebradas* and walk them out. Streambeds and arroyos sometimes cut down through the soil layer to expose a bed of rocks which can give you strike and dip. You'll see several small hills that rise above the jungle canopy. These are volcanic plugs, which must be remnants of igneous rocks that pushed up through the sedimentary section. You can climb them to get the lay of the land. Except for that, it's intuition and seeps."

"Dr. Hayes said to pay attention to the seeps," said De.

"The Indians call them *chapapotes*. You'll find lots of seeps around the base of the volcanic plugs. Some seeps are dried asphalt and some still bubble oil and gas. When you return to Tampico, let's kick around if they mean anything more than a breached seal. As Chester observed, not much production has been found by drilling next to seeps."

"We'll need to review every well that's been drilled in the *huasteca*. Do we have information on all of them?"

"Our files only cover El Aguila's wells. Most were dry holes. They may not be too helpful."

"*Anything* will help," De replied and turned to Jim. "Jim, ask Hippolito if he knows the way to Tierra Amarilla."

Hippolito must have understood some English because he pointed his chin toward the north and spurred his horse up a beaten path. When his own horse followed, De turned backward in his saddle to wave goodbye. "We're off, Hop! I'll see you in a couple of weeks. Let's the three of us discuss the geology after I've had a chance to look over the country."

"We could use a geological discussion," replied Hop, laughing as he waved at the riders. "Good luck!"

The trail from the river landing was well-worn. It skirted the edge of the small town past large fields and then led directly to an opening in the dense jungle. When they rode into the trees and thick undergrowth, De felt as if he'd been encapsulated by vegetation. No breeze stirred. He heard cicadas, he thought, but even those sounds grew silent as they rode farther into the jungle.

The silence, he realized, was the most unusual aspect of this darkly-shaded world of deep green tones.

He looked up through the canopy at speckled patches of sunlight and saw another canopy of trees high above the first. He stared at the understory and realized how traversing off the path would be difficult if not impossible. He speculated that most of the exploration so far had been along trails or down the rivers because of accessibility. What a different world, a silent emerald world. The immensity of the challenge to map the geology of the coastal plain slowly sank in.

They traveled for several hours and just before dark came upon the edge of a grass savannah. The view opened onto a rolling plain with scattered undergrowth marked by deep arroyos. The transition from jungle to grassland was fairly abrupt. De guessed the jungle had been cleared to open the land up for grass and cattle. In the distance a cone-shaped hill rose above the landscape. He surmised it was one of the igneous extrusions that Hop described, and he wondered how it might have re-shaped the subsurface when it extruded to the surface.

They continued traveling the open country until twilight faded to a faint half-light illuminated only by the waning moon. Capella shone bright directly overhead. Later Orion would be rising in the eastern night sky, trailing Aldeberan and the Pleiades in their ancient track.

De had no trouble following Hippolito's pointed sombrero as it bobbed along at the front of the pack train. Riding in the darkness with no requirement for engaged thought or conversation, De reflected on the last two days. He wondered what brought Don Luis to such an isolated locale as Tamiahua and under what condition the two young ladies who served him dinner worked. For some, he thought, Mexico might offer more than land or minerals to exploit. His mind flashed to an image of Nell and he smiled to himself. Would she move to a place as foreign as this? Would Mexico be too exotic, too far from her home and family? Underneath these pleasant speculations ran the vexing challenge: how to unravel the subsurface? How could he locate a well with the expectation of finding oil when the jungle covered up all the clues? Dr. Hayes' recommendation to stick close to seeps troubled him. Finding significant oil production was more complicated than drilling near seeps or it would already have been discovered and he wouldn't be here.

Lights flickering in the distance caught his attention. When they rode closer he saw they were kerosene lanterns hung underneath the covered porch of a large, two-story hacienda. Hippolito rode to an ornate iron-grill gate set in a thick-walled stucco fence that surrounded the house and shouted a greeting. The front door opened and a slight, narrow-faced young Mexican sporting a mustache strode across the porch and squinted to the edge of the light.

"*¿Quien es?*"

Jim answered in Spanish and the man walked down the front steps and opened the gate. "*Bienvenidos,*" he said. To Jim he rattled orders that were relayed to Hippolito, who nodded and took the horses' reins. De stepped off his horse, rubbed his legs, and walked to the gate.

"Hello. I'm Everette DeGolyer with El Aguila Oil Company," he said, extending his hand.

"With El Aguila, yes. My name is Manuel Pelaez. Please, welcome to our house." Manuel shook his hand and gestured for them to enter. He stood a head taller than De, and wore leather boots that came to his knees. Upon entering the house, Manuel directed De and Jim toward a large library. The shelves were filled ceiling to floor with books. Embers glowed in the fireplace. Even in the tropics, November evenings were cool.

"Are you the American geologist? I was expecting someone older." asked Manuel frankly.

"Yes, but I've studied with one of the best-known geologists in the world, Dr. Williard Hayes."

Manuel nodded approvingly and then spoke to a servant who returned with a tray of glasses and brandy, which he offered to his guests. After asking about the ride and their health, Manuel acknowledged the late hour and said, "It is a long distance from Tuxpan by horse. A small meal has been prepared for you. I will leave you to wash and eat and will join you for dinner tomorrow. Tonight, it pleases me to welcome you."

"It's good to be here," responded De. "*Muchas gracias* for your hospitality." Jim thanked him at greater length in Spanish.

Manuel Pelaez nodded politely and after the brandy was finished, left De and Jim to dine by themselves. For De, it had been a long day, a day full of new sights and smells and sounds. After eating he told Jim he was headed to bed. Jim said he'd check on Hippolito and wouldn't be far behind. De climbed the stairs to his room, washed with soap from a bowl on a nightstand and snuggled between clean sheets, tired but content. He immediately thought of Nell, and of how thrilled he was to be here, on an adventure of the first order. Finishing his degree in Norman didn't hold a candle to Mexico. He felt conflicted, though. Would she follow him to such a different world?

Chapter Three

November 1909

De awoke the next morning refreshed and happy. He couldn't remember ever waking up when he wasn't happy. Today he felt especially energized. He shaved, dressed, and walked downstairs. Hearing Jim's voice, he followed it to the kitchen. Jim was chatting with the cook, who was serving him hot tortillas after she flattened the dough with a wooden rolling pin on a table, shaped the tortillas into a circle, and cooked them on the hot stovetop.

"Good morning, Jim. Nice place, isn't this?"

"*Buenos días, jefe.* Yep, sure is, for being in the middle of nowhere."

"It's interesting that Manuel speaks pretty good English," said De.

"Yep, he sure does. Ain't these the best *tortilias* I ever ate?" He had added a fourth syllable and winked at the cook. "De, I'm taking a liking to this job. Now don't be thinking you can do without me just because Manuel speaks a little English."

"Don't be thinking I don't need you."

"Good, because no Spaniard will take my place."

"Spaniard? Manuel is Mexican."

"He and his brothers are the Spaniard types who own the land, rule the roost, and leave the work to the peons. Scratch one of these *criollo* Spaniard types and you'll find an old conquistador."

Jim walked past him to the back door and looked out toward the barn. "I haven't seen our chatty *mozo* this morning. Do you realize Hippolito hasn't spoken a word since we met him?"

"I wouldn't call him a talker."

"Ha. Maybe I can get him to say a *dicho* for us."

"Maybe in his culture, silence is golden."

"You're funny, *jefe.* Here, have a *tortilla.*"

After breakfast Jim and Hippolito loaded De's duffle bag onto one of the mules and soon were headed directly across the country toward the distant hill that rose above the gently-sloping landscape. *Cerro Pelon,* Manuel had called it. De noted that the hacienda was on the flank of a grassy plain that sloped down to the east in a series of terraces. Spread before them, the grassy ridges undulated between arroyos striking north by northeast. They followed the edge of one of these arroyos, which Hippolito pointed to and said succinctly, '*Arroyo Chico*'. It spilled into a much larger arroyo, which he called back over his shoulder and said, '*Arroyo Grande*'. Jim rode his horse beside De and said, "See there, our *mozo* does speak. That's four words in two days. I was afraid we had us a deaf mute."

"Probably he understands everything we say," replied De softly. "Why don't you ask him something?"

"Good idea, *jefe*," and Jim spurred up to Hippolito and started a conversation. At Hippolito's reply, Jim threw his head back and whooped. "You're a good one, sure enough," he said in English and rode back to report to De.

"Well, what did Hippolito say?"

"I asked him why he didn't talk much. He replied '*en boca cerrada no entran moscas*.'"

"What does it mean?"

"Flies don't enter a closed mouth," said Jim. "Pretty good! Can you believe we have a fellow who only speaks *dichos*? De, we've got ourselves a real character here. I may learn to speak in proverbs myself. The next challenge is to get old Hippo to smile. Have you ever seen such a somber *sombrero*?"

De smiled and shook his head at his interpreter. As they rode through the countryside, occasionally De would step off his horse, take his rock hammer, and scramble down into the arroyo. Jim and Hippolito waited patiently until he emerged. Once he came back with a handful of crumbling shale that he handed to the *mozo* and showed him how to put the rock samples in small cotton sacks that he had removed from the duffle bag. De wrote on the sacks and put them in the saddle bags. They crossed the deeper arroyo and there in front of them was a shrub-covered hill rising more than 300 feet from the plains.

"Let's climb it," said De. "I want to get a lay of the land." As they rode around its west flank, suddenly De shouted, "Wow, would you look at that!" He pointed down to a pitch-stained patch of ground less than a foot in diameter filled with a dark liquid. "It's a seep, a *chapapote*!"

"You've already found oil," commented Jim dryly.

De jumped down and scooped up some of the oil. He rubbed it between his fingers, sniffed it and put a small pinch in his mouth.

"How does it taste?" asked Jim. De didn't reply but took out his notebook and started writing.

"Mr. De, do you know the story about the *hombre* who grabbed his friend's arm and said, 'whoa, watch your step there, *amigo*, that could be cow poop you're about to step in.'"

De looked up at his interpreter, astride his horse, one leg over the saddle horn, hat shoved back on his head.

"Is this a joke?"

"The *hombre* rubs it between his fingers just like you did, smells it just like you did, and then takes a bite just like you did and says 'Whoa, *amigo*, don't step in it. It *is* cow poop.' Ha ha ha." Jim clearly enjoyed his own jokes. "Better not drink that stuff, De. You'll grease up your insides."

De reached into his duffle bag and withdrew a small jar. He filled the jar with oil from the seep and then said, "Come on, let's climb the hill. Hippolito, bring your machete *por favor*."

They tied their horses to a thorny shrub and, with Hippolito in the lead clearing the thick brush with his machete, they pulled and scrambled up the steep slope. De pounded the rocks with his hammer like a crazed blacksmith. Finally, he thought, we've found a rock. He took notes in the small pocket notebook, labeled each rock sample, and then pointed toward the summit. The last part of the ascent was nearly vertical. At the top they gazed out over the vast expanse.

"Pretty view, ain't it, boss?"

"Sure is," said De. "Miles of thick shrub and there," pointing east to a green horizon, "nothing but jungle. Every bit of bedding is covered with soil and vegetation," he sighed.

"Boss, the rocks on this hill are sure enough black and heavy. What kind of rock is it?" asked Jim.

"Mostly basalt, which is igneous and means one time the rocks were so hot it was molten, like lava. This rock," and he held up a grey-black chunk, "is metamorphosed limestone, which means the heat from the igneous rock altered the surrounding limestone into something more like marble. Look across the landscape there. Do you see a couple of more hills like this one? When the molten rocks formed these hills, this area must have been plenty hot."

"Hotter than a hot tamale," agreed Jim. "It looks to me like the lava would burn up all the oil."

"Good observation. Molten rocks are hot enough to cook out the oil but didn't. We know that because of the seeps."

"Drinking the oil might help you figure it out, do you think? Kind of like an old mexicano I know in South Texas who eats peyote buttons raw. Says it makes him see things."

De continued. "The question is when was the oil generated."

"What difference does that make?" asked Jim.

"To understand the geology we have to think about when events occurred. Timing can be everything. First we have to figure out what the subsurface looks like now. Just because the ground is flat on the surface doesn't mean it's flat in the subsurface. All sedimentary rocks, but mainly limestone and sandstone, hold oil and were laid down horizontally in layers, the older layers on bottom and younger layers successively on top the older beds. But sedimentary rocks often are shoved around after they were deposited. They don't stay horizontal. So we need to figure the topography of a certain buried rock strata, the one that holds the oil. And we need to determine if the oil moved into the rocks before they were shoved around, or afterward. That's where the timing comes in."

"It all looks flat to me," said Jim, gazing out over the country, "except for the good grass country close to the hacienda. Did you notice the cattle? They're standing knee-deep in grass but look half-starved. This coastal grass must not be nutritious."

De had noticed the cattle, all Brahma-crossed with long legs and flopping ears. He looked to the horizon and pondered what the landscape could tell him. To the west he gazed at a thin, blue line of distant mountains.

"Are those the sierras?" he asked.

"The Sierra Madres Oriental," replied Jim. "Boss, can you tell me what you're looking for? Maybe old Hippolito and I can help out."

"We're looking for buried domes, what we call anticlines."

"I've heard of anticlines," said Jim.

"It's where the oil is trapped." De had surmised the sedimentary beds next to *Cerro Pelon* must dip in all directions away from the hill because the molten lava pushed up through the sedimentary strata, tilting the beds away from the extrusion.

"If you'd show me and Hippo an anticline, we'll know what to look for," Jim suggested.

"I'd like to show you an anticline, but in this country everything is covered with soil and vegetation. In the Rockies, whole mountains of bedded rock are exposed to the surface. There it's like reading a book in ancient script. With a little imagination you can piece its history together. Here, the clues are hidden. One of these days we need to head to the sierras," he said, pointing to the west. "The rocks that produce oil underneath here may be exposed at the surface up in the mountains. If we can examine rocks on the surface, we can understand them in the subsurface."

"Just say 'go', and old Talky will lead the way," responded Jim, nodding toward Hippolito. "Let me ask you something stupid."

"No question is stupid."

"What is a beached seal?" asked Jim. "I heard you and Mr. Hop talking about a beached seal yesterday at the boat dock."

"A beached seal? I don't have any...oh, do you mean *breached* seal?"

"If that's what you and Mr. Hop were talking about."

"Ha. Jim you were paying attention. We were talking about a *breached* seal. That's an oil reservoir that has leaked because its top seal which traps the oil has been broken. Think about this: several millions of years ago, before this basaltic hill we're standing on was here, the oil was in place underneath us in a buried dome or anticline. Then a few million years later, up comes hot igneous rocks right through the middle of the anticline. What would that do to the oil?"

"When hot rocks punched through your anticline it'd either cook the oil or spill it out. Ah, your breached seal. I get it. Is this what you geologists do, sit around and dream up what happened millions of years ago?"

"It takes some imagination," admitted De, "but it also takes information. Here we have seeps and an igneous plug. They're nothing but clues. For now, all we can do is find as many clues as possible on the surface and try to figure out what they're telling us about the subsurface."

"With so few clues you could dream up a great story."

"You're right. Here we have *chapapotes*, so we know oil was formed sometime in the past and came up to the surface. We need to determine if the oil is just a residue left from a breached seal or if it's what we call 'live' oil. That's why I took a sample."

"You wouldn't want to be caught drinking dead oil, would you?"

De looked at Jim and caught the sparkle in his eye. "Nothing but live oil for me. That's the kind you can sell."

"Live oil for me, too," agreed Jim with a grin.

They spent the rest of the day slowly scouting the area, walking in a circular path first about a quarter mile from the basaltic hill and then in larger and larger circles away from the hill. When they found a second *chapapote* in a shallow arroyo, De climbed a tree to get their bearings from the hill. He calculated the line between the two seeps and pointed Hippolito to head directly away from the hill on the same azimuth. Soon they found two more *chapapotes*.

"You're good," said Jim, impressed with their success. "You keep this up, De, and we won't have to do any drilling. What do these seeps tell you?"

"They're along one azimuth. The only straight lines on the surface are formed along faults. So I'm thinking the seeps line up because the oil leaked up a buried fault. A fault is a long, linear crack in the rocks."

"What formed the fault?"

"That's another piece of the puzzle we need to figure out. Was the fault in place before the molten rock penetrated to the surface, or did the hot lava pushing through the sediments cause the fault?"

"Mr. De, this ain't science. It's like the plot of a murder mystery. I can't believe an Englishman would hire a man with your credentials as a cook to play detective with a bunch of rocks."

"It *is* a little like a murder mystery," agreed De. "Putting the pieces of the puzzle together into a coherent explanation is the key."

Chapter Four

November — December 1909

It was late in the afternoon before De told Hippolilto to head back to the hacienda. The mule's pack was laden with small cotton sacks of samples, mostly basalt from *Cerro Pelon*. The last part of the trip was again lit by moonlight. Even in the dark it was easy for Jim and De to follow Hippolito's bobbing sombrero. When they rode up to the hacienda, Manuel met them on the front porch.

"Welcome back. How was your day?" he asked.

"Delightful!" exclaimed De. "It couldn't have been better!" He dismounted, handed Hippolito his reins, and extended a hand to Manuel.

"Please, come in." Manuel spoke to Jim in Spanish.

"My English needs some wine," said Manuel. "Please join me for a glass in the library in thirty minutes. Dinner will be served afterward. I would like to understand how you look for oil."

"Shall we mention the taste test?" Jim asked De.

De smiled and nodded acceptance of the offer to Manuel. He climbed the stairs to his room, washed, changed into clean clothes, and arrived downstairs in the library before the others. Its tall shelves filled with books made De feel like he shared the room with strangers, long-dead authors who could fill him with wonder and knowledge if he could only read what they had written. De was fascinated by such an extensive collection. When Manuel and Jim entered the library, De asked about the books.

"Our father was a collector," replied Manuel. "He loved to purchase books about the early days of the Spanish Conquest."

"I have a great curiosity about your country's past as well. It was very different from the United States."

Manuel spoke at length in Spanish and Jim interpreted. "*Señor* Manuel says our histories are not so different. The southwestern United States belonged to Spain and to Mexico. Many people consider it to be rightfully Mexican."

De didn't know how to respond so he only smiled. Manuel continued speaking with animation, after which Jim interpreted. "He says too often political boundaries disregard history, culture, and language."

"Jim, please tell *Señor* Pelaez that I am curious how the boundaries of this property were determined," said De.

Jim spoke to Manuel, who gave De a sharp glance and again spoke in Spanish.

"He says when Spain ruled, all land belonged to the sovereign. Land grants were approved by the king or viceroy. The king deeded Tierra Amarilla to their ancestors, the Gorrochoteqius. The land covered several haciendas in existence today, Tierra Amarilla, Cerro Azul, Alazan, Potrero del Llano, Cuchilla del Pulque, Palma Real, Cerro Viejo, and Llano Grande."

Manuel continued to speak and Jim interpreted. "When Mexico became a country, the Spanish land grants were validated by the Constitution. Since much of the land in Mexico had never been surveyed or claimed, a law was passed which provided first for surveying the unclaimed lands, and then for selling it. *Hacendados* who purchased the land cleared it and made it productive."

Manuel continued speaking in Spanish and Jim again interpreted. "*Señor* Manuel says he is surprised someone so young could be experienced enough to explore for oil. He asked if you have found oil in other places."

"Tell him I have not. Petroleum geology is a new science. Most oil today was discovered by drilling near surface seeps, but we know that finding oil is more complicated than drilling near seeps. I studied under a man who believes in the anticlinal theory. Instead of looking for oil seeps, we now know we should look for anticlines."

Manuel spoke and Jim said, "He wants to know what is an anticline? Do you want me to give the answer?"

De saw Jim's smile and continued. "Tell him an anticline is a buried dome that traps the oil. Tell him that oil and gas are found in porous sedimentary rocks, generally in sandstones or limestones. By 'porous' I mean rocks that have enough pore space to hold oil or water, which is retained within the rock matrix, like a sponge holds water. When porous sedimentary beds are folded into domes or anticlines, oil is trapped within the rock in the dome. Since oil is lighter than water, it rises to the top of the dome. The lower part of the dome or anticline usually contains salt water."

Jim interpreted De's explanation. Manuel silently nodded. De went on to explain that the oil is trapped inside the anticline by an impermeable seal, often a shale, that prevents the oil from leaking out. Although he could tell that Manuel Pelaez did not fully understand, De continued, pausing occasionally for Jim to interpret.

"Determining when the oil migrates into the anticline is critical. If it migrates through the porous rock before the anticline is formed, no oil is trapped. So we need to understand the timing of when the oil migrated and when the anticline formed."

Manuel spoke in Spanish and Jim again interpreted. "*Señor* Manuel says it is complex. He wonders how you will find anticlines on Tierra Amarilla."

"That is the challenge," agreed De. "After examining your property today, I realize it is a very big challenge because most of the surface is flat-lying soils that obscure the deeper subsurface horizons. However in Arroyo Grande I observed shale beds that are not horizontal, which may indicate a buried hill. If beds of rock are tilted, the angle and direction of the tilt can be projected into the subsurface and may hint at a buried anticline. Since an anticline is a dome, beds of rock will tilt away from its apex in four directions, which we call four-way dip. Perhaps when *Cerro Pelon* penetrated the sedimentary rocks it pushed the horizontal layers up and away from its core, tilting the rock in four directions and thus forming an anticline where oil is trapped."

Manuel spoke to Jim, who nodded in agreement with his statement. "Manuel says finding oil is a treasure hunt."

De laughed. "Yes, and the treasure is buried deep beneath the surface so we can only guess from little clues where it is hidden."

Manuel spoke again and Jim continued his interpretation. "*Señor* Manuel asked what will happen if you find oil on their property at Tierra Amarillo."

"It is hard for me to say," answered De. "We must not only find oil, but we must find oil in commercial quantities, which means enough to pay for all the costs of transporting, shipping, and refining. Tierra Amarilla is far from oil markets. If we find it in sufficient quantities, the oil will have to be transported to the river, barged to tankers, and probably shipped to Texas for refining. Tell him the companies who explore for oil take a great deal of risk. We must spend millions of dollars not knowing if we can find oil, and even if we find oil, we must find enough to pay to extract, transport, and refine it."

Manuel spoke again and Jim interpreted. "And if this occurs, Manuel asks, what will happen to Tierra Amarilla? Will this not change their way of life?"

"I am hired to find locations to drill for oil," responded De, looking at Manuel. "If I am successful, it has the possibility to bring you and your brothers great wealth."

Manuel spoke at length in Spanish to Jim. "*Señor* Manuel asks if the foreign oil companies will help the Mexican people, or will the money flow only to the oil companies? He asks if the wealth that you hope to find should not belong to Mexico? His family will receive only a small percent. What does the country receive? Do foreigners not gain wealth by exploiting the people and the country's resources?"

Jim listened more and then continued. "*Señor* Manuel says under President Díaz, foreigners have built railroads across the country so they can charge high prices for moving goods." Jim paused while Manuel continued to speak, then he interpreted. "In the city, foreign-owned companies charge high fees for gas and electric lights. Asphalt from Tampico is now paving streets in Mexico City and Guadalajara. Peasants perform the work and the oil company receives the money. Waters-Pierce is the only company allowed by President Díaz to provide refined petroleum products to all of Mexico, a monopoly that must be broken."

"*Señor* Pelaez," said De, "I cannot answer your concerns. I am here to look for oil. If our endeavors are successful, it will benefit your family and all of Mexico."

"My two brothers and I have many discussions about these issues," replied Manuel in English. And in rapid Spanish he spoke again to Jim. "In a country with no capital and little technology, who else but foreigners can develop railways or power and light plants or sanitation works? Mexico must industrialize. Yet some of the money should be used to educate the people. What foreigner will spend money for educating poor Mexicans? There is no profit in it."

"The United States began to modernize only fifty years ago, after our civil war," replied De. "In such a short time, compare America's wealth to Mexico's. Now it is Mexico's time."

Manuel spoke animatedly to Jim. "He says transitions in Mexico have always been paid with the blood of the people. If oil is discovered, blood will flow."

De looked at Manuel and said to Jim, "Please tell *Señor* Pelaez I hope this time the transition will be with the sweat of our people, and with the currency and expertise of foreigners, and not with the blood of his people."

Manuel shrugged and said in English, "A toast," raising his wine glass. "To finding oil on Tierra Amarilla."

The three raised their glasses, touched them, and drank the wine.

"And to my host," responded De. "We appreciate your hospitality." He looked at Manuel. "Manuel, I was born in a sod house, a house made of dirt. People in America and people in Mexico are not so far apart, not in distance and not in our desire to help our people. To Mexico," and he raised his glass.

His toast pleased Manuel Pelaez. Later that evening, De lay in bed pondering Manuel Pelaez's speech. He reflected on his own background, and how in America opportunity was available to those with the hustle and know-how to grasp it. Did such opportunities exist in Mexico? Perhaps America and

Mexico were farther apart than his toast suggested. Then his thoughts turned to Nell, as often they did in the evenings. What was she doing right now, he wondered? Was she thinking of him as he was thinking of her? Sweet Nell. He could see her in his mind's eye, smiling. He could almost hear her voice and feel her warm red rose kiss. Slowly he drifted off to sleep, dreaming of when he and Nell could see each other again.

For the next two weeks, De, Jim, and Hippolito rode off into the countryside before daylight, and returned to the hacienda late at night. During the day De walked out every ravine in search of beds of rock that might show a dip angle, anything other than flat-lying beds. Hippolito walked in front, hacking the underbrush with his machete. Jim followed in the rear, often commenting on the rigors of oil exploration.

"And to think I left the South Texas brush country for this," complained Jim good-naturedly. "Here I'm afoot a hundred miles from nowhere in the bottom of a windless arroyo manhandling your damn survey rod. If this was South Texas I'd be sitting horseback, whistling a lullaby and waiting for Saturday night. Lord, what was I thinking?"

"You're learning the oil business from the ground up, aren't you?" said De. Jim had shown an interest in what De was doing and constantly fired questions at him. "Think of this arroyo as a classroom."

"If you call this learning," replied Jim. "At least the girls in town think cowboying is romantic. I'm in need of some romance."

Hippolito pointed his machete to a thistle, and warned, "*Mala mujer.*" He indicated by gestures it could cause a painful irritation.

"*Mala mujer,*" repeated De. His Spanish was good enough to understand the words. "Is Hippolito talking about the plant or about bad women?"

"He's talking about that nettle," Jim said and pointed to a plant with purple blooms. "It stings if you touch it, just like the *señoritas*. Which is a different kind of sting, the good kind. Mr. De, maybe you and I could find us a couple of *malas mujeres*, what do you say? It'd cheer us up."

"Not me," said De. "I left a girl in Norman."

"Norman is a long ways from the bottom of this arroyo," Jim replied. "We could call it Spanish lessons. It'd do your vocabulary a world of good."

De smiled and said he didn't think so.

In Arroyo Grande between what Hippolito called Arroyo Tlasolaco and Monte Chico, De whooped with excitement. He had found bedding and he instructed Hippolito to chop away all the underbrush until he could measure the strike and the dip of the beds with his Brunton compass.

"Now what about this particular rock has you so excited?" asked Jim. "It looks exactly like the other rocks you've beaten to bits with your rock hammer. Why can't we look for your precious rocks on the hills? There's a breeze up there and I prefer the view."

"We're looking for any beds of rock that are not in the horizontal plane. See that bedding plane? It dips at an angle," replied De, pointing to a thin bed near the base of the arroyo.

"So it does, so it does," nodded Jim. He watched as De laid the Brunton compass against the rock bed, and measured the angle.

"What are you doing there, *jefe?*"

"I'm measuring the dip angle with a Brunton compass. See this little protractor looking bob? See the angles? You hold the compass against the rock and this bob measures the degrees from horizontal. It shows," and he leaned over to look closer, "six degrees northeast dip."

Jim looked over his shoulder. "So what?"

"So the beds of rock are at an angle. Project the angle and the direction into the subsurface and we can begin to visualize the subsurface. If we can find similar beds that all dip away from a point, what we call four-way dip, we've found ourselves an anticline."

"Lord, there's that word again. Do you think we can find one down here in this arroyo?"

"No, but if we map enough dip angles, we might find one. This is just a clue. If you're going to become a geological assistant, you need to understand how to use a Brunton compass and you have to put your feet on the outcrop, even if it's in the bottom of an arroyo."

"The way I look at it," said Jim, "if a cook can make a geologist, why can't a cowboy? Maybe I missed my calling. Still, getting more excited about rocks than *malas mujeres* seems like something we should keep to ourselves."

"All it takes to be a geologist is a keen sense of observation," said De. "Why don't you ask Hippolito what he thinks of oil exploration?"

Jim spoke to Hippolito, laughed, then said to De, "Hippolito says '*Donde menos se piensa, salta la liebre.*'"

"What does that mean?" asked De.

"Where you don't expect it, a jackrabbit will jump up. He thinks we're looking for jackrabbits."

"I think he understands what we're doing. You have to put your feet on the outcrop and work every section. After the field work, I'll go back to the office and put all the data on a map which shows the topography and the direction and degree of all the dips. Then who knows, maybe out jumps the jackrabbit."

The final night at the Pelaez hacienda, Manuel laid out a huge meal. Dinner lasted several hours. Jim's contribution as interpreter and humorist kept the atmosphere light and the conversation lively. Afterward Manuel gave De a guided tour of the library, pointing out his father's first editions with a reverence that De appreciated. When they departed the next day, he felt like landowner relationships were in good shape at Tierra Amarilla.

By the time they returned to Tampico it was the Christmas holidays. The small enclave of foreigners celebrated together, but without Nell, De's festive mood was dampened. He confessed to Jim how badly he missed her.

"So you've been bitten by the love bug? My condolences. It's a sad state of mind," said Jim.

"I asked Nell to marry me before I came to Tampico, but she refused."

"Now why would she refuse you? What kind of woman would pass up a chance to marry a cook?"

"She said she wouldn't marry me until I graduated from the university."

"Does she think you can't make her a living?"

"She already has her degree. She was my German tutor at the University of Oklahoma."

"You know what distance does to the heart, *jefe*. Old Hippolito would have a *dicho* for it."

"I can't keep her out of my thoughts," said De. "Nell may not know it yet, but I'm going to marry her."

Chapter Five

January 1910

January 18, 1910

Geological Report for Tierra Amarilla

Topographically the Tierra Amarilla region is a basin somewhat open at the west but otherwise, with the exception of the sharp canyons of Arroyo Grande, surrounded by high ridges and hills. In the center of the basin the very prominent volcanic plug, Cerro Pelon, rises to a level of some 120 meters above the surrounding valley.

The Tierra Amarilla property is prospective because of its chapapote seepages of live oil. Sixteen such seeps are discussed in detail below. Seepages 1-5 are on Solio Hacienda, an oil property of the Ebano Company. From the foregoing conditions, it has seemed to be desirable to fulfill the following conditions in making the location for the Tierra Amarilla Well No. 1.

First, the well should be as near to Cerro Pelon as possible.

Second, the well should be on the west side of the line of faulting and a desirable distance (75 m) from it.

In the fulfillment of these conditions, I recommend that the spot 250 feet N. 35 degrees W of the large seepage at locality VI be the location for Tierra Amarilla No.1. This place is marked by a stake, set in a mound of stones. It is about 50 feet from Arroyo Grande and about 25 feet above it. Arroyo Grande will be the source of water supply, both for boiler and domestic use. A wagon road has already been constructed from Laja Camp (Tumbadero) by way of Temapachi and both this camp and well sites have been cleared. Firewood can be secured in sufficient quantities in the immediate vicinity of the location.

Signed. E. De Golyer, Geologist

Dr. Hayes put down the paper. He had arrived in Tampico at the end of January and was reviewing reports by the three geologists. "De, did you map an anticline? You don't mention it."

"Yes, sir." De showed Dr. Hayes an illustration of an igneous plug.

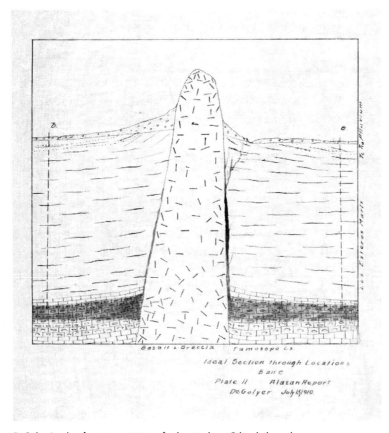

DeGolyer's subsurface interpretation of volcanic plugs. Oil is darker color.

"As my cross-section indicates," De said, "there is dip away from *Cerro Pelon*." He pointed to the cross-section. "The alignment of seeps suggests a buried fault. Structurally it appears we have an elliptical flat-top dome whose longer axis strikes in an east-west direction. Since all the beds on the surface dip away from Cerro Pelon, it leads me to conclude when the igneous intruded through the sedimentary section, four-way dip was established. There are active seeps of live oil along the fault which means all the oil hasn't leaked due to a breached seal. Thus we have an anticline pierced by an igneous plug with live oil seeps on the flanks. It's a good place to drill."

"Why drill so close to *Cerro Pelon?*" asked Dr. Hayes.

"When the igneous plug pierced the sedimentary rocks, it should have fractured the adjacent limestone, which would bust it into breccia and so increase flow rates."

"Have you read Chester Washburne's report on the general stratigraphy of this area?"

"Yes, sir, but without knowing what the producing horizon might even be -- limestone, metamorphosed limestone, maybe even igneous if you believe what Hop thinks about Furbero -- it's premature to consider stratigraphy."

"Chester wrote the report last November with the help of Geoff Jeffreys, one of the Brits who worked for the firm until a few days before you arrived."

"I'd like your ideas on the regional geology, sir," requested De.

"Our main task for now," said Dr. Hayes, "is to gather as much site specific data as possible and then to place it into a regional context. We do not have enough data points yet to understand the regional picture."

"Without a regional picture, all I can recommend now is to drill a well as close to Cerro Pelon as possible," said De.

"With so many seeps of live oil and the evidence for four-way dip, I agree with your recommendation," answered Dr. Hayes. "It's a reasonable place to drill a well. I'll recommend the location to Lord Cowdray. Is this the first well you ever drilled?"

"Yes, sir," replied De.

"Let's hope it produces oil."

"I'm not worried about it producing oil," replied De confidently, "but the rate is unpredictable. It can make two barrels a day or ten thousand barrels a day."

"Let's hope it's at least a hundred barrels a day," responded Dr. Hayes. "Establishing production is critical. El Aquila has drilled enough dry holes already."

De nodded in agreement and Dr. Hayes continued, "Mr. DeGolyer, I'd like you to return to the field and map a prospect that is now drilling. About the time you arrived last November, we spudded a well on a property a few miles southwest of Tierra Amarilla, on Hacienda Potrero del Llano. Ignacio Pelaez, Manuel's brother, helped us negotiate a lease on the property with his cousins. Geoff Jeffreys did the original geological work. He mapped an anticline and I would like your confirmation of his work. Jeffreys is a good geologist, but he never found anything significant for El Aguila."

"When do you expect the Potrero well to be down?"

"Within thirty days. We're drilling it with a cable tool rig. They're at 1700 feet. We ran 13 inch casing at 78 feet, 10 inch casing at 1183 feet, and 8 inch casing at 1567 feet. While you're on location be sure to take samples of the cuttings. We need to analyze the stratigraphy."

"Yes, sir. Dr. Hayes, I appreciate your confidence in me. I would like to ask, sir, if I could extend the trip from Potrero del Llano over to the Sierra Madres?"

"You want to go to the mountains?"

"According to a report by L. V. Dalton, who mapped the sierras a few years ago, I expect the rocks we are drilling in the subsurface are exposed on the surface in the sierras. Examining crushed cuttings from drilling wells is not the same as walking the rock outcrop. I need to measure the thickness of the bedding and look for stratigraphic variations and compare them to the subsurface."

"Certainly, Mr. DeGolyer. Take your *mozo* and Jim and let me know what you find. I'll require a written report within a week of your return."

The next day De and Jim packed their gear for the trip. They intended to catch the crew boat at the plaza wharf. Jim confided that he was ready to leave town.

"This city life is killing me," he told De. "Last night I lost a month's wages playing a game of monte with some sure enough slickers."

"Gambling your money away is not exactly the road to fame and fortune."

"I know, I know. It's the old primrose path."

"Do I not, as some ungracious pastors do, show you the steep and thorny way to heaven?" asked De with a smile.

"Well, some of us ungracious followers take a path that twists and turns a tad. I'm not running from responsibility. If you'd hang out at the cantinas like I do, you'd hear all the latest rumors. Sitting in the office working on your precious maps and pining for your sweetheart ain't no way to keep up with the competition."

"I have too much to learn in a short time to be tomcatting around with you, Jim. Besides, I miss my Nell."

"Lovesick and moonstruck. Lord Almighty, you're in bad shape," said Jim.

"You're such a romantic."

"The reason I can make fun of you is because I haven't been bitten yet. By the way, Mr. De, I was talking to one of the Huasteca hands about a well they're drilling a few miles northeast of Tierra Amarilla. They call it Juan Casiano."

"And?"

"It's near some of our leases."

"Can you get information on their well?" asked De.

"When the drilling hands are not in the field, they hang out in the bars. If you act a little interested, they'll tell you everything they know. Is there some particular information you'd like about the Casiano well?"

De realized the significance of Jim's suggestion. "Jim, you have a great idea. Do the drilling hands have access to geological data?"

"Doheny doesn't use geologists. They tell me he prefers a dowsing stick to geological theories."

"We know so little about the regional picture, any data you can gather will be helpful clues for me, Jim. How would you like, as part of your official duties, to keep up with the competition, to find out whatever you can about their wells and where they're buying leases?"

"It would be easy enough, Mr. De. You're teaching me to ask a million questions. Most people are flattered to answer."

"I'll clear this with Dr. Hayes," said De, "but I'm certain he will agree. Your scouting information can become part of my monthly report. We need the data and you need to stay away from the monte tables."

"Where do you think I get my information…in the cathedral? While you're here in the office dreaming up what's under a half mile of solid rock, I'll be in the bars keeping up with Huasteca. Jim Hall: interpreter, packer, peon, palm reader, and oilfield scout. I need a business card."

"Ha. What you need is to provision us with enough supplies for a two week trip to the sierras. I'll see you in the morning at the crack of dawn down at the wharf."

"Mr. De, you're a good man and there aren't many of us left."

De, Jim, and Hippolito were at the Potrero del Llano No. 1 on their way to the Sierras when it drilled into pay on February 5, 1910 at 1933 feet. The well came in flowing by heads that lasted ten to fifteen minutes. The well would quit flowing for a half hour or more and then would discharge again.

"What do you make of it, Mr. De?" asked Jim. He was excited. "We struck oil, didn't we?"

De didn't answer. He was busy taking samples of the rock cuttings from the bailer as it was emptied into the mud pit. "Here," he said to Jim, "Wash these samples with water, put each clean sample in one of those small cotton bags, and write the depth on the label."

By measuring the oil as it flowed into a reserve pit, De calculated in twenty-four hours the well could produce 400 barrels, not enough for commercial production so far from a pipeline and a refinery. Jim hadn't moved. "Yes," De said finally, when he looked up at the smiling redhead, "it's exciting. Now hurry and wash those cuttings. I need to see what the pay looks like."

By noon the next day the well had been temporarily capped. It would only flow in spurts. De figured the oil was about 15 API gravity, less viscous than El Ebano oil. The problem was it wouldn't flow enough. Did this mean the whole anticline would have the same characteristic?

"We found oil," said Jim. "What's so bad about that?"

"It won't sustain a flow, which is a puzzle. Maybe we're close to some good reservoir rock," replied De. "Dr. Hayes arrives back in Tampico today. I'll wire him to come down and take a look. I know he'll expect a recommendation from me. I'm afraid the main question can't be answered yet."

"Which is?"

"Is the well commercial? Think of all the costs to transport the oil to the Gulf. Is this a one-well phenomenon that spits a few barrels and quits, or is it an anticline large enough, and the reservoir rock good enough, to justify spending a lot more money?"

"You're asking me?" asked Jim.

"Yes," said De. "What would you do if it was your well?"

"You're sounding like you wished it was a dry hole."

"I'm not wishing it was a dry hole, but I have to make a recommendation to Dr. Hayes."

Jim grinned. "I'd put some more chips on the table and draw a card."

"This isn't a game of monte," replied De.

"I didn't finish," Jim said. "Then I'd wait for the hand of God to see who won."

Dr. Hayes arrived at the Potrero well site two days later. De had already double-checked the surface expressions of the strikes and dips. The west side of the anticline looked to have steeper dips than the east flank. He made a few refinements, but generally agreed with Geoff Jeffreys' interpretation. He also noted how many live oil seeps were along the east bank of the river. An igneous plug like Cerro Pelon was not too distant but did not extrude through the anticline. Seeps were present over a large area, and the four-way dip indicated the presence of an anticline elongated north-south. De walked Dr. Hayes around the entire prospective area, confirming the dips and strike with his

Brunton compass. Afterward they reviewed his maps.

"The bedding on the banks of the river shows ten degrees west dip." De pointed to the map. "The side creek 600 meters north of the location shows bedding that dips to the east at five degrees. South dip is here," and he pointed a half-mile south of the well. "North dip is harder to peg, and is probably across the Buena Vista on Alazan. We won't know where the crest of the anticline is without drilling at least two more wells, one north and one south of the No. 1. What we do know is that we have a large oil saturated anticline that hints at good reservoir characteristics."

Dr. Hayes studied the map and nodded in concurrence. He reminded De of an elder statesmen, formal, button-down, proper. Even in the field Dr. Hayes wore coat, vest, and tie.

"Show me samples of the pay, please Mr. DeGolyer."

The samples were ready for examination. Dr. Hayes looked through the microscope at length, moving the crushed bits of limestone around with tweezers.

"Did you note the rhombic crystals?" he asked De, his eye still glued to the eyepiece.

"Yes, sir. What do they indicate?"

"Crystal-lined cavities, which might indicate good porosity."

"What age is the pay zone, sir?" asked De. "Is it the Tamasopo?"

"If my correlations are correct, yes, it is the Tamasopo limestone, which is Cretaceous in age and is the same zone that blew out at Dos Bocas." Dr. Hayes continued examining the samples and finally looked up from the microscope. "There is only a small amount of visible porosity, isn't there?"

"I've not seen enough cuttings from wells to know, sir," admitted De.

"It's a dilemma, Mr. DeGolyer. The well is a teaser. Walk away now and we'll never know what we found. Yet drilling another well may be throwing good money after bad."

"Yes, sir, that's my thought exactly."

"What do you recommend, Mr. DeGolyer?" asked Dr. Hayes.

De had known for two days the question was forthcoming. "We could drill another well. Maybe the next one will be better. But it's my recommendation to drill four more wells at the same time, one in each direction from the No. 1."

Dr. Hayes was clearly surprised. "Four wells at the same time…that's aggressive don't you think, Mr. DeGolyer?"

"A four-well rectangular pattern will confirm the structural configuration of the anticline. I would stake locations to the east and west and slightly closer to the first well than those to the north and south to fit the elongated direction of the anticline."

"What if the next wells perform like the first one? It would be a huge loss for Lord Cowdray. These wells cost $25,000 each."

"Unless we drill all four offsets to the No. 1, we will never answer the question about how big or how good the anticline can be," replied De. "By drilling all four wells, we'll gain a much better understanding of the structural configuration of the anticline, and also of the stratigraphy and the nature of the Tamasopo. Is the reservoir rock uniform? Will one side of the anticline exhibit higher producing rates than another?"

Dr. Hayes took out his pipe, filled it with tobacco, deliberately tamped the tobacco firmly into the bowl, and finally lit it. De remained quiet. He had the same reservations about his own recommendation that Dr. Hayes was pondering.

Finally Dr. Hayes said, "It *is* a dilemma. To ascertain a predictable geologic model that will support the rest of our exploration program, we need to understand the Tamasopo. Four wells, though, Mr. DeGolyer, four more wells…"

"Drilling next to seeps hasn't worked," said De. "We have to drill anticlines, and we need more answers about the Tamasopo."

"You're right about needing more answers," agreed Dr. Hayes. "And the only way to answer the questions is with the drill bit. Walking away now makes no sense, but a recommendation to drill four wells at once is a big order."

"Dr. Hayes, we know it is an oil-saturated anticline. It appears to be large. If the next two or three wells are no better than the first, the question will remain unanswered whether one more well in the undrilled direction would unlock the key to the stratigraphy. It's no time to tiptoe one well at a time. Four wells or none."

All day Jim had been hanging around the two men. He hadn't understood all that they discussed, but now he nodded his head in agreement.

The two spent the rest of the day measuring sections along the river banks and the side creek, and batting around possibilities. Jim followed them, listening to their geological banter, but didn't intrude in their discussions. He paddled them across the river where De showed Dr. Hayes slight indications of west dip on the Alazan hacienda, which El Aguila also had under lease. De told Dr. Hayes if the Potrero anticline extended that much farther north, it would be sizeable.

Their field work endorsed De's recommendation: drill four more wells back-to-back.

Before he left the site, Dr. Hayes told De he would lay the dilemma before

Lord Cowdray. Drilling one well at a time was the safest way to determine whether the anticline was commercial. However failing to offset the first well in all four directions would leave unanswered the basic stratigraphy needed to determine if the Tamasopo was a viable reservoir. He instructed De to run samples on the next wells, to prepare well logs from the samples, and to send him a written report on each well and show how each zone in each well correlates to that in the other wells.

That night De turned over in his mind his recommendation to drill four wells at once. He had struggled with the implications of his recommendation but knew in his heart he was correct. Examining outcrops in the Arbuckle and Rocky Mountains had taught him that limestones can be heterogeneous. In Montana he had observed how a few feet could mean the difference between a porous limestone and one as tight as flint.

The next day Dr. Hayes returned to Tampico to catch the train to San Luis Potosí and then on to Mexico City to meet with Lord Cowdray. De, Jim, and Hippolito set out from Potrero for the mountains with a long string of pack mules loaded with two weeks of supplies. De was elated to be headed to the mountains. He whistled as he followed the pack train. Hippolito was in the lead riding a small burro. De had instructed him first to head to the plateau in front of the mountains west of Valles. Hippolito called it the Sierra del Abra.

They traveled by trails, most large enough for oxcarts. The Díaz government required that landowners maintain the trails through their lands. By connecting the villages with a good trail system and patrolling it with his *rurales*, Díaz was able to extend the reach of his control. Even though the Indians complained that the *rurales* abused their power, peace had prevailed for more than thirty years. When they passed through Indian villages, De noted how poor the people were. Villagers lived in thatched houses and scratched a living from small plots planted in corn. Most villages were inhabited by women and children because the men worked at the haciendas or for the oil companies.

De surmised that until the oil play came along, little had altered their way of life since before Cortez. As he rode along, De pondered how to improve the life of peasants. Manuel had told him more that three-fourths of the people of Mexico were illiterate. He bet illiteracy among Indians was even higher. Educating their children had to be part of the answer. Sending native children to school far from their families hadn't worked in the U.S. Maybe he'd ask Hippolito.

When De saw bedding, he would jump from his horse to examine the rocks, pound them with his rock hammer, label the samples, and put them in the pack gear. He often scribbled in his notebook as he rode.

De loved this kind of field work. Riding horseback provided a wholly different perspective than tramping the ground. From the back of a horse he could see farther and pay better attention to the regional topography. Looking at the country with a view for the geology made him feel like a latter-day conquistador, this time conquering not the indigenous cultures, but the secrets hidden deep beneath the surface.

The Sierra del Abra loomed larger as they rode west. It stood three hundred meters above the surrounding landscape, a narrow, north-south elongated plateau of limestone in front of the much higher Sierra Madre Oriental. They camped at a spring near the base of the plateau. De closely examined the limestone that the spring gushed from. Dalton's report on the sierras called it the Tamasopo, the same as the pay in the Potrero well. Springs poured from the limestone all along the base of the plateau. He traveled to several sites where the clear water poured out in huge quantities, forming deep pools of emerald green water before cascading to lower elevations. The springs convinced De that the rock had good reservoir qualities. If the limestone was porous enough to absorb rainwater and channel it to large springs on the surface, those same characteristics could become an excellent reservoir rock for oil production in the subsurface.

Late each day thunderheads built towering anvils in the afternoon sky. As the sun sank behind the western mountains, sky hues changed from soft blue to amber, fading after sunset to dove grey and finally to a deep navy blue. The entire heavens became an upturned bowl lit by thousands of brilliant stars. A gibbous moon on the eastern horizon rose, each night closer to the horizon, like a huge floating pumpkin in the sky.

In the evening after a day on the outcrop, their routine soon became unspoken and efficient. Hippolito unloaded the pack mules, unsaddled the horses, started a fire, and began cooking. Jim hobbled the livestock and gathered firewood. De raised the tent and lit a kerosene lantern to review his notes while they were still fresh on his mind. In the margins he would draw cross-sections showing the bedding planes he had mapped on the surface and extrapolating the beds into the subsurface.

For a week they camped on the Sierra del Abra. De first mapped the topography and then measured thicknesses of the rock beds, marking the information on his plane-table and calling for Jim to move the rod to a new location as he mapped the southern nose of the plateau. He agreed with Dalton that the lower member of limestone, where the springs gushed clear water, was the Tamasopo. The realization that it could be an excellent reservoir rock raised his confidence that the oil play south of Tampico was not a fluke.

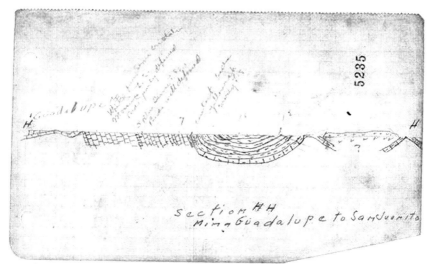

DeGolyer's interpretation of subsurface

"De, you're treating me worse than a Chinaman," complained Jim good-naturedly. "Holding this rod is worse than roping steers on foot. I'd rather be an interpreter than a rod man."

"You're a fine rod man, Jim, a man of many talents. See how most of these beds dip away from the sierras. I've seen the same on the Front Range of the Rockies. I wouldn't be surprised if the uplift or compressional force that created the Rockies didn't form these mountains, too."

"It must have been some awful powerful force to bend rocks like that," commented Jim. "A crow bar wouldn't nudge this plateau a quarter inch."

"Probably it happened very slowly when the rock was buried and hot, which could make it less brittle. Don't think in human scale. We're dealing with geologic scale. Think about moving this entire sierra at the rate that your fingernail grows, maybe an inch a year. Does that make it easier to understand?"

"You're still bending rocks and moving mountains."

"Yes, but slowly, very slowly and over millions of years. See those bedding planes that are shoved up vertically? They were laid down horizontally in a marine environment."

"In the ocean?"

"That's right."

"Lordy, De. You're telling me these rocks you're beating to pieces were laid down in the bottom of the sea. And then you're telling me they were shoved up here to make this mountain we're standing on. We're probably a thousand feet above the coast."

"Yes, and what I'm also trying to figure out is when it happened."

"What difference does that make?"

"See these beds of rock, the folded ones? I think the rocks are middle or maybe lower Cretaceous, just like the Rockies. If these folds were formed after the Cretaceous in the Tertiary like I think, we can deduct that the anticlines that we're drilling in the subsurface were formed at the same time and by the same forces. Look here. This is probably the same limestone we're drilling at Potrero." He showed Jim a chunk of limestone he had broken with his rock hammer. "See those stains. What do they look like?"

"Oil."

"It's dead oil, but oil nevertheless. Did it migrate through here after the rocks were folded or before, or maybe it's being formed *in situ* in the rocks."

"So what?"

"If the oil migrated through the rocks before the anticlines were formed, they wouldn't be filled with oil, but with salt water."

"Selling salt water could be a challenge," said Jim with a grin. "There's plenty enough in the ocean."

De laughed and continued. "The whole Sierra Madre Oriental runs north-south through this country. Sierra del Abra runs north-south. Remember which direction we mapped Potrero?"

"North-south. Tierra Amarilla was more east-west."

"Which is a hint that Tierra Amarilla was not formed by the same forces and at the same time as this plateau and the sierras were formed, or when the Potrero anticline was formed."

"Mr. De, do you ever get hungry? You fill your mind with this geologic big-think and forget about your stomach. Are you trying to starve us to death?"

"It *is* getting late," admitted De. "Let's stop for lunch."

They sat down in the shade of an oak tree, broke out the tortillas that Hippolito had prepared, and rolled them around tasty strips of goat meat dried with hot chili peppers. De commented how much he liked the peppers, the hotter the better.

"Wait until tomorrow," replied Jim. "You may change your mind."

When they broke camp at the foot of the Sierra del Abra, De directed Hippolito to head to the high mountains. Only a few trails penetrated the steep mountain front, trails that were only wide enough for a horse or mule. They climbed steadily, their horses and pack mules grunting with exertion. Hippolito would stop occasionally to let the panting animals rest and re-tie loose packs. Finally they topped out onto a high mountain meadow more than three thousand feet above the coastal plain. The air was cooler. They pitched camp near a clear-running stream with a view into a distant valley. That night the wind howled in the trees and the temperature dropped. Jim kept adding wood to the fire Hippolito had built.

"I don't know why the *indios* won't build a big fire," Jim said. He added some logs and walked over to Hippolito and passed on his thoughts, then walked back to De with a laugh.

"Old Hippo has a dicho for every occasion."

"What did he say?" asked De.

"He said *'las lumbres que yo he prendido no las aspaga cualquiera'*."

"Which means?"

"The fires that I have started can't be put out by anyone."

"What does he mean by that?" asked De.

"I think he's saying no one can take his place, meaning he doesn't think you and your rock hammer and me and my survey rod could find where to camp or firewood to burn. You wonder what he thinks we're doing up here in the mountains."

"He probably thinks we're *loco*, beating on rocks, measuring section all day," said De.

"Thank goodness he keeps it to himself."

"Jim, ask Hippolito if he'd like the Indian children to attend school."

Jim raised his voice so Hippolito could hear. Hippolito was bent over stacking wood, but when Jim asked the question, he stopped and looked at the two Americans.

"*Bonito es ver llover aunque uno no tenga milpa.*"

"What did he say?" asked De.

"He said it's beautiful to see the rainfall even if he doesn't own a farm."

On the tenth day while they were traveling along a limestone ridge, De jumped off his horse, grabbed his rock hammer and started pounding away. "Would you look at this!" he exclaimed, and held up a piece of red-stained rock.

"It looks like a petrified ice cream cone, jefe. What is it?"

"A rudist!" De pointed at his feet. "It's a rudist colony!"

"You don't say," said Jim.

"Rudists are bi-valve mollusks that live in shallow water," De said. "Look! This whole ridge is one big rudist colony!"

"A rudist colony," repeated Jim and shook his head. He looked up and down the ridge. It was solid red-stained fossils like the one De held up.

"You've sure enough found yourself a rudist colony," commented Jim. "Mr. De, maybe you better not let anyone but me and Hippolito know how much these rocks get you excited. Hippolito already thinks you're crazy. We don't want the word to spread."

De spent the afternoon diligently hammering on the outcrop. He kept filling up small cotton sacks with rock samples and asked Jim to label them for him. He noticed that Jim's writing was slow and tentative.

Later, after De had filled a dozen or more sample bags, he looked up and down the ridge and asked Jim, "Do you notice anything interesting about our rudist colony?"

"These fossils have probably been here a million years without a worry in the world, bless their hearts, and then you show up with a rock hammer and start beating them to bits. What else should I notice about your rudist colony?"

"They only cover an area maybe a hundred yards wide. And they're completely cemented together."

"You forgot to mention they're red."

De grinned. "Jim, we're standing on an ancient reef. I don't know why the rudists are rust-colored, but the fact that they're cemented together tells me something changed after they were deposited. A colony of individual rudists should have preserved a lot of pore-space even after they were buried. Cementation is a bad sign."

"Cementation?" asked Jim.

"Fluid won't flow through these rocks."

"If they weren't cemented together, they would have fallen off the mountain."

De stared blankly at Jim for a moment. "That's an interesting observation, Jim. You're beginning to think like a geologist. What if the talus slope of the reef is the place to drill a well for uncemented reservoir rock? I'll have to think about that possibility. It may be the problem with the Potrero well."

"What does the Potrero well have to do with this?"

"Don't you see, it's the same Tamasopo! If we can find a reef in the subsurface, and if we can find where the rocks are not cemented together, we'll know where the good reservoir rock is in the Tamasopo."

"Is that one big *if* and a little *if*, or is it two big *if*'s?"

"Figuring out what happened to the Tamasopo after deposition is part of the puzzle," De said. "Jim, you made a good observation."

"My mother always said I was observant."

De laughed, moved back from the ledge, and started walking toward a rock bluff that rose thirty or more feet high. He moved along its face and squatted down next to a shaded opening.

"Jim, would you look at this?" De said.

"What do you have there, *jefe?*"

"It's a cave. Let's check it out."

"You better watch for rattle bugs," warned Jim. "They love to hole up in caves like this."

De wadded dry grass and sticks into a makeshift torch, lit it and crawled on his belly through the opening. In a few minutes he crawled back out.

"Wow, it's huge. I can't see the back. The ceiling must be fifteen feet tall."

"Without lanterns you better stay out of there, Mr. De. One of these days we can come back and do a little exploring. We need to get on back to camp. It's getting dark on us. You've loaded the mule with so many rocks, he can barely budge."

As they rode back to camp, De kept turning over in his mind the reef, the cave, and the springs. For certain the Tamasopo was not a massive dense limestone. If he could find an anticline in the subsurface where the Tamasopo had caves, or was an uncemented reef, the production could be fabulous.

When they arrived in camp, long after dark, Hippolito quickly heated the meal he had prepared hours before and served them as soon as they sat down at the campfire. De ate silently, contented after a great day of discovery on the outcrop. The pieces of the puzzle were beginning to fall into place. The streams proved the Tamasopo had excellent reservoir qualities, but why was the reef cemented? After supper, lying around the campfire before calling it a night, Jim regaled De with stories of his days chasing cattle. De laughed and shared his cigars. Hippolito silently smoked a cigar and listened to the banter, but never laughed or made a comment. Still, he kept close to the campfire and seemed to enjoy the company.

De rolled into his sleeping bag and thought of Nell and of the geological clues that were coming together in his mind. He wished she were here to share his excitement. He stared up at the stars sparkling bright across the wide swath of sky. Venus shone in the south, glimmering in the night sky, obscured occasionally by a patch of cloud, but mostly so brilliant he thought he could touch it. He puffed on his cigar and mused at what brought him to this spot on earth. It was a long way from Norman, Oklahoma.

The more he examined these rocks, the more confident De felt about finding significant oil production for Lord Cowdray, if he could only figure where the good reservoir rock was in the subsurface. His mind kept returning to the springs. What secret did they hold?

At the end of the second week they rode off the mountains down into

Tamazunchale, an Indian village on the south side of the Rio Moctezuma in the foothills of the sierras. At the town center a large church stood next to a plaza. De was surprised at its size. He asked Hippolito to pull up the horses so that he might examine its ancient stone and plaster construction. No sooner had they walked to the intricately carved front door than they were surrounded by a crowd of children.

"Why the reception?" De asked. The children spoke a language that De knew was not Spanish.

Hippolito said the children were *huastecan*. They pointed to Jim's hair. They had never before seen a redhead.

Hippolito led De and Jim to a house made of hand-hewn planks and told them there would be beds here. Hippolito unloaded their sleeping gear onto the porch and said he would take the animals to the *potrero*.

"Did he say *potrero*?" asked De.

"Yep, it's not far."

"What does it mean, *potrero*?" asked De.

"It means 'pasture'. I thought you knew that," said Jim.

"Potrero del Llano. Pastures of the plains," said De. "It sounds biblical."

After washing with a cloth dipped in a pan of water, which only removed the outer layer of dust from the day's ride, De and Jim strolled to the plaza. The locals were holding some kind of religious festival. A procession passed. First an Indian priest carried a cross and a wooden statue of Christ with grotesque features and a feathered crown. Rusty nails were hammered into its hands and feet. The bloodstains looked real to De. A double line of masked Indian men followed the cross. When the Indian priest entered the church, the followers broke out of procession and surrounded the two Americans, circling faster and faster. The wooden masks they wore were in the form of deer heads, bull heads, and bird heads. Each man held a painted wooden dagger with colored feathers attached to the handle. The masked men danced closer and closer to the two foreigners, circling and muttering a chant that rose into a crescendo. Some shook gourds in their faces and made passes with their wooden daggers as if to stab them. De looked at Jim and raised his eyebrows. Finally, the Indians gave a shout, removed their masks, and held out their gourds for an offering. De put some coins in the gourds. After receiving the money the Indians laughed and held up their coins, spoke to each other in an unfamiliar language and finally scattered, some going into the church, others taking the hands of women dressed in colorful clothes who had followed the procession.

"What was *that*?" asked Jim. "I thought we were about to be scalped."

"It wasn't high mass," answered De. "Four hundred years of Catholicism hasn't erased their own religion."

"Catholics here sure don't act like Catholics in South Texas," observed Jim.

By the time De and Jim returned to Tampico, Dr. Hayes had met Lord Cowdray in Mexico City and wired that the Chief had approved the drilling of four more wells at Potrero del Llano. Detailed instructions were given to build a permanent camp, to construct a railroad line and to lay a six inch pipeline from Potrero to Tanhuijo on the south end of the Tamiahua Lagoon, more than twenty miles away.

De was surprised at the report. He had only recommended drilling four wells at once, and certainly had not recommended that El Aguila build a pipeline and railroad without knowing what the wells would produce, or *if* they would produce. He questioned Tom Ryder, El Aguila's superintendent in the Tampico office, about such a large commitment. Mr. Ryder answered that the Chief had a great deal of confidence in the new team.

"We'll soon find out if you Americans are better geologists than the British," he said. De could tell he wasn't joking.

De asked what facilities would be required for a permanent camp. Mr. Ryder explained that the Potrero camp would consist of an office and six houses for the drillers and company personnel, as well as a blacksmith shop, an ice plant, cold-storage plants, a water distillery, an electrical plant, a sawmill, a machine shop and a boiler shop.

De was astounded. "Should Lord Cowdray spend so much money before we know if the wells will produce?" he asked. The result of his recommendation to drill four wells at once was staggering.

"In June the rainy season sets in. Lord Cowdray and Mr. Body thought it best to construct the camp as soon as possible. We'll move another cable tool rig and a Hammil rotary rig to Potrero as well. Dormitories will be needed for the workers, and also a medical facility."

"How many workers are you talking about?"

"We will hire three hundred now. When the rigs arrive, we'll add more."

De again expressed his surprise at such a huge commitment.

"You can never accuse the Chief of small thinking," replied Mr. Ryder. "I hope a six-inch pipeline is big enough," he said without smiling.

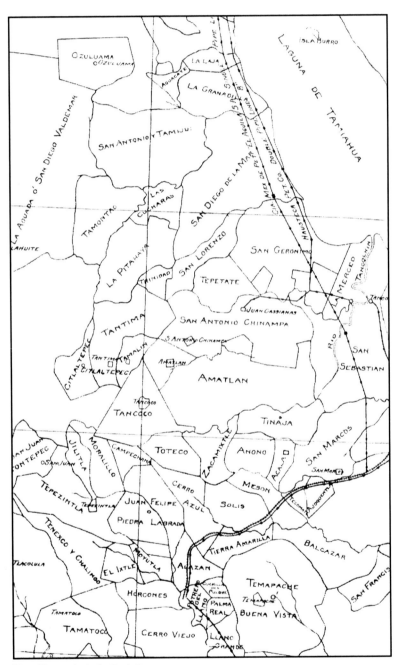

Map of haciendas in the South Zone

Chapter Six

February — May 1910

During the next three months Dr. Hayes directed Hop, Chester, and De to re-map the El Aguila properties that had been studied by their British antecessors. Every two to three weeks, the three geologists would meet in Tampico and share their information. De began putting the topography and strikes and dips onto a regional map. Hop and Chester agreed with De that the Tamasopo could have excellent reservoir qualities in the subsurface, but each had differing opinions about where and if good reservoir rock could be predictable.

"There is no predictability in geology," claimed Chester. "Look at the results of all the wells drilled by Huasteca at El Ebano. Each well performs differently than the one next to it, yet they're not three hundred feet apart, and out of twenty wells, there is a single good one."

"Drilling next to a poor well increases the odds of drilling a poor well," answered De. "Isn't that predictability?"

"What about drilling next to Potrero No. 1? It isn't exactly a barnburner," replied Chester.

"When Potrero No. 1 flows, it flows a large quantity of oil and then loads up and kills itself. To me, that means it could be close to some good rock. We saw indications of cavities in the cuttings. I didn't recommend offsetting a two-barrel a day well."

"What seems smart to me," said Hop, "is to stick close to good wells. Practical is more important than predictable."

"But without predictability, every wildcat is a stab in the dark," said De.

"So let somebody else do the stabbing," replied Hop. "Why drill a wildcat? When someone makes a good well, all we need to do is drill next to it."

"Hop, you know the problem with that idea," said De. "El Aguila owns more than half a million acres. *We* have to drill the exploratory wells."

"Maybe not," said Hop. "We could contribute acreage and let somebody else contribute drilling money. We split the acreage so both have half of what's good, but El Aguila doesn't pay drilling costs for what's bad."

"Hop, I like your idea, but El Aguila has to drill the wildcat. Can we find success simply by avoiding failure?"

"De, you end every conversation with more questions than answers."

De, Jim, and Hippolito spent most of the next four months mapping the properties that El Aguila already owned or had under lease near Potrero del Llano. With Hippolito's help De located the smaller *quebradas* or streambeds, which he walked out with Jim, who handled the survey rod. Hippolito managed the machete and pointed to *mala mujer* thistles that were so painful to bare skin, and occasionally to a rattlesnake, which Hippolito treated with reverence. He refused to kill the serpents but instead gave them a wide berth until they wriggled out of the path. Hippolito soon learned the kinds of terrain De looked for, and guided them to arroyos or streambeds where there was the possibility of finding bedding planes.

In the middle of an afternoon while they were mapping Cuchilla del Pulque, one of the *estancias* not far from Potrero del Llano, an Indian rushed from the jungle and started talking excitedly to Hippolito. Hippolito translated to Jim.

"The fellow says his wife and baby are sick," Jim told De. "He wants us to give her some medicine."

"Where is she?"

"At his house in the jungle somewhere," answered Jim. "Mr. De, she could have cholera or some other contagious disease. Out here if the *curanderas* can't cure them, they just die."

"We'll try to help," said De, without giving it another thought. "Tell him to show us the way."

The Indian led them on foot along a narrow trail through the dense foliage. At a small sunlit opening in the jungle they came to a thatch house. When they rode into the clearing De heard a baby's cry. He dismounted and hurried to the thatch hut.

Inside a young woman lay on a bed of leaves covered by hides. De looked around for a chair or stool. The only evidence of the modern world was an iron pot on a tripod over a smoking fire. The woman's husband spoke to Hippolito, who translated to Jim in Spanish.

"He says the baby is sick," Jim told De. "The mother has a fever."

"Let's take a look," said De. He removed his knapsack, knelt beside the woman, and felt her forehead. "She's running a high fever. All I have is aspirin. What about the baby?"

Jim felt the baby's head, placed the back of his hand against the mother's cheek, stuck out his tongue to show her to stick out her tongue, and then pulled down the bed covers. Her breasts were dried and caked.

"The baby isn't sick, he's hungry," said Jim. "I've seen mother cows with the same problem."

"What do you do for them?"

"The same thing I'll do for this Indian woman."

Jim took from his saddlebag a clean cloth, a bar of soap, and a jar of ointment. He soaked the cloth in warm water from the pot over the fire, and with the soap gingerly cleaned the woman's caked breasts while she stared at him wide-eyed and watchful. Flakes of dried skin stuck to the cloth. Jim covered both his hands with ointment and began massaging her breasts. After a few moments he gestured for the husband to mimic what he was doing.

Jim told Hippolito he'd leave them the ointment. "Tell him to rub it on several times a day. She'll be giving milk in no time."

When they left the house, the man was effusive in his thanks. They didn't need to speak *huastecan* to understand gratitude. De told Jim he was impressed with his practical knowledge of medicine.

"Dry tit is common with young heifer cows," Jim said as he tied the saddle bags behind his saddle. "Today was the first time I ever held a woman's breast with her husband watching."

De laughed. "Hippolito and I won't tell anyone. We'd hate to hurt your reputation."

The next week they began mapping the topography and measuring strikes and dips with the Brunton compass on Los Horcones, an *estancia* that adjoined Potrero del Llano to the west. It was owned by the Suara family and had been divided into 1200 shares, which were fragmented by fifth generation cousins, now scattered all over Mexico. The *estancia* to the south, Cerro Viejo, had signed leases with both Huasteca Petroleum Company and with El Aguila. Until the title to both *estancias* could be cleared, no drilling operations were planned.

When the manager of Los Horcones learned that Americans were on the property, he sent word that they must leave immediately. De directed Hippolito to take them to the hacienda's headquarters so he could discuss the issue. When they arrived, De asked Jim to tell the manager that they worked for El Aguila, and that they had authority to study the geology because El Aguila had the hacienda under lease. The manager shook his head emphatically and told them they were not allowed on the property. De walked to the pack mule, removed his plane table, set it up in the front yard, and began examining the topography, whereby the manager shouted at them to leave. Without speaking a word, Hippolito walked behind him and slapped the flat blade of his machete across the man's buttocks. The manager was astounded. No Indian had ever confronted his authority. Without speaking, he turned and stomped back into the house. Hippolito picked up the tripod, folded its legs, and put it over his shoulder.

Jim looked at De. "What do you think about old Hippolito, *jefe?*" He was as surprised as the ranch manager at Hippolito's action.

"I think Hippolito just handed us permission to map Los Horcones," replied De.

Hippolito's face remained expressionless.

"Silence doesn't mean subservience, now does it?" De said, and patted Hippolito's arm.

"*El que busca, halla,*" commented Hippolito and turned to fetch the horses.

Jim nodded in agreement. "He said whoever looks for trouble finds it."

In April 1910 a stunning political development rocked Mexico. Francisco I. Madero, scion of one of the country's wealthiest families, announced that he would challenge Porfirio Díaz in the fall election. Over the last two years, Madero had become Díaz's chief critic. He published a daring book that criticized Díaz for his increasing authoritarianism, and for giving away too many concessions to foreign companies. Madero's book became a runaway bestseller in Mexico, and he attracted huge crowds as he began campaigning for the presidency.

As the season turned to late spring, the temperate winter days grew warmer and the heat and humidity began to rise. De sweated out his clothes and wondered what the heat would be like later in the summer. Temperatures in Oklahoma and the Rockies could warm up, but not with such stifling humidity. Los Horcones had not proven promising, but De was excited about Cerro Viejo. He intended to recommend to Dr. Hayes that efforts be made to cure the title so El Aguila could drill a well.

When De and Jim returned to Tampico, tired and dirty from another field trip, the two cleaned up and met Hop and Chester in the bar of the Southern Hotel for a drink. After downing a couple, Jim invited them to accompany him to the Club Mariposa.

"It's the classiest cantina in Tampico, world headquarters for the oil patch."

"World headquarters?" repeated Chester.

"Sure is. All the oil magnates hang out there, not to mention some of the prettiest *señoritas* you've ever laid your eyes on."

With Jim as guide, the three young men followed him to the Mariposa, a short walk from downtown. It was situated on a bluff overlooking the Panuco River and had an outdoor terrace. Inside, a local band played *huapango* music. Jim described it as a cross between *mariachi* music and *conjunto* music. "It's dancing music," he told his young geologist friends. "Do you boys know how to twirl the girls?"

De, Chester, and Hop didn't reply but looked interested.

"Here, I'll show you. See those young ladies next to the bar?" Several *señoritas* lounged in an area toward the back of the bar.

"You go up to one, ask her to *baile*, and then get after it. They bring the girls here for dance partners. You'll need to buy them a drink, which is how the house pays for the privilege."

De, Hop, and Chester nodded but no one moved.

"It's the best way in the world to improve your Spanish," continued Jim. "I learned Spanish from *señoritas* in the bars when I was just a kid in Mexico City."

With that, Jim tucked his pant legs into the top of his boots, which he called his pumpers, pushed back his cowboy hat, walked over to the prettiest *señorita*, and started a conversation. When the music began, they twirled like polka dancers on the wooden dance floor. Soon De, Hop, and Chester joined the other foreigners, mainly young Americans, who were dancing with the *señoritas*.

De's dance partner told him her name was Chelina. Over the loud and lively music De struggled to think of things to say, sticking to the present tense. Chelina giggled at his word choices, but understood him and answered his questions with simple responses.

De liked her smell. It reminded him of the gardenias in the plaza his first night in Tampico, gardenias mixed with a slight scent of sweat. On a slow dance she pressed against him and called him her 'cherry'.

"¿*Compra una bebida?*" she asked after a few dances, and De said '*Claro*' like an old hand and walked to the bar and bought drinks. When the band took a break, the four couples sat together. Jim insisted that no one speak English, and then he and the girls laughed at the others' broken Spanish. Chelina whispered in De's ear.

De raised his eyebrows at Jim. "What's she saying?" Chelina spoke rapidly to Jim.

"She wants you to take her to one of the rooms in the back. It'll cost you more than a drink."

The realization sank in that Chelina was not just a dancing girl. De felt slightly awkward but not embarrassed. No, he told her, only *baile*. Jim winked at him and said, "If you boys don't throw a little more money around, our ladies won't think you're the oil magnates I told them you were."

"We better learn enough Spanish to keep you from misrepresentation," replied De. When the band started, he told the others he would walk back to the Southern.

At the Southern bar, De had a drink by himself and thought of Nell. What would she think if she knew he was in a place like the Mariposa? Surely she'd heard stories of the oilfield boom towns, and the girls who followed the booms. De had always felt secure, taking Nell's love and constancy for granted, even with the vast distance separating them. But he began to wonder, did Nell take his fidelity for granted, or did she worry about him? He wished he could hold her right now and talk to her, to reassure her that he would always be her man. But she was so far away, and his new world was so very different, and yes, very enticing.

Less than a week later De stepped to the desk at the Southern Hotel and asked for messages and his key. The clerk handed him a letter.

Norman, Oklahoma
April 5, 1910

Sweetheart De:
I am sending today to the best sweetheart a girl ever had a talisman, which is to mean to him that the greatest love of which I am capable is given to him – and by the talisman in itself that I have the supremest trust in him of all men.

My hope and daily prayer is that he may be guided from all temptation and that he may be kept from all desire of evil in attractive or unattractive guise.

If this talisman, consecrated with a kiss from lips kept sacred to him, will help in any way to strengthen him against things which would tend to make him the less noble and true-hearted, I shall be glad for the day that the thought was suggested to me.

Should the talisman prove to my sweetheart that I am true to him day in and day out forever and that he of all men is uppermost in my heart, mind, esteem and confidence, I shall be more than repaid for the slight breaking of tradition it has been to me to send the talisman.

May Heaven keep us as true to one another henceforth as we have been in the past.
Your Nell

The letter made De's heart ache to see her. Work in the field kept his mind occupied but at night in camp or when he worked late in the office in Tampico, his mind involuntarily turned to Nell. After the night at the Mariposa, De felt guilty that he had enjoyed the dancing. He read Nell's letter again and wondered what had prompted her to write it. Was she worried about his morals or his fidelity? Admittedly the young prostitutes in the cantinas were attractive, and his thoughts might be less than noble, but never his actions. It had been more than six months since he had wrapped his arms around Nell. Their separation, he decided, was a test of his character, and a test he was determined to pass.

The three young geologists continued the geological field work on El Aguila properties based on instructions sent from Dr. Hayes in Washington D.C. After working in the field for two to three weeks, mapping an area or a hacienda, each returned to Tampico and spent a few days plotting the information gathered in the field onto maps and writing a report. By early June the summer rains made field work difficult. Dry streambeds were swollen to the banks with muddy flood water. The heat and humidity were stifling. Wood ticks and mosquitoes discovered every bit of uncovered skin. Plane-table work was slow and cumbersome in the mud.

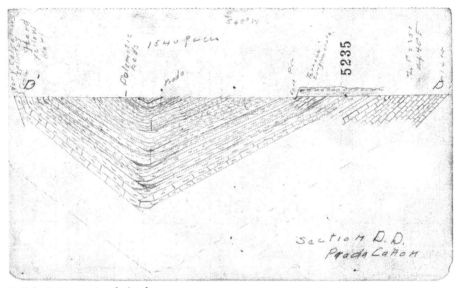

DeGolyer's interpretation of subsurface

Jim finally told De that he and Hippolito were going to mutiny.

"We didn't hire on to be in the navy, *jefe*. Why don't we head back to Tampico? I'll do some recon work there on the competition. You can work on your maps." He spoke to Hippolito.

Hippolito replied, "*Después de la lluvia, sale el sol.*"

De thought a minute and then interpreted, 'after a rainstorm, the sun will shine'. De laughed. "You're right, Hippolito. Jim, let's head to Tamiahua. Stomping around in the mud isn't doing us any good."

They returned to Tamiahua and spent the next day with Don Luis Kenyon, who always appreciated their company. His maid washed their clothes and brought hot water to a big tin tub for bathing. Clean and refreshed, their spirits lifted. The next morning De and Jim waved down the company launch and left Hippolito on the bank with the horses. When De arrived early to Tampico, he found Hop alone in the office.

"I didn't expect you back so soon," said Hop.

"I tried to finish mapping Los Naranjos, but it's too wet to plough. We couldn't cross the streams, the arroyos were running full bank, and the mosquitoes have grown big as turkey vultures. Hop, I stopped in to see Mr. Ryder but couldn't find him. Do you know where he is?"

"Mr. Ryder left for Mexico City and will be gone two weeks," Hop replied. "The Chief called him in for talks with the politicos. The Madero thing has them worried."

"He'll be gone for two weeks?"

"That's what he told me."

"Then I'm catching the train tomorrow for Oklahoma."

"You're what?"

"I'm going to ask Nell to marry me."

"You are *what?*"

"I'm going to ask Nell to marry me," De repeated.

"You can't just take off for Oklahoma without permission."

"There's no one to ask," said De. "I'll be back in two weeks. That's my plan."

"Have you told Nell your plan?"

"I didn't know I had the opportunity until five minutes ago."

"You're going to leave without permission to ask a girl to marry you who doesn't know you're coming?"

"I mapped as much of Los Naranjos as I could. Until the rain slows down we can't do anymore field work. Dr. Hayes is in Europe and Mr. Ryder is in Mexico City for two weeks."

"De, you should tell somebody besides me," suggested Hop.

"I'll go without pay."

"You are crazy *enamorado.*"

"Dr. Hayes said I would be moving to Tuxpan. I won't have another chance to go to Norman for months."

That night Chester also returned from the field. The three geologists dined together at the Colonial Club and Hop told Chester of De's plan. De pleaded guilty as accused and admitted he had already packed. Chester suggested De's rationality was distorted. Wouldn't they all appreciate the company of a nice girl, but Tampico was no place to bring anyone you cared for.

"It must be the heat and humidity," said Chester. "It's affected your good sense." But De repeated that his mind was made up.

The next morning when they accompanied De to the train depot across the canal, Hop asked De to bring Nell's sisters. "Nell will need the company and so do me and Chester."

"I'll be back in two weeks," replied De with a confident grin. "Married and with my new bride."

"You better not give her the straight skinny about life in Tampico," suggested Chester. "And for heaven's sake don't tell her about Tuxpan, or about doing field work for two weeks at a time, or about coleopterans as big as her arm. She'll probably turn you down anyway."

"Cheerful Chester," retorted De. "I'll tell Nell how my two friends couldn't wait to meet her."

"That's a fact," said Hop. "Honest, I hope it works for you, De. Good luck and God speed. This place could use some ladies."

As the train pulled out of the station, Chester shouted, "Bring her sisters!"

Chapter Seven

June — October 1910

When De arrived by train in Laredo, he wired Nell that he would be in Norman the next day and had important issues to discuss. He paced nervously throughout the train on the way to Oklahoma, chewing cigars and trying to picture the encounter to come. He knew that Nell loved him, but she had said, repeatedly, that they couldn't marry until he finished his college degree. De wondered how much of this came from Nell, and how much was due to her parents. Although Mr. and Mrs. Goodrich seemed to like De, he knew that they saw him as somewhat impetuous, having rushed off to work in Mexico, rather than building a career for himself in a more conventional fashion. Even if he could somehow convince Nell to say yes, how would her parents react?

Late the next afternoon, dressed in his best suit, he arrived at the Goodrich home. Norman was not as hot as Tampico, but De felt sweat dripping as he stepped onto the porch. Nell opened the door before he could knock. Their eyes met and De's heart skipped. Yes, he thought, yes, you're the only one, and you have always been the only one.

He reached for her and Nell flushed. They hugged without saying a word. De was so choked he could barely whisper hello. After a brief kiss, she led him inside to visit with her parents. De had brought a large bottle of Mexican vanilla for Nell's mother, and a box of Cuban cigars for her father. After some polite chatter, they sat down to dinner, and De was delighted to see that Nell's mother had prepared his favorite, chicken and dumplings.

After dinner De took Nell for a walk and formally proposed. She accepted without hesitation, which surprised and pleased him immensely. He had expected a discussion about his plans for graduating from college and a career after the Mexico job. Nell's simple 'yes' erased all his self-doubts. They kissed a long, lingering warm rose kiss.

"Are you parents okay with this?" he asked.

Nell nodded. "They know what I want, De. They know what I need." De didn't know exactly how she had done it, but he realized that Nell had already cleared the path for them.

"We'll be living in Mexico," De said, "at least until my contract is up in November. Would you mind moving to Mexico?"

"Oh De, of course I won't mind. Since last October I've thought about you every single day, alone in that wild country."

"We won't be living in Tampico," De said. "Dr. Hayes is moving me to Tuxpan, which is about sixty miles south of Tampico. Tuxpan is, well, it's rustic, no electricity, no paved streets, only a few Americans. Would you mind living in Tuxpan?"

"We'll be together, won't we, love? Living in Norman won't give us a chance to make our own way together. Papa already has ideas about a career for you. When you're contract is up, we can return to Norman and you can finish your degree. In the meantime, Mexico will be our adventure."

De didn't mention the field trips, or the heat, or the bugs. He also assumed El Aguila wouldn't mind if Nell accompanied him to Tuxpan.

Nell's parents worried about her moving to Mexico. Her dad suggested she stay at home until November, but Nell insisted that she would be fine. Seeing that nothing would deter her, her parents relented. De at least had a good job, and the prospects of a good career in the oil business when they returned from Mexico.

Ten days later, on June 10, 1910, they were married in her parent's house. Within two hours the young couple left for Laredo and from there took the Montezuma Express to Monterrey and on to Tampico. Nell carried only two suitcases. It all happened so quickly, and Nell was so certain everything would work out fine.

The train ride from Nuevo Laredo through the Chihuahuan Desert was terribly hot and dusty, and became hotter when they reached the coastal plains. On the second afternoon a tropical downpour fell in curtains of rain. Afterward the heat and humidity became almost unbearable. Nell put her head out the window and stared across the great expanse, allowing the wind to stir her hair.

The train arrived late at night in Tampico less than two weeks after De had departed. No one met them at the station. De ordered a *cargador* to carry their luggage to the Southern Hotel and there asked Mr. Fouts for the best suite.

The next morning De took Nell to the El Aguila offices. He stuck his head in Hop's office and introduced Nell. Hop stood and extended his hand.

"Since we arrived here last fall, De has talked about one thing, about his beautiful Nell," said Hop. "Now I understand. It's so good to meet you at last. Welcome to Tampico."

Nell had dressed in her Sunday best. She extended her hand and told him that De's letters had often mentioned Hop and that she was happy finally to meet him.

"Have you seen Mr. Ryder yet?" Hop asked De.

"Not yet. Is he back?" De asked, raising his eyebrows.

"Not happy," replied Hop. "I gave him your reasons for leaving on such short notice."

"Don't worry, Hop. All I have to do is introduce him to Nell," De replied confidently.

After chatting with Hop a few minutes about the wells, De and Nell walked down the long hall to the corner office. De stuck his head in the door. "Hello, Mr. Ryder, I'd like you to meet my wife, Nell."

Tom Ryder rose from his chair. "Mr. Hopkins informed me you had left for Oklahoma," Mr. Ryder said, looking sternly at De. When Mr. Ryder looked at Nell, his voice softened and he extended a hand. "Welcome to Tampico, my dear, and to our offices. We are so pleased that you accepted the proposal of your rash young husband. Bets were made whether you would agree to marry."

"There was never any doubt about whether, Mr. Ryder, and only some question about when. It's a pleasure to finally meet you, sir. De has told me what a fine man you are." She shook his hand firmly. Nell was shorter even than De, her posture was erect, her blue eyes shone under blond curls, and her smile was enchanting. De marveled as he looked at his bride. He could see that she was smoothing the path ahead for them yet again.

"Yes, well thank you," replied Mr. Ryder. "Where are you staying?" he asked De.

"At the Southern."

"I hope you find it suits you, Mrs. DeGolyer."

"It is perfectly fine. Mexico is so exotic."

"Do you speak Spanish?" asked Mr. Ryder.

"No, only German. I will learn Spanish, though. De is already teaching me."

"De has some field work to do for Dr. Hayes," replied Mr. Ryder. "De, we're sending you to Tuxpan tomorrow."

"Dr. Hayes told me we would be moving to Tuxpan," answered De. "Nell will be going with me with your permission."

Mr. Ryder looked surprised. "Accommodations there are a bit, well, a bit rustic."

"It will be fine," insisted Nell. "You're very kind, Mr. Ryder, and we both thank you from the bottom of our hearts for your understanding. De told me he was sorry you weren't here to ask your permission to leave for Norman."

Mr. Ryder smiled slightly for the first time and looked at De. "We started Potrero No. 4 the day after you married. We're drilling it with a cable tool rig, and will move the rotary rig to No. 5. You're to look after both wells and stop the drilling one hundred feet above the Tamasopo. Our plans are not to drill into the Tamasopo until the pipeline has been completed. Rains have slowed the construction."

"Yes, sir," De said. "When do you think the pipeline will be completed?"

"Work won't pick up until the end of September, so I expect it will probably be December. While you were gone we finished drilling the Potrero Number 2 and Number 3. Both tested small quantities of oil, about like the first well."

This came as a terrible blow to De. He had expressed his doubts to Nell about El Aguila spending so much money, building a pipeline and railroad before they even knew if the wells would produce.

"Potrero No. 4 or No. 5 could make good wells, sir," replied De. "It's too soon to condemn the property."

"Yes, well, we'll see. Now please excuse me, Mrs. DeGolyer," said Mr. Ryder. "It has been my pleasure to make your acquaintance. My wife lives in Mexico City. She says Tampico is a bit too malarial for her. I hope you don't mind the rural life as much as she."

"I'll be fine," said Nell cheerily. "Tampico is so charming."

"I hope you do not find Tuxpan uncomfortable. De will be spending quite a bit of time in the field. Are you certain you want to accompany him to Tuxpan?"

"Yes, I'm sure."

"If Tuxpan is not agreeable to you, Mrs. DeGolyer, please come back to Tampico and stay in the Southern or the Imperial. My wife and I find that our separation is quite acceptable. It makes the time together more meaningful. De, one more thing," continued Mr. Ryder. "Would you check on Huastaca's Juan Casiano No. 6? It should be down next month. Dr. Hayes telegraphed that he would like an update on the well in your monthly report. Jim Hall reports that Huasteca's first five Casiano wells were not promising."

"Yes, sir, and thank you again for allowing me time off to get married."

Mr. Ryder smiled. "I didn't exactly give you permission, now did I, Mr. DeGolyer? By the looks of it, though, you made a wise decision. Mrs. DeGolyer, please forgive me for being so abrupt. If there is anything I can do to help you, please call on me. Are you *sure* you wish to accompany your husband to Tuxpan?"

"Sure as sure can be, thank you sir. It is so exciting to be in Mexico, and to meet you. Thank you from the bottom of our hearts for your understanding."

Mr. Ryder smiled again at Nell. Like the other Scots in the office, he didn't regularly show pleasure.

After introducing Nell to Mr. Ryder, De and Nell returned to Hop's office and De shut the door.

"Mr. Ryder said the Potrero No. 2 and No. 3 were no good. Is that correct?" asked De.

"Yes," Hop replied. "Both tested about like the first well."

"Oh Lord, Hop, what if the next two test the same?"

"Then I'd say you found predictability in the Tamasopo," answered Hop.

"And a ticket back to Oklahoma," said De.

"De, didn't you tell me it wasn't wise to build a railroad until the four wells were tested?" asked Nell.

"Yes, Nell, but it was built because of my recommendation. No telling how much Lord Cowdray has spent."

"You told me four wells or none, didn't you?" asked Nell. "It still seems reasonable to me."

"It did to me, too, before the last two were drilled," answered De. "Hop, the next two wells may be all of our tickets home."

That afternoon De gave Nell a tour of downtown Tampico, the two plazas, and the old residential area on the bank of the Panuco River. He told her to buy whatever she wanted from the vendors at the Plaza de la Independencia. "Tuxpan has only a small market," he explained. "Mr. Ryder wasn't exaggerating when he said it's rustic."

"He said you would be in the field. Will field work require a lot of your time?" asked Nell.

De shrugged and said he would have to be at the location when the No. 4 and No. 5 Potrero wells were drilling. He hoped the railroad from Tuxpan to Potrero would be finished soon, which would reduce the time it took to return to Tuxpan from the Potrero camp.

That evening De introduced Nell to Chester Washburne and Jim Hall. They met in the bar of the Southern. Both young men were clean shaven. Jim wore a new shirt and new boots. Hop joined them later in the evening for dinner.

"Has De told you to sleep under mosquito netting?" Chester asked Nell.

"Yes, and to wear long-sleeves and a handkerchief around my neck during

the day," said Nell

"Are you taking cinchona bark?" asked Chester. "Tuxpan doesn't have a pharmacy."

"What would that be for?" asked Nell.

"For malaria," answered Chester.

"Miss Nell, there are bugs in the tropics as big as your foot," Jim said.

"Jim is teasing," said Hop.

"At night every insect in the jungle starts marching toward kerosene lanterns," continued Jim, "an army of six-legged creatures marching to the flame."

"Perhaps De and I will learn to read by moonlight," Nell replied and laughed.

"Cockroaches big enough to carry a pound of butter on their back…"

"Jim, stop it," De said. "Nell will have nightmares."

"It's not all that bad," Hop said. "Nell, if you don't like Tuxpan, you can move back to Tampico. Women in the Methodist church have organized a club. You would fit right in and feel more at home here in Tampico."

"De and I will be fine in Tuxpan," Nell replied. "We're not moving there permanently. Hop, what do you do when you're not working at the office?"

"I read, and I write a little poetry," answered Hop.

"Hop went to Cornell," De explained, "where he learned to appreciate the higher art forms. Geology is a secondary pursuit."

"Not any more," Hop said. "Miss Nell, we're happy you came to Mexico."

"Maybe your sisters will visit you," added Chester.

The next day at dawn De and Nell caught the company launch from the dock at the foot of the plaza. All their possessions fit into three suitcases. Nell held De's arm tightly as they made their way across the muddy Tamiahua Lagoon. When they reached Tuxpan, De stepped from the boat onto the rickety dock and directed two boys to carry their luggage. The newlyweds walked the muddy trail to town behind the *cargadores*.

"Do we have reservations at the hotel?" Nell asked.

"I wouldn't exactly call it a hotel. It's a room above the market. We have cots, sweet lady, and the room has a nice view of the river."

Tuxpan's main street was as muddy as the trail. Nell held her dress up so the mud wouldn't soak the lining and looked at the row of simple wooden buildings with shallow front porches. Bright-colored roosters were tethered to poles in front of many of the houses. Hens, chicks, and pigs wandered the streets, as did children, who looked at Nell, spoke rapidly, and pointed to her blond hair. De stepped into a cement building with a hand-painted sign marked *mercado* and spoke in Spanish with a lady in one of the vendor stalls.

The market smelled to Nell of rotting food. She gazed around at all the bins of fruits, vegetables, woven mats, hammocks, and footwear in the various stalls. One merchant sold meat from an un-refrigerated tray. Flies buzzed and lit on skinned hindquarters hung from the ceiling in rows behind his counter.

De ordered the two boys to carry their luggage up a narrow stairwell above the market. As they entered, Nell saw there was no lock on the door. De pushed it open with his foot and said with apprehension, "This is it, love, our little ranchito. What do you think?"

"Oh," said Nell, looking around. She stifled a sob. "The light comes in nicely from the window. Is there electricity?"

"Only kerosene lanterns," answered De. Nell recalled what Jim had said about the flame attracting bugs.

"Beaner, love, I know it's nothing fancy. One of these days we'll own a house. We have to sleep under the netting." He pointed to two cots. Metal frames suspended mosquito netting above the cots.

"How long will this be our home?" Nell asked.

"Only until the Potrero wells are down, only a few months. Tomorrow we can buy some flowers and brighten up the ranchito."

Nell started sobbing. De was perplexed, and then overcome with solicitude. "It's a bit rustic," he said anxiously.

"You call this rustic?" Nell said, wiping her eyes and looking around. Plaster peeled from the walls. She could smell the market below. "Is it safe?" she asked.

"I bought a pistol for you to put under your pillow when I'm away."

Nell started crying again. "I'm sorry," she said. "I had no idea."

De felt dreadful. It was the only available room in Tuxpan. The floor had been scrubbed, a colorful tablecloth draped the small table. Two chairs made of rawhide stood against a wall. He knew the room was rustic, but at least it was clean. He told her he would put latches on the door before they went to bed.

Nell straightened her shoulders and attempted a smile. "It's an adventure," she said at last. "I'll be fine. I, well, I didn't know what to expect."

Nell had been so enamored with Tampico and so enlivened by the boat trip. De looked around and now saw what Nell saw, the small inconveniences: a chamber pot under the cot, jars of water for drinking, a bucket and dish of soap for washing.

De told her the company had built a telephone system between Tuxpan and the camp at Potrero. It didn't work yet, but there was hope they could soon communicate with each other while he was in the field.

"If the phone doesn't work, I'll send you letters by the company packet."

Nell tried to smile. "How long will you be in the field?"

"No more than two weeks at a time."

She stared at him with disbelief. He had never told her how long he would be in the field.

"When will you go to the field?"

"The day after tomorrow."

"Will you be back by the Fourth of July?"

"I'll be back as soon as I can, Beaner. You know how much I'll miss you."

"I'll miss you even more." She looked around the room and took a deep breath.

Two days later De left Tuxpan for the Potrero camp. He had introduced Nell to the wife of one of the American vanilla farmers and hoped that they would become friends. He felt terrible that he couldn't offer Nell a nicer place to live and promised her as soon as possible, they would move to Tampico.

After sobbing to herself most of the first night, Nell showed no more misgivings. When she said 'I do' she knew their marriage would be an adventure, and told herself that adventures were what you made of them.

The morning he left for the field, De hugged Nell for a long spell, and told her she would be with him in his heart when she wasn't beside him. The summer monsoon had set in again. Rain fell in sheets like buckets overturned from above. As he rode off, he kept looking back at his beautiful young bride, dressed in a white cotton dress in the shelter of the market, waving back at him as he and his *mozo* rode down the muddy street and out of town.

Even though the Potrero camp was only twenty miles from Tuxpan, it was a long day's horseback ride through the jungle. They had to cross several swollen streams. When De finally arrived at camp, he said hello to Sam Weaver, the company superintendent, who directed him to throw his belongings on a bunk in one of the company dorms.

Beginning the next morning, De watched the No. 4 slowly drill ahead. The wooden beam rose and fell, creaking loudly as it lifted the drill bit from the bottom of the hole by a steel cable connected to the beam. When the beam dropped, the bit pounded and pulverized the rock at the bottom of the hole. The driller kept the hole full of mud to prevent caving. Every few hours he ran the bit out of the hole by spooling in the cable with gear works run on a steam engine fired by a boiler that was a hundred yards from the rig. The driller would replace the bit with a bailer, run the bailer back in the hole, mixing the mud

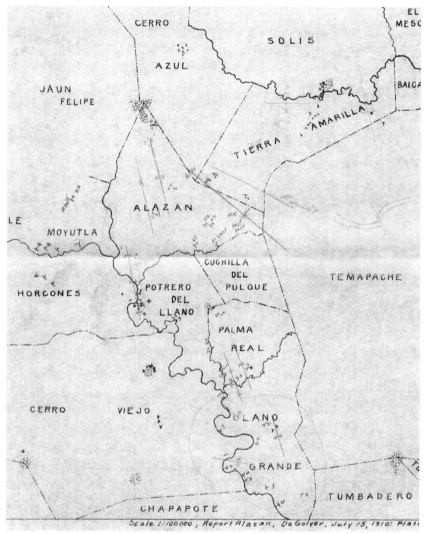

Haciendas with anticlines noted as straight lines with short perpendicular arrows

system and catching samples from the bottom, and then trip out the hole.

De took the cuttings from the bailer, washed them and analyzed the small bits of rock under a microscope. De prepared a well log showing each formation and its thickness on a one-inch-to-five-foot scale, color-coded separately by lithology, the shales grey, sandstones yellow, and limestones blue. When each well's sample logs was laid out next to the others, De would compare bed thicknesses and thereby calculated the structural relation with the other wells. The No. 4 was running structurally lower than the first three wells, which worried him. Lower down the flank of an anticline could encounter salt water instead of oil.

De tried to phone Nell every day, but the phone never worked. He wrote her letters and poems. With each passing day, the folly of his impulse to marry her and bring her to Tuxpan sank in. It was no place for a young bride, alone in such a remote and inhospitable locale. Why hadn't he thought more about their living conditions? He should have waited until his contract was up to ask her to marry him. Dejected and self-disgusted, he mechanically went about his job, but thought again and again how he might make it up to Nell.

On the first of July De typed his monthly report to Dr. Hayes. He read it twice before sealing and sent it by courier to Tuxpan. He felt the report was a good template, and much improved over the report he had sent for Tierra Amarilla.

```
Potrero Del Llano Camp
July 1, 1910

    The hacienda Potrero del Llano is an old
lease of the Aguila Company situated in the
canton of Tuxpan, State of Veracruz, Mexico. It
is about seven kilometers west of the village
of Temapache and about twenty two kilometers
northwest of Tumbadero, the nearest company
supply camp.
    The western, northern and southern boundaries
of the hacienda are fairly well defined, since
they are either streams or ditches, but the
eastern boundaries from El Terreno to the
crossing of the Potrero-Tumbadero road with
the Arroyo Bacarillo are very indeterminate.
The haciendas Potrero, Cuchilla del Pulque, and
Palma Real are and have been owned by the same
family and the subdivision is only a legal one,
having been defined by will.
    The property topographically is one of low
relief. The western and southern parts occupy
the very gentle sloping shale valley of the Rio
Buena Vista, while the eastern part occupies a
portion of the limestone ridge called "Cuchilla
del Pulque". About the most noticeable feature
of the entire area is a long low rounded hill,
```

Cerrito Palma Real. The elevations as shown on the maps refer approximately to sea level. They were brought by a line of trigonometric levels from the Tamiahua Lagoon.

There are two routes by which supplies are brought into the Camp. The old route which is being abandoned at the present time is to bring supplies to the port of Tuxpan by boat, thence to Tumbadero by the Tuxpan River (30 km) and by wagon road a distance of 25 kilometers to Potrero camp. The new route, which is being used at the present time, is to bring supplies from Tampico through the Tamiahua Lagoon by boat to within about three km of Tanhuijo camp. From this camp they are brought by wagons to Potrero, a distance of about 40 kilometers. A survey has been made and construction is now going on for a Decauville track, pipeline, wagon road, and telephone line from Potrero to Tanhuijo and thence to Tamiahua. Potrero is connected with Tuxpan by telephone and from there with all other points by telegraphic.

There is very little timber of a size to be of use in rig building, with the exception of a few narrow strips along the arroyo, although almost the entire property is covered with a thick brush or second growth. The most common tree is the palm. A great many lemon trees grow in the valley of the Rio Buena Vista.

The only source of water supply for either boiler or domestic use is the Rio Buena Vista, which dries into pools before the rainy season.

There is no place in the immediate vicinity of Potrero del Llano where any sort of geologic section can be compiled. As a result of my observations, however, I am inclined to accept the section given by L.V. Dalton for the region of Northern Vera Cruz, for this report, and with some modifications from time to time, for the entire region.

The Tamasopo Limestone does not outcrop in the vicinity of Potrero del Llano but is probably the oil bearing limestone which forms the reservoir of the Potrero pool. The logs of the Potrero Wells No. 1 and No. 2 showed 30-50' of bluish limestone at the top of the formation. Immediately under this bluish limestone comes the hard white (probably dolomitized) limestone in which the oil occurs.

Resting upon the Tamasopo limestone are the Valles beds, a series of limestones, shales and marls. The only thing in the logs of the Potrero wells which one recognizes in Dalton's description of this formation are the reddish shales of the No. 3. These beds do not outcrop in the vicinity of Potrero.

In ascending sequence above the Valles are the Los Esteros marls, the Comales beds, the Carvajal group, and the Temepache beds, which form the high ridges and hills (except those of volcanic origin) which occur in the region.

In the extreme eastern part of the hacienda is Cerrito Palma Real, a low hill of volcanic origin. It is composed of a volcanic breccia which is almost covered with vegetation. The breccia is quite typical of that rock, of which most of the smaller volcanic necks or plugs of the region are formed. The breccia, being composed to a great extent of limestones and baked shales, breaks down easily under the action of the weather and forms the low rounded knobs which are almost covered with vegetation and are so prominent topographically.

Structurally Potrero is situated on the crest and east flank of a northwest-southeast trending anticline. The dips are very low, increasing a bit as one gets farther from the axis of the fold. The rocks are perforated by the volcanic plug Palma Real. It is probable that a fault or fissure passes close to the axis of the anticline. The only evidence of the existence of such structure is the fact that the chapapote seepages occur in a more or less regularly aligned zone.

The wells which have been drilled (Nos. 1, 2 and 3) have thrown but little light on the structure of the field. The dips are very low and with the present crude method of measurement the logs can easily be twenty feet in error. Twenty feet in this field makes all of the difference in the world in the interpretation of geologic structure from well logs.

Exploration for oil in Potrero hacienda was first undertaken because of the great number of chapapote seepages and amount of chapapote cemented gravels which occur in the western part of the property. There are more than a hundred separate vents through which chapapote and gas are, or have been given off. These are probably supplied by the same or by comparatively few channels from the oil reservoir. About two kilometers north of the No. 1 in a report written in 1907, F.W. Moon describes an active seepage. It is probably that this seepage came from the same sources as the Potrero seepages. About two kilometers south is Cerro Chapapotal, an old volcanic neck or plug along whose contact with the sedimentaries rise several very large and very active seepages. This is on the Cerro Viejo property which is at present in litigation.

Potrero No. 4 is being drilled at the present time with cable tools. The rig has been built for Well No. 5 which is to be drilled with rotary tools.

During the visit of Dr. C.W. Hayes to Potrero camp in February 1910, it was decided to locate the exploration wells of Potrero field according to a system of rectangular coordinates 300 meters by 420 meters. The new scheme is to locate the wells 300 meters apart on a system of squares. A judicious selection of wells located according to either scheme is the most economical drainage of the oil rock, so that the drainage areas do not needlessly overlap each other.

Signed E DeGolyer

De's work on the wells, which drilled twenty-four hours a day, kept him busy running samples from the bailer, washing them, examining them under a microscope, and describing each zone's lithology, thickness and color on a sample log. When his mind wasn't occupied with the well, he thought of Nell, plucked from her familiar surroundings in Norman and a week later alone in Tuxpan. It had been nearly two weeks since he had left Tuxpan. Every day he wrote her a letter. Neither the camp telegraph nor the telephone worked. He missed her terribly and worried how she had adjusted to such a sudden and wrenching change, from the warmth and security of her own home and family and now all by herself with no friends in a location as remote and foreign as Tuxpan. Finally, after nearly three weeks without hearing from her, he received a letter. He eagerly tore open the envelope.

Tuxpan
Tuesday night
July 5, 1910

My Very Own Sweetheart, De:

> *I have just finished trying to phone you, my sweet. I ran all the way back from the ranchito to get to the phone, but it didn't work. Now I'm in our room in my kimono waiting to sit on your lap and to be put to bed so that I can lie on your dear arm til I go to sleep – the very sweetest place for my head that I can think of. This is more of a love letter than I have ever written to you before, dearest, but it is all straight from a heart so full that I had to write it even if I had no way on earth to send it.*
>
> *My husband, this is the first letter I've written to you, do you know it? And do you also know that I love you more now than I have ever done in the five years I've known you. I didn't know there was anything so big and powerful that it could make one lost without her mate and that could make one want to go to bed at dusk so that the night would bring another day nearer her husband's coming.*
>
> *I am trying awfully hard not to want to be foolish and to be brave and let you go when you must, but, my best beloved, when a girl leaves her home, her family, her friends –all to go to live with the one man – she wants to live with him. I shan't be at all surprised if I don my riding habit in the morning. A little matter of being in bed a week*

with sore muscles is nothing compared to the joy of having your very
man to rub the sore places and pet you and put you back into shape
again.

If that letter for the keys dare be anything but a really truly love
letter, I am liable to be absent when you come. I've had to say my
prayers by myself, eat by myself, and sleep alone and you must come by
Friday.

Dearest, when I've been married at least a month I think I can let
you go for five days, but now – for my sake, come Friday. I don't want
to be unreasonable but I am very lonely and very much in love with the
sweetest man on earth, which is my very own husband. Love to you in
a thousand tender caresses from the Woman Who is Yours Alone.

Signed Nell

De read the letter again and again. The next morning he taught a young
drilling hand how to catch samples from the bailer, how to wash and label them
and put them in cotton sacks so De could examine them later. By noon he had
shaved, changed into a clean shirt, and left by horseback for Tuxpan.

Nell's surprise and delight to see him overcame his misgivings for having
left her alone. Her natural cheerfulness had returned. While he was away she
had made friends with two American women, wives of vanilla farmers. After
lingering in a long embrace, he repeated to her again and again how much he
loved her and wanted her to be happy, that this separation would not last.

"It's why we married. Life is no good without you, Beaner. When the Potrero
wells are down and our contract is up, we'll return to the States and I'll find a
regular job with the Geological Survey."

"I don't like living without you either," Nell replied. "I understand how
important your career is, but surely we'll find a way to avoid lengthy separation,
promise?"

When De arrived back at Potrero camp after three days at Tuxpan with
Nell, Jim was at the rig waiting for him.

"Good to see you, Jim," De said and smiled as he stepped off the saddle. De dusted the back of his pants with his hat and walked up the wooden steps.

"Playing hooky, were you?" winked Jim. "With a wife as handsome as Miss Nellie, you'd have to hog tie me to this rig to keep me from riding home every night."

"I know. Married two weeks and shipped to the middle of a scrub-brush jungle. It doesn't seem right. Nell is holding up, though. She's such a sweetheart. Now, what about the Casiano report? Did you find any information?"

"That's why I came back so soon. It doesn't take long to ask a few questions," said Jim and handed over the report. "This recon work is easy."

De was surprised that the report was typed. "I didn't know you could type."

"I only finished the third grade. I had it typed."

"Should I ask who typed it?"

Jim didn't offer an answer. De read the report silently.

```
Juan Casiano Property
July 12, 1910


    Estancia Juan Casiano lies 95 kilometers east
and south of the Port of Tampico. Apparently,
the first attention directed to Juan Casiano
was by the Garner-Barber Asphalt people, who
in 1902 secured some 80,000 acres of oil and
asphalt leases in this general region to exploit
the asphalt of the seepages on the Juan Casiano
estancia. In 1906 the leases were transferred
to E. L. Doheny, who in 1907 organized Huasteca
Petroleum Company. During 1908 this company
commenced drilling operations on the Juan Casiano
No. 1. During the later part of 1909 wells no.
1 and 2 were brought in for only a small amount
of production. The Huasteca Company commenced
laying an eight inch line to Tampico after the
first well.
```

De looked up at Jim. "You say that Doheny started laying the pipeline from the coast before they knew what kind of production they had?"

"Yes, *jefe*, it seems to be how they operate down here in Mexico. It keeps the peons off the streets."

"And I thought we were wildly optimistic to be laying a six inch line from Potrero. At least Potrero No. 1 flowed 400 barrels per day." Jim shrugged and De kept reading.

```
The next three wells were dry, no. 3, no. 4, and
no. 5.
```

"Who did their geology?" asked De.

"No one. Mr. Doheny told them to drill in the middle of the seeps. That's how he found La Brea in California, that's how he drills El Ebano, and that's how he drills Casiano."

"And that's why he just drilled three dry holes," said De. "I can't imagine not keeping sample logs and mapping at least the top of Tamasopo." He kept reading.

```
On July 8, 1910, when the total production
from the first five wells was 326 barrels of
oil per day, Casiano No. 6 was brought in at
approximately 18,000 barrels of oil per day.
```

De looked up. He couldn't hide the excitement in his voice. "That was four days ago. Is this accurate? It would be by far the best well in Mexico."

"That's what my sources tell me," answered Jim confidently. "They wouldn't let me near the location, but I have ways of finding out."

"Jim, this report has to be absolutely accurate. I must telegram Dr. Hayes and Lord Cowdray today."

"It's accurate. Next to their camp where their workers live are a few cantinas. It's a pretty rowdy crowd. I spent a little money with the *señoritas*, which I'll be submitting on my expense account."

"This is the biggest thing that's happened since Dos Bocas, and you're telling me you got the information from a prostitute?"

"I wouldn't quote my sources if I was you, but I'm telling you, Mr. De, it's as accurate as reading your mail," Jim said and grinned. "And, speaking of news, guess what else has happened since you've been honeymooning out here in the jungle? Ol' Díaz had Madero arrested, and the young rabble rouser's locked up in a Mexican hoosegow. Looks like there won't be much of a presidential election this year after all."

"I can't believe Díaz did that," said De, shaking his head. "It destroys the credibility of his government. Even those who supported him are going to begin questioning him now."

"I couldn't agree more, *jefe*. Mexico's modernizing, but the government ain't."

"That's a recipe for disaster," said De. "Now, tell me everything you heard about Casiano No. 6." Rumors and exaggerations were common fare, and De had some doubt about the accuracy of the reports, but he had come to trust Jim. He decided to send the telegram to Dr. Hayes and Lord Cowdray.

The Chief immediately telegrammed back: 'Good Work. Keep information tight. Check leases next to Casiano property. Cowdray'

De had never communicated directly with Lord Cowdray. He had only been charged with mapping the local geology of specific properties owned by El Aguila and with looking after the Potrero wells. The telegram was clear, though. De ordered Jim to check for any small tracts near the Casiano well that might be unleased. Leases were filed for record with the government in Tampico, but most companies would not file them, knowing that a clerk in the recording office could tell competitors where they were leasing. Talking to landowners on the ground was the best way to gather information about leasing activity.

Jim returned three days later and said that the closest unleased tracts were along the River Estancia, more than a mile from the No. 6 Casiano.

"The Casiano wells are in a narrow valley that opens onto the river bottom. The tracts I'm talking about are down river about a mile."

De asked if this would be northwest or southeast of the wells. He felt like most of the anticlines ran north-south or canted to the northwest-southeast. Jim replied that the tracts were a mile east of the location.

"Without mapping the area, I couldn't recommend buying the leases," responded De. "They are probably not on the Casiano anticline."

"Word must have leaked about the well, or at least a rumor, because while I was there two hustlers showed up. One was an Irishman who spoke good Spanish. The other was a fellow from Pennsylvania named Joe Trees with an outfit called Benedum and Trees."

"Did you find out who they worked for or which tracts they were working on?"

"No, but I could."

"El Aguila owns a lease on a large tract a few miles from the Casiano estancia."

"Which one is that?" asked Jim.

"Los Naranjos. We bought it last year, but I haven't finished the detailed mapping yet."

"Los Naranjos," repeated Jim. "Do they have orange trees on the hacienda?"

"Yes, and lemon trees like here in the valley," said De. "Contact the owners of Los Naranjos. Tell them El Aguila will be evaluating their property immediately. Go back to Casiano and report anything you hear about the well, and especially if it starts making salt water. If any more landmen show up, try to find who they work for and where they're leasing." He didn't know if Lord Cowdray's telegram had authorized him to take charge of scouting the well, but if Casiano No. 6 was as good as Jim reported, other properties in the area could be, too. He felt confident Dr. Hayes would agree with his decision. "Let me know anything you can find out about the well, but especially if it starts making salt water."

"I'm you're man on the ground, *jefe*. Scouting well information beats lugging a survey rod through a rattlesnake-infested arroyo. I'll need Hippolito's help, too."

"Sure. Have you seen him lately?"

"He's teaching me *huastecan*. I told him I only wanted to learn *dichos*, so I could talk to the natives like he talks to me. They'll think I'm the second coming."

"Jesus spoke in parables, not in *dichos*."

On September 11, 1910, Casiano No. 7, across the narrow valley from the No. 6, blew in from less than 1900 feet. It was a gigantic well, spewing oil over the derrick and hundreds of feet in the air. The roar could be heard for miles. It flowed wild for ten days at more than 30,000 barrels per day before it was brought under control. An early attempt to close it in was made, but as the valves were turned, the pressure rose to 585 pounds per square inch and oil began to flow through fissures in the earth for a considerable distance around the well. The valves were opened until the pressure dropped to 290 psi and the new seepages became inactive.

De was mapping Los Naranjos Hacienda near Casiano when news came of Casiano No. 7. He realized what it meant, that this oil trend was not a fluke. What the Dos Bocas well had hinted at two years before, the Casiano wells proved for a certainty: the Tamasopo was a world-class petroleum reservoir.

De simultaneously realized that understanding the Tamasopo limestone was paramount to making more discoveries. The Casiano wells had found reservoir quality, as good as the springs of Sierra del Abra. How could he predict where else in the subsurface the Tamasopo had such excellent reservoir quality?

De quickly calculated the revenue from the Casiano No. 7. With oil selling for 55 cents a barrel, the well would generate six million dollars a year, a fortune beyond any he could imagine.

Dr. Hayes sent word by telegram that he would be in Tampico after Thanksgiving and wanted to check out the big Casiano wells. In light of the recent news, Mr. Body from Mexico City decided to visit the Potrero camp by way of the Casiano wells. When he arrived at the camp, Mr. Body told De that rumors were rampant, but all reports were that the two Casiano wells were producing 25,000 barrels per day. Doheny was buying tankers and had announced a refinery in Tampico. Mr. Body also dropped some surprising news.

"We're moving you back to Tampico. Dr. Hayes sent word that you are to map as much of the area around Casiano as possible. He asked that you coordinate Mr. Hopkin's and Mr. Washburne's activities. You will be in charge of the project."

De was delighted and relieved by the news of their move to Tampico. Nell had been such a trooper to accept his long absences and primitive living conditions. 'Rustic' had become a joke between them, a description used for everything from toilet paper to toothpaste. De was also pleased with his new responsibility. He would soon be twenty-four years old. His decision to accept the job in Mexico had provided a world of experience, which he hoped to use as a consultant when his contract with El Aguila was completed.

As soon as Mr. Body left Potrero camp, De rode all night to share the news with Nell that they would be leaving Tuxpan. She had worked hard to make the ranchito above the market bright and cheerful, hanging new drapes of colorful fabric, scrubbing the floors, walls, and ceiling. She had screen doors with locks installed and bought several kerosene lanterns to light the space at night. Living on the second floor offered some sense of security, but she slept with the pistol under her pillow. Even though she had made friends with several wives of vanilla plantation owners, she still missed De desperately when he was away.

When Nell heard the news, she broke into tears. "De, I'm so happy we're moving to Tampico. I know you'll think I'm silly," she sniffed, wiping her eyes, "but I will miss our little ranchito in Tuxpan. It's our first home. You won't be spending so much time in the field, will you? And we can find a home in Tampico, a home of our own, can't we?"

"Yes, Beaner," he said. "The Potrero wells will keep us in Mexico until year end. Then we'll move back to Norman and I'll finish my degree. In the meantime, we'll look for a house in Tampico close to work so I won't be far from you every day. We can eat together, sleep together, and…" He wriggled his eyebrows and Nell flushed.

De and Nell rented a large house only a block from El Aguila's office. After Tuxpan, life in Tampico seemed to Nell absolutely cosmopolitan. Her happiness and cheerfulness in Tampico were palpable. Now that he didn't spend so much time in the field, both had a new appreciation for married life.

"De, dear," said Nell, "I spoke with a lady at the Novaris Club, a Mrs. Hodgson. Since I play the piano at the church, she asked if I would give her lessons. Several of her friends would like to learn as well."

"What a swell idea, love. Can you use the church's piano?"

"The Reverend was enthusiastic. He thought piano lessons might gather in more Methodists. Have you noticed all the newcomers?" asked De.

"Isn't this town becoming an American outpost!" exclaimed Nell.

De laughed. "The Casiano wells have put Tampico in the news. Guess what Jim saw yesterday?"

"I can't imagine."

"An automobile, a Model T Ford. Jim said the fellow driving didn't so much as tip his hat."

"My goodness, an automobile in Tampico," said Nell. "Electricity, cars… technology is hard to keep up with, isn't it?"

Hop easily accepted De's new position of authority. After the Casiano wells, De was more determined to predict reservoir quality in the Tamasopo. Hop agreed with him that the Tamasopo could be a fabulous reservoir, but disagreed whether the data they were collecting could add predictability.

"It took six wells to find decent production on Casiano," Hop observed. "Who but Doheny has that kind of perseverance, or money?"

"I'm not suggesting there won't be dry holes," said De, "but we have to play the probabilities."

"Play the probabilities? With so few wells, what probabilities are you talking about?"

"Think of oil exploration as a murder mystery, said De. "Clues and false clues, plots and subplots. Our job is to find oil by eliminating the extraneous."

"Good God, De," said Hop. "This is oil exploration, not literature."

"Throw in some of the characters we deal with, like Jim Hall and Manuel Pelaez, and you tell me it isn't a detective story? Hop, have you seen Chester? I told him I needed the report on Solis by yesterday."

"Chester spends as much time socializing with the landowners as mapping the outcrop. He'll be back in town in a few days."

De didn't answer. He was still thinking about the Tamasopo.

"Finding oil *is* like a murder mystery, and like a treasure hunt combined," De sighed. "So few clues, such big rewards. It's us versus Mother Nature."

Hop laughed. "If it's us against Mother Nature, we're outgunned. Anyone who hides her treasures under a half mile of sediments and cackles at our inept efforts must be a contemptuous old bitch."

On September 16, 1910, Porfirio Díaz and his government celebrated the one-hundredth anniversary of Father Hidalgo's cry for Mexican Independence from Spain. For the previous two months, Díaz had lavished the capital with pomp-filled ceremonies. Although the centennial was the stated reason for the celebrations, in truth much of the activity focused on glorifying Díaz himself.

On September 27, with Madero imprisoned in San Luis Potosí, the eighty-year-old Díaz declared himself the winner of the presidential election, and he was sworn in for his eighth term.

In October, Madero escaped from the prison and made his way to San Antonio, Texas. There he issued his Plan of San Luis Potosí, which proclaimed Díaz's election a fraud, and called for an armed revolution.

De instructed Ed Hopkins and Chester Washburne to spend the remainder of October and November locating seeps in the area surrounding Juan Casiano. De sensed that Chester didn't like taking orders from him but he dismissed Chester's attitude and encouraged his two friends to gather as much geological data as possible. Mr. Body approved paying the natives money to show them seeps. In the meantime De spent most of the next two months with Jim and Hippolito working on Los Naranjos hacienda.

When he wanted information about a well, De would ask Jim to see what he could find. More often than not, Jim would bring back well data or information about the leasing activity. When he couldn't come up with the information on a specific well, Jim told De he could swap for it.

"You mean you want to give El Aguila's data for someone else's data?" asked De.

"Seems sensible to me," replied Jim. "It's not like we don't already own half a million acres. I would only swap well-for-well."

"I'll have to think about swapping," said De. He knew Mr. Body did not approve of sharing El Aguila's well information.

De placed all the surface and subsurface information onto a 1:100,000 regional map. As the topography, basaltic plugs, wells, and seeps were spotted, the blanks began to fill in.

Daily more and more foreigners streamed into Tampico by train and by steamer. Jim reported that leasing activity had picked up, especially between the Dos Bocas well and the Casiano property. What had once been an area where only Huasteca and El Aguila competed for large haciendas, now several companies were snooping around, questioning landowners about their lands and seeps, and buying leases. De felt they had little if any geological support except for proximity, which was not necessarily bad, but was not based on scientific principals. Jim told De that some of the newcomers inquired where El Aguila and Huasteca were leasing but that he kept lease information confidential. De strongly agreed, explaining to Jim that no matter what other information he might share, Jim must never discuss where El Aguila was buying leases. A great deal of geologic input went into recommendations to buy a lease. Telling others where they were leasing would give away months of geological work. Shortly after he had reiterated that Jim keep their leasing information confidential, De received a letter from Dr. Hayes.

October 17, 1910
Washington, D.C.

Dear Mr. DeGolyer:

You have doubtless been impressed with the difficulties encountered in securing leases on reasonable terms in the vicinity of active operations or where some properties have already been leased. These difficulties are increased by the prevalent idea that the Aguila has unlimited money and is bound to have the leases at any cost. The Company is thus handicapped and must secure its perfectly legitimate ends through indirect means. Moreover the Company has been exploited in one way or another in the past by its land agents.

In view of these conditions a new plan is being tried. Mr. Ralph Cullinan, of whom you have doubtless heard, is engaged in taking leases in northern Vera Cruz and these will eventually become the property of the Aguila Company. His relation to the company is known only to Mr. Body, Mr. Ryder, and myself. It is obviously essential that this relation should be known to the smallest possible number of persons and you will of course impart the information to no one whatsoever and drop no hint which might lead anyone in or of the Company to suspect that Mr. C is in any way connected with the Company.

I am writing this at Mr. Ryder's suggestion in order that you may be in a position to advise Mr. C as to the desirability of leasing particular properties concerning which he may be in doubt.

Mr. Ryder will inform Mr. C that you are in the confidence of the Company in this matter and Mr. C will confer with you in regard to his operations. You are authorized to use your own judgment without waiting for special instructions, in visiting and examining properties which may be of interest, but all examinations should be made in such a manner as not to connect you with Mr. C. In all correspondence with the Mexico office you well refer to Mr. C as though he were an outsider.

I have assured Mr. Ryder that your discretion is equal to your scientific judgment, of which he has the highest possible opinion.

Very truly yours
C.W. Hayes

De locked the letter in his safety box and told no one about it, not even Jim.

As the three geologists gathered field data and met weekly to discuss each other's ideas, De's regional topographic and subsurface map was slowly filling in. The consensus of the young geologists was that surface seeps were sometimes but not consistently indicative of underlying anticlines. Igneous plugs were also associated with seeps. All three geologists agreed that igneous plugs had penetrated the sedimentary strata after the anticlines were formed. They argued at length if the plugs had extruded to the surface along pre-existing faults, or if their extrusion was a random occurrence without correlation to a pre-existing fault. They also argued whether the beds immediately overlying the Tamasopo Limestone were Cretaceous or Tertiary age.

"What difference does it make?" asked Hop. "De, you're too theoretical."

"Rudists and other fossils date the Tamasopo as Comanchean, or mid- to lower Cretaceous. If the overlying Valles sands and shales are Tertiary, there are several million years of missing sediment."

"So?"

"So don't you see, it means the Tamasopo was exposed to the surface for several million years?"

"So what does it matter?" asked Hop.

"How would exposure to the surface for several million years alter the limestone?" answered De with a question. "Do you remember the limestone outcrops we mapped in Montana?" Hop nodded and De continued. "Some of the limestone exposed to the surface had large dissolution cavities."

"Exposure to the surface would alter the rock, but not uniformly," added Chester.

"Rain water is slightly acidic," continued De, "which would dissolve cavities in the limestone. In our small sampling of the Tamasopo, we've seen rhombic crystals. Dr. Hayes believes these are indicative of cavities. Some of the Tamasopo samples are dolomitic. What process caused the dolomite?"

"There you go again," said Hop.

"From the samples we've seen, the top of the Tamasopo is a dense bluish limestone. The dolomite is thirty to fifty feet into the formation. Why wouldn't exposure to the surface alter the limestone at the contact where the rain fell, rather than fifty feet below the top?" asked De.

"For every question you answer," said Hop, "two more come forth."

De laughed and continued. "Maybe acidic rain water seeps down to a less resistant dolomitic zone that more easily dissolves. I mapped the Tamasopo in the Sierra del Abra and the Sierra Madre Oriental. There are large dissolution cavities in the limestone. Remember the huge cave I told you about?"

"The cave probably formed more recently," said Chester. "After all, the limestone in the Sierra is exposed to the surface now."

"The rock face inside the cave was a brecciated mess, as if the cave was part of a much larger system. I think the cave was ancient, formed before the uplift that caused the sierras."

"De, what are you getting at?" asked Hop.

"The Casiano No. 7 well has been making 12,000 barrels a day for more than a month, which means the Tamasopo has huge storage capacity within the rock matrix. How is that possible? If we can figure where caves are in the subsurface, we can predict where the good rocks are. Find good rocks on an anticline, and we have another Casiano," explained De.

"Dos Bocas flowed better than Casiano," said Chester, "and it turned to salt water in two months. We won't know how good the Casiano wells are until they produce at least a year."

"With every lease hound in the States flocking to Tampico, we don't have a year to decide whether it's another fluke. Jim says they're paying $2000 an acre for small tracts next to the river. Can you believe it?"

"El Aguila already has more than half a million acres in fee or under lease. The ones who got here first got the best tracts at the cheapest price."

"And we took the greatest risk," added De. "Think of the infrastructure that Huasteca has put in, and look at El Aguila, constructing field camps, laying pipelines, building railroads and refineries. Except for Cerro La Pez near El Ebano and now Casiano, neither company has a lot to show for the millions spent."

"It takes deep pockets to play this game, doesn't it?" said Hop.

"Deep pockets, plus what Jim calls big *cojones*," added De. "Which is why we need better ways to predict the subsurface."

"Oil seeps and surface dips aren't a lot to hang your hat on, much less to drill a $25,000 well, but it's about all we have," said Hop.

"Jim thinks anyone who believes they can predict what's buried under a half mile of rock is touched."

"I've been accused of worse," said Hop.

Chapter Eight

November 1910 — February 1911

When De heard the news, his first reaction was incredulity, but within minutes as the news sank in, confusion turned to melancholy. A feeling that he hadn't been up to the challenge swamped his natural cheerfulness. He walked home in the middle of the afternoon, hours before his usual arrival. Nell looked up alarmed. "De, what is it? Are you feeling badly? It's not malaria, is it?"

"Word came from Tierra Amarilla today," replied De. "The No. 1 is a dry hole."

"Oh, darling De, I'm so sorry." Nell gave him a hug. "You were so certain it would produce. What happened?"

"I don't know. I located it on a buried fault next to Cerro Pelon with active seeps practically bubbling oil, just like Huasteca's Cerro La Pez well. I figured the volcanic plug had fractured the adjacent limestone so the oil would flow at high rates. I never even considered a dry hole."

"Did it not produce anything?"

"Nothing. Not one single barrel. Not a spit of oil."

"One dry hole doesn't matter, does it, not in this business? You told me so yourself."

"I know, I know, but the location made such good geological sense. Maybe Chester and Hop are right, maybe there's no way to predict the subsurface. Look at Edward Doheny. He has the best production in Mexico, and he doesn't even use geologists."

"Darling De, finding oil is more than luck. You'll figure it out. Honestly, one dry hole only puts you one well closer to the next producer."

De smiled at his bride. He knew she only wanted to cheer him up. "We may be headed to Oklahoma sooner than I planned," he said and sighed. "I just don't understand how it could be a dry hole."

"De, darling, you mustn't let it get you down. Why don't we go to the

Colonial Club and celebrate your first dry hole?"

De tried to smile. "*Celebrate* a dry hole?"

"Yes," replied Nell, "We'll celebrate the knowledge you gained."

"The Scots at the office seemed pleased that Tierra Amarilla was dry."

"Oh, De, that's not true," answered Nell. "Your success is everyone's success, and your failures are their failures, too."

"If your intent is to cheer me up, you beauty girl, it's working. Looking at you works even better. You make me think I'm the luckiest man in Tampico, even if I just drilled my first dry hole."

Nell flushed and gave De a warm rose kiss, the kind he liked the best. At the Colonial, De's spirits rose. Sadness for him was like a spring rain shower. It never lasted long.

"Here's to your first dry hole," said Nell, holding up a glass of wine. "Didn't you tell me Mr. Doheny drilled nineteen wells before he found a good producer?"

"I can't imagine the mental anguish. Can you imagine drilling nineteen poor wells in a row? He was using his own money, too," replied De.

"Let's drink to science," said Nell, "and to figuring out the geology of the Tamasopo." She clinked her glass against De's.

"Surely science will prevail," De said. Nell's blue eyes shone so brightly and her support was so sincere, he already felt better. Luck, he thought, was indefinable and unscientific, but nevertheless, he felt lucky with Nell.

"Beaner," said De a little more cheerfully, "Dr. Hayes sent a telegram today. He arrives in Tampico the second week of December. I can't wait for him to meet you. He'll understand why I left Tampico for Norman last summer without asking permission."

"Why is he visiting Tampico?" asked Nell. De detected a hint of anxiety in her voice.

"To review our progress and he wants to see Potrero. The pipeline will be finished soon so we'll be drilling out the No. 4 and No. 5. He also wants to visit Tierra Amarilla and Furbero."

"Will you go to the field with Dr. Hayes?" Nell asked.

"Yes, of course."

"Oh De, Dr. Hayes will be here over the holidays. You'll be in the field over Christmas. You can't! It's our first Christmas."

De immediately saw Nell's point. Tampico was no place to be alone for Christmas.

"Oh my goodness, Beaner, I see what you're at. I hadn't given it a thought."

"You didn't give it a thought? Don't you care about something besides your career? You *can't* be gone our first Christmas. I spent four months in Tuxpan by myself. You promised you wouldn't be gone when we moved back to Tampico."

"I can't tell Dr. Hayes I won't accompany him."

"Why not? Your contract is up in November," Nell said. "Aren't we moving back to Norman?"

"Nell, Dr. Hayes promoted me. I'm in charge of the whole Potrero operation. I can't walk away from that. This is a huge opportunity for us. There's no way I can quit now."

Nell looked down at her empty glass and didn't reply. De continued talking, trying to shake her out of her mood, but for the rest of the evening she only spoke in one-word replies.

Two weeks before Christmas Nell began the long journey, alone, back to her parent's house in Norman. When they said goodbye, De could feel the disappointment in her hug. Two days later Dr. Hayes arrived in Tampico. De and Jim accompanied him in the company launch to Tuxpan. From there they traveled by horseback to Tierra Amarilla. De showed Dr. Hayes the samples from the No. 1. All were oil saturated, but the Tamasopo was so dense and welded by heat that no fluid would flow through the rock. The well had drilled into metamorphosed limestone instead of fractured limestone.

"Dr. Hayes, what do you think went wrong?" asked De.

"The geology adjacent to a plug is more complex than you thought, Mr. DeGolyer. My guess is that the igneous rock, when in a molten state, can flow horizontally into less resistant zones just as easily as it can push up vertically through them to the surface. The interface with the sedimentaries is not always a smooth and even transition zone."

De had envisioned the molten intrusion to act like a hot spear penetrating upward through limestones, shales, and sandstones.

"We need to drill another well, Mr. DeGolyer," concluded Dr. Hayes.

"What if we drill another dry hole?" asked De. "Drilling a seep next to an igneous plug didn't work."

"We're learning, though, Mr. DeGolyer. You said yourself about Potrero, walking away after the first well would leave the oil field for someone else to discover."

"It takes so much money," sighed De.

"It also takes tenacity," responded Dr. Hayes. "Tierra Amarilla No. 1 is another data point. Look at it that way."

After a long day reviewing the alignment of the buried fault and the active seeps, both were convinced that one well didn't condemn Tierra Amarilla, and both agreed another well should be drilled a distance from the basaltic plug and closer to an active seep that bubbled oil.

Toward evening they left the field and rode to the Tierra Amarilla hacienda. De had sent word ahead that Dr. Hayes would be arriving to look over the well. Manuel Pelaez was expecting them and, when they rode up, greeted them amicably at the front gate. As soon as De introduced Dr. Hayes, Manuel inquired about the well. Dr. Hayes told him that he and De were disappointed.

"I was hoping it would make my family rich," Manuel replied.

"We'll drill more wells," answered Dr. Hayes, "For some reason, the rocks here are not as good as we expected. Oil is present, but the rock properties are missing."

"The rock properties are missing? I do not understand."

"The oil can be *in* the rocks, but not be able to flow *through* the rocks. We call the property that allows fluids to flow through rocks 'permeability'. It's the nature of the Tamasopo to have erratic permeability, and the nature of the business to drill dry holes," explained Dr. Hayes. "No matter how much science we conduct before a well is drilled, there is only one way to determine if our science is right. We must drill a well. The results often teach us more humility than hope."

Before the meal Manuel met them in the library for drinks. De's attention was pulled to the old and rare volumes that lined the shelves. While Dr. Hayes and Manuel talked, De examined the leather and vellum covers with reverential affection.

"You are interested in my father's collection, *Señor* DeGolyer?"

De looked up. Manuel was standing beside him.

"Yes. I'm fascinated with your father's books. Why did he start collecting?"

"He was interested in others' thoughts and research. There is much wisdom in these shelves."

De agreed. The book he held looked like a treatise in Spanish about the ancient Greek world.

"The book you are holding is very rare," said Manuel. He took it from De's hands and carefully opened a crinkled map. "It is a first edition about Theophrastus, an ancient Greek who studied minerals."

"Really?" said De. "Was your father interested in minerals?"

"As you can see by his collection, his interests were wide-ranging."

"I wish I could have met your father," said De. "His love of books intrigues me."

On Christmas day, Manuel, Dr. Hayes, and De shared a bountiful meal. Their conversation was polite, but was constrained by language barriers. De couldn't help but think of Nell, in Norman with her family, having a Christmas meal with family while he was here in Mexico with Dr. Hayes.

Early the next morning, De told Dr. Hayes that he had been thinking about the Tierra Amarilla well. It had been drilled on an anticline. Seeps were evident, as well as faulting. "Our biggest problem is not finding anticlines, but finding an anticline with good reservoir characteristics. We need to learn more about the stratigraphy of the Tamasopo."

Dr. Hayes agreed, and De continued, "The wild card in the whole play is the quality of reservoir rock. Dos Bocas and Casiano tell us the Tamasopo has excellent characteristics. We need to figure out the geology so we can predict where it occurs. It can't be random. It must result from geologic processes that covered a large area."

"At this stage it's all hints and innuendos," said Dr. Hayes. "For now, Mr. Hopkins is correct. Until we have a better understanding of the Tamasopo, staying close to good reservoir rock makes sense. Proximity is practical but it's not science. I'm anxious to see your report on Los Naranjos. It's our closest property to the Casiano well."

"I should finish mapping Los Naranjos early next year, but I can tell you, I like what I see already. There is little bedding to map, but I'm intrigued with a change in soil types that indicates a buried anticline."

"Perhaps we'll be able to parlay Huasteca's success with one of our own," said Dr. Hayes. "When will the Potrero wells be down?"

"We started deepening the No. 4 two days ago. I estimate we are about 100 feet from the Tamasopo and should be down when we arrive at camp. It appears to be structurally low to the No. 1. I'm afraid my recommendation to drill four wells at once has wasted Lord Cowdray's money."

"Mr. DeGolyer, you said yourself that all four directions must be drilled. If all five wells are non-commercial, we will learn a great deal about the stratigraphy of the Tamasopo."

"The Chief may not think understanding stratigraphy is worth the price."

"I'm sure he prefers paying for wells that produce oil. Don't give up too soon, Mr. DeGolyer. Finding oil is never easy."

When they arrived at Potrero camp, the Potrero No. 4 had not reached the Tamasopo. After checking the samples, De report it was definitely running low to the No. 1. Running low meant closer to salt water.

"Should we suspend drilling?" De asked Dr. Hayes. "The well is already low to the No. 1."

"How low is too low? Now is no time to stop, Mr. DeGolyer," said Dr. Hayes. "We'll keep drilling."

In the afternoon they saddled up again and returned to Tuxpan, arriving late at night. They stayed at the room above the market, De and Nell's ranchito. De reminisced about his and Nell's honeymoon days there. Her decorations were still on the walls, a reminder of good times which seemed so long ago and simpler. She'd sent him a wire after arriving safely in Norman, but other than that, he'd heard nothing from her.

Early the next morning they ferried across the Tuxpan River and took the narrow-gauge train to Furbero. When they arrived at the Furbero field camp, a telegram awaited them that announced the Potrero No. 4 had come in late the night before on December 27, 1910, and was flowing wild.

De said they should immediately return to Potrero, but Dr. Hayes insisted they examine Furbero.

"But Dr. Hayes, Potrero came in!"

"It will take a few hours for the well to clean up. We'll be back in plenty of time."

Impatiently De showed Dr. Hayes samples from the latest Furbero wells.

No matter how often De suggested they return to Potrero, nothing would rush Dr. Hayes.

"The producing zone is igneous, all right," said Dr. Hayes of a rock that he was holding.

"Yes, sir. It's an odd reservoir, isn't it Dr. Hayes?"

"I'm convinced the igneous activity in the region is more recent than the compressional forces that formed the anticlines. Active seeps tell us that migration of the oil is ongoing."

"But how can an igneous rock produce oil?" asked De.

"My guess is Furbero is a deep-seated laccolith which created a dome. Migrating oil rose to the highest point and filled whatever pore space available, in this case into fractured igneous," said Dr. Hayes.

Try as he might, De couldn't hurry Dr. Hayes into returning to Tuxpan until late in the afternoon. When the ferry was halfway across the river, De spotted Jim waiting for them on the far river bank with two saddled horses.

"How much is the well flowing?" De yelled to Jim as they pulled up to the dock. He was unable to hide the excitement in his voice.

"The *hombres* who came in here this morning to hire more help were covered head to toe in oil and said it's flowing sky high. *Mucho fuerte*, plenty strong. It sounds like another Casiano."

Jim relayed that Lord Cowdray had wired instructions for Robert Sterling, an engineer in their Tampico office, to take charge of the well and had ordered Dr. Hayes and De to meet him immediately in Mexico City. De was terribly disappointed they wouldn't go to the well.

He and Dr. Hayes rode horses hard for a day and a half, crossing the coastal plains and up onto the central plateau to reach a train in San Luis Potosí that took them directly to the capital, bone-tired when they arrived and without a change of clothes or a bath. Lord Cowdray was at the station in Mexico City to meet them.

He shook Dr. Hayes' hand and when introduced, shook De's hand firmly. His bald head towered above De. "This sounds like a big one, Dr. Hayes." Lord Cowdray couldn't conceal the excitement in his voice, a voice which projected a natural sense of authority. "As best we can measure, oil is flowing four hundred feet into the air. The derrick has already come down."

"Good Lord!" De said, unable to contain his excitement. "Four hundred feet!"

"You're the young man who located the well?" asked Lord Cowdray.

"With the direction of Dr. Hayes," replied De.

"Your recommendation to drill four wells has proven sound, young man. After the first two, I had my doubts, but it was the correct call. Mr. DeGolyer, you are my lucky talisman." Turning to Dr. Hayes he continued. "This train returns to San Luis Potosí and back to Tampico. I will leave you two here. I must go to the Potrero camp immediately to cap the well. We cannot risk another Dos Bocas. Communication from here is too unreliable."

"We'll return with you," suggested Dr. Hayes.

"No, no, no, Doctor. You've been underway three days already. Go to the El Aquila office in the city, clean up, buy some clothes. I've told Lady Cowdray you would have lunch with her tomorrow. I insist. She is expecting it."

De looked down at his and Dr. Hayes' filthy clothes. "We prefer to return with you, sir," he said earnestly.

"No, I insist. I hope to God this is not another Dos Bocas. We must control the well before it ruins itself. Thankfully it has not caught fire. After Dos Bocas we moved the boilers several hundred feet from the derrick so if a well blowout like this occurs, it won't catch fire. Dr. Hayes, I'll want you to return to Washington as soon as possible. If the well is as good as we expect, you need to make arrangements for tankers. We don't have the refinery capacity to handle the crude. Your top priority is to put together a plan to handle the oil. Contact the Texas refineries. I've told Mr. Body you will work with the American companies. Mr. Body will be working with the British."

They talked only a few more minutes before the train sounded the steam whistle. Lord Cowdray jumped aboard as it pulled from the station. "Mr. DeGolyer, as soon as you've rested, come to the well," he ordered. "I hope to have it under control in a few days."

After a hurried goodbye to Lord Cowdray, De said in exasperation, "Dr. Hayes, how could Lord Cowdray think we shouldn't return with him to Potrero? We've got to return to the well. I'll go if I have to ride horseback the whole way!"

"He's the Chief and the Chief said lunch with Lady Cowdray," replied Dr. Hayes calmly. "Now we should go downtown and buy some new clothes. I'd rather return to the well, too, Mr. DeGolyer."

"The most important well El Aquila has ever drilled, and we're to attend a luncheon with Lady Cowdray!" De was exasperated.

The lunch with Lady Cowdray included Sir Reginald Tower, the British minister to Mexico, and Governor Landa y Escandon, the governor of Mexico's federal district. Dr. Hayes did not attend. Earlier that morning he took the first train back to the United States. His last words to De were to keep him informed about the well.

The luncheon group politely peppered De with questions about the big well. He felt uncomfortable fielding questions as if he were the expert while the real work to be done was back at Potrero. Most of the discussion, however, was about the Madero riots. Governor Landa y Escandon condemned the uprising.

"Like a coward, Madero fled the country to the U.S., from where he foments rebellion against our government. Orozco is a puppet unworthy of being called a Mexican. President Díaz will deal with the rebels who proclaim revolution."

After the meal they toured the city in the governor's new car, one of the few in Mexico City. De felt like an intruder among royalty. When he was dropped at El Aguila's downtown office, De asked Mr. Body about the Madero uprising.

"Who is Orozco?" De asked. "Is the uprising serious?"

"Pascual Orozco is a supporter of Madero" answered Mr. Body. "Yes, it is serious. Orozco has turned Madero's protest into violence. He is hailed as a hero in Chihuahua City. They say thirty thousand turned out in the streets to greet him as a conquering Caesar. Yes, Madero's rebellion is very serious indeed, Mr. DeGolyer."

"How about the well? Any word yet?"

"No new developments. Lord Cowdray should be at the wellsite tomorrow morning and will take charge of the operation."

Lady Cowdray insisted that De stay another day to attend more social events which had already been planned before the well blew out. De realized he was filling a social void left by Lord Cowdray. Lady Cowdray introduced De as the young man who had discovered the great runaway well, which by now had made all the newspapers.

De could barely contain his impatience. He politely answered all the questions, and when finally was released from his social obligations, caught the next train back to Tampico. There Hop and Chester informed him the well continued to spew a huge volume of oil.

Potrero No. 4 blowing out

It was almost a week after the well blew out before De finally rode up to Potrero camp. He couldn't believe the scene. The well spewed oil hundreds of feet in the air with a howling roar, a primal force of nature emitting from the bowels of the earth. Thick, black viscous oil covered the landscape for hundreds of acres around the well. Every bush, tree, and patch of land was coated in black ooze. Lakes of oil filled every low-lying depression.

Hundreds of workers had been enlisted from all the nearby villages, haciendas and the town of Tuxpan to help build earthen holding ponds. Their clothing was covered in oil. White bosses whose shouts could barely be heard over the din from the well directed the work. The Buena Vista was now a river of oil. Oil had already reached the Tuxpan River and was moving like a great flood tide toward the Gulf.

Lord Cowdray had personally taken charge of the operation. Field headquarters were built upwind more than a quarter mile from the well. The roaring this far from the well still required that all communication be shouted. De was dumbfounded by the spectacle.

"I've gauged it as best as we can," Lord Cowdray explained over the roar. "It's flowing somewhere between 100,000 and 110,000 barrels per day, bigger than Dos Bocas. This makes it the largest well in the entire world. I have assigned most of the men to build earthen holding ponds." He pointed to an oil-stained topographic map. De had noticed hundreds of workers building huge dams across the creek north of the well.

"Mr. DeGolyer, you are to help construct flumes through which the oil will flow from the ponds to the river. I've designed them such that the oil will rush through so fast that when the river catches fire, the flames could not follow up the flumes. I intend to light the oil on the Tuxpan River above the bar to keep it from pouring into the Gulf. It is imperative we keep the flames away from the wellhead."

"How can you possibly cap such a force?" asked De over the thunderous roar.

"My engineers are building a device to shove over the well. We call it the Bell Nipple. One of your countrymen from Texas has used such a device to cap smaller wells. Two weeks are required before the Bell Nipple is ready. In the meantime, we will save as much of the oil as we can. When completed the ponds should hold two million barrels. Mr. Ryder will show you exactly what to do. Jump to now."

For the next two weeks De was in charge of building flumes. The work was close to the well. Every day he and the workers who had been enlisted to help him were soaked by the oily deluge.

The federal government issued an edict requiring all able-bodied men in the area to join the effort, a result of Lord Cowdray's connection with President Díaz. After the first week many of the workers left but were forcibly returned by the *rurales*. Manuel Pelaez brought all the ranch hands from Tierra Amarilla and surrounding haciendas. Indians were recruited from every village within miles of the blowout until more than three thousand workers were involved in the gargantuan effort to contain the well.

Huge piles of clean clothes were brought daily for the workers. A temporary camp was hastily built a safe distance from the blowout to supplement camp housing. After dark De helped with the chow lines in camp. Food was served all day, the men rotating in shifts. The scale of the project was greater than anything De had ever imagined.

After two weeks working near the wild well, De was relieved to be assigned to help an engineer lay out a route for a new pipeline. The newly completed six inch line could only carry 12,000 barrels per day, much too little for the one well. Lord Cowdray wanted the new pipeline to avoid Tuxpan, which meant two river crossings instead of one. Since De had made a topographic map of much of the area, he was assigned to choose the best route for the pipeline to gravity-drain to Tuxpan bar. His new assignment removed him from the roar, filth, and confusion next to the well. De finally found time to send a report to Dr. Hayes.

> January 13, 1911
> Friday the Thirteenth
> Potrero del Llano
>
> Dear Doctor:
>   I have put off the letter up to the present date in the hope that I would be able to write to you and say that the well has been closed in, but as the attempt to close it has been postponed until tomorrow, I will describe it to you as best I can.
>   The log of the well shows the following entry. Well No. 4: We struck oil at 1911 feet. The well broke loose absolutely without any warning, throwing the bailer, which was in the hole at the time, clear out of the hole. The boilers got shut down at once. The oil blew in at 2 a.m. Dec 27, 1910.
>   After I returned to Potrero, I met the driller, Lou LeBarron, in Tierra Amarilla and an expurgated edition of his account might be of some interest. It was somewhat as follows:
>   "I had just come on the blankety blank tower and we had a blankety little blank blank gas. I run a little water in the blankety blank of a

blank but she wouldn't mix. I says to Shannon, 'Stick the blank blank pipe in the blank bailer and tie up the blank dart. We run in some more water and I stuck my hand over the blankety blank hole and felt a little gas. I says to Shannon, see what a little blank water will do. Jist then the old blank shot the bailer up against the roof and the blank blank blank thing come down through the derrick roof. Shannon fell out backwards through the blank forge room and by blank blank blank I crawled through the blanked little hole under the bull wheel and run my blankedst out into the monte but I couldn't hardly get to camp and the blanked thorns tore my face and blankety blank blank I wuz gassed. I crawled on my knees a trying to get the blanked fire out on the boilers when I wuz gassed. I'll tell you, it's the blankedst blank biggest well I ever worked on and the gas is so bad that I wish that I hadn't ever seen the blanked blank thing and the blanked blank blank gas certainly is bad."

The best part of it is that the boys said that they think that Lou was only frightened and not gassed. He was on the lease two days after the well came in but he didn't go near it again.

Your name has grown great as a prophet on account of your recommendation to go on with the well as the oil might be encountered at any time. Only about five feet were drilled since we visited the well on the morning before we left Potrero.

The casing is in excellent shape and an attempt will be made to shut it in tomorrow. The scheme to be used is one by Mr. Laurie. The men are wearing Mexican clothes and working in the oil. One can go near enough to put your hand in it. Lord Cowdray has been there all day every day, wearing a slicker, hip boots, and a sou'ester.

The oil rock, of which I have several excellent samples, is very similar to the oil

rock of No. 1 and No. 2. It is fossiliferous and
contains a great many cavities, crystal lined.
While it shows some evidence of brecciation, I
am inclined to think that the cavities are the
thing. I will send you the samples soon.

The well is the same now as when it first
came in as nearly as can be estimated. Various
estimates have been made. Lord C thinks that the
well is 100,000 barrels at least. I myself think
that the well will finally prove to be between
thirty and fifty thousand barrels. No oil is
being saved yet. The well did not increase from
10,000 to 100,000 barrels as we understood.

I am working on some leases with our friend.
Lord C wired for Ickes and I suppose that he
will be put on engineering work. Tierra Amarilla
has been shut down indefinitely. We are working
toward getting a lease on about half of Juan
Felipe. If successful, I think that it will be
taken up before Alazan.

I understand that six inch pipe has arrived
and is being sent out to camp. I have recalled
your warning that the well is apt to be of high
pressure.

I will write to you again as soon as anything
of importance occurs.

Yours respectfully,
Everette DeGolyer

The first attempt to cap the well was a failure. The pressure was too high, the Bell Nipple too lightweight. The engineers and workers who tried to place the Bell Nipple over the well could only work next to the spewing eruption for a few minutes in relays. Overhead roofing installed next to the wellbore was inadequate to deflect the deluge of oil from the workers who tried to move the Bell Nipple in place. The mixtures of oil and gas choked their throats and stung their eyes. After the first attempt, Lord Cowdray ordered much larger overhead protection and instructed his engineers to reinforce the Bell Nipple with additional iron and to redesign the pulleys that would slide the cap in place.

After more than a month of struggle by thousands of workers to contain the flow, Lord Cowdray ordered oil on the Tuxpan River to be ignited in order to keep the giant oil slick from reaching the Gulf. Great billows of black smoke rose as high as cumulus clouds. The workers at the well site understood what it would mean if the burning liquid overtook the flumes and ignited the flow at the wellhead. The earthen dams had at last been completed and the half-mile long ponds began to fill with oil. Rows of posts were driven into the middle of the holding ponds to gauge the fill rate and quantity of oil. All the while the great gusher spewed oil high into the sky. Ditches channeled the oil into the ponds. The rate the ponds were filling validated Lord Cowdray's estimate of more than 100,000 barrels per day.

If the oil coming from the wellhead caught fire like it had at Dos Bocas, all chances of capping it would be next to impossible. Confining the fire to the river became paramount to capping the well.

When the oil was ignited, De was put in charge of more than a hundred men to build dams across the Buena Vista River. He enlisted Jim to be his assistant. The urgency of their action increased as the fire's leading edge moved upriver.

Lord Cowdray no longer called men in from the field to discuss the situation at his field headquarters. Instead he issued hand-written orders and had them delivered to the lieutenants in charge of the various operations so that work in the field could continue day and night. The day after the fire was ignited, De received a note from Lord Cowdray.

> Mr. DeGolyer:
> The men will not be paid today. Advise them that the authorities tell us the men must remain at work until the fire is extinguished and we must not pay them til then. Otherwise the men will leave. They can have some payment on account but we must hold the regular pay back. What rate of flow have you in the 80-foot length of flume and what width is it? Make the best terms possible with the woman feeding the men. Fifty cents a day for three meals per man should be a fair charge under the circumstances. But do the best possible, threatening that you ask the rurales to see that she feeds the men and have the local jefe or judge tell us what we must pay her. This only if she be too unreasonable.
> Cowdray.

De was astounded at Lord Cowdray's note. Not to pay the thousands of workers who had spent days fighting the runaway well was asking for rebellion.

"They ain't going to like this," said Jim when De told him to interpret the letter to the men and to the cook. "Working outside in the rain is no fun. Working outside when it's raining oil is bad, no good, muy *malo*, you know what I mean? And then you want me to tell them they ain't getting paid until the well is capped? It could cause a revolt. I may lead it myself."

"Tell them if everyone does their job, the fire will be contained. El Aguila will pay them the full amount owed. Tell them we must cap the well and can not allow them leave until it is capped. If you have to, tell them the rurales will insure they stay at work."

"The *rurales* already arrested several who left for home. They brought them back to camp with busted faces. One had a broken arm. Lordy, why did I ever leave South Texas?"

> Mr. DeGolyer:
> Word has reached us that your dam is not holding very well. If the current where you are damming is too swift you had better select a point where it is slower, trying to fell the trees so they will fall where you want them. It requires a little engineering study to get the dams just right to serve the proper purpose. Mr. Weaver and about 100 men are on the way towards La Ceiba and will put up dams there also, fighting the fire bit by bit to hold it in check.
>
> Cowdray.

De had written to Nell of the exciting news regarding the well, but he was unable to provide many details, as El Aguila employees were prohibited from giving any specific information about the well, especially in letters or telegrams to the States. Still, De made it clear that he had experienced a great success, and he hoped that this would mitigate her disappointment in not being able to spend the holidays together.

He sent Nell several follow-up letters, assuring her of his love and disappointment in not spending their first Christmas together, but no incoming personal correspondence was allowed at Potrero, so he received no word from her in reply. As conditions worsened, it became clear that he would still be in the field for weeks to come. De decided it was best to wire Nell, telling her that she should stay in Oklahoma longer because he had no idea when he'd be able to return to Tampico. His inability to explain in further detail was maddening. He could only hope she understood the critical necessity for him to remain at Potrero.

Oil from the spewing well continued to fill the huge twenty-acre earthen ponds. Black clouds from the burning oil filled the air with smoke. The earthen dams kept most of the oil from spilling into the Buena Vista until the ponds filled. Still the river, its bank, and most of the countryside were covered in flammable ooze.

"*Jefe*," shouted Jim to De over the well's roar, "If you had told me a year ago this was part of the job of being an oil maggot, I'd have stayed in South Texas. To hell with fame and fortune. This ain't no way to make a living." His face looked permanently coated by the black residue. His clothes were oil soaked, the same as all the workers, as were his boots. De didn't look any better.

"We can't just let the well blow until it puts itself out. They think the next attempt will work. Would you look at this spectacle?" For miles all he could see was black earth, black men scurrying about, and a black sky filled with black smoke, as if the whole scene had been plunged into purgatory. The fire downriver was still burning, but the flumes had worked, stopping the flames from moving farther upriver to the well.

> *Mr. DeGolyer:*
> *Mr. Ryder advises that he finds the oil will not fire up a quick current. Therefore our programme must be to form earth or rock dams and to concentrate the flow of oil into one quick flowing stream. This means making the dams where you can get the current. The stream of oil should be, say, about one meter wide.*
>
> *I note your men are knocking off at nine. Arrange for them to be out again in the morning to make another dam at a suitable point lower down. Weaver is out with all the men from here and from the pipeline and railway fighting the fire from where it is as it moves upstream. You with your gang should work downstream.*
> *Cowdray*

Fighting the fire on the river bought them enough precious time until the next effort to cap the well could be attempted. The Bell Nipple was now more than ten feet tall and had been skidded under the protective roof. Two eight-inch flow lines were attached to the Bell Nipple to divert the flow as soon as the Bell Nipple was in place. Lord Cowdray gave the word to the men at the wellhead to start moving the Bell Nipple over the well. Slowly slowly, by ropes attached to winches and pulleys, the Bell Nipple inched into place. As it moved over the wellbore, the force of the flow lifted it up from its footings. More iron rail ties were quickly jammed on for added weight. Finally, on the sixtieth day after the blowout, the Bell Nipple moved over the wellbore. The gigantic spew into the air ceased. Oil filled the Bell Nipple and began flowing down the eight inch lines.

The instantaneous silence caused the mass of men to stop and stare. For two months the well had been an untamed force of nature, drowning out all other sound with its howl and drenching every surface within hundreds of yards from its spewing fountain of oil. Now suddenly silence had fallen and the runaway flow was contained. No one shouted for joy. The relief and exhaustion were too great. The mass of men moved toward the well. Lord Cowdray ordered them to go to the river to fight the fire, but with the Bell Nipple in place, the threat of fire was past. The giant well had been capped.

Potrero No. 4 wellhead and flares

Earthen ponds with gauges to measure flow

117

Chapter Nine

March — May 1911

"Here you are, Mr. DeGolyer." Lord Cowdray handed De a letter. De read it and smiled with pleasure.

"Thank you, sir." The raise in pay was very welcome. Two hundred dollars a month in gold seemed like an enormous sum. "Nell and I appreciate your generosity. I also deeply thank you for naming me Chief Geologist."

"Chief Geologist you are. It was your recommendation that we drill four more wells at Potrero that made El Aguila a viable oil company."

"My recommendation or my luck?"

"Either one suits me. Luck is part of the business world, and indeed is part of life. I like to have lucky people onboard. Besides that, Dr. Hayes tells me you have good judgment, which is as hard to find as a good producing well."

"I appreciate your confidence, sir."

"We choked the No. 4 back to 45,000 barrels per day. It's been flowing at that rate for more than a month. With the other Potrero production, we now produce more than 50,000 barrels per day. We have two and a half million barrels stored in the earthen pits at Potrero. I've been buying every barge on the Texas Gulf Coast to help move the crude from the pipeline outlet at Tamiahua Lagoon. Dr. Hayes has contracted a dozen tankers to move the crude to Texas refineries. We will build a second refinery in Tampico, the largest in Mexico. Our Minatitlan refinery on the Isthmus can handle only a fraction of the volume."

"Even with a larger refinery, how will you market so much petroleum?"

"I have asked my son Clive to take charge of marketing the oil to Great Britain and the Continent. Their navies need the fuel oil. Your Navy thinks that diesel from Mexican crude produces too much smoke. Nevertheless, the demand for crude will only grow. It's the most efficient fuel. Three and a half barrels of diesel provides the same heat energy as one ton of coal. The whole world will soon convert to petroleum."

"Does this change our strategy here in Mexico?" asked De.

"Not at all. Finding this quantity of production will certainly stretch our need for capital. With my and Mr. Doheny's production, Mexico is now one of the world's greatest oil producing countries, which has political implications. Those are things I have to worry about. You, Mr. DeGolyer, need to find El Aguila more oil. I have great faith that you will do so."

"I have some ideas that may direct us toward the best reservoir rock. Finding good production is more complex geologically than just drilling seeps or anticlines. Furbero and Tierra Amarilla are anticlines, but their production doesn't match Potrero or Casiano."

"I am confident that you and Dr. Hayes will solve the puzzle," said Lord Cowdray. De could sense that he was getting ready to end their meeting. He took a quick breath, and then spoke.

"Sir, I have a request. It may seem a bit odd."

"Yes? What is it? Speak you mind, Mr. DeGolyer."

"Sir, I have not finished my university education. When I came to work for you, I needed only a few more months to complete my degree in geology at the University of Oklahoma. I would very much like a leave of absence to finish my degree at the university. Shouldn't a Chief Geologist have a university degree? Do you agree, sir?"

"Well, DeGolyer, that *is* an odd request," said Lord Cowdray, who was clearly taken aback. "The day I announce you are my Chief Geologist, you ask for a leave of absence."

"Yes, sir."

"Mr. DeGolyer, you are twenty-four years old. I have great plans for your future. In the past ten years I have hired many scientists who purport to be geologists, including Anthony Lucas, who discovered Spindletop, and a string of others with degrees from Cambridge and Oxford. A college degree doesn't mean you can find oil. A geologist who can find oil is rare. After Potrero, I place my trust in your abilities rather than in a college degree. But if you insist, my answer is 'yes'. When you have confirmed with Dr. Hayes enough locations to keep the rigs busy for six months, you may return to Oklahoma to finish your degree."

"Oh, I can't thank you enough, sir." De was ecstatic. "The University of

Oklahoma is the leading university for petroleum geology. Professor Gould stays abreast of all the latest development in the great oil fields of Oklahoma. I'll learn a lot that is applicable here. It won't be wasted time, I assure you."

"In that case, I will keep you on the payroll, as assurance that you will return when you have completed your degree."

"Sir, Nell had not wanted to marry me until I finished college. Now I will fulfill my promise to her. Allowing me to return to the university and on full pay is extraordinarily generous. We can't thank you enough, Lord Cowdray."

"I will expect, Mr. DeGolyer, that your thanks will be in the form of more discoveries for El Aguila."

Despite receiving two wires from De telling her to stay in Norman, Nell returned to Tampico before the well had been capped. When they finally met in March, after nearly three months without seeing each other, De was relieved that she was loving and cheerful. Neither mentioned their tiff before Christmas. When he told her the news of returning to Norman to finish his degree and on full pay, Nell was overjoyed. He repeated that he never wanted to be apart during the holidays.

With his new responsibilities as Chief Geologist, De spent long hours in the office, pulling together all the data from the Potrero wells and trying to integrate it into a regional picture. Every day at noon De walked the short distance home to eat with Nell. Their Chinese cook shopped in the market and for lunch prepared fresh meals for the young couple. In the evenings he and Nell walked to the Colonial Club or to the Southern Hotel for a drink and dinner together. Afterward he would return to the office and pore over the data.

"De, love, I can't believe the number of people arriving in Tampico!" Nell exclaimed one evening as they dressed for dinner.

"Tampico has turned into a boom town," De agreed. "More foreigners arrive every day by train and steamer. Yesterday a bunch rode in on horseback all the way from Texas."

"It's all because of your great discovery. Everyone thinks they will get rich in the oil business, don't they?"

"Jim says the cantinas are making more money than Potrero No. 4."

"I have never see so many cantinas or heard so many languages," said Nell. Tampico was such a quaint place when I arrived last June. Now traffic clogs the street – people, horses, mules, merchants for everything from drilling rigs to ladies' hats. There is even an automobile dealership. Did you hear that the mule-drawn trolley fell over on the curve yesterday? No one was hurt. The passengers just shoved it back upright, lifted it onto its track, and appropriated another mule to tow up the grade from the river. Mr. Sterling said the city government is planning an electricity plant. Electricity, can you imagine?"

"The oil activity is causing big changes, not just in town but in the countryside, too. Last year most of the rural people lived off fishing and agriculture. Now they're moving to the oil fields to work. The *haciendas* paid them 25 centavos a day. The oil field pays them one peso a day and provides medical services. The owners of the *haciendas* are not happy."

"It will never be the same ever again."

"Change can be a good thing, sweet Beaner. There is another change in the office, which I hate to see."

"What's that, love?"

"Chester Washburne turned in his resignation. He wants to work as a consultant."

"That's too bad," responded Nell, "but I'm not surprised. I had the feeling Chester resented that you should become Chief Geologist."

"Chester is a good geologist. I once gently scolded him for spending too much time socializing and could tell he disliked it."

"When you start out as equals, it's difficult for some to accept you as their boss. How does Hop feel about your new position?"

"He seems fine with it. He told me someone had to throw water on my theories and I said he was the perfect choice."

"Change is in the air, De love, isn't it? So much change so fast."

Change had indeed arrived at Tampico. The hotels overflowed with men talking oil business, rumors of the latest wells and leasing activity. With every hotel and hostel booked, many of the newcomers pitched tents or moved into the countryside. The impact was even greater at Tuxpan, which had fewer facilities to handle such an onslaught of foreigners. Dozens of cantinas sprang up all over Tampico's and Tuxpan's commercial districts and adjacent to every drilling camp. Money and whiskey flowed freely night and day. It was a young crowd, mostly male, and a rough crowd. Raffish adventurers from all over the world arrived – white, black, olive, red-faced, oriental. German, Italian, French, and even Japanese could be overheard in the cantinas and hotel lobbies. Crowds packed the two plazas. By dusk every *posada* and bar was overflowing with fortune seekers. Some were oil men who worked for the companies, most were only opportunists: young men looking for a way to break into the game, lawyers looking for legal work, roughnecks who worked on the rigs, prostitutes that cropped up in every boom like wildflowers after a spring rain.

Jim explained to De that the new influx of ladies in the cantinas was opportune for his job as oil field scout. "The way I look at it," he explained, "hanging out in bars is just another form of education. You can get your education in the classroom or you can get it from a book. I get mine in the cantinas."

De smiled. "What kind of education would you be talking about?"

"You study rocks and history. I study human nature."

De laughed. "Are you sure you don't visit the cantinas as an excuse to socialize with the pretty *señoritas?*"

Jim protested. "Now don't start preaching at me, *jefe*. As good looking as some of these dark-eyed lasses are, if they taught Sunday school, I'd be on the front row. Anyway, my motives are business, not pleasure, and I don't sample the goods. The girls tell me who will talk and who won't."

"Where in the world do the girls come from?" asked De. "Nell thinks it is tragic for young women to be exploited."

"Every single one has a story," replied Jim. "For most it's their only option. What can a young *señorita* do with no family to help, no husband, and a baby to feed? It's a way to survive. They all dream of finding a good husband."

"Do you pay for the information?"

"Ha. Nothing is free, *jefe*. I buy a drink or two and listen. With thousands of men pouring into the city, the price of accurate information has gone up like everything else."

"What news have you heard lately? Anything from Doheny's group?" asked De.

"No, but the East Coast Company is drilling their second well at Topila. They're also leasing on the other side if the river.

"The Panuco, across from town?"

"Yep," responded Jim. "Lease hounds are buying tracts along the river. It's a wildfire of activity. The first East Coast well made a small producer. They must be hoping for bigger production."

De shook his head. "This play has broken wide open, hasn't it?"

"Oil is not the only thing that's broken wide open," said Jim. "Did you hear what happened in Juarez? Orozco and Pancho Villa have taken the city and now Madero's in control. I don't know how much longer Díaz can remain in power."

"President Díaz has kept the country stable for the last thirty years. With the new oil production, money will be flowing into all levels of the society. The Indians and peasants will eventually have access to a better way of life, just like at home. Creating wealth is the best way to prevent revolutions."

"Except this ain't the U.S. of A.," replied Jim. "The upper crust depends on the layers. Keeping the peasants in their place is part of the formula. That's what's odd about this fellow Madero. He's from one of the richest families in Mexico and yet he claims to care only about the peasants. They say he listens to spirits. Why would anyone trust a fellow who receives directions from a Ouija board?"

"I asked Manuel Pelaez why Madero is so popular." said De. "Manuel says because he's big on land and worker reform."

"Which means taking land from the *hacendados* and giving it to the peasants," said Jim. "It ain't going to happen without a bloody fight."

"Given time, as the tide rises the workers will share in the prosperity."

"That may not be soon enough for the *maderistas*. Like I said, boss, Mexico ain't the U.S. of A."

"And Tampico is no longer the sleepy fishing village it was when we came here a little over a year ago," De concluded, "which means we need to figure out the geology before somebody else breaks the code. Jim, I need the logs on the last two Casiano wells. Tell your contact with Huasteca that I'll trade them for the logs on our last two Potrero wells." Since De was appointed chief geologist for the company, his push for more data overruled Mr. Body's concern for confidentiality.

"Now you're talking," replied Jim. "I can keep up with the drilling and leasing activity from the cantina talk. Accurate well logs have to be swapped."

"Let me know if Huasteca is willing to trade."

Three days later, De called Hop and Jim into his office, closed the door, and showed them a letter from Mr. Body that had been sent to Lord Cowdray about the situation in the capital.

May 18, 1911
Mexico City

Lord Cowdray:

Since I wrote you last we have had a most anxious time in the city here – not knowing what was going to take place, and fearful of mob violence, for there are only three thousand soldiers in the whole of the Federal District, and last Saturday the rebels took the town of Huachinango, only a few miles away from Necaxa, and it was anticipated they would cut the transmission lines, so much so that the Government bought up all the acetylene lamps so they could light up the barracks and the city arsenal, and it was feared that if the transmission lines were cut the men who would be thrown out of work and the factories would be very violent. Threats also have been made to blow up bridges on the Interoceanic and Mexican Railroad if General Reyes attempts to travel over those lines, and it is significant that the Government sent a warship to Havana to take General Reyes off the German steamer by which he was traveling, and it is not known at present at what port he will land. Felix Díaz, the president's nephew, had to go down to Tehauntepec and ride four days overland to get to the City of Oaxaca, as the southern region is in the hands of the rebels. There is a band of rebels also at Valles ready to break rail connection with Tampico if ordered by the Maderistas. The horrible remarks which have been publicly made about the President are too disgusting to write you, and there is a very bitter feeling which is very general. The looting which took place at Pachuca a few days ago was disgraceful, but this was done by the mob, and not the insurrectos, who came in afterwards and restored order.

I was sorry to have to wire you yesterday regarding the insurgents entering Temepache and cutting our telephonic communications to Potrero. I hesitated whether I should send you this news, not wishing to worry you too much, but I thought it better to advise you. A message in from Tuxpan this morning states the line is still cut, and it is probably by this that the news of the armistice has not yet reached them. Our Alvarado train was held up on Sunday by the rebels at Salinas station, and the one rurale who travels the train was disarmed and the train allowed to proceed.

I will keep advising you by cable of any important events, but shall not wire otherwise. In conclusion I may state there is a very triste and

Hop looked up at De and shook his head.

"What do you think?" asked De.

"It is not good news," replied Hop. "The *rurales* are throwing in with the *maderistas*. Orozco and Villa control Ciudad Juarez. Chaos is breaking loose all over the country."

"Jim, what have you heard?"

"I met an attorney new to town by the name of William F. Buckley. He and his two brothers came down to ride the boom. They opened a law office to handle land disputes. He seems to be connected to the political scene. There is a rumor that Madero is being financed by Waters-Pierce to overthrow Díaz. I'll confirm it with Will."

"Waters-Pierce, the American company?" asked De.

"Yep, they're a branch of Rockefeller's Jersey Standard."

"Why would Rockefeller want to disrupt Mexican politics?" asked Hop.

"I'm no one to tell you what's on Mr. Rockefeller's mind," replied Jim, "but if we've found as much oil as you say we have, it could attract the likes of Jersey Standard. Every other oil company from the States is moving down here. If Waters-Pierce financed the Madero rebellion, Jersey Standard could obtain important oil concessions from Madero."

De thought for a moment. "I still don't see why anyone would want to disrupt a stable regime. Chaos is not good for business."

"The Doheny men think Lord Cowdray's relationship with President Díaz is too cozy."

"Doheny has done very well under the Díaz regime, too," Hop said. "He's no one to claim favoritism."

"Stirring the stew could make for opportunities. Mr. Doheny's own people say he's mean as a coyote and a tee-totaler," continued Jim. "Would you trust a man that doesn't drink or smoke?"

"I never would have guessed that Casiano and Potrero would have such an impact," said De.

"Money is pouring into this one-horse town like rain off a roof," said Jim. "In the last two months Americans, Germans, Japs, Dutch, and French have opened consulates. Tampico is a pot of stew all right, and you boys got her to cooking."

"I had my doubts about the play," said Hop, "but Dos Bocas, Casiano, and Potrero tell us a lot of oil is left to be found."

"Which has political implications, according to Buckley," added Jim. "If Díaz is overthrown, the new regime could kick out the oil companies."

"Not peacefully," responded Hop.

"I don't see it happening," said De. "The locals don't have the capital or the expertise to operate the wells, much less to handle the transportation or refining. It doesn't make sense that they would confiscate our properties. I'll ask the Chief if he wants to include an assessment of the politics in the monthly report. I'm sure Mr. Body is informed about what is happening in the capital, but he should know about local politics, too. Jim, you'll need to add that to your list."

"First I'm your rod man on the outcrops, next I'm a scout for the competition, and now I'm supposed to keep track of local politics. *Jefe*, you're going to keep me up all night. Tell the Chief the boy needs a raise, would you? The new pair of boots he bought me is nice, but with all the new duties, my expense account is outrunning my pay."

"I'll recommend a pay raise, Jim. Keeping track of our competitors and the politics will keep you busy. Have you heard from Hippolito? I haven't seen him since Potrero No. 4."

"No, but he was happy as a blue jay on a June bug after the Chief gave him the bonus for keeping his *indios* on the job."

A week later, on March 25, 1911, President Díaz resigned. It was the same day that the first refined oil from Mexico was exported abroad.

May 27, 1911
Mexico City

Dear Lord Cowdray

The riot which occurred on Wednesday afternoon and started from the Chamber of Deputies, when it was found out that the President had not resigned, as was expected, was most serious. The papers here are keeping matters as quiet as possible, presumably by reason of the orders of the new President, but had it not been on account of the deluge of rain on Wednesday night, which helped to disperse the rioters, things would have assumed more serious proportions. The number of killed has not been reported, and the number of wounded was great. On Thursday morning I happened to be working with Adams in his office, and about ten o'clock the rioters passed in front of the Aguila office, carrying timbers and branches of trees, and packing cases, the object clearly being that they were going to burn someone's house, as they had the previous night endeavored to burn the imparcial building. The cavalry, who were riding alongside, as soon as they found the mob was depositing these things in front of Mr. Limantours' new house charged them with their sabers drawn and when the rioters got one of the cavalry off his horse and were carrying him away they opened fire, killing one man close by the Iron Horse, and another directly in front of Mr. del Rio's house. The mob then took to their heels and ran around by Rosales into Calle Colon where you will remember Riba has his office. The cavalry turned back to meet them by the side street and fired a volley, ostensibly over their heads, but this resulted in the killings of four more men. The number of wounded we have not been able to find out. The shooting and cavalry charges continued for probably another hour, when the mob was dispersed. Later on in the day the mob reunited and the Government arranged with some of the Maderistas, who are just coming to town, that the latter should get out on their horses and try and pacify the people, which they did with very good effect. The whole of the shops was shut up for the entire day, and great uneasiness was felt but fortunately no very serious disorders occurred. Yesterday when the new President de la Barra took his oath, though the demonstrations were numerous, they were quite peaceable. There was a big demonstration last night of students, but they kept the peace.

I am copying DeGolyer who should immediately secure our properties from raids by bandits.

Yours respectfully,

John Body

The next week marauding bands of armed men sacked El Aguila's oil camp at Furbero, taking all the food and livestock. No one was harmed, even though the marauders held rifles on the El Aguila employees. As a consequence, De spent the following week working on security for El Aguila's producing wells. He ordered that the wellhead of the Potrero No. 4 be encased in a large cement housing to prevent tampering with the valves.

"Shouldn't we arm the camps?" asked Jim. "We can't depend on the *rurales* to protect us."

"Let's hope the change of regime is peaceful," responded De. "Until the new government is in control, we may experience some banditry, but so far there has been little violence against the oil fields."

"It's just a matter of time," said Jim. "The *federales* here in Tampico don't have the manpower. We'll need to provide our own security."

"Let's see how it plays out," responded De. "We're not the only one in this boat. One more item, Jim. Next week Nell and I are headed to Norman to finish my degree. While we're gone, send me a copy of your monthly reports. Be sure to include any political developments that affect our operations."

"So you're headed back to Oklahoma?" smiled Jim. "Why do you put such high merit in a college degree? I didn't finish the fourth grade and look at me."

"Finishing college has been a long-term goal. Besides, the university is doing research on carbonate reservoirs in Oklahoma that will apply here. While I'm away, Jim, I expect you to keep me posted."

"Don't worry about me keeping you posted, Mr. De. Sending you reports will improve my writing. I figure if I'm ever going to get about in this world, I need to learn the Queen's English better. One of these days I may go back to school myself. By the time you get back from Oklahoma, we'll have this shop running like a Singer sewing machine. Now, don't you go to Oklahoma and never return to Tampico."

"I'll be back," De said and smiled. "This is the world's hottest oil play. Why would I leave it now?"

Chapter Ten

June 1911

Jim entered the Cantina Mariposa close to the waterfront. He liked the large covered veranda overlooking the river. The muddy waters of the river teemed with boat traffic. From the shade of a booth, a friendly hand waved at him. Jim walked over, pushed his hat back, and nodded to Edward Lynton.

"Hey, Edward, good to see you. Who's the lady?"

"Isn't she beautiful?" Edward's arm was around a young *señorita*. "She's the prettiest thing in Tampico. Sit down, sit down, *amigo*. Let me buy you a drink. Jim meet Lourdes."

Jim tipped his hat and sat down. It was late afternoon. The bar was already half-filled with roughnecks and hookers. The big crowd wouldn't start arriving until dark.

"Any word on the East Coast well across the river, Edward? Their first well last March wasn't all that good."

"It drilled in last night making a thousand barrels a day. Not as good as your Potrero well, but better than a poke in the eye."

"Who's the money behind East Coast?"

"You'll have to ask your buddy Will Buckley. He keeps up with the players. I'm just a man on the ground scratching for an opportunity."

"Are you finding any?" asked Jim.

"I bought three small tracts along the river, paid $1000 gold for each and already sold one for $6000. You don't need to drill an oil well to make money in this play. All I need is a good rumor. Is Aguila leasing along the Panuco? It's a hot lease play."

"We don't buy small tracts or trade leases," responded Jim. "El Aguila sticks to big haciendas where there's running room if we find something good."

"A strategy which keeps the likes of me out of your hair," replied Edward. "All I want is a good rumor and some tracts small enough for my pocketbook, and I could care less who finds oil or how much. The money is in the trading, not in the drilling."

"You play a different game than El Aguila, Edward. My boss believes he can unlock the key to finding oil. I never knew anyone could love rocks as much as DeGolyer does. He calls them stone diaries written in code and he spends his waking hours trying to break the code. Who else has been buying around the Panuco well?"

"Everybody in town owns leases in the area: Kirkland, El Vado, Mexican Gulf, Sill and Sawyer, Chijoles, Veracruz Mexican, Panuco Excelsior. It's all small tracts. Lots of bad title, too. Nobody has a controlling interest. That's another reason your friend Will Buckley will like the play. He's probably already searching for tracts with bad title."

"What would we do without lawyers? How you doing at the monte tables?"

Edward waved a hand in the air with a dismissive gesture. "Don't bring up monte. Luck comes and luck goes, just like the tide. I've learned to roll 'em when you're hot, and to pull 'em in when you're not."

"Any news about the *maderistas?*"

"I hear all of Madero's compatriots who helped him overthrow Díaz will be looking for the payoff. If he doesn't deliver, out he'll go."

"Do you think the regime change will hurt the oil play?"

"That's another question for Buckley," said Edward. "The natives are still mad we took Texas and that was seventy-five years ago. They don't like us here, but now that they've tasted what oil can buy, they can't live without the money."

"Oil has sure stirred the pot," agreed Jim.

"As soon as they can, the Mexicans will kick us out," predicted Edward. "It's their country. Which is another reason to make money trading royalty and leases instead of drilling for oil. I'll take my profits with me. Yours will stay in the ground until they're confiscated."

"Mexico couldn't operate an oil field if they wanted to. They need our money. We need their oil. Seems like a fair swap. And look at you," Jim said winking. "With such a lovely lady in tow and a good rumor, you're sitting mighty pretty yourself."

Jim rose and paid his respects to the young lady. He didn't know Edward's source of information, but in a town rife with rumors, he had found it to be reliable. Jim left the bar and walked a few blocks to the Campana Building. He opened a door with the sign 'Buckley and Buckley'. Seeing no one at the front desk, he walked down a hall and stuck his head into the first office. The occupant, a thirty-year old man with a full head of hair, looked up. "What brings you around so late in the day, Jim? Looking for legal advice?"

"Looking for something a little wetter than advice," Jim said.

Will Buckley laughed, "Would you care for a drink?"

"You never know when it'll be your last," replied Jim. When the drink was poured he raised his glass and tipped it toward his friend and continued, "Have you heard about the well across the river?"

"The East Coast well across the Panuco?"

"*Si*. A friend of mine said it came in last night."

"Who's your friend?" asked Will.

"Edward Lynton. He showed up in Tampico a couple of months ago. He was working for the Consolidated Copper Company in Sonora but they closed the mine after a bloody worker's strike, so he moved to Tampico to check out the oil play. He's been trading leases and royalty and told me the East Coast well came in last night flowing a thousand barrels a day."

"I hope he's right," said Will. "I ran title on some of those tracts. They're a mess. Few plots have been deeded. Most are claimed solely by possession. Many of the owners never married. Heirs are unknown and scattered to the seven winds. Families have swapped and sold tracts over the years. None has been surveyed. It'll take a lot of title work to figure who owns what."

"Which must be an opportunity for a man like yourself," Jim said with a smile. "You wouldn't end up with any of the leases would you?"

Will Buckley grinned. "Now Jim, I'm here to *cure* title, not to acquire it."

Jim laughed and continued, "Do you know who is behind East Coast?"

"They're the old Leland Stanford bunch from California. In 1909 they started the Southern Pacific of Mexico. East Coast is their subsidiary. We do some work for them. They have deep pockets."

"What do you think of the Madero situation?"

"Like everyone else, I'm apprehensive. Will he tax petroleum? Will he obstruct the way we do business? Will he nationalize the minerals? No one has the answers."

"My friend told me Waters-Pierce financed the Madero revolution."

"Henry Pierce would sell his mother for a wooden nickel, but I doubt that he financed Madero."

"No matter what you thought of Díaz," Jim continued, "for thirty-five years the country has been peaceful. When Madero showed up the riots broke out."

"Passing the baton has never been easy for young countries," said Will. "Given Mexico's history of blood and violence, the change so far has been relatively calm."

"Change down here ain't particularly a democratic endeavor."

"Who cares about democratic endeavors?" asked Will. "Last month the Supreme Court of the United States busted the Standard Trust into thirty-eight companies. Our own legal system can dictate change the same as a Mexican revolutionary. Governments are our worst enemies."

"Why do you figure Madero's revolution is so popular? Thousands show up at his rallies."

"Messiah movements have cropped up throughout history. Show me a culture with an underprivileged class, and I'll show you a dilettante who convinces them to follow him because he promises to eradicate their worries and woes. The messiahs all have the same problem: they can't carry out their promises. Madero promised freedom from poverty and corruption. Unlike Christ, who promised it would happen in the next world, Madero promised it would happen in this world in the next thirty days."

"Is the Madero movement like a religion?" Jim asked.

"Religion, faith, idealism. They'll all send you to the same place. Madero can't deliver so he won't last unless he turns into a dictator like Díaz. If idealists prevail, they tend to become what they overthrew. Madero was smart not to declare himself president. De la Barra is a figurehead, but at least he was part of the elected government, which signals to me no radical changes for a while. When Madero runs for president in October, he will be elected, which then legitimizes the change of regime."

"Where do you think this will end?" Jim liked Will Buckley's predictions. He enjoyed his new scouting duties, and enjoyed asking questions of knowledgeable people.

"¿Quien sabe? Jim, your guess is as good as mine. It is odd Madero is from the privileged class. The upper one percent controls virtually all the wealth in Mexico so they have the most to lose. Once you turn the tiger loose, no telling where it'll end."

Jim chatted for a few more minutes, finished his drink, and thanked his host. "I better run. The bright lights are calling. Thank you again, Will." He walked back to the El Aguila building, nodded a good evening to the night clerk, took out a paper and pencil, and laboriously began writing the monthly report.

Within a week a frenzy of activity surrounded the Panuco well. Leases and royalty near the well were bought and traded and then swapped again. Wells that cost $25,000 were sold for $1,000 or more for each one percent, a four-fold mark-up. The local newspaper crowed about oil's impact on the future of Mexico. Half a dozen companies moved rigs to drill their leases. Unlike Potrero, development of the Panuco Field was an uncontrolled, haphazard melee by individuals, small companies, promoters, syndicates, and anyone else with an ownership map and an oil lease. Wells were opened at full capacity to capture as much of the oil as fast as possible.

De smiled as he read Jim's monthly report. Even though he was taking double the normal course load, De found time to direct Jim and the geological activities from Norman. Dr. Gould's classes were absorbing, particularly ones related to karst topography. Yet however much he enjoyed the academic world, it didn't compare to the excitement of the oil play in Tampico.

```
Monthly Report*
   'June 1911: People are spending money around
here like it's horse hockey and they own the whole
herd. The last three wells at Panuco came in for
more than a thousand barrels a day. It's a feeding
frenzy from the field to the cantinas. Last night I
watched a man lose a half interest in a 500 barrel
a day well at a game of monte and he wasn't even
upset, said he'd go drill another one next week. At
least a dozen rigs are going up. Across the river
the derricks look like a windmill factory. I have
enclosed sample logs on three wells.'
```

De wondered how Jim had acquired copies of the sample logs. A brief scan confirmed that the producing zone was the Tamasopo Limestone.

*Not authentic report

'Will Buckley says Madero promised too much. He says it's too early to know how the change will affect the oil companies but to expect the 1899 law that allowed oil exploration without taxation to be amended unless the oil companies let it be known they won't pay taxes. Except for the raid on Furbero, everything has been quiet on El Aguila properties. I'll make a recon trip with Hippolito to find out what's happening in the countryside. Here in Tampico it's all rumors. Ignacio Pelaez told me his brother Manuel was one of Madero's supporters. Last fall Manuel organized a group of the large ranch owners in the Huasteca to support Madero. I'll talk to him soon, as directed by your honor. Signing off, your obedient servant,

James H. Hall.

Jim sent word for Hippolito to meet him at the landing in Tuxpan and the next day took the company's early-morning fast launch through the Tamiahua Lagoon. Boat traffic was more congested than ever. Even the merchants had caught oil fever. As more people poured into the region, prices for goods had risen with demand.

When Jim arrived in Tuxpan, Hippolito was at the landing, dressed the same as when Jim first saw him, in a white loose-fitting cotton shirt, cotton pants tied at the ankles, a red sash tied at the waist and a conical-shaped sombrero.

"Hippolito, *buenos dias, amigo. Listo?*" Hippolito nodded. "*Entonces vámanos.* Let's go." Hippolito nodded again but didn't say a word.

"There you go, talking my ear off," Jim said to Hippolito in English. He waved a dismissal to the launch driver, tied his small duffle on the back of his horse, and stepped onto the saddle. "To Tierra Amarilla, Hippolito."

"*Poco a poco se andan lejos,*" replied Hippolito. Jim smiled. Always a *dicho*, he thought. 'Little by little we go a long way'. He's right as usual.

They rode through the middle of town. Tuxpan had also caught oil fever. New false storefronts and two-story hotels had been built in the two weeks since he had last been here. A shanty town had sprung up at the town's edge. Several new cantinas and brothels lined the main street, most of them constructed with canvas stretched over a wooden frame. Unlike Tampico, where many of the streets were being paved with asphalt from the Ebano wells, Tuxpan's streets were quagmires from the summer rain. Jim stopped by the telegraph office to check for any messages and lingered for a while to overhear conversations. He had tried to hire the telegraph operator to keep a log of who telegraphed, but so far the operator had refused. This time he upped the offer and could tell the operator's refusal was not as emphatic as before.

Within an hour they left Tuxpan headed to Tierra Amarilla. As they rode along, Jim would throw out a *dicho* in Spanish. Without looking back, Hippolito would offer the phrase in *huastecan*. Jim struggled with the pronunciation. It was difficult for him to hear the tonal differences. Finally he told Hippolito, "You're making my head spin, *amigo*. I think I'll stick to Spanish."

"*Arrieros somos y por el camino andamos.*"

Jim laughed. Hippolito's *dichos* fit every occasion. 'We're mule drivers and we're walking on the same road'. In the U.S. we say 'we're all in the same boat'. Personally, I'd rather be driving a mule.

Toward dark he recognized a familiar landmark. Cerro Pelon rose up from the flat landscape like an enlarged version of Hippolito's sombrero. In the fading light he saw several derricks in a line extending from Cerro Pelon's west flank. He knew they were located along the fault that he and De had mapped on their first field trip. So far none of the wells were outstanding. Total production for Tierra Amarilla was less than six hundred barrels per day, but with the phenomenal production at Potrero, extending a branch pipeline to Tierra Amarilla had made it commercial.

Outside the compound's perimeter a muddy street separated a row of wooden cantinas. Two company men with rifles nodded as he and Hippolito passed through the gate. The company camp was laid out in perfect rows and consisted of wooden structures built on stilts with front porches and thatched roofs. He rode up to the first and hailed. A freckled-faced man nearly as wide as he was tall came to the door and waved him in. Jim directed Hippolito to take the horses to the stables.

"I'm Charlie Johnson. Call me Stump. Come on in." Jim guessed Stump had to weigh close to three hundred pounds. "Will you spend the night?" asked Stump. "We have plenty of bunks."

"Sure," said Jim. "After riding a boat and a horse all day, my backside needs a break."

Stump held open the door and Jim shook his hand as he squeezed past. Stump showed Jim to a bunk and then walked with him next door to the dining facility. Chinese cooks and houseboys had shined it to a spotless sheen. Stump yelled into the kitchen and hot coffee arrived immediately. He told Jim to order anything he liked. Jim asked the Chinese cook to throw a steak on the grill and fry up some onions and potatoes.

"The last time I was here we didn't have a Chinaman to order around," he told Stump. "Me oh my, how I do love civilization."

As he was eating, Jim noted Tierra Amarilla's transition. Electric lights from a generator lit the company compound. Even Tuxpan, which was getting electricity, couldn't match the modernity of the camp. Jim could see the lights of dormitories for the rig workers and for those who oversaw the saw mill and the ice plant. A water treatment plant and a blacksmith shop were on the far end of the compound.

"This is a small operation compared to Potrero," said Stump. "Have you been there yet? Potrero has a cafeteria, a hospital, housing for fifty company men and two hundred workers. There are more whores in the cantinas next to the Potrero camp than in Tuxpan. They can smell money, can't they?" said Stump. "I swear if we found oil in the Arctic, there'd be an igloo whorehouse next to the rigs."

"Have you had trouble finding hands?" asked Jim.

"Not a problem. The hacienda owners complain they can't get help anymore because the oil field pays a peso a day, four times what they pay," answered Stump. "It's free enterprise, ain't it? If we didn't pay more than the haciendas, we couldn't get the workers."

"Why do you allow cantinas so close to camp?" asked Jim. Not a hundred meters separated the compound gate from the row of cantinas.

"The girls go where the money flows. The workers are on twelve-hour shifts. When they're not on the rig, they're in the cantinas.

"I'm all for dancing girls," replied Jim, "but maybe they should stay in town. Any problems with the rig hands mingling with the *indios*?"

"Only when the *indios* get drunk. When they're sober, they're good workers, but let the greasers swallow a little *aguadiente* and they turn *puro loco*, crazier than wild animals. We keep guards on duty at the cantinas twenty-four hours a day, paid by the company."

"Why don't you just shut off the whiskey and close down the cantinas?"

"We'd have a revolt on our hands. The only way to keep roughnecks in the jungle is to keep the whores nearby. The cantinas probably make more money than the oil wells."

"Sounds to me like the company should get in the whore business," said Jim. "This could be a perpetual money machine. Pay the roughnecks every two weeks and two weeks later the company has all the money back, less a little slice for the ladies and the drinks. I'll bring it up to the *jefes*."

"Here comes your steak," said Stump chuckling. "After you eat, I'll show you around the camp."

The next morning Jim and Hippolito saddled up and rode to the Tierra Amarilla hacienda headquarters. Within a mile of the house, a dozen armed horseman pulled up on the trail beside them. Jim nodded to them and said he worked for El Aguila, and that he wanted to speak to *Señor* Pelaez. The leader was very cordial, but kept his men placed on either side of Jim and Hippolito. When they arrived at the front gate of the house, Manuel Pelaez was on the porch waiting for them. He already knew of their arrival.

"*Señor* Pelaez, it's Jim Hall with El Aguila," Jim greeted him and introduced himself.

"*Bienvenidos*." Manuel walked to the gate and opened it. He nodded to the leader of the escort, who turned his troops around and headed back toward the oil field. Jim stepped off his horse, dusted his pants and extended his hand.

"I was in your neighborhood and thought I'd stop by."

"Yes, welcome. Please, come in."

Hippolito, who would never be welcomed inside the house, attended the horses. Jim and Manuel walked into the house. Nothing had changed since his last visit. Manuel Pelaez said to join him in the library after he had washed up. When he walked into the library, Manuel offered Jim a glass of brandy.

"*Salud*," Jim said and raised his glass.

"*Salud*."

"How was your journey?"

"Fine. Who are the escorts?"

"They are friends. Since so many foreigners are here and so much money is in the oil camps, the rurales are unable to patrol the area with sufficient men. We *hacendandos* hired them for our own security."

"From the bandits or from the central government?"

"Perhaps from both," responded Manuel without a smile.

"Your brother Ignacio is doing a fine job for El Aguila," said Jim. "He has helped us acquire several valuable leases."

"Ignacio is a good lawyer, and he knows much about the haciendas in this area."

"He filed suit for us against Doheny on the Hacienda Cerro Viejo."

"Yes, he told me. Cerro Viejo has had title problems for many years. Our grandfather signed the first oil lease on Cerro Viejo to Cecil Rhodes in 1876."

"Cecil Rhodes?"

"Yes. His group drilled wells on Hacienda Cerro Viejo near the *chapapotes*. They found only a small amount of oil. The owners of the hacienda are my cousins, the Gorrochoteguis. A few years ago the widow Gorrochotegui signed a lease with Mr. Doheny's group. She was duped. The lease is invalid. Your company, El Aguila, then took a lease on the hacienda and received signatures from all my Gorrochotegui cousins."

"Yes, both El Aguila and Huasteca have claims on Cerro Viejo. Since Potrero came in, the property is of much greater interest to us. Huasteca threatens to move a rig on Cerro Viejo even though we believe we own the lease."

"How do you say in your country…possession is the law?"

"Ninety percent of the law," answered Jim.

"In Mexico, it is one hundred percent. And how are the wells on Tierra Amarilla?"

"We finished our fifth well on your hacienda," said Jim. "I am here to check on the drilling. So far, we have not found a big producer on your land, but we are still drilling."

"Where is your short companion, the amiable young geologist?"

"*Señor* DeGolyer is back in the United States finishing his university degree in geology. He'll return in a few more weeks. Our owner, Lord Cowdray, named him Chief Geologist after we got the Potrero well under control."

"All of my men worked on the well for your Lord Cowdray," said Manuel. "Did you see the well while it was blowing out? What a force of nature! I could not imagine that it could be capped. I thought it was another *Dos Bocas*."

"Yes, we all did, too, but the Bell Nipple worked. DeGolyer is figuring ways to keep wells from blowing out. You hate to see all that oil flow down the river and catch fire. It's like burning thousand peso bills."

"It made a waste of the land, and the river, too, but soon enough the jungle will reclaim itself," Manuel commented. "More important is the wealth it will bring to Mexico."

"In the meantime we have moved several drilling rigs to Potrero. May I ask you a question about politics? My superiors would like your opinion."

Manuel's expression did not change. "*Claro.*"

"Your brother Ignacio told me that you support Madero."

"Yes, it is not a secret. Díaz depended too much on foreigners for capital and on his *científicos* for advice. He was wary of the Americans but trusted the English and especially your Lord Cowdray. Limantour preferred the Germans. I do not trust Hugo Scherer or any of the Germans. Díaz should not have considered granting a concession to the Japanese for Magdalena Bay, which is not so far from your San Diego Bay. Why provoke the Americans? And he would never provide for succession. When he chose Corral, it was clear that chaos would ensue if Díaz died in office. Last September's centennial celebration was nothing more than ostentatious self-aggrandizement at a cost of millions. Díaz's last election was a fraud. Madero ignited the country with his motto to negate the election."

"Since then has there been banditry in this area? Our Furbero camp was sacked," observed Jim.

"In Mexico there have always been individuals who would take advantage of an opportunity," responded Manuel. "But with the help of the other *hacendados*, we have not had trouble. As you saw, we provide our own security."

"Díaz was president for thirty-five years," said Jim. "Do you think Mexico is better off because of him?"

"Díaz served a purpose in our history, but his time has passed. He held power too long. As in your country, longevity breeds corruption. Mexico industrialized by selling out to the foreigners. You control the mines, the smelters, the railroads, the oil fields."

"At least there was peace and security."

"With the *científicos* in control, no hacienda was safe from confiscation. *Rurales* imperiled the countryside."

"And the peasants, will they be better off?"

"*Los indios?*"

"Under Díaz the hacienda owners were deeded Indian lands."

"What do you mean by 'Indian lands'?" asked Manuel. His voice rose in a subdued rebuttal. "They had no legal ownership. They scratched a living from the jungle. Our Mexican government recognized the original land grants from Spain. The remaining lands were surveyed and patents were issued from the government to owners who purchased the land, the same as in your country. We have cleared much of the forest and made it productive with cattle ranching. Many *haciendas* allow *indios* to live on the land in return for clearing the forest. We call it *cuente zacate*, 'in exchange for grass'. Many Indians trade their work for the right to live on the land. Some *indios* have bought land from the government and maintain communal property, the *condueñazgos*."

"Will Madero help the Indians?"

"The Indians are uneducated. The church controls their aspirations through faith in the next world. In this world, without education they will live in poverty and ignorance."

"Perhaps they hope for a better life in this world."

"Perhaps. Are there more questions your Mr. DeGolyer wished to ask?" Jim understood this to be an end to the questioning.

"Those are all my questions, *Señor Pelaez*," Jim said. "Thank you for sharing your knowledge."

"Shall we drink to your next well on Tierra Amarilla? May it be as good as Potrero," said Manuel. They touched glasses. "Please give my regards to Ignacio."

The next morning Jim and Hippolito saddled their horses and rode to Potrero. "Would you look at that!" he said to himself as they rode up to the camp. Half a dozen cable-tool rigs were drilling, their lift beams slowly rising and falling, pounding the drill bit into the earth. He also saw the Hamill rotary rig. Mr. De told him it could drill much faster than the cable tool rigs, but needed repair much more than the reliable cable tools. Already the pipeline to Tuxpan Bar was carrying more than 50,000 barrels per day of crude oil for El Aguila. A pipeline along the ocean floor pumped the oil to tankers anchored in deeper water a mile offshore. The huge earthen pits at Potrero had been supplemented by steel tanks. More than two and a half million barrels of oil were in storage. Dozens of derricks stood over well sites that had already been drilled. Denuded of plant life, the land was barren, blackened by the millions of barrels of crude. Jim barely recognized the wellsite where the great well had blown out.

"Hippolito, can you believe your eyes?" said Jim as much to himself as to the *mozo*.

"*Sacar dinero hasta de las piedras.*"

Jim laughed. "In English, we say 'to squeeze blood out of a turnip'. Your *dicho* is better, 'to get money out of rocks'."

Sam Weaver, the Potrero superintendent, gave Jim a tour of the camp and facility. Jim asked him about security.

"We have a security force in camp. They mainly break up fights at the cantinas. No arms are allowed in camp."

"Have there been any problems since the *maderistas* took power?" asked Jim.

"An ambush was attempted on the payroll wagon last month. The guards drove them off and no one was hurt. I've asked Mr. Body for more armed guards to protect the payroll. In the countryside they say there is unrest, but here it's business as usual."

"How's the Number Four?"

"Steady as a rock at 45,000 barrels per day."

After spending the day at Potrero, Jim told Hippolito they would return to Tuxpan early the next morning. During their ride back to Tuxpan, Jim asked Hippolito what he thought of all the cantinas and the young Mexican girls serving as prostitutes.

"*Con dinero hasta la mona baila.*"

Jim told him it was the same in the States, 'with money even the monkey dances'. On a whim, Jim asked Hippolito, "What do you think of Madero?" He had asked the same question of everyone else.

"Last year a comet lit the night. The day Madero arrived at the capital, an earthquake shook the ground."

Jim glanced over his shoulder at the *mozo*, whose face was as impassive and expressionless as ever. Jim had seen Haley's comet last year and he had read about the earthquake. It was the first time Hippolito had not spoken a *dicho*.

Chapter Eleven

July — September 1911

In June De received his degree in geology. He had been tagged as the richest student in the University of Oklahoma because of his salary from El Aguila. Their stay in Norman had been happy and enjoyable, especially for Nell, who missed her family when she was in Mexico. Her father was concerned about the Madero uprisings and the safety of his daughter if the new election scheduled for October 1 turned violent. De assured him they were safe, that El Aguila provided adequate protection for its employees.

Back in Tampico, De's work directing daily field operations resumed immediately. With several rigs running, mapping and updating the fields as they developed took up more and more of his attention. He seldom had time to go to the field. To handle field operations De hired two field geologists, Charles Hamilton and Ben Belt. Under De's directive, rock samples from cuttings were taken every ten feet. As soon as a well reached total depth, detailed sample logs for each well were brought to the Tampico office for his review. He also required that exact temperatures of the oil and salt water of the producing wells be measured daily, as well as each well's flowing pressure and daily production. If he needed a competitor's well log, De would ask Jim to trade El Aguila logs for the logs of other company's wells. By summer's end, before the rains began to slacken, he had proposed several locations for Dr. Hayes' approval.

In August Lord Cowdray telegraphed De to meet him and Dr. Hayes in the capital. There the Chief expressed pleasure with the enlarged operation. Even with so much more oil being sold in the world market, the price of crude was holding steady at sixty cents a barrel. While De was in Mexico City, Lord Cowdray met with Francisco Madero, and reported that he was confident the transition would not materially affect their operations.

"The last thing the Chief said was to find more oil," De reported to Hop. "Next year he wants to build Mexico's largest refinery in Tampico."

"Did you hear that Standard Oil bailed out Doheny?" asked Hop. "Standard contracted to buy two million barrels of crude per year for five years from Huasteca."

"The Chief and Mr. Body discussed it. Lord Cowdray said he prefers to sell refined products. He is meeting with the British admiralty next month to reach a long-term agreement on fuel oil for the British navy."

"The British navy…you're kidding."

"Lord Cowdray said Admiral Jack Fisher convinced Churchill to convert all British naval ships from coal to fuel oil. It will create a huge world demand."

"You can't fault the Chief for thinking small, can you?" mused Hop.

"He wants us to find another Potrero. Too many of his assets are riding on the shoulders of one well." De paused. "I told him we've only scratched the subsurface." De chuckled at his own joke.

"He wants me to check out leasing a *hacienda* in the Mata del Peso area," De continued, "so I'll be headed there next week. He also wants us to provide an accurate projection of how much each of El Aguila wells will produce in the future."

"I see you've been plotting each well's daily production." said Hop.

"All we now know is how much oil the wells have already produced. We need to determine how much more oil each well will produce, how quickly it declines, and if there is a maximum rate we should maintain to recover the most oil. Perhaps we will be able to predict salt water encroachment. With close to 50,000 barrels per day production and the Chief spending huge sums of money to build a refinery, we need to learn more about what we've found."

"Isn't finding oil hard enough?" asked Hop. "Figuring out how much a well can produce will be an even bigger guess."

De agreed. "With enough data, maybe we can discern patterns. It *is* an odd business, isn't it, looking for something buried a half mile deep and then trying to figure out how much oil we can produce from rocks we can never see?"

When De told Nell he would be in the field for the next three weeks, she decided to accompany her mother on a trip to California and she booked passage on the *Iparanga* for Havana and on to Galveston. With rebel armies holding most of Chihuahua and large parts of Coahuila, travel by train had become very dangerous.

A week later De, Jim, and Hippolito were in the countryside examining the outcrops in the Mata del Peso area. After a few days in the field, De developed a headache that wouldn't go away. He took an aspirin, but the headache remained and he began feeling very nauseous. Nevertheless, he resolved to keep working, believing he had a mild flu that would soon abate. Two days later, he felt increasingly weak, but he waved off Jim's inquiries. They returned to the campsite in the early evening, where Hippolito had built a roaring fire. De sat heavily on the ground, and out of habit, pulled out his notebook. After scribbling a few notes, the pencil fell from his hand and he leaned over on his side.

"*Jefe*, you're looking green around the gills," said Jim, who had come over to check on him. "Are you sure you're feeling all right?"

"*Poco poco*," whispered De. He was shivering.

Jim touched De's forehead. "You've got a raging fever, boss."

"I've felt better," said De.

"Here, let me help you in the tent," said Jim. "Where's your aspirin?"

"In my kit," said De. "But I've already taken a bunch of it – no good." Jim laid De on his cot, covered him with extra bedding, and brought him plenty of water. That night De sweated through his bedding, delirious with a high fever. The next morning De was even worse. Jim talked to Hippolito, who nodded and pointed to the jungle. The two loaded De on the saddle with Jim riding behind him to hold De up. De was conscious but couldn't speak except to grunt.

"You're sicker'n a dog, *jefe*. It's two days ride back to Tamiahua. You need help now. Hippolito knows a *curandera* he says can cure you."

Hippolito guided them through the jungle until they came upon a thatch hut in a small clearing. The Indian family who lived there helped De off the saddle and took him into their house. Hippolito spoke to an older woman. She examined De, first putting her head to his chest, then holding open his eyelids to examine his pupils. Jim thought to himself this was no time not to have modern medicine and worried that De might not make it.

For three days the old woman nursed De. She held his head and made him swallow potions concocted from dry leaves boiled in water. *Sustos*, the *curandera* repeated to De, and mumbled other words over her patient that Jim couldn't understand.

Jim asked Hippolito for an explanation of *sustos*. Hippolito moved his hands around his head, indicating demons.

Finally after three days, the fever broke. When De regained consciousness, he looked at Jim and Hippolito. "Where am I?"

"You've been plenty sick, *jefe*. You've been out of your head. You told us all your secrets."

De smiled weakly. "I don't have any secrets."

"I was kidding, Mr. De. The old woman here cured you. You were sure enough sick."

De wanted to know what kind of medicines the woman had ministered to him. She showed him the leaves of several plants. Weak as he was, De placed some of the leaves in his field book for later identification. He determined to learn more about the local plants that the natives used for medicine. The woman and her family spoke Teenek and understood only a little Spanish, so he could not express his thanks in words but only in expressions of gratitude. When De, Jim and Hippolito left, De gave them what little money he had. By the time he finally reached Tampico, he was still weak but the fever had passed. In Tampico the American doctor diagnosed malaria and prescribed daily doses of quinine.

"No wonder the British drink this with gin," he told Hop two days later over a gin and tonic at the Imperial Bar. "Juniper juice is the only way to choke down the quinine. And it does go with a good cigar."

"We're just glad you're back alive," said Hop.

"Well, now that I'm back, I'm anxious to know, did you finish mapping Amatlan?"

"I'll need a couple of more weeks. It looks promising."

"Isn't Amatlan close to Hippolito's village?" asked De.

"That's right," answered Hop. "Zacamixtle. What a Gomorrah."

"Is it?" asked De. "The last time I was there it reminded me of Tamiahua."

"Zacamixtle now hosts gambling parlors, cantinas, brothels, every delight a roughneck could dream of. I wrote a poem about it." Hop took a folded paper from his pocket and handed De a typed page.

Zacamixtle

A mushroom growth in the monte

With its huts of split bamboo

The village of Zacamixtle rose

And her careless bosom drew

Outlaws, gamblers and prostitutes
Chatting their song, age old
Wherever the money is free,
"There shall we harvest the gold."

So the roulette wheel was mounted
Cantinas opened their doors,
And mud-stained boots went waltzing
Across the dance hall floor.

A million stenches taint the air
When she swelters in the heat,
While the babies, dogs and buzzards
Fight for refuge in the street.

The native sees with wondering eyes
The boomtown's startling growth.
The white man loathes her filthiness
But she curses and holds them both.

Shoulder to shoulder at night they crowd,
The white man and the brown,
Pushing and cursing and shoving
Along the streets of the town.

Men from the camps of the companies
Stained with the marks of their toil
Wearing hats that are gray with mud
And boots that are black with oil.

Drinking and dancing and laughing

Spending with lavish hands,

While the peon jealously watches

These men from another land.

The spirit of Zacamixtle hangs,

Low over the sweating throng,

Bidding them snatch their pleasures

Heedless of right or wrong.

Like a young queen with her power

Watching her courtiers play

Reckless, cruel and extravagant,

Snatching what pleasures she may.

De looked up. "Hop, I'm impressed. I had no idea you were a poet." Hop shrugged in response.

"Jim told me Zacamixtle was quite a watering hole for those in search of brown-eyed delights," De said.

"It makes Tampico look like a church camp. Mixing oil and *aguadiente* makes a dangerous brew."

"Jim tells me the natives resent *gringos* messing with their women. Do you think it's a problem?"

"Two nights ago I watched a drunken Indian stumble into a cantina with a machete," related Hop. "He tried to lop off the head of a big roughneck from Texas. The Texan knocked him flat with one punch. The Indian lay on the floor for several minutes. No one paid him any attention, as indifferent as to a cockroach. When the Indian stood up, he attacked the roughneck a second time and the second time the roughneck knocked him cold, dragged him out the door, and threw him in the mud."

"Was that because of a woman?"

"I suspect so. 'While the peon jealously watches' may change to 'while the peon jealously takes revenge.'"

"Oil booms attract a tough crowd," said De.

"The roughnecks better watch their backside," Hop continued. "There are more Indians than *gringos*."

"Thank goodness the Indians are unarmed," said De. "With so much change so fast, the situation could become volatile."

"What do you mean 'could'?" asked Hop. "What do you call Madero's revolution?"

"You're right," said De. "The mobs that rose up like a tidal wave to follow Madero suggest more unrest from the underclasses than we understand. The question is, will they always submit to the powerful, like they have for centuries?"

"They resent foreigners, yet they like our money," said Hop. "They resent the upper class, yet they accept their servitude. It's an interesting contradiction."

De handed Hop a cigar. "I don't know what to think of the politics," said De. "So far, it hasn't affected our operations, but we'll see."

"We'll see," repeated Hop. "Did you finish the report on Mata del Peso? I'd like to look at it."

De picked up the geologic report and shoved it across the desk to Hop. "I'm interested in what you think about the Jeffrey well," said De. "It changed my geological concept somewhat."

August 26, 1911
Report on Mata del Peso

The rocks outcropping in the Mata del Peso lands are Tertiary lime and sandstones. The topography of part of the lands is that of low rolling hills and that of the remainder is very flat, caused by the alluvial plain of the Arroyo Estancia and the Rio Tancochin.

I was unable to determine any favorable structure, the few dips and strikes obtainable indicating that the rocks are probably slightly folded but in general, dipping normally to the south and east. Altogether, the land in question is geologically very similar to an equal area in Tanhuijo or San Marcos. Regarded simply as a wildcat lease upon which we are to do the exploratory drilling ourselves, I would not recommend its leasing, even at one peso per hectare.

The closest well in operation to the land in
question is the lease to the Electra Company
(Jeffreys) well which is about two miles east.
I doubt if either this well or one on the Mata
del Peso lands would ever reach the Tamasopo
limestone under present drilling conditions.
It is probable that the depth of the Tamasopo
limestone is at least 3500' to 4000'.

Respectfully, E. Degolyer

"Just because the Mata area is deeper doesn't mean it won't produce," said Hop, after he put down the report.

"Depth increases the costs and therefore the monetary risk. But the anomaly with the well is that it is west of the producing trend yet the Tamasopo is much deeper than I expected."

"Why did you expect it to be shallower?" asked Hop.

"I had imagined we were drilling the ancient continental shelf-edge and that as we move west from the producing trend toward the sierras that the Tamasopo would be shallower since it outcrops in the mountains."

"Another false clue," said Hop, "the mind of man versus Mother Nature."

"There *has* to be a geological explanation why Tuxpan is better than Ebano, and why Potrero is better than Tierra Amarilla."

De spent the next week working on the regional map that he kept on the draft table behind his desk. As more data points from wells were spotted, the blank spaces on the map slowly filled in. The big puzzle remained: why do some anticlines have giant wells, and others only mediocre wells? And why on the same anticlines with giant wells are there mediocre wells and dry holes? He told Hop that in order to understand the stratigraphy they had to determine the limestone's original deposition, and then to figure out the subsequent alterations to the rock. Dr. Hayes believed the Tamosopo limestone was an old land surface and the Valles beds lay unconformably upon it. De agreed with Dr. Hayes and thought the rudists colonies on the outcrop explained its original deposition.

"The rudist colonies tell me reefs were present in the area. Perhaps we're drilling a reef complex, but not one at a continental shelf-edge. In any event, the subsequent alterations to the rock altered the stratigraphy."

"Why do you think what happened after deposition is so important?" asked

Hop.

"The cavities in the Tamasopo are the key. The immense size of some of the larger solution cavities can only be guessed at," De reasoned. "Along the scarp from the plateau of San Luis Potosí great caves have formed. There is also a line of immense springs along the base of Sierra del Abra. I haven't yet figured how the exposure of the Tamasopo and later alteration of the limestone occurred, but I'm convinced the cavities were dissolved after the Tamasopo was exposed to the surface. We need to find a pattern for greater predictability."

"Add a hundred million years of sedimentation on top of the Tamasopo," responded Hop, "and you've altered the limestone in ways that are simply unpredictable."

"I'm not giving up on a predictive model."

"The smartest strategy is to play proximity," said Hop. "Practicality should always outweigh theory."

"Whatever processes that deposited and later altered the Tamasopo occurred on a regional scale, which means there is predictability *if* we can break the code."

"As soon as you think we can predict reservoir quality, we'll drill another dry hole."

"Hop, your skepticism anchors my ideas."

"Is that your way of saying 'thanks'?" asked Hop.

De smiled at his friend, shuffled around the stacks on his desk, and picked up a piece of paper. "Guess what, Hop? You're not the only poet working for El Aguila," he said. De showed Hop the paper. "Take a look," he said.

"I can't read your writing."

"Shall I read it?" De didn't wait for Hop's response, but put down his cigar and read aloud.

The Grand Canyon
(Lines from a geologist upon reading the Book of Job)

"Who hath cleft a channel for the water flood

Or a way for the lightning and the thunder?"

Roar of senses desert stilled,

Mighty chasm, soul depth chilled

Painted seas of ages dead,

Pigments laid in giant beds,

Riot color, clay and stone

Own the Makers Hand Alone.

"Where wast thou when I laid the foundations of earth?

Declare if though hast understanding."

Beliefless beauty of barren rock,

Bed on bed and block to block,

Water chisel, a grand deep tool,

Horizon line and star marked rule

Sculped a thousand ages through hoary old, dawn-pin new.

"Who hath laid determined the measures thereof, if thou knowest?

Or who hath stretched the line upon it?"

Angle, curve, break, serpentine

Column, peak, long straight line

Buttressed banded canyon wall

Dome and pinnacle, spire and hall

Talus slope and hard rock cliff

Deep gray red gorge through granite sift.

"Whereupon are the foundations thereof fastened?

Or who laid the corner stone thereof?"

Hazes purple gulfs below

Blazing blue, green, indigo

All the endless colors play

Deep-burnt red, dull brown, and gray

Silver glisten sheaf of light

Black-blue, gray, and purple night.

"When the morning stars sang together,

And all the sons of God shouted for joy."

De put down the poem and looked up. "What do you think?

"De, you've got the mind of a geologist and the heart of a poet."

"I wish I had the *gift* of the poet. Thanks, Hop. It takes a geologist to see poetry in the subsurface, doesn't it? Who else would look for treasures buried miles beneath the surface by a hand mightier than ours?"

"The more obscure the clues, the more room for poetic imagination," Hop observed. "Just remember, De, there's nothing like a dry hole to ruin a good theory."

A week after returning from Mata del Peso, De received two letters from Nell on the same day. She was still with her mother in California. When De read them, he was so elated he wrote back to her immediately, and then ran to the Southern Hotel to announce the news and hand out cigars.

> *September 26, 1911*
> *Dearest Beaner:*
>
> *I got two letters from you last night from California and dear it is the most wonderful news. Oh dear, life is so many many things. I would have given anything to have had you with me during this month. Sweet, if you don't buy yourself some things in the way of clothes, I am going to be most disappointed and dearest, I don't want you to buy me any masonic ring nor cigarette case nor anything of the sort. Now don't think I'm any little angel but am just saying these things to make my halo feel better but honestly dear, I can't think of any ring or anything that affects me in any but a perfectly indifferent manner except you and I'd lots rather spend what we can spend on you. All*

this is from a perfectly selfish standpoint because I don't believe that anything will make me feel half so good as to feel that you are one of the best groomed women that I know. I like to wear old clothes a good deal but I like new ones at times and dear, I absolutely love to see your things, the nicest. I love silk stockings and fine underwear for beaners and nice parasols and lots of shoes (especially that aren't scuffed and when the buttons are whole) about ½ dozen pairs at least and I hate corsets that stick out like a shelf all the way around the top. You know dear, that there are some things like shoes that you will have to wear, even if you are going to have a baby.

I could keep on writing I guess but when your trunk comes home, I'm going to be mad if there isn't evidence of about $100 gold at the very least in things for you. I don't believe that men fall in love with other women on account of their clothes but I'll bet that a lot of them admire other women's clothes. Beaner, I'll spank you nothwithstanding if you don't do what I said. If you do, I'll be happier than 100 masonic rings and 50 cigarette cases.

Dear, I've been wondering if you wouldn't rather go from here to Oklahoma and live with your mother for the last month and a half month afterward than going to San Antonio. I'll bet you would because there would be people to love and take the tenderest care of you instead of strangers. You tell me. Beaner I'm loving you, oh so hard. I love you very very much.

Your man, Everette

"Now that you're going to be a father," Jim told De, "you better start stashing the cash. The little ankle biters will cost you a fortune."

"Jim, you should get married and have a few kids yourself. Nothing is better for a man than a good woman and a family."

"If I could only find a good one," concurred Jim. "But how could I explain to a wife that my job is to hang around cantinas and talk to the *señoritas*?"

"Ha, maybe you're right. One of these days you'll find the right woman. But as long as you're hanging around cantinas, let me ask, did you swap a log for the last Panuco well?"

Chapter Twelve

October 1911 — March 1912

In October 1911 the first-ever free elections in Mexico were held. Madero and his running mate, Piño Suarez, won by a huge landslide. Madero's victory raised hopes across Mexico that the transition would be peaceful. But things began to fall apart. Within three weeks of Madero's inauguration, Emiliano Zapata and sixty of his officers signed the Plan of Ayala, denouncing Madero and declaring that the land, woodlands and waters usurped during the Porfiriato by the *hacendados*, the *cientificos*, and the chieftains under the cover of tyranny and venal justice would forthwith become the property of the villagers. By January 1912 other leaders who had joined Madero in the rebellion against Díaz were grumbling that the revolution had been betrayed. In Chihuahua, Pascual Orozco was disgruntled that the *maderistas* got the rewards for which his ragged bands had fought. In Coahuila, Venustiano Carranza was claiming the government had no authority to order his troops to disarm and demobilize. In Sonora, Alvaro Obregon said his Yaqui soldiers had not fought to keep the same corrupt policies of the past. In Nuevo Leon, General Bernardo Reyes, and in Veracruz, Porfirio Díaz's nephew, Felix Díaz, talked of open rebellion. Only the old stone-faced, brandy-drinking Indian, Victoriana Huerta, remained loyal.

Jim was seated across the desk from De. The summer monsoons had abated and with the drier air a faint trace of autumn lifted their spirits.

"Lord Cowdray asked for another report on the security of the oil fields," De told Jim. "With Madero taking over, the Chief wants to know if the *rurales* are keeping the countryside safe and what recommendations we would make for our own security. Bandits and rebels are sacking haciendas in other parts of Mexico."

"I'll check with the other oil companies," said Jim. "There are so many rumors in town you don't know what to believe. Buckley says since Díaz was booted, the *rurales* take the law into their own hands. I'll make a round to the field and let you know what it looks like from the ground."

"What else does your friend Buckley say about the new regime?"

"If Madero and the congress pass the proposed tax law, he says the oil companies should refuse to pay taxes."

"Buckley thinks the oil companies should refuse to pay taxes?" repeated De. "Lord Cowdray says it's better to put up with an outstretched hand and keep the oil flowing than to have the revolution spread to the oil fields."

"Outstretched hands have a way of wanting more," observed Jim. "Here in Mexico we call it *la mordida*, the bite."

"The Chief lent Madero's uncle $100,000 to buy the opposition newspaper in Mexico City," said De. "When the president's relative asks for a loan, what are the options?"

"If I was producing 50,000 barrels a day," said Jim, "I could afford some options myself. But it's still *mordida*. By the way, Doheny is moving a rig on Cerro Viejo."

"*What?* Even though we are contesting his title?" De was surprised at such a rash dismissal of a clear title. "If his title is invalidated, any well he drills will be handed over to El Aguila."

"No one ever accused Doheny of lacking *cojones*," said Jim.

"El Aguila should ask the courts for an injunction."

"I'll bet Doheny already paid the judge in Tampico a *mordida*," answered Jim.

"If a rig is moving in, we need to move fast," replied De anxiously. "I'll wire Mr. Body to do whatever it takes to speed up an injunction."

"Maybe it'll be a dry hole," said Jim. "There's nothing like a dry hole to cure title."

"It's on trend with Portrero," said De. "I want El Aguila to drill Cerro Viejo."

"Mr. De, I'm headed to the field next week. Why don't you come along? You can talk to *Señor* Pelaez about his cousins, who own Cerro Viejo."

"I think I will, Jim," said De. "I'd like to talk to Manuel Pelaez about Madero's problems, too. The country is falling into chaos."

"Chaos? I wouldn't call this chaos," said Jim. "Not yet, anyway."

"Well, maybe you're right," said De. "In its first fifty years Mexico survived worse politicians than the ones we have now. I'm reading about Antonio Lopez de Santa Anna. He was a rogue."

"Mr. De, is there any subject you're not interested in?" asked Jim.

"Understanding Santa Anna's character may tell us something about the Mexican culture. Judging by almost any canon of criticism, Santa Anna was a scoundrel, yet his constant comebacks indicate there was something about him out of the ordinary. He was elected president of Mexico eleven non-consecutive times and set the high mark for courage under fire, corruption, and duplicity."

"Really?" asked Jim. "I thought his only claim to fame was handing over Texas."

"An article published last year in "The Nineteenth Century" gives an account of some famous bandit in the vicinity of Mexico City, who desiring to disgrace old Santa Anna, succeeded in catching his young *señora* while out taking the air in the state coach. He stripped her and all of the coachmen and outriders of their clothes and sent them back to the Presidential Palace undressed. The lady took to her bed in high fever and his Serene Highness went out and hung the first three hundred people who had firearms. Is his behavior a manifestation of an indiscriminate cruelty endemic to the Mexican culture, or is it only indicative of Santa Anna's character?"

"I'm no one to fuss about Santa Anna's character," answered Jim. "If it wasn't for his yellow rose, I could have grown up eating beans and tortillas in an adobe house on the Nueces River in Mexico. Instead I grew up eating beans and tortillas in an adobe house on the Nueces River in Texas."

De and Jim were at the Potrero camp when the company moved the drilling equipment to a new drill site, one of De's geologic picks on Alazan hacienda across the shallow, silty Buena Vista River from Potrero. Two thousand Mexican workers packed everything on mules: boilers, thirty-foot pieces of steel casing, lumber to build the rigs, tin to build the boiler and belt houses, steel, rope, tools, food and supplies for the teamsters, roustabouts, and roughnecks. The string of mules was a mile long.

"It's like moving an army." said Jim.

"What an operation!" said De. "It was so easy to draw a circle on a map. This gives me a real appreciation for what that means."

They spent the next three days observing the move. A vanguard of men with machetes cleared the path. Crossing the river was a major challenge, accomplished by homemade barges loaded high with the equipment and supplies. Mules balked and threw off their packs. Muleteers cursed and repacked. Slowly the whole procession made its way through the jungle to the new location, which had been cleared by hand saws and machetes. As the supplies arrived on site, carpenters, boilermakers, tank builders and mechanics began to assemble the boiler and derrick, to build temporary crews' quarters, and to dig pits for the drilling fluids.

"Your next location," Jim said to De, "pick a site close to a road. Lord Cowdray will need two-dollar oil just to pay for this one move."

"I mapped Alazan on the same anticline as Potrero, but it could be a separate anticline. It's so close to the No. 4, we have to drill it. I've said before, this is no game for the faint of heart."

"Or for the short of pocket," finished Jim.

The pregnant, glowing Nell had returned to Tampico in fine form. De wasted no effort in spoiling her as much as possible. He left the office often to check on her, and he made sure that she had the best, freshest food that Tampico had to offer. He worked to prepare a nursery for the baby in their home, and consulted with Nell on how it should be decorated. De worried about Nell's small frame carrying what looked like a very large baby. They had hired an experienced midwife to help, but De wondered if they should have a doctor on hand, in case anything might go wrong.

"Stop worrying, dear," Nell told him. "Mother is arriving next week, and our midwife is the most highly recommended in the city. As for me, I'm tired but healthy, and I'm happy and ready."

"I'm sure it will go fine, love," replied De. He didn't want to express misgivings about the local hospital if anything went wrong.

Back at the office, De handed Hop a bound brochure. "Hop, if you would, please look over this report[1]. "The Chief asked me to put it together for the British government. It seems our success has raised interest all the way to Whitehall."

[1]see Appendix One

"First the British admiralty wants the oil. Now the British government wants a report."

"I suppose we've made an impact," said De. "Read the report and let me know if you find errors."

Hop thumbed through the brochure. "Where did you find the history of the oil business in Mexico?"

"Jim's friend Edward Lynton handed me a trove of old newspaper articles and private reports. He has friends who offered histories of their haciendas. I've been digging around in church archives. The research has been enjoyable. We're not the first to see the potential of the seeps."

"Maybe not the first to *see* the potential," said Hop, "but we're the first to realize the potential."

"Our timing was fortunate," replied De. "If the world hadn't switched from coal to fuel oil in the last few years, what would you do with 175,000 barrels a day of crude oil?"

"It's been only a year since Potrero No. 4 blew out. What a difference a year makes," said Hop.

"After Potrero No. 2 and 3, I told Nell we'd be moving back to Norman by the first of the year. After Potrero No. 4, I told Nell our kids would grow up speaking Spanish."

Chapter Thirteen

March — December 1912

The Rose

Although the way be long,

The immortal Rose of Beauty shall not die,

Yester'en it blossomed in the sunset sky.

Tonight it bloomed within the poet's song.

And I could tell of what it symbol is,

Just as it lived upon my loved one's breast,

God kissed, it passed to Him again in rest,

This beauty flower is that with Him it lives.

De laid the poem on the pillow. Nell was finally sleeping. He knew how exhausted she must be. He laid her sister's letter next to the poem, softly kissed her forehead, and quietly left the room.

March 26, 1912
My dear Nell and De:
I can never tell you how sad we have felt since mamma's letter came today. I know it is awfully hard to have to go through such sorrow and

suffering but I can't help but think it is better for the child to be taken when it was than after you had learned to love and know all its little ways. Since everything is for the best, I suppose we will live to see the reason for this — although that doesn't make it much easier for us at the present time. It seems that all things in this world were not meant to turn out right for everybody. Nell, you must be really careful and get strong and well again — that is the important thing now. I am so glad mamma could be with you for there is nobody like a mother when we feel so disheartened and sad. I guess you realize that more than I do. I must stop but will try to write more soon. De, let us know how Nell is all the time and take good care of her. I would love to be with you both tonight but my heart is anyway.

Lovingly your sister, Callie

De felt sadness for Nell's mother, too. She had been so helpful, and was as devastated as Nell. The baby looked healthy, a perfectly formed little man, red-skinned and crying. The midwife took him away and within minutes brought the news. He had stopped breathing. Was the midwife at fault? Why hadn't he asked a doctor to be present? A pervading guilt filled his soul. Why, he asked himself again and again, hadn't he insisted Nell return to Norman to have the child?

Jim dropped by Will Buckley's office. The monthly report was due and he needed information on local politics. "Will, De has been out of commission and I need to send the chief a monthly report."

"I heard about the baby," said Will. "Please send my condolences to De and Mrs. DeGolyer."

"They've had a rough time. At least Nell is in good health,"

"Which matters more than anything else," said Will. "Now what were you asking?"

"De sends a monthly report to Dr. Hayes and Lord Cowdray. In the report I update him on local politics, oil activities by other companies, and security. Any news along those lines?"

"It's clear to me that Madero is in trouble," answered Will. "Can he keep it together? Your guess is as good as mine, but I have my doubts. All this preaching by Zapata, Carranza and the rest about land redistribution is a ruse to mobilize peasants behind their own ambitions. Land reform will never happen in Mexico without blood staining the land by the bucketful. The reformers dangle it in front of the peasants like a priest holding a crucifix. A poor and uneducated underclass is a dangerous tool."

"What about Madero's new tax of twenty centavos per ton on oil produced?"

"I've said a thousand times to my clients, crack the door and a flood will pour in upon us. Oil companies should act as a group and refuse to pay. The government cannot drill the wells or operate the oil fields, so we have bargaining power, at least for now. Madero supports the labor unions. Now that they formed the Longshoremen's Guild of the Port of Tampico, the next thing they'll be calling for is a strike."

"Edward Lynton says a strike didn't work at Cananea," said Jim.

"If Taft or Teddy Roosevelt is elected, it would precipitate an intervention by the U.S. The Madero administration has squandered the treasury from a $65 million surplus to a debtor nation in less than a year. It's been a heyday for the porkers. The exchange rate is falling against other currencies. This country is coming undone at the seams."

"Will, you're a bundle of good tidings."

"You asked for my thoughts. So what's happening in the oil patch? Any good news there?"

"Have you heard about the Tampico Oil Company well at Chila Salinas? It looks like it'll make a well."

"They just keep finding more, don't they?" said Buckley. "I recently formed Pantetec Oil Company, not to compete with my clients, but if I can pick up a little royalty here and there, it could complement the legal work."

"Complement the legal work or replace the legal work?"

"The line between a conflict of interest and protecting our clients is not a thin one. I won't compete with my own clients."

"Have you heard that the Topila wells are already turning to salt water?"

"Already? Those wells were drilled only a year ago. Has DeGolyer figured out what makes good oil wells turn to salt water?"

"Mr. De is working on that very problem. He cut back Potrero No. 4 to 37,000 barrels of oil per day to be conservative."

"To be conservative. Even after choking it back, that one well is making, let me see." He scratched on a piece of paper. "It's making $750,000 a month. What a fortune!"

"You forget how many dry holes we drilled to find the one Potrero No. 4."

"Right, but still..."

"But still. Will, one more thing and then I have to run. Have you heard anything about German agents working in Tampico? A friend of mine says a couple of Germans who claim to be roughnecks are asking about every well that's drilled, how much oil it produces, its depth, and who operates it. They say they're looking for work but are asking questions that no roughneck would care about."

"They sound like Jim Hall," laughed Will.

"I don't have a German accent. Mr. De says by the end of the year Mexico will become the world's third largest producer of petroleum."

"With that kind of production, agents are bound to be sent here by foreign governments to keep tabs on the oil. By my last count there were 89 companies organized for operations in Tamaulipas. And I'd guess in the last two years at least $150 million has been spent looking for oil. The whole industrialized world is watching the Tampico oil play."

"Why do foreign governments care what happens in Tampico?" asked Jim.

"The Kaiser's navy, like all the others in the world except ours and Russia's, is dependent on foreign oil, so it wouldn't surprise me to see German agents watching what we're doing, and Japanese, French, and Dutch, too"

"Lord, the next thing you know foreign navies will be patrolling the Gulf of Mexico," said Jim.

"For two hundred years the world was dependent on coal, which is abundant in every developed country," explained Will. "In the past decade, in the past five years, the industrialized world became dependent on fuel oil. Petroleum seems to occur only in a few places in the world. Its location alters world politics. Countries will fight to protect their sources and supply lines. Keep *that* in mind the next time you see a German sipping a *cerveza* at Rosie's."

"The talk at Rosie's doesn't lean toward world politics," said Jim with a grin.

"If Woodrow Wilson is elected in November, heaven save the United States," continued Will Buckley. "Wilson is an academic do-gooder. Will he have sense enough to understand what all the other foreign powers realize about the importance of Tampico crude oil? William Jennings Bryan, the old populist who Wilson says he'll nominate for Secretary of State, is a pacifist and Wilson is an idealist. Can you imagine two less capable leaders?"

"I'm more worried about the natives," said Jim. "Revolution is in the air. But speaking of Rosie's, I'm off to evening vespers. Thanks again for the help, Will. I should sign your name to the report this month. You're making me look informed."

"Jim, if you weasel as much information from all your friends as you do from me, you could be a spy for the U.S. government," laughed Will as he waved goodbye.

After the baby's death, Nell left for Oklahoma with her mother. She and De had decided that it would be best for her to recover in Norman, surrounded by her family, since De would be so busy at work over the next several months. The letters De received from her suggested a despondency De had not known in Nell. They reported none of the usual news or observations of people. He sensed her sadness, and he felt that, at some level, she blamed herself for the tragedy.

At home in the evening, De's steps sounded like hollow echoes against empty walls. He removed the decorations in the baby's room and put them away in the attic. De still felt the child's presence. If it hadn't cried at birth, would he feel differently? Was human consciousness nothing more than a result of evolutionary succession? He knew it had to be more, a miracle, the touch of God's hand. But how then could life be so fragile? He ached to hold Nell.

Lord Cowdray called for a meeting with De and Dr. Hayes in Mexico City. After De showed them his updated regional map, Dr. Hayes praised his work. Mr. Body groused about sharing such data with competitors, but De assured him no one but the three parties in that room were privy to the map. Swapping individual logs only exchanged micro viewpoints. Putting those points into a coherent regional picture was the real reason to swap their own well data for others. The more data he received, he told them, the more he preferred the Tuxpan area for future exploration.

Before returning to Tampico, De walked into a rare books shop in the Mexican capitol. He picked through the dusty shelves for hours, pulling books and opening the ancient pages with their musty smell, oblivious to everything but the books. He felt a connection to the long-dead authors. Did their words conquer the finality of their own mortality? It seemed that only moments had passed when the clerk approached him and politely indicated that it was closing time. De glanced outside and was surprised to see that darkness had fallen. He hurriedly purchased an edition of Wordsworth, and read it on the train ride back to Tampico.

A simple Child,

That lightly draws its breath,

And feels its life in every limb,

What should it know of death?

Whither fled the visionary gleam, he wondered, and where now was the glory and the dream?

Hop dropped by his office the next evening after his return from Mexico City. "De, it's seven o'clock. You're looked peek'ed."

"What's peek'ed?"

"In need of a drink," answered Hop. "I'll buy at the Southern."

"Ok, sure, Hop."

The bar was loud and crowded. The two found a table in the back. Hop held up two fingers to the waiter. "De, when does Nell return?"

"Not soon enough," said De. "The house is lonely."

"Is that why you've been working so late? Your light is on every time I pass your office."

"I've been analyzing the Tamasopo."

"Still chasing rainbows, are you?"

"Hippolito says I'm chasing jackrabbits. Who knows, one of these days a jackrabbit might pop out."

"De, Nell is with her family, but I'm worried about you."

"I'll be fine, Hop. Really. It's a kind thought, though. Thank you. I'll be fine."

With Nell in Oklahoma, De contemplated quitting El Aguila and becoming a consultant. Working for a salary was no road to financial independence. With that doubt lingering on his mind, in mid-May he was asked to join Lord Cowdray, Dr. Hayes, and J.B. Body on the German liner "Prinzessen Cecile". Aboard ship they held daily conferences on the developing oil fields. When asked hard questions about the competitions' activities and successes, De did not change his mind about the quality of the reservoir rock in the South fields compared to those in the North. After two days, De convinced his bosses that their attention and money should be concentrated south of Tampico in the Tuxpan area, where the best wells were being drilled. Although he still couldn't explain geologically why, only a relatively small area held the best wells, the Potrero and Casiano class wells. De's presentation of the economics showed that finding one or two more wells of that quality had by far the largest impact on the company's revenues. No other competitors except Doheny had comparable wells or comparable lease positions. Before they disembarked in Veracruz, the Chief authorized spending a million pesos for leases in the southern region.

"De, I like your science," he told his young employee. "I like your convictions, and I like your luck. I'm giving you common stock in Aguila valued at 2500 pesos. If ever you care to sell it, I will pay you 5000 pesos."

Lord Cowdray's generous offer erased De's thought of resigning from El Aguila. Starting his own oil business, De knew, required an enormous amount of capital.

"The bosses sometimes focus on what the competition is doing," he wrote Nell. "The Chief believes in luck. I believe in it, too, but good science increases the odds of being lucky. Now that we're shareholders, what's good for El Aguila is good for us. I miss you terribly. Hurry home to Tampico."

In spring, Orozco openly rebelled, and Madero sent Huerta to put down the revolt. The old Indian fighter did his job, enlisting Pancho Villa. Within a month Huerta ordered Villa to be shot for insubordination. Instead, Madero had Villa imprisoned in Mexico City, where he was held without trial. By May, Huerta had crushed the Orozco revolt. In March, President Taft embargoed arms sales to Mexico. In September, Ambassador Henry Lane Wilson addressed a stern note to President Madero, warning against shipments of arms slipping into Mexico from Germany.

When Nell finally returned to Tampico, De's spirits lifted immediately. Her good nature had returned and with it his own. They both avoided discussions about the baby. For now, it was better to leave the baby as an unspoken presence in their hearts. De and Nell welcomed the regularity of their own routine in their own house. Regularity and routine, De thought, offered solace and a sense of simplicity that restored balance and happiness.

The rainy season made field work nearly impossible. Drilling was progressing slowly in Tierra Amarilla, Alazan, and Potrero. Before the monsoons ended exploratory drilling for the season, one of Hop's recommendations, Tanhuijo, came in as a small producer.

By the end of September, the drilling schedule picked up and with it, De's workload. He was busy making geologic cross-sections when Jim rushed into his office.

"De, have you heard about Tuxpan?" Jim handed him a telegram. "Felix Díaz and several hundred armed compatriots rode into Tuxpan this morning and took over the town."

"The ex-president's nephew?"

"The same. We just received this telegram from Charlie Melick."

```
October 16, 1912
10:45am
```

```
Please advise that General Felix Díaz took
possession of this place this a.m. All the
banks are closed, also the custom house and the
following federal employees are under General
Díaz's orders: the arsenal, the war vessels
"Bravo", "Morelos" and "Veracruz", the military
hospital and barracks which contained about a
half a battalion. He entered this city with
the mounted cavalry, one hundred and ten armed
infantry, seventy armed rurales, besides about
one hundred and forty volunteers without arms.
The city police, about three hundred on foot and
mounted, are under his orders and are keeping
peace. Not a shot fired, all business of this
terminal going as usual with the exception of
fiscal wharf on account of the collector giving
instructions to suspend about 8 am. I am informed
that the collector has been notified to call at
revolutionary headquarters and also that the J.
Politico has been displaced. The predominating
grito is "Viva General Díaz!"
```

When De looked up, Jim continued, "The telegraph wires were cut shortly after we received it."

De ordered Jim to take the fast launch to Potrero. "Make sure we have guards posted around the wellhead of Potrero No. 4. Then go to Furbero, Tanhuijo and Tierra Amarillo camps as fast as you can. Their telegraph lines have probably been cut, too. I hope the violence doesn't spread to the oil fields. Report back to me as soon as you can."

When Jim returned three days later, he reported that all was quiet in the camps. Felix Díaz and his troops had not disturbed the oil companies' property or personnel. The oil still flowed from the pipeline terminus at Tuxpan Bar to the waiting tankers.

Within days the Madero government had shipped federal troops by rail under the command of General Victoriano Huerta to put down the insurrection. Fighting on the outskirts of Tuxpan was rumored to be heavy.

After more federal reinforcements arrived, Felix Díaz and his band of rebels were defeated. Jim reported that Felix Díaz had believed he could capitalize on the rising discontent within the federal army. He also had hoped the oil companies would rally to his support because of Madero's tax on oil, which he promised to rescind. However upon hearing of Díaz's rebellion, Mr. Body announced to the federal government that it was El Aguila's policy to support the legitimately elected government.

"There was one more twist," added Jim.

"What's that?"

"Manuel Pelaez fled to San Antonio."

"Why in the world?"

"He was a conspirator with Felix Díaz," explained Jim. "When Felix Díaz lost, he must have figured it was better to beat it to San Antone than hang around and be hung. Huerta sent Felix Díaz to prison in Mexico City. He'll probably be shot while attempting escape, which is the Mexican way of handling political opposition."

"I thought Manuel supported Madero."

"The last time I saw him, he told me he didn't think Madero could hold the hounds at bay."

"The hounds, as you call them, just won't give Madero time, will they?"

Two days later De walked into Jim's office and handed him a cigar. "Have you heard about the Alazan well?"

"Which one?"

"Number Four, my lucky number."

"The first three were dry."

"You don't have to tell *me*. We watched them move the location to the No. 1, remember?"

"Sure do. It looked like army ants on the move."

"After three dry holes, Dr. Hayes and I decided we needed to drill one more Alazan well," said De. "The top of Tamasopo on the first three wells was oil saturated and confirmed the anticline. All we needed was to find the porosity."

"You've chased that jackrabbit before."

"Potrero camp telegraphed the morning report. Alazan No. 4 flowed 19,000 barrels yesterday and is still cleaning up."

"Whew, 19,000 barrels! Mr. De, congratulations! The Chief will be happy as King Harry. Good lord, what's he going to do with all the oil you're finding?"

"He formed another company, the Eagle Oil Transport Company, Ltd. and ordered twenty tank steamers, each with a 250,000 ton capacity."

"El Aguila will soon have our own navy!" exclaimed Jim. "Look out Shell Oil. Speaking of Shell, they just opened a subsidiary in Tampico."

"Royal Shell, the Dutch company?" asked De.

"Buckley tells me five years ago the Royal Dutch combined with the British company Shell Oil Transport. Now the Chief's own countrymen are competing with us. Their new company is named La Corona. They have already optioned 150,000 acres near El Ebano and are talking to Hacienda San Jose de las Rusias, which owns more than a million acres north of Ebano. Are you sure we shouldn't jump in the North play?" asked Jim. "The leasing is hotter there than in the South. We could tie up de las Rusias if we move fast."

"Shell will be tough competition," De acknowledged. "They're scientific oriented. Maybe I'm wrong, but there is nothing in the North fields around El Ebano that looks as promising to me geologically. I'm beginning to see a pattern in the Tamasopo. We'll stick to the Southern fields between here and Tuxpan."

"Potrero No. 4 could have been luck, but after Alazan No. 4, I'm putting my money on the little short man with the oversized head," Jim said with a smile. "Shell Oil better look out."

Will Buckley was at his regular place in the Cantina Mariposa overlooking the river. A striking young Mexican woman sat beside him. "Jim, may I introduce you to Josephina Flores Jacinto. Miss Flores, my friend *Señor* Hall."

Jim tipped his hat and smiled. "Will, you're a man of many accomplishments." In Spanish he continued, addressing the young lady. "*Señorita* Flores, it's my pleasure. How did you come to know Mr. Buckley?"

"Mr. Buckley has been speaking with my family about purchasing our minerals."

"Purchasing minerals from your family?"

Will interrupted. "Before a well has been drilled, of course. I have told Miss Flores her family should sell part of their mineral interest because of its title problems. Her mother already sold her mineral interest, subject to an oil and gas lease that she also signed."

"What title problems?" asked Jim.

Will continued in Spanish, intentionally including the young lady in the conversation. "According to the records, many years ago before the French invaded Mexico, five families purchased forest lands now known as Cerro Azul. Their common land covered some 23,000 acres and has since been divided into individual tracts. Miss Flores' family owned one tract of more than five thousand acres. It was leased to a land agent named Genaro Avendano several years ago. Have you heard of him?"

Jim shook his head.

"Avendano flipped it to another agent, Enrique Julvecourt, who in turn sold it to Huasteca back in 1906. At that time Miss Flores' mother and her husband, Hilario Jacinto, agreed to extend the lease for thirty years. Doheny paid them twenty-five thousand pesos, an unheard of sum at the time, and committed to drill a well within five years. In June 1911, after your company's Potrero No. 4 came in and just before the lease terminated because a well hadn't been drilled, her father was stabbed to death.

Jim whistled. "That's a serious accusation. Why do you think so?" He directed the question to the young lady.

"Because my father would not extend the lease," she answered. "In December 1911 after my father was killed, my mother Eufrosina agreed to sell Cerro Azul to Mr. Doheny for five hundred thousand pesos. She took the money and moved with my two brothers to Los Angeles, where she draws a pension from Mr. Doheny."

"Why would Doheny move them to Los Angeles?" Jim asked, looking at Will.

"Your guess is as good as mine, but perhaps so he can be certain that none of the Flores heirs, including Miss Flores, can convince their mother to contest the sale."

"I've heard of hard ball but this takes the cake," muttered Jim.

"Money will test men's mettle, don't you agree?" asked Will.

"What would *you* do if Mr. Doheny offered to pay you half a million pesos?" asked Jim.

Will smiled. "I wouldn't wait until the offer reached half a million pesos. Miss Flores' mother must be quite a good negotiator."

"Half a million pesos...that's a quarter million dollars. It's an extraordinary sum to pay before a well has been drilled. DeGolyer said Cerro Azul has some good seeps. It's next to our Alazan tract and west of Tierra Amarilla."

"And just north of Potrero de Llano. That's why I'm interested...close-ology is my geology," Will explained.

"But why," continued Jim, "do you think Miss Flores owns an interest? You said Huasteca bought the minerals from her mother."

"Oh, they did," said Will. "But if a well is drilled, and if it is productive, I will have a legitimate cloud on their title."

"Is a cloud on their title worth a knife in the back?" asked Jim.

"They never found the assassin," said Josephina.

"If Huasteca drills Cerro Azul and if it makes a well, you better start looking over your shoulder," Jim warned Will.

"My price is much less than a half million pesos," replied Will. "If I sign up all the heirs and quitclaim the interest to Huasteca, I clear the title for Mr. Doheny. What's a good title worth?"

"Doheny is drilling a well on Cerro Viejo, which is close to where you're talking," answered Jim. "El Aguila has what we believe is a valid lease. Even though we have contested his title in court, Doheny is drilling ahead. He doesn't seem to care about a clear title."

"I'm betting he *prefers* a clear title," replied Will. "In this case, he's not up against El Aguila, but against a lawyer willing to talk. For a reasonable compensation, I will assign him my interests and his title is undisputed."

"And if Miss Flores decides not to sell to you?"

"Then she shoulders the risk of a dry hole," replied Will. He was happy Jim had asked the question.

"Will, you're playing a different game. Betting you can sell a clear title to someone like Doheny who drills Cerro Viejo without clear title is mighty risky odds."

"It's not every day you can buy a clouded title under five thousand acres in a hot oil play."

"Money tests men's soul, doesn't it, Will?" asked Jim. "I hope to God I don't have to take the test. My knees start shaking just thinking about half a million pesos."

De kept his promise to Nell about Christmas. They would go to Oklahoma for the holidays. Before they left Tampico, De wrote a 1912 yearend report. "Since Edward Doheny opened the modern phase of exploration in 1901, a total of 252 wells have been drilled in the Tampico region. In the past year, the pace of exploration jumped exponentially. Forty-two wells are drilling. Discoveries continue to be made, although the number of high-volume wells remains small. The political situation is troubling. Pancho Villa, who was locked up with Felix Díaz and General Bernardo Reyes, escaped Santiago Tlateloco prison and fled to the United States. Rumors are that the new Woodrow Wilson administration is talking with Villa in case Madero is overthrown".

When he finished the report, De reflected that he had turned twenty-six. He had been in Mexico three years. His understanding of the subsurface was far greater than when he arrived, yet so much remained unanswered toward what he considered a predictable model for exploration. After the baby's death, he and Nell were closer and more tender with each other. Yet De worried that she would be happier living in Norman near her family. Lord Cowdray treated them with kindness and respect, and paid him far better than any job back home. De was making more money than even the senior staff at the U.S. Geological Survey. It was also true that the opportunity to be at the center of such an extraordinary oil play might never occur again in his lifetime.

Chapter Fourteen

February — April 1913

In early February 1913, several Army generals rose up against Madero and freed Felix Díaz and General Bernardo Reyes from prison. Large numbers of the military joined their rebellion and stormed the presidential palace to remove Madero. In the general melee, General Reyes was killed but those troops still loyal to Madero under General Huerta held the palace and repelled the rebels. With the palace under siege and the rebels' strength increasing, Huerta asked for command of the government defense. Madero consented.

Ten days of tragedy ensued, *La Decena Tragica*, in which the capital erupted into a bloodbath. The palace was fired upon with machine gun and cannonade. Thousands of soldiers from both sides were killed, innocent civilians were slaughtered, gunned down in the streets and in their homes, often caught in the crossfire between the factions. Pillage and looting ran rampant. A state of fear and lawlessness gripped the capital city. To prevent the spread of disease, piles of corpses were stacked and burned in the streets. General Huerta refused to bring reinforcements from outside the capital, claiming they were untrustworthy. The U.S. Ambassador, Henry Lane Wilson, shuttled between meetings with Madero and leaders of the rebellion.

After ten days of siege, General Huerta invited Madero's brother Gustavo to dinner for a discussion of what Huerta deemed great importance. After the meal Huerta gestured to the guard to arrest Gustavo and at, the same time, ordered the arrest of Madero and his vice president.

The old Indian fighter, himself an Indian, had betrayed his president. Before dawn, Gustavo Madero was brutally tortured, his only eye gouged out before he was shot and stabbed by his drunken captors. Later that morning Huerta drove to the U.S. Embassy where Ambassador Wilson, with seeming complicity, introduced him to the other foreign diplomats as the new provisional president.

Later the same day General Huerta sent a message to Madero. If he and Vice President Piño Suarez would resign, their lives would be saved. Madero signed the resignation but was not released as promised. Three days later Madero and Saurez were taken to the palace stables and shot "while attempting to escape". On February 18, 1913, General Huerta took over the presidency.

"De, what does the Chief think this means for the oil fields?" Jim asked. "Huerta's reputation is a man who keeps no promises."

"Immediately after Madero was arrested," De replied, "Mr. Body met with Feliz Díaz, who The Chief hoped would become president. When Huerta was declared president, Mr. Body telegraphed that the new government must be cultivated and that we're not to take sides."

"Cultivated?" exclaimed Jim. "This ain't no vegetable garden. Are we going to arm the camps or not?"

"It's against the law to import arms without permission," said De. "Last year El Aguila received permission to import ninety carbines and nine thousand rounds."

"But the Chief only wants to distribute them to the payroll and security guards," said Jim. "We need to arm the camps."

"We are to depend on the government to provide security," replied De.

"I wouldn't bet my tulips on the *federales* protecting me," said Jim. "Tell the boss men we need more rifles and permission to carry pistols. We have to protect ourselves."

"The bankers and the clergy have rallied to Huerta. Maybe he can put an end to the chaos."

"My Mexican friends say you can't trust that old Indian to light your cigarette," said Jim. "They say he sits in a bar all day drinking cognac and issues orders for *la ley fuga*...the fugitive law, 'killed while trying to escape'. He's a bad *hombre*."

"Sounds just like the *porfiristas*, doesn't it? And the *maderistas*, and the rest of the *huertistas*," said De.

"Huerta is worse than the rest," responded Jim. "He doesn't have enough *rurales* to protect us if he wanted to. Did you hear that bandits rode into East Coast's Panuco Camp yesterday and stole horses, food, and money?"

"What?" exclaimed De. "A direct attack on the oil camps?"

"They didn't kill anyone," said Jim, "but pour a little whiskey down their gullets and we better *cuidado* watch out because bullets will fly."

"As long as no one is harmed at the camps, Mr. Body says we're to keep the camps open and the rigs running," said De. "Maybe Mexico needs a strong arm. Madero tried to rule by persuasion. Huerta may do a better job ruling by fear."

"Killing your enemies just makes more enemies," said Jim. "What about Nell? Will she return to the States?"

"Nell wants to stay here. We'll see how it plays out," answered De. "Huerta decreed all foreigners and their properties will be protected. For assurance, I saw on the teletype that President-elect Wilson will move some battleships to the Gulf."

"Battleships? As shallow as the Gulf is, a battleship couldn't anchor within five miles of shore. Why do we need battleships?"

"To evacuate Americans if the political situation gets out of hand," said De.

"If it gets out of hand, how do we get to the ships? Swimming five miles is a problem if you're like me and can't swim."

De smiled. "We'll have the launch ready to evacuate ladies, children, and non-swimmers first."

"Now you're talking," said Jim. "I'll stick with the women and children."

"Jim, any news on Huasteca's Cerro Viejo well?"

"The bar talk is that Cerro Viejo is looking good. I don't have hard data yet, but I heard the story from reliable sources. What about our injunction?"

"It hasn't been issued yet. I am afraid the regime change has delayed the proceedings."

"With the regime change and everything else in a turmoil," De said, "Doheny will pull the well as hard as he can and drill as many wells as he can before any injunction can be issued and enforced."

Jim and Will walked into the Mariposa. Jim pointed to a well-dressed man wearing a bowler hat. "Have you met the Reverend William Bayard Hale?" asked Will.

"Yes, I've had the misfortune," replied Jim.

"He showed up in my office last week claiming we're all going to hell for drinking and whoring and robbing the natives of their mineral rights. Good men like you and me, Jim, come to Mexico to make an honest *peso*, and his stripe shows up, a self-righteous, self-proclaimed man of the cloth, and tells us we're sinners. Any play as hot as this will attract a little riff-raff, a scattering of scoundrels and slickers, even outright criminals. It's all in the stew when so much money is sloshing around. But when the preachers show up, we better put our hands in our pockets. Can you believe he introduces himself as the *Reverend* William Bayard Hale? He's no more a reverend than I am."

"You're safe in that regard, Will,"

Will laughed. The two stared at the preacher, who was lecturing a young man, no doubt Jim bet, for sins of the flesh.

"Should I rescue the poor fellow?" Jim asked.

"Consider it your Christian duty," answered Will.

Jim rose and walked to their table. "Reverend Hale, how are you doing this fine morning?" Jim said and tipped his hat.

The Reverend looked up and glowered. "Yes. And what is it you want? Can you not see I am having a private conversation?"

Extending his hand to the young man, Jim said, "Hello, I'm Jim Hall. Would you join us for a cup of coffee," and nodded to where Edward sat. "After you finish listening to the preacher, of course."

The man didn't smile but offered his hand. "Ludwig Witke," is all he said with a heavy accent. Jim shook his hand.

"Ludwig is German, Mr. Hall. Do you speak German?"

"Not me, Reverend."

"We're having a private conversation, can't you see?"

"Well, in that case I'll be moving on. Sorry to disturb you two."

Jim walked back and sat down by Will, who was smiling widely.

"Did he thank you for saving him from salvation?" asked Will.

"The Reverend Hale would talk to a guinea hen in high Dutch if he thought he could squeeze a dollar donation for the glory of God," replied Jim. "No telling what he's trying to beat the fellow out of. They're speaking German. A friend told me the Reverend was a friend of President Wilson, but I'm suspicious. He seems too comfortable with the Germans."

In December, President Wilson announced to Congress the United States would not recognize General Huerta as the legitimate leader of Mexico. El Aguila continued to develop Potrero and Alazan. Production from new wells continued to be erratic, but when De laid sample logs of only the good wells beside one another, from Casiano to Potrero, an idea began nagging at his mind.

"Hop," said De, "I had lunch yesterday with Ezequiel Ordoñez, Huasteca's geologist."

"I thought Doheny didn't trust scientists," Hop responded.

"Ezequiel Ordoñez has worked with Doheny since 1903. *Señor* Ordoñez is mainly a hard rock scientist, and is especially interested in volcanoes. He told me the story of how he saved Doheny's bacon."

"He saved Doheny's bacon?" repeated Hop. "How's that?"

"When Canfield and Doheny came to Mexico, Señor Ordoñez told me they drilled nineteen wells next to seeps near Ebano with very little success. Most of the fortune they made in California was drilled up. Ordoñez had completed a study of the El Ebano area for the government, and urged Doheny to drill a well at the foot of Cerro de la Pez, a volcanic plug. His theory was that next to the volcanic plug there would be a brecciated zone of limestone that had been busted up when the plug penetrated the sediments. He was right. The La Pez No. 1 was completed for 1500 barrels per day from 1600 feet."

"Proof again that it only takes one good well."

De continued. "I located the first well at Tierra Amarilla at the foot of the Cerro Pelon volcanic plug on Tierra Amarilla, hoping to find a similar brecciated zone. The well was a dry hole. Proof again that predictability is a scarce commodity."

"After drilling nineteen non-commercial wells on random picks next to seeps and then drilling one good well on a geologist's recommendation, you wonder why Doheny doesn't trust geologists?"

"Men with big egos mainly trust their own instincts," answered De.

"Then why did he hire Ordoñez?"

"To look after their contract with Jersey Standard. Have you heard, Hop, that the Chief wants to open more exploration offices. He has too many assets concentrated in Mexico.

"Will he open an office in the United States?" Hop asked. De detected eagerness in his question.

"No, but El Aguila will open an office in Cuba," replied De.

"Really?" said Hop. "What would you think if I applied for the job of general manager? Would you recommend me?"

De paused for a minute and looked at his friend. "Of course, I would, Hop. Would you want to leave Tampico?"

"I'd jump at a chance for a manager's position," answered Hop. "My future here is to stay with El Aguila and work as your assistant."

"I see you point. Lord, I'd miss our discussions. You're the one who throws water on all my theories."

"Sounding boards are a dime a dozen. There's another reason, too. Have I told you, De...I met a young lady last week. I can't get her off my mind."

"A young lady?"

"Amy Longcope."

"And?" prompted De.

"And she is governess to the Mayberry's girl. And the most gorgeous and lively lady I have ever met."

"What would Miss Longcope think of your being transferred to Cuba?"

"The Mayberry family is moving back to Houston. The situation here is too dangerous for their children. Amy will return with them, which makes my heart sick, but so long as I'm in Tampico, I'll never see her. I was hoping the Chief might open an office in Houston. Havana would be wonderful, too. Who would the Cuban manager report to?"

"Directly to Dr. Hayes. It would be a great opportunity, Hop."

"De, would you tell Dr. Hayes I'd like the job. Would you do that for me?"

"Of course I would. I hate to see you leave Tampico.

"If I am offered the job, Amy could visit Havana. I'll tell her before she leaves for Houston."

"I'll wire a recommendation to Dr. Hayes today, Hop. The *Iparanga* sails for Havana a week from tomorrow. If he agrees, you should be ready."

The next morning Jim walked into De's office and announced the news. "Hop asked Amy Longcope to marry him!"

"What!" exclaimed De. "He hasn't known her a week!"

"I heard the news from a friend of the Mayberrys," said Jim. "They're marrying next month in Houston. It's the old love bug. One bite and he's a goner."

"I was with Hop yesterday afternoon. He didn't even mention marriage."

"He just asked her last night."

"He met her a week ago and has asked her to marry him?" De was incredulous.

"You told me a good woman is hard to find, and when you find one, grab hold with both arms."

"Jim, but a one-week acquaintance! Hop is more, well, more like an engineer. He's skeptical and deliberate. Let's head to the Imperial. The subject deserves a more contemplative respite than El Aguila's offices. I'll buy a round. Hop should have told me."

"He's packing for Havana. I'm sure he'll tell you before he leaves."

Security in the countryside continued to deteriorate. More oil camps were robbed by bandits. Governor Carranza of Coahuila started an open rebellion. Rebel armies sprang up in the west under Obregon, in the north under Pancho Villa, who had returned from the U.S. after Huerta's coup, and in the east under Pablo Gonzalez and Candido Aguilar. They had one common bond: the removal of Huerta the Usurper. To legitimize their insurgency, they proclaimed themselves *constitutionalistas*. The *zapatistas* in Morelos continued their fight against the federal government as well. To put down the rebellions, General Huerta increased the size of the federal army, and the attendant cost.

As the fighting spread, Mr. Body asked De for another assessment of the security of the *monte* to determine if the camps should be shut down. He also wanted to determine which, if any, faction was in control.

The next day, Jim and Hippolito rode in silence toward the mountains to Ixhuatlan and Chicontepec, beyond the railroad being built from Tampico to Furbero and on to Veracruz. Bandit activity had shut down its construction.

"Hippolito, you interested in lunch?" asked Jim. They had ridden since sun-up without a word spoken. "No need for a long lecture, mind you," continued Jim. "I'm only suggesting we stop and rest our bones. Just a nod of the head will do."

He wasn't sure if Hippolito understood sarcasm. At a break in the wall of foliage, the *mozo* pulled up his horse and the pack mule and led them off the trail through the overgrowth until they came to a small clearing next to a large tree whose trunk was fluted into fans half the height of a man. Without speaking a word, Hippolito stepped down from his horse, and unpacked the saddle bag. Jim dismounted, led his horse to the tree and looked up. He figured the first limb was fifty feet above the ground. Putting his hands on his waist, he leaned back and stretched. Hippolito took his reins and led the horses and pack mule to a stream further into the jungle.

"What did the *jefes* mean, 'assess the security in the countryside'?" Jim muttered to himself. "Do they expect me to ride up to a bunch of bandits and ask for their credentials?"

After a short lunch, the two lay down between the roots of the huge tree. Jim put his hat over his eyes and soon was snoring softly. Hippolito leaned against the tree and lit a hand-rolled cigarette. Shortly a noise coming from the direction of the trail prompted Hippolito to turn his head and listen. He heard approaching horsemen.

Hippolito lightly pushed on Jim's shoulder to awaken him. Jim shoved his hat back from his face and looked up at Hippolito. He, too, heard horsemen and quickly rolled behind the tree trunk away from the riders and pointed for Hippolito to move behind him and to lie down. Jim glanced in the direction of their own horses and the pack mule. They were hidden from the trail. In a few minutes several riders filed by. From the occasional glimpse through the foliage, he saw they were armed. Some had belts of cartridges slung over their chests. All carried new German Mausers. One white man rode in the back of the file. Jim was surprised to recognize the young German he had seen with Reverend William Bayard Hale at the Mariposa.

They waited several minutes until the sound of the passing horsemen faded to a silence broken only by cicadas. Jim stood up cautiously and indicated for Hippolito to remain behind. He wished again for a revolver. The *monte* was too dangerous to be traipsing around unarmed like some ignorant sheepherder, he thought. Isn't it just like the boss men to send him and Hippolito unarmed into the country while they sat safely in their offices? He crept back toward the trail and listened a long time for any other horsemen. When nothing materialized, he walked quietly back to Hippolito.

"Hippolito, old buddy," he said, "I don't know what those boys were up to, but I'm glad we didn't make their acquaintance."

"*A quien Dios quiere, le llena las casa de bienes.*"

"Yes, well, I'd feel better about who God likes if I had a sidearm. Come on, let's head up the trail. Do you know where the next village is?" Hippolito slightly nodded his chin and moved to gather their horses and the mule.

They rode on the trail in the direction the armed men had come from, their senses now alert. After half an hour, Hippolito reined in his horse and dismounted. He motioned for Jim to wait and he disappeared into the jungle. When he appeared again, Jim hadn't heard his approach. Without speaking, Hippolito stepped to his horse, swung into the saddle and rode forward. After threading their way along a trail for another half hour, they came to a small village. Two thatch houses were smoldering. When the Indians saw Jim they ran in fright until Hippolito spoke out to them. Jim could tell they were distraught. They were mostly women and young children. Jim asked Hippolito what happened and in broken Spanish, Hippolito explained that the horsemen had demanded food from the villagers. When one of the bandits took a sack of corn, an old woman protested. He shoved her to the ground, seized two of the younger women, took them to the huts, and he and his friends raped them while the other bandits ate food from pots cooking on the fires. When the bandits left, they threw burning logs from the fires onto the thatch houses.

"Who were they?" Jim asked Hippolito.

Hippolito shrugged. "Not from the *huasteca*."

"Who was the *gringo?*"

Hippolito shrugged again and then said, "*Ya me voy.*"

"I'm going with you," said Jim. "I've assessed the security all I need. The countryside ain't safe, not for Indians, not for Hippolito, and not for me."

At Zacamixtle Jim and Hippolito parted ways. Hippolito was preoccupied with moving his family into the jungle before nightfall. Jim said a quick goodbye and rode out of the village. He felt even more uneasy now that he was alone. He decided to stop at Huasteca's Casiano camp for the night.

When he approached the Casiano camp, Jim heard loud laughter and shouts coming from drunken men in the cantinas. He gave them a wide berth, trotted his horse past the company gate and up to a dormitory. Inside a few American roughnecks were playing cards. He saw they were drinking whiskey, which he knew was strictly against Huasteca Petroleum's rules.

"Where is your superintendent?" Jim asked.

A tall square-headed youngster looked up, pointed out the door, and said he was in the building next to the flagpole. Jim walked outside and spotted the building. The office was dark and the door was locked. Down the valley he saw electric lights on the derricks. Work was still ongoing, but, like El Aguila, crews were reduced to a skeleton workforce who had volunteered to stay for extra money. He walked back to the dormitory and asked if he could spend the night.

"Sure," replied the youngster. Jim thought he couldn't be fifteen years old. "You want to play some monte?"

"No thanks," Jim replied. "I'll just throw my bedding on one of the cots." He walked out the front door, untied his horse from the hitch and led it out of sight of the dorm into a grove of zapote trees. By the time he returned to the dorm with his bedding, darkness had set in. As he stepped on the porch he heard a gunshot from the direction of the cantinas. Once again he wished he had a revolver. The poker players scarcely looked up when he walked by and unrolled his bedroll on a cot in the back of the dorm. He lay down in the dark but the roughnecks kept him awake, cussing at unwanted cards and hooting when a hand was won.

Jim had dozed off when shouting jerked him awake. Several drunken rebel soldiers were in the dorm, pointing their rifles at the card players. Jim saw one of the card players reach for his gun. A shot rang out and slammed him against the wall. He fell to the floor writhing and holding his side. The other card players raised their hands.

Jim lay still, unseen on his cot in the dark. The Mexicans shoved the roughnecks against the wall. One grabbed the money on the table. Another ordered in Spanish for the roughnecks to take off their clothes. They understood because they began undressing, warily watching the Mexicans. The wounded man groaned. Blood ran from his side, but he was still conscious.

The Mexicans gestured for the Americans to throw their clothes in a pile, including their boots, and ordered them to take off their underclothes. The roughnecks glanced at each other but obeyed. The drunken Mexicans made fun of their white skin. One said they should treat them like they treated the Chinamen two weeks ago. Jim had heard the story. Two Chinese had been shot and left on a trail. The soles of their feet had been skinned, probably before they were murdered. The square-headed kid lowered his hand to his crotch, prompting a rebel to shout and gesture with his rifle to keep his hands above his head.

"*Mira!*" shouted one of the Mexicans and pointed to a large beetle crawling up the young man's upper thigh. The Mexican laughed and said to his *compadres*, "I'll shoot it off." He was taking aim just as a Mexican officer broke into the room. The officer was sober and demanded they drop the clothes and leave. The soldiers let go the clothing, but kept the boots and the money. The officer ordered them again to leave. As they sullenly filed out, he stepped over the wounded man and followed his men out of the dorm.

When their voices receded into the distance, Jim jumped from his cot and ran to the front of the dorm. The other roughnecks were kneeling by their wounded friend. Jim pushed past them and examined the wound. "Is your doctor still in camp?" he asked.

"He left two weeks ago," replied the youngster. Jim leaned over the prostrate man and examined the wound. The bullet had entered his right side above the hip. Jim unbuckled the man's belt, removed his shirt, ripped apart a bed sheet, folded it and placed the compress on the wound.

"He'll need a doctor. You," he pointed to the square-headed kid, "what's your name?"

"Amon Robertson."

"Go get a bucket of clean water."

Amon nodded and ran out the door.

"You," Jim said to another man. "Hold this against his wound. I have some dope to stop the bleeding." Jim handed the compress to the man and ran to his saddle, opened the saddle bag, and seized a jar of ointment. The square-headed kid returned with a bucket of water and clean rags.

"If this can cure a horse, maybe it can cure our *compadre*," said Jim as he started cleaning the wound. After examination, he saw the bullet was only a flesh wound. It had missed the hipbone and any vital organs. Jim covered both bullet holes with the ointment and placed clean rags over the wound.

"There. Hold these rags in place." Jim had wrapped a long piece of sheet gently around the man's waist and around the bandage. "At first light, take him to Potrero. El Aguila has a doctor at their camp. It's a long ride, but he should make it."

The men were relieved. When one pressed the others to grab their rifles and go kill some greasers, Jim stated the obvious. "The cantinas are full of drunk Mexicans who far outnumber you. Better to stay here, put out a guard, lock the gate, and be prepared in case they come back."

Jim's good sense prevailed. The wounded man was conscious and in pain, but the bleeding had stopped and unless infection set in, Jim said he would live. Before daylight they helped him onto a saddled mule. A second man rode behind and held him upright. Jim saddled his own horse, rode past the gate, and gave a wide berth to the cantinas. He could still hear drunken laughter.

"Have you heard the news?" De looked up at Jim. "Manuel Pelaez has returned."

The past two months had seen more and more bandit activities. Marauding bands, often drunk on *aguadiente* and calling themselves *constitutionalistas*, terrorized the countryside. Entire Indian villages had fled to the mountains. After Jim's report on the lack of security, Lord Cowdray immediately ordered that no more geological field work would be conducted until the security situation stabilized. Charlie Hamilton and Ben Belt, the two geologists who worked for De, were to stay in the company's well-guarded camps and run well samples.

"Really? Where is Manuel now?" asked De.

"Probably he's back at Tierra Amarilla."

"I wonder what he means to do."

"Good question," replied Jim.

"Yes, well I'd like to talk to Pelaez myself. Since the Chief's directive for no more geological trips to the field, I'm office bound," groused De. "The Chief doesn't want his geological staff to be killed or kidnapped."

"Did he mention his scout staff?" asked Jim.

"Charlie and Ben may be re-assigned to Haiti or Cuba," De continued. "Rumors are rife that El Aguila will open offices in Trinidad and Venezuela."

"A change of scenery might not be bad," replied Jim. "Mexico is a mess."

"A new play in a new country without competition has a certain allure, doesn't it?" said De. "The political situation in Mexico can't get worse."

"Don't bet on it," said Jim.

"And we still have undrilled anticlines to test," said De. "Next month a rig is moving to Los Naranjos. If the geological theory I'm working on is correct, it'll make a great well. Just as things are rolling the country falls apart."

"Reports from Sonora and Coahuila sound like Huerta's armies are whipped," said Jim.

"Nevertheless, there has only been random violence against the oil companies here in the *huasteca*," said De.

"It's random until it happens to you," responded Jim.

"You'd think one of the rebel leaders would move an army to the *huasteca*. Maybe that's why Manuel Pelaez is back. Jim, can you bring me the report on the latest Cerro Viejo well by next week? In spite of our lawsuit, Doheny is drilling more wells in Cerro Viejo."

"I will doublecheck my contacts, *jefe*. The rumors are conflicting."

"Good. And find what you can about Manuel Pelaez."

"Sure will. What's that on your desk? You writing poetry again?"

De looked down at a piece of paper. "Since I'm stuck in the office, I scribble a few lines every now and then."

Jim picked it up and read aloud:

Sand

Child of the rocks and waters

Wanton with waves and wind

From the ice-masked coast of Labrador

To the brazen beaches of Ind

Of your powers of abrasion

We require no persuasion

Whether riding a blizzard

Or in some chicken gizzard.

Jim laughed. "What does 'wanton with waves and wind' mean? I understand the chicken gizzard part."

"Waves and sand, like a playful seductress, carry the sand."

Jim laughed. "Good poem, Mr. De. Like a playful seductress. You inspire me."

"Hop got me started writing poetry. It's entertaining."

"Have you heard from Hop?" asked Jim. "Is he married?"

"Yes, safely married, but it was a close call. He sailed to Mobile and was held in quarantine until the last minute."

"Held in quarantine?" repeated Jim. "I swear. That'd make a monk anxious."

"He arrived at his own wedding only three hours before the ceremony."

"Time enough to say 'I do', was it?" asked Jim.

The next day, De and Jim left Tampico to visit Manuel Pelaez. De had not been in the field for four months. When he told Nell he would be visiting Tierra Amarilla, she was anxious about him leaving. Tampico was swirling with stories of marauding rebels who robbed and killed everyone they saw. De assured her that their trip would be safe. Before sunrise, as he said good-bye, Nell gave him a lingering hug.

"You'll be careful?" she asked.

"Don't worry, Beaner," he said. "I'll be careful."

Their launch left the dock adjacent to Plaza Independencia on the Chijol Canal and traversed the canal and the lagoon to Tamiahua, where they picked up Hippolito. Their old friend Don Luis had long-abandoned the village and returned to the States. A few more miles took them to the lagoon's southern end where it narrowed into a second canal that connected with the Gulf above Tuxpan Bar. Halfway down the canal a dozen or more men on either side waved them to shore. Jim directed the launch driver to pull over. When the boat bumped the canal bank, two armed men jumped onboard, told them they were soldiers in the Carranza army and asked to see their credentials. De and Jim showed them their identification. The two searched the boat and, finding nothing, stepped back onshore.

"¿Quien son? Who are you?" asked Jim as they pulled away.

The grizzled leader spat, laughed, and holding up his rifle shouted "*Viva Carranza!*".

When the launch had pulled away and moved beyond rifle shot, Jim asked Hippolito if he thought they were *carrancistas*. Hippolito replied, "*No todos los que chiflan son arrieros."*

"Not all who whistle are mule drivers. So you think they were bandits, not *carrancistas?*" Hippolito raised his eyebrows but said nothing.

Hippolito led him and Jim on a different route, this time through the huge Hacienda Temapache. De assumed that Hippolito was avoiding bandit activity along the more direct route. Jim had told him Manuel Pelaez had been chosen president of Temapache by his fellow *hacendados*, which gave him control over all the countryside between Tuxpan and Tierra Amarilla.

The ride was long but uneventful. Just at dark they rode in single file past the guards at the Potrero gate and directly to Sam Weaver's office. Sam greeted them warmly, showed De and Jim to a dorm, and pointed Hippolito toward worker's housing. Early the next morning, Sam escorted De to the ten-foot tall cement housing built around Potrero No. 4. De inspected the valve and wellhead system and was satisfied it was secure from tampering. When De sat on the cement ramp, Sam took his photo. Before noon they rode on to Tierra Amarilla and late in the evening recognized headquarters from the kerosene lanterns flickering in the darkening twilight. Riders who escorted them the last few miles left them at the gate to the house and told Jim that *Señor* Pelaez would not be there until tomorrow. *Señor* Pelaez had left orders for the cook to serve them dinner.

The next morning De and Jim walked into the kitchen and were served *huevos* in a spicy picante sauce and hand-rolled tortillas cooked on top of the wood-burning stove. Jim expressed admiration for the chatty cook's food and asked about *Señor* Pelaez. She told him with pride that her *patron* was now the leader of eleven owners of haciendas, *criollos* who had joined with *Señor* Pelaez, to form an army.

While waiting for Manuel, De spent the rest of the morning thumbing through books in the library. He removed an ancient leather-bound volume and unfolded long-unopened maps. It was a history of Mexico by Villagra, dated 1610. De wondered how many years it had been since the maps were last unfolded. Their accuracy and detail surprised him. He pondered how people dismissed works by predecessors as out-dated and unimportant until treasures such as this brought to life the level of inquiry and intelligence of authors so long dead.

Late in the afternoon Manuel Pelaez arrived at the hacienda with a half dozen armed escorts. He dismissed the men, strode to the porch, talked briefly with the houseboy, and sent word for De and Jim to meet him in the library.

Manuel said after a brief greeting, "Please excuse my tardiness. It has been a long time since we met," he said to De. "What brings you gentlemen to Tierra

Amarilla?"

"Our superiors asked us to assess the security of the oil field," answered De.

"And what have you determined?" asked Manuel.

"Our camps are in good order," said De. "We should give you credit. You have raised an army to control the rebels."

"Our troops are not an army," replied Manuel, "only a security force. We are left to protect ourselves. General Huerta's *rurales* are required in other parts of our country."

"Lord Cowdray, our chief, would like to know if you support General Huerta."

"Yes, I support General Huerta," replied Manuel.

"Are Huerta's *rurales* not in control of the countryside?"

"No one is in control of the countryside. That is why I and the other *hacendados* have raised our own security force, a small group of trustworthy people, my brother Alfredo, also Alfonso Sanchez from Tanhuijo, Daniel Herrera, and a few others."

"All are owners of haciendas like yourself?" asked De.

"Yes, of course. It is for our own defense."

"Do you think it is safe for El Aguila to keep the camps open?"

"If proper safeguards are taken."

"Uprisings against General Huerta by the *constitutionalistas* have swept the country into open revolt."

"Yes, I am aware of the uprisings. They are fostered not for the benefit of Mexico, but for the enrichment of those who plunder our country in the name of patriotism."

"Can order be restored without more bloodshed?" asked De.

"A hundred years ago three hundred thousand of my countrymen died to free us from Spain. Perhaps more will die in this revolution. Blood is our inheritance, and our deliverance."

Manuel then turned the discussion to the oil activity in the *huasteca*. De was surprised how much he knew about the Tierra Amarilla and Potrero wells. He must have good sources, De thought, because his information was accurate.

"I am disappointed, *Señor* DeGolyer," said Manuel, "that Tierra Amarilla makes so little oil, compared to Potrero and Alazan. They are very close."

"Close does not always matter in geology," answered De. "I am still struggling with the reasons."

When it came time to leave, Hippolito guided them back to their launch by an indirect route, avoiding the major trails and railroad. No bandits were encountered and nothing eventful occurred. De reported, however, that peace and security in the countryside were fragile, and probably temporary.

Nell was overjoyed at his safe arrival. That evening after dinner, De and Nell adjourned to the screened courtyard to share stories of their day's activities. In the twilight's defused afterglow, De liked to smoke a cigar and read while Nell sat knitting in a chair near him. Their house was shielded from the busy street by a high wall, which muffled the sounds of Tampico's hustle and bustle. After his bout with malaria, De transplanted a lime tree, *tilia mexicana*, to their courtyard. The *curandera* had used *t. mexicana* flowers in the tea she brewed to cure him of the high fever. Now its flowers released a faint fragrance which filled the courtyard with a delightful aroma. De was enjoying a new biography on Benito Juarez in Spanish. He still ran into a few rough spots while reading, but his understanding was improving all the time. Books about Mexico's turbulent history fascinated him.

"I went to the doctor today," Nell said quietly.

De set his book down. "You did what? Are you okay, Beaner?"

Nell nodded, smiled, and reached for his hand. "De, love, I'm going to have a baby."

De stood up. "Oh, Nell," he said. "How wonderful!" The tone of his voice expressed both joy and anxiety.

"This time, it will be fine," she assured him.

They agreed that she should return to her parents' home in Norman, and that De would join her prior to the baby's birth.

"You won't miss the birth, will you?" she asked.

"We have several wells drilling, but I'll be there long before the baby is born,"

"Do you think Lord Cowdray would ever open a Houston office?" Nell asked. "Mexico is in such chaos. The revolution could come to Tampico any day now."

"Which is precisely why you need to be in Norman," said De, kissing the top of her head. "Safe and sound with your parents."

"De," said Nell, as tears glistened her eyes, "it seems like we're always apart."

"It won't always be this way, Beaner. I promise."

Chapter Fifteen

May – September 1913

Despite the increased banditry in the countryside, the rigs continued to run. In late May, Penn Mex Oil Company discovered "Alamo No. 1" sixteen miles southwest of Potrero, extending the productive area of the Southern Zone. The exchange rate dropped from fifty centavos to the dollar to thirty-two centavos. Roving bands who were purportedly *constitutionalistas* controlled the countryside while the *huertistas* controlled Tampico and Tuxpan. The federal army grew from fifty thousand to more than two hundred thousand as General Huerta faced rebel armies under Obregon in the west, Villa in the north, Gonzalez and Aguilar in the east, and Zapata in the south. The deteriorating economy failed to provide enough revenue to support the larger army. Stories were rampant about pillaging the great haciendas in Sonora and Coahuila, but none of the *hacendados* in the *huasteca* were ransacked.

In May 1913, General Manuel Larraga and two hundred troops appeared at Huasteca's camp at El Ebano. Claiming to be a *constitutionalista*, he arrested the superintendent, confiscated supplies, demanded a loan of five thousand pesos, and took all the rifles in camp. He then moved to La Corona's Panuco camp and plundered it as well.

"It's a bad development," De telegraphed Mr. Body. "General Larraga professes loyalty to Carranza. It is one thing for El Aguila to provide protection against small bands of bandits. It is another to confront a sizeable army. If more Constitutionalist troops move into the area, the countryside will soon be under Carranza's control, while Tampico remains under the control of Huerta's troops. Manuel Pelaez has forces near Tierra Amarilla and Potrero. Who should we support?"

Mr. Body's response was to support all sides. Expediency and the continued flow of oil did not take sides. Directions to De and the field operations were to handle each situation separately, but not to provoke violence by arming the camps. They were an oil company, not a trained military force. Mr. Body did, however, order the temporary closing of all El Aguila camps except Potrero and Los Naranjos.

"Will," Jim asked, "would you say Mexico is ripping itself apart?" Jim had dropped by Will Buckley's office while gathering information for his monthly report.

"Right before our eyes. Our new President Wilson refuses to recognize Huerta so his government can't secure loans from the U.S. He is thus driven to extort taxes from the oil companies and loans from Europe. Failure to recognize Huerta encourages every two-peso bandit to call himself a Constitutionalist and continue fighting."

"Mr. De told me Huerta asked Lord Cowdray to put up a million dollar loan."

"In the United States we call that a political contribution. Will Lord Cowdray make the loan?"

"I expect the Chief will, what's the word Mr. De used, equivocate," replied Jim.

"What does your Lord Cowdray think of Huerta's proposal to raise the export tax by fifty percent?" asked Will.

"The Chief and I don't exactly talk on a regular basis. I've only spoken with him once and that was when he asked me to pass the salt at one of the chow lines on the Potrero blowout. I inquired if he wanted the pepper, but he must not have heard my question. What about Huerta's export tax on oil?"

"If he increases it to eighty-six cents a ton as proposed, taxes will equal half the price the oil companies receive. It'll make all but the highest producing wells non-commercial. Kill the goose that laid the golden egg…I wonder how you say that in Spanish?"

"I know just the man to ask," replied Jim. "Any other news? You're always full of good tidings."

Jim, how about this?" Will held up a newspaper. "Last week in his speech on August 27 before a joint session of Congress, President Wilson explained John Lind's mission to Mexico. He sounds like a professor lecturing a college freshman class.

Mexico has a great and enviable future before her, if only she choose and attain the paths of honest constitutional government. War and disorder, devastation and confusion, seem to threaten to become the settled fortune of the distracted country. As friends we could wait no longer for a solution which every week seemed further away. We offer our good offices, not only because of our genuine desire to play the part of a friend, but also because we are expected by the powers of the world to act as Mexico's nearest friend. It is upon no common occasion, therefore, that the United States offers her counsel and assistance. All America cries out for a settlement.

Do you want me to keep reading?" asked Will. Jim nodded in the affirmative.

A satisfactory settlement seems to us to be conditioned on: the immediate cessation of fighting throughout Mexico; security given for an early and free election in which all will agree to take part; the consent of General Huerta to bind himself not to be a candidate for election as President; the agreement of all parties to abide by the results of the election.

Will put down the Tampico *Tribune* and looked across the table at Jim.

"Surely Wilson didn't think Huerta would simply give up the presidency, announce elections, declare himself a non-candidate, and that the fighting would stop," commented Jim.

Will shook his head. "*Señor* Gamboa, the Secretary of Foreign Affairs, rejected the entire offer, if that's what you call it." Will continued reading from the newspaper.

We would earnestly urge all Americans to leave Mexico at once, and should assist them to get away in every way possible – not because we would mean to slacken in the least our efforts to safeguard their lives and their interests, but because it is imperative that they should take no unnecessary risks when it is physically possible for them to the leave the country.

What do you think of that, Will?" asked Jim. "When the president tells Americans to leave, maybe it's time we left."

"Since the revolution started, more than sixty Americans have been killed, and only three Mexicans have been brought to trial. All three were acquitted.

It's time our government protected its own citizens."

"I've been telling my bosses we need to arm ourselves."

"Huerta has to go," said Will emphatically.

"If Huerta falls, who will replace him?" asked Jim.

"My guess," said Will, "is if the *constitutionalistas* win, the country will divide. Carranza would control Coahuila and the *huasteca* and the *veracruzana*, Villa the north, Zapata the south. I can't imagine those three working together."

"It's the same old Mexican story, isn't it?" said Jim.

"Convulsive violence seems to be a cultural predilection. Since the Olmecs populated this hallowed ground, every century the Mexicans have held a rendezvous with bloodshed."

"You wonder if it would be different if the country was populated by Chinamen?"

"If Huerta falls, it'll be worse before it gets better," predicted Will. "And whoever has the upper hand needs the revenue from the oil wells."

"Will, you're always full of good tidings."

"Unlike you oil types, who are too optimistic, I am realistic. Banco de Paris lent Mexico twenty million pounds. After Huerta runs through the loan, he will raise taxes. After he raises taxes, he will suspend payment on foreign loans."

"Isn't that short-sighted?"

"Without money, he can't pay his troops. The purchasing power of the peso is falling like a rock. Without purchasing power, he can't pay interest on loans or buy arms. For Huerta it's a downward spiral. His only salvation is a quick victory on several fronts, and I don't see that possibility. For him, it's just a matter of time."

"My friends in Chihuahua and Coahuila say his armies rape, pillage, steal, and burn everything in their path like it wasn't their own country. The rebels in turn open the jails, levy loans against the rich if they don't kill 'em first, and sack their haciendas. If half the stories are true, and I've seen photos to believe them, I wouldn't want to be a Mexican, rich or poor."

"I've seen Casasola's and Horne's photographs, too," replied Will. "Peasants hanged from telegraph poles for miles. Photographers are having a heyday selling postcards of executions and atrocities. Armies led by barbarians with no rules, no morals, no consequences to their behavior except that murder and revenge engender more of the same.

"I'll drink to that," said Jim. "So what's the solution?"

"The solution is American intervention," replied Will. "I'm sailing to the States next week to convince the American government to intervene. Ed House in Austin is an old friend of mine. He is now an intimate of President

Wilson. I intend to enlighten Mr. House about the situation in Mexico. Wilson desperately needs to listen to Americans who live in Mexico and who understand the situation."

"Lord Cowdray believes American intervention would result in nationalization," Jim said.

"Yes, well your Lord Cowdray has certainly benefited from painting the Americans as self-interested, while he switches sides from Díaz to Madero to Huerta in order to keep his concessions and the oil flowing."

"As an impartial judge, I'd say 'so far so good' for El Aguila."

Will Buckley smiled. "You, my friend, are the very model of impartiality. Edward Lynton told me last week about your impartiality in sharing El Aguila's data that has been on the streets for weeks in return for the latest logs of your competitors."

"Just doing my job," said Jim. "I swap data without regard to benefit. Edward has an uncanny ability to buy mineral rights under good wells, have you noticed?" Jim rose and said, "I need to be moving along, Will. After you return from the States, let's catch up. I'll buy the drinks."

"That would be a first."

"You're the man with the single malts. When I buy we'll be drinking *agaurdiente*." Will laughed again and shook his head as Jim rose and wished him well on his trip.

De wasn't sure what to expect when he saw a telegram from Oklahoma on his desk. He tore it open, fearing the worst. He read the telegram anxiously. Its message was brief. "Nell has malaria. Please come home."

De immediately wired Mr. Body and was granted permission for a ten-day leave. He caught the next ship to Mobile, but the trip to Norman nevertheless took three days. By the time he arrived at Norman, Nell was better. Her fever had broken, and the doctor said the baby was not in danger. He stayed for only four days. The morning he packed to return to Tampico, Nell's father berated De for taking his daughter off to Mexico.

"De, I'm sorry what papa said to you," Nell said. "He didn't mean it."

Why *had* he left her in Tampico the first time she was pregnant? Couldn't he get a job anywhere but Mexico? Where were his priorities, with his job, or with his family?

"He was right," said De.

"De, it's our lives and our decision."

"Beaner, Beaner, Beaner," sighed De. "Tell me what to do."

He held both her hands in his and looked in Nell's eyes. He had never felt so indecisive, so torn between a career and a family.

"Go back to Tampico, De. The baby is due in three months. I can manage. I believe in you."

De nodded. He looked down, still holding her hands, and reflected how Nell's calm certainty provided a bulwark against his own doubts. He kissed her forehead.

"You need me here," he replied quietly.

"I can manage," she repeated.

"Yes," he said, looking up into her blue eyes, "I know you can manage. Beaner, I love you so very much. You're my rock and my compass."

"I hope that's a compliment," Nell said and smiled, and he kissed her again, this time on the lips, a warm red rose kiss.

The next day De left for Tampico. Her father's words still rang in his ears.

De was reading the report when Jim dropped by his office. The Naranjos No. 1 had drilled the top of Tamasopo and tested 700 barrels a day.

"Mr. De," said Jim. "Good to see you back. How was the trip home?"

"Fine, Jim. Nell is much better. The visit was too short."

"She's in good hands and in the right place," said Jim. "Tampico is no place to have a baby. It sounds like you've done it again, *jefe*. I heard a rumor down the hall about Los Naranjos."

"I was just reading the report. Yesterday it tested oil but we only drilled the top ten feet of the Tamasopo. If my hunch is right, it'll be a lot better if we drill fifty more feet. I ordered them this morning to deepen the well. We'll know more in a couple of weeks. Where is everyone? I leave for a week and when I return the office is half empty."

Jim explained that the office staff had been trimmed back. While he was gone, General Huerta's railing against America had reached a high pitch. Talk of killing *gringos* was common. The illegitimacy of his usurpation reached a new level when Huerta dissolved the senate and placed the members of Congress in jail.

"The next shoe will fall soon," predicted Jim. "The peso fell to twenty-nine cents to the dollar, barely half its value a year ago. Mexico suspended payment on the national debt, just like Will Buckley predicted. And there seem to be an awful lot of Germans sniffing around."

Jim told De he had been forwarding reports to their Mexico City office, purportedly disseminated by Waters-Pierce operative Shelburne Hopkins, no kin to Ed, that Lord Cowdray helped Huerta overthrow Madero, that Cowdray had brought about British recognition for Huerta, that Huerta gave El Aguila new oil and railway concessions, and that Cowdray was about to sell his interests to Standard Oil. All of the reports were untrue, but in a climate of chaos and disorder, rumors reigned.

A week later Jim was standing at De's desk again. "Did you test the well?"

"Which well?" asked De innocently.

"Don't kid me, *jefe*. Los Naranjos No. 1. You were deepening it a few more feet, remember?"

De leaned back in his chair. "Jim, I would have told you last night but I wanted to test your sources. Here, have a Cuban. I'd still like to keep the lid on the data for a few days until we finish some title work on an adjacent tract, but yes, after deepening fifty feet, yesterday it flowed something between forty and fifty thousand barrels of oil."

"Fifty thousand! *Hijo, jefe!* De, you just keep doing it!"

"I waited to test it until my lucky number four rolled around. Yesterday was October 4. 'Four' keeps coming up in spades for me. Good geology and good luck go hand in hand."

"Call it luck or call it science, either one works for me," said Jim.

"The oil business is a combination of skill and luck," replied De. "If you are lucky enough, you don't have to be skillful, but no matter how skilled you are, you have to be lucky. Without intending to crow," De continued, "Los Naranjos secures Aguila's rank as one of the world's great oil companies. With Los Naranjos, we're no longer dependent on one well or one field."

"Los Naranjos is four miles south of Huasteca's Casiano wells. Is it on the same anticline?"

"No, but the rocks look just as good, and I'm beginning to see a pattern."

"De, if you keep this up, you could single-handedly flood the world oil market."

De laughed. "That's not a worry. Every well declines, some much faster than others, and although Potrero No. 4 still shows no sign of depletion, one day it will, too. Depletion is reality."

Jim leaned back and blew cigar smoke. "The day after you discover a 50,000 barrel a day well you are worrying about depletion."

"We can't rest on our laurels. Look at Topila. Several of those wells flowed more than ten thousand barrels a day and went to salt water in a year."

"Well, I'm betting you'll find plenty more. Congratulations on Los Naranjos, *jefe.*" Jim was elated.

"Thanks. It's a good feeling to find oil using scientific methods, a method that adds predictability. Jim, isn't Hippolito from Zacamixtle?"

"Sure is, but he took his family to the sierras, so he doesn't stay there. Why?"

"What do the minerals look like around Zacamixtle? Are there any large tracts?"

"I'd bet the minerals are cut to pieces," said Jim. "Why do you ask?"

"No good reason yet. Would you start checking ownership of mineral interests for us? I'm just thinking about trends."

De had been thinking about the immense springs at the base of Sierra del Abra, those he had seen on his field trip to the mountains three years ago. He wished Hop was around to discuss a geologic concept that was nagging at him.

"Well, Mr. De, I'll bet good money on your trends. Lord Cowdray has to believe you're the smartest geologist in the world."

"Or the luckiest," said De, thinking of both oil and Nell.

Chapter Sixteen

October — November 1913

In October General Candido Aguilar arrived in the Southern fields and ordered the cessation of all drilling. Jim was in Will Buckley's office and told him the news.

"Who is Candido Aguilar?" Will asked. "This country has more generals than privates."

"Carranza's son-in-law," answered Jim, "and the provisional governor of Veracruz."

"Last spring it was Larraga at El Ebano. Now it's Aguilar in Tuxpan."

"Larraga had only a couple of hundred troops. They say Aguilar has three thousand."

"Three thousand!" exclaimed Will. "Larger than your friend Manuel Pelaez's army."

"Manuel ain't no fan of Carranza. Aguilar has been recruiting workers from the oil camps, promising if they join his *constitutionalistas* they'll share in the looting and the women."

"As if sharing women and looting is constitutional," Will said.

"It has a certain appeal to the recruits, don't you think?" answered Jim. "The Chief wants me to have another chat with *Señor* Pelaez to assess his measure of Aguilar. I'm headed to the field tomorrow. With my freckles and red hair, maybe they won't confuse me for a *huertista*. I don't exactly look *puro mexicano*."

"Tell them your mother was an Irish catholic," suggested Will.

"I'll tell them the Pope sent me. What's your prediction, Will? You said two years ago Mexico was falling apart."

"It's worse now than I ever imagined. The whole country, north to south, has let loose the barbarian horde upon itself. There is scarcely any commerce between the different parts of the Republic, owing to the irregularity of train service. The price of foodstuffs and clothing have advanced from ten to fifty percent."

"Is there any way Mexico can hold together?"

"Had it not been for the Monroe Doctrine, Mexico would probably today be enjoying the blessings of justice and peace and prosperity as a dependency of some European power."

"European power? What are you talking about, Will?"

"The idea of a democracy prevailing here is simply out of the question. The state of public morality is so low, and their idea of political privileges is so debased, any vote can be bought for centavos. A monarchy, where some attention and respect are paid to law, would be far preferable."

"Madero was elected by a landslide. His election wasn't bought."

"He was probably the first president in the history of Mexico who was the choice of the majority of the Mexican people, and he was undoubtedly the most incompetent president in modern Mexican history. He promised a great deal, doubtless in good faith. A great majority of the people of Mexico were convinced that they could quit work within ninety days after the inauguration of President Madero. They were severely disappointed. Thirty days after his election, there was never a more unpopular leader."

"Wasn't it because his lieutenants broke with him and they took their followers?"

"You're right, Jim. The discontent of the people was exploited by professional revolutionary leaders, who based their campaigns ostensibly on the failure of Madero to comply with the program set out in the Plan of San Luis Potosí. A majority of men who are now fighting Huerta, or rather who are devastating the country, are the same men who first rebelled against the Madero and Díaz governments."

"It seems to me poor Mexicans are just killing other poor Mexicans. What about the *criollos?*"

"In this country there exists no sympathy between the few people of Spanish blood and the great mass of Indians. They hardly look on each other as Mexicans. The lower classes are as much oppressed now as they were 400 years ago. The laws are framed by the rich for their own benefit. What these people need most, and what they desire most, is food and clothing, and the consequent privilege of educating their children."

"The same as in America."

"Except if you were born in Mexico, Jim, you would have no opportunity to be anything except what your father was."

"Then I'd want to revolt, too. So how do you fix a broken pot?"

"There is but one solution, and that is American intervention. Given the lawlessness, the ravaging of property and murder of thousands, of *hundreds* of thousands of their own citizens, intervention would be humane."

"But what if it ain't what the Mexicans want?" asked Jim. "Maybe they remember the Alamo, too. My Mexican *amigos* had rather waltz with a bear than reach a hand across the Rio Grande."

When General Aguilar's rebel troops first arrived in the Huasteca, owing to their lack of artillery, the federal troops repulsed them handily. General Aguilar responded by falling back onto the oil camps. He moved his headquarters to the abandoned El Aguila camp at Tanhuijo and, to announce his presence and authority, sent armed men to every oil camp in the vicinity, including Potrero and Los Naranjos, and demanded that representatives of the oil companies meet him at his headquarters to discuss policies

Well before dawn, Jim loaded his gear in the company launch. He had instructed the launch driver to meet him on the dock before the merchant traffic clogged the narrow Chijol Canal. With the disturbances in the countryside growing more frequent, the early morning market at the Plaza Independencia was smaller, but still drew a crowd.

"To Tuxpan," he instructed the launch driver. They backed from the docks and moved slowly forward, able to see clearly enough in the moonlight. Several companies' payrolls had been robbed by rebels calling themselves *constitutionalistas* in the narrow Chijol Canal. As a result, Mr. Body had forwarded instructions for the launch to carry no money, food, or supplies. All food, supplies, and the company payroll were sent to the camps by sea to the Tuxpan Bar and up the Tuxpan River to the juncture with the Buena Vista. From there a large group of armed company guards traveled to the company camps at Potrero and Los Naranjos.

Jim carried letters of introduction to the general from Mr. Body. He had again asked permission to carry a weapon, but Mr. Body had nixed his request.

The boat ride down the Chijol Canal and the length of Tamiahua Lagoon passed without incident. The launch stayed far enough from shore so that no rebels could hail them. At the southern end of the lagoon, however, the boat was constrained into the narrow canal that led to the Gulf near the mouth of the Tuxpan River. With the canal banks less than fifty feet apart, any bandit could halt them without difficulty. Jim's only defense was his fluent Spanish and his own wits, but nevertheless he wished he carried a pistol.

Halfway down the canal a group of armed men waved a large flag and indicated for the boat to approach the bank. His boat driver slowed the launch and pointed it toward the men. When the launch was a few feet from the canal bank, the leader yelled '*Viva* Aguilar! *Viva* Carranza! *Muerte los huertistas!*" Jim took off his hat. He hoped his mop of red hair would hold the firing squad off until he could explain his mission.

When the boat touched shore, a grizzled rebel jumped aboard and pointed a 30-30 Winchester at his chest. Jim produced the letter from Mr. Body. The man took the letter and called for another to read it. The letter was written in Spanish, addressed to General Aguilar, and stated that James H. Hall represented El Aguila, and was present in fulfillment of the summons by General Aguilar. The leader ordered several of his men to search the boat and the cabin. They rifled through every cabinet, opened the lid to the motor, and finding nothing, motioned the boat driver to proceed down the canal.

Jim asked for the letter back but his request was dismissed. When the boat reached Tanhuijo, Jim was surprised at the size of the rebel encampment. All the company's buildings were occupied by soldiers. Campfires sent smoke into the windless air far beyond the boundary of the camp. Several soldiers met them at the dock, and ordered him to follow. As he was marched through the Tanhuijo company camp, Jim heard gunfire in the direction of Tuxpan. He passed ragged groups of soldiers comprised mainly of Santa Maria Indians from Papantla, fifty miles south of Tuxpan, whose reputation as rapacious fighters was widespread. All were well-armed, some with American rifles, but many with new German Mausers. When they walked past the cantinas, he heard laughter and women's voices. As the procession wound its way to the General's headquarters, throngs of rebel soldiers stared at him suspiciously. When they passed the company store, he saw the door was open and the shelves were empty.

Arriving at what had been the camp superintendent's office, Jim and his escort climbed the wooden stairs and walked into the offices. One soldier acknowledged his escort, walked to the office in the back, knocked, spoke with someone inside the office, and motioned for Jim to enter.

The General, a *mestizo* sporting an extravagant mustache and a swarthy visage, sat behind a large desk. "You are the representative of El Aguila?" demanded General Aguilar.

"Yes, sir. Mr. Body, our general manager, sent a letter for you." Jim nodded to the man who had taken the letter, who handed it to the General. He glanced at it and passed it to another officer.

"General Carranza does not recognize the validity of the Huerta government. Huerta is a usurper and must be removed," stated the General forcefully.

"Yes, sir," replied Jim. He figured the less he said the better.

"Your oil companies have pillaged the resources that belong to the people of Mexico. You do so with no legal authority. The Díaz government that gave you permission was illegitimate. The government of the Usurper is illegitimate."

Jim said nothing. Discretion demanded no response.

"Under my authority, conferred by General Carranza, I order you immediately to cease drilling. Until a new government and a new constitution are in place, foreign oil companies must cease all operations."

Jim remained silent. He suspected the General's words were only bluster before he asked for a bribe.

"In addition," continued the General, "you must stop producing all oil immediately. You must close all oil wells. No more oil is to be exported until you provide costs for the protection that our army provides."

Jim didn't mention that the protection the General offered was protection from depredations by his own troops.

"In addition, El Aguila, and the Huasteca Oil Company are to pay 200,000 pesos each, to be brought to me no later than seven days from today," concluded General Aguilar, rising from his chair as he made the final demand.

Jim acted nonplussed. "I will report your requests to my superiors," he said.

"Understand me, *señor*, these are not requests," replied the General. "They are demands by General Carranza and must be met immediately. I have instructed my troops to confiscate all arms in the oil camps and other necessary supplies, for which my troops will sign notes. Tell your superiors that any foreigner found with weapons will be shot as an enemy of the people and a supporter of Huerta."

"Yes, sir."

The General looked at the letter. Jim wondered if he could read.

"Who is Mr. J.B. Body?" asked the General.

"Mr. Body is our general manager. He is at El Aguila's office in Mexico City."

"Tell your Mr. Body that I summon him here to my headquarters. I do not wish to speak with messengers."

"Yes, sir."

"One more requirement. El Aguila must close the refinery in Minantitlan. It is controlled by the *huertistas*. And tell your Mr. Body that he must bring 120,000 pesos for unpaid taxes on the refinery. This is not a request."

The General issued the directives in a manner that left no room for negotiation. Still, Jim thought, this is Mexico. It served no one's purpose, federalist or rebel, to stop the flow of oil. The General nodded to the man who brought him to the headquarters, and the man motioned for Jim to follow him. They left the office without further comment from the General. Jim was escorted back through Tanhuijo camp to the boat where they were met by the same group of scruffy guards that hailed them in the canal. Jim stepped onboard and upon instruction from one of the guards, the launch driver backed out and turned the launch north toward Tampico. At the same place where they had been pulled over earlier in the day, the boat stopped and their passengers disembarked and joined the guards left behind. The launch driver slowly backed and turned the launch up the canal toward the lagoon. When out of earshot range, Jim said to the boat driver, "I'm happy to be rid of our guests."

"Sí, señor," said the driver. "Yo también." Jim felt safer yet when the boat moved into the open water of Tamiahua Lagoon, and he instructed the boat driver to drop him off at the small village of Tamiahua.

Jim left the boat and walked up the single dirt street. Most of the habitations were empty. Few villagers were on the street. All the game cocks had disappeared as well. Jim walked into a cantina and the sole occupant, the bartender, looked up. "Where is everyone?" Jim asked. The bartender shrugged his shoulders.

"Bring me a horse." The bartender stared blankly until Jim took a coin from his pocket and put it on the counter. The bartender picked it up, moved from behind the bar, mumbled for Jim to wait, and walked out. In a few minutes he returned with a sway-backed horse. It had a halter but no saddle. Jim swung his leg over the horse's back and kicked its ribs.

He followed a familiar trail toward Los Naranjos through Zacamixtle. Before he rode into the village, Jim dismounted, tied his horse and walked cautiously into the village. Like Tamiahua, it too looked abandoned. He stepped to the thatch house that belonged to Hippolito and walked inside. Embers still smoked in the hearth. He stepped outside, shouted Hippolito's name, and when no one answered, turned back to town and rode to a cantina. An old man sat in a chair swatting flies with a piece of paper. Jim thought it odd that the only residents remaining in the villages were bartenders. Perhaps their profession conferred neutrality. He asked where everyone had gone. The man waved his hand toward the back wall and pointed. "Las montañas. Mountains," he repeated in English.

"Hippolito, ¿donde está?" He thought the man might know Hippolito's whereabouts.

The bartender shrugged his shoulders. Jim took a coin from his pocket and passed it across the table. "Tráigele aquí. Bring Hippolito. Dígale es Jim." The man put the coin in his pocket, rose, and left without saying a word. Jim sat in the chair so he faced the door, and waited. In less than an hour, Hippolito walked into the cantina, followed by the bartender.

"Hippolito, good to see you," smiled Jim. "I was hoping you would come." Hippolito nodded.

"I want to show you my horse. She's a sway-backed beauty." He led the way out the cantina. When they were out of the bartender's hearing, Jim looked over his shoulder. Hippolito's expression never changed.

"I just came from the rebels' headquarters in Tanhuijo. Do you know of General Aguilar?"

Hippolito nodded in the affirmative.

"What do you hear of him?"

"Los indios son malos."

Jim agreed that his Indians were bad types. "He claims he is a *carrancista.*"

Hippolito did not respond.

"Do you think his troops will attack Tuxpan?"

Hippolito nodded in the affirmative.

"Do you think he will attack Tampico?"

Hippolito again nodded in the affirmative.

"You never were a man of many of words," said Jim in English. In Spanish he said, "Hippolito, I'm headed to Potrero."

Hippolito responded, *"Cuidado. Mucho cuidado."*

You don't have to tell me to be careful, thought Jim. When everybody but me is armed with guns and *aguadiente*, I'm as cautious as a rich man in a confession booth.

"Where is your family?" Jim asked.

Hippolito nodded his head toward the *sierras.*

Jim arrived at Los Naranjos just at dusk. Several rebels armed with Mausers stood outside the front gate. He told them he worked for El Aguila and they allowed him to pass. He walked through the nearly empty compound to the main office. The superintendent greeted him, gestured for Jim to take a seat, and asked in a soft voice how things were going.

"Not too bad, on the whole," replied Jim. "How are things here?"

"The rebels moved into camp two days ago. They stripped the store and took most of our livestock, and signed notes for payment. They assure me when Huerta is overthrown, the notes may be presented to the new government.

Jim explained what General Aguilar had demanded, that the wells be closed until further notice, and that instructions from the Tampico office would be forthcoming. Afterward, Jim retired to a dormitory and threw his gear on a bunk bed. Two rig hands who were lying on their bunks scoffed at the rebels.

"The greasers ain't running me off," one of them said.

"What if they have a rifle and you ain't got one?" asked his friend.

"Sonofabitch point a rifle at me and he ain't long for this world," the roughneck said gruffly. Jim didn't tell him how many rebel soldiers he had seen at Tanhuijo camp.

The next day Jim borrowed a saddle and rode on to Potrero. When he walked into Sam Weaver's office, two armed rebel soldiers rose from chairs. Their dirty boots had muddied what had been spotless floors. One asked him what he wanted and he explained that he was sent by General Aguilar to discuss the company's operations. He was directed to the superintendent's office, and when he walked in, Sam rose and greeted Jim warmly.

"What do you make of our new friends?" Jim asked Sam in English.

"They act like they own the place, don't they?" replied Sam.

"How about the drilling crews?" asked Jim.

"We're down to two rigs. There are less than fifty of us to run the whole show. When the word spread that Aguilar and his *indios* were in the neighborhood, our workers disappeared."

"I just came from General Aguilar's headquarters. He demanded that all drilling was to stop until Aguila pays the back taxes."

"Stop drilling? We could lose the holes."

"Until we have the situation resolved, Sam, that's what you'll need to do. He also wants us to shut in the wells."

Sam didn't like what he heard. "We can probably shut in all the wells except No. 4. Does El Aguila intend to pay the taxes?"

"It ain't my decision, Sam, but I'd say something needs to be worked out *pronto*. In the meantime, we better not aggravate the boys." Jim nodded toward the soldiers. "Is there any liquor in camp?"

"Two weeks ago I threw out whatever the men had stashed. We bought the whole inventory from the cantinas, then broke the bottles and poured it out. You never heard such a howl."

"That was smart, Sam. As soon as the Chief decides what to do about the General's demands, we'll send word to you. In the meantime, you better make preparations to stop the drilling and shut in the wells."

After Jim returned to Tampico and reported to De, Mr. Ryder, the new El Aguila manager, asked De, "Do you think he meant what he said about closing in the wells?"

"Jim said the General made it clear: it's not a request," said De. "He has three thousand troops to back him up."

"What about General Aguilar's demand that Mr. Body meet him in Tanhuijo?"

"He said it was not a request."

Mr. Ryder said Mr. Body would not meet with the General. "We will have to find an excuse for him. I'll draw up a schedule to close in the wells. If we slowly choke them back, maybe no damage will be done."

Mr. Body's return telegraph directed De to follow General Aguilar's orders. The telegraph was only one terse sentence. De figured Mr. Body assumed their telegraph wires were read by rebels and federalists alike.

Within minutes after the Potrero No. 4 was shut in, the pressure on the casing rose to several hundred pounds. Fissures radiating from the wellhead started spewing natural gas. Sam Weaver immediately opened the well and when the casing pressure was reduced, the fissures ceased spewing gas. As a result of No. 4's response, the remaining Potrero wells were not shut in.

El Aguila and Huasteca Petroleum jointly made a 10,000 peso payment with a promise that more would be forthcoming. Mr. Body reiterated that Aguila's Tampico office was to cooperate with the *carrancistas* in the field, and with the *huertistas* in Tuxpan and Tampico. Necessity required that they operate with both factions. After the money passed hands, the oil flowed as before, but in deference to the demands of General Aguilar, El Aguila, Huasteca, and Waters-Pierce agreed not to sell fuel oil to any of the Mexican railways within federally controlled areas.

Chapter Seventeen

December 1913 — February 1914

De read the telegram. General Aguilar's troops had taken Tuxpan and were now pushing toward Tampico. Rumors had been rampant for more than a week about the fighting around Tuxpan. If only a small portion of the rumored atrocities were true, General Aguilar's Santa Marian troops were ransacking the entire region, the *hacendados*, *rancheros*, and the villages. He knew what would happen to young women, and hoped they had moved into the jungle or to the sierras.

"Is this reliable information?" De asked Jim.

"I have friends in town who support Carranza and who are in contact with General Aguilar's army. They say his troops will be in Panuco within a week."

"Will they attack Tampico?"

"You can bet on it," answered Jim.

"As long as Tampico is under the control of General Zaragoza and his federal troops, we have to accede to their authority. But if the *constitutionalistas* win, Mr. Body says we are to switch loyalty. What are the other companies doing?" asked De.

"La Corona moved their managers aboard the Dutch cruiser *Kortendaer*."

"Our cruisers and gunboats are in the Panuco and Tamesi rivers, as are the German's and the Dutch," said De. "The *Virginia* is anchored three miles offshore to evacuate us if necessary."

"The Mexicans may need our oil but they may want our blood in the bargain," observed Jim.

"They're not the only ones who need our oil, if the other battleships are any indication," replied De. American, British, German, and Dutch dreadnoughts also were anchored off Tampico.

A second telegram arrived, this one from Oklahoma. De ripped it open. "Nell fine," it read. "No baby yet. When are you coming home? Mexico in flames."

De set the telegram down. He wanted to be with Nell more than anything, but he couldn't just walk away from his responsibilities. Even more, he knew that he was closing in on the key to the Tamasopo. This was no time to abandon Tampico. He sent a telegram back to Nell stating all was quiet in Tampico, and that he would be home soon.

In the middle of the night, a week later on December 9, 1913 the rebel troops under General Aguilar attacked Panuco, across the river. Rifle and machine gun fire could be heard at all hours of the day and night. Immediately after the fighting began, El Aguila sent word for all the employees to proceed to the Custom House to be evacuated to British merchant ships lying in the Gulf.

With Mr. Body's permission, El Aguila's office was opened to take in displaced foreigners. By the end of the first day's fighting, more than ninety women and one hundred fifty men were crammed into the new five-story El Aguila building, the tallest in Tampico. The front doors were sandbagged and lookouts were placed at the side doors and on the roof. Two small American cruisers, *Tacoma* and *Chester* plied the river. A German gunboat likewise patrolled up and down the river. Although all foreigners were considered neutral, if the fighting reached Tampico, their neutrality could not guaranteed that marauding troops would not harm them.

"I carried my telescope to the roof," De told Jim on the afternoon of the second day of the siege. "Do you want to watch the fighting?" he asked Jim.

Jim was surprised at the offer. "Sure do."

The two climbed the stairs and walked out onto the roof.

"We ought to charge admission," said Jim when he saw the view from the roof. "This is better than *sombra* seats at a bullfight *corrida*. They ought to be playing *La Macarena*."

"You can spot the rebel soldiers," said De, pointing to a throng of activity across the river. "The national troops are in the trenches over here," he pointed to this side of the river, "the ones with blue-striped trousers. One of their artillery batteries is sited in the telescope. Take a look."

Jim looked through the eyepiece and saw men near an artillery piece. While he watched, they fired a howitzer, which jerked backward in its traces and threw a long spurt of smoke from its muzzle. The national troops were evidently outnumbered, but they nevertheless held a superior position, and possessed artillery. Everywhere he looked across the river, Jim saw rebel soldiers running about, hunkering down when crossing open areas. He swiveled the telescope to watch a large group of rebels gather near small boats in a tributary, out of sight of the *federales*.

"Do you see the boats in the small tributary?" asked De.

"I was just looking at them," replied Jim.

"I imagine it's their invasion flotilla. Aren't these great seats?" De said and turned to Jim. As he did, his hat flew off his head. No wind was blowing. Puzzled, De walked across the roof and picked it up. "Would you look at this?" Holding up the hat, De poked a finger through a hole.

"That's a bullet hole, De. We better get the hell off the roof!"

De ducked behind the parapet and held the hat in his hand. "Would you look at this?" De repeated with astonishment.

"*Jefe*, this is no way to test your luck," said Jim. "The *federales* think you're spotting for the *carrancistas*. The *carrancistas* think you're spotting for the *huertistas*."

"I wonder who fired the shot?" De asked. He was still astonished. The bullet had passed through the crown of his hat. "Close call, but no cigar," he finally said and ducked into the stairwell.

The next day De asked Jim if anyone had contacted the U.S. military to make sure communications with the naval ships had been coordinated. "Maybe we should communicate directly with the Navy. Jim, could you make it to the river and wave down one of our gunboats?"

Jim nodded.

"If anyone stops you, tell them you work for El Aguila."

"I'd rather tell them the Pope sent me," replied Jim.

"Since our telegraph communications are interrupted daily, we could be on our own. It looks to me like the fighting will move to this side of the river. We should be prepared to evacuate." De expressed his misgivings about depending on the English to evacuate them.

"I'll see what I can do about contacting our navy," said Jim. "You wouldn't know the admiral's name, would you? I'd hate to address a man of his standing as 'hey, you.'"

"Admiral Frank R. Fletcher. His flagship is the *USS Virginia*."

"I've never spoken to an admiral before."

"If you could wave down one of our gunboats on the river, hand them the list of Americans here in the building, and work out a way to signal if we need evacuate. I've already sent the list to Consul Miller."

Jim donned a sombrero, exited the El Aguila building and stepped to the far side of the street. The streets were nearly empty. At every intersection he stopped and watched the side streets before moving across. He made his way to the wharf without incident. Once there, Jim remained inside a warehouse until he was able to wave down the German gunboat *Ceciele*. The German officers spoke enough English to understand his wishes to be taken to an American gunboat. When they dropped him alongside the *Chester*, Jim told the officer in charge that the situation in El Aguila's building was under control and handed him a list of the names of the Americans. The officer assured Jim that the list of people and his report on the situation would reach the admiral. At Jim's request, they waited until after nightfall to drop him off at the company wharf. In the darkness, he made it back to El Aguila's building and reported to De and the others in charge of their refugees.

"The officer on our gunboat told me it was standing orders not to evacuate Americans until specifically requested by our consulate. Evacuation, he fears, would send a message to the *federales* that we think they will be defeated."

De mulled. "Does that make us hostages of the *federales?*"

"The problem with taking sides," said Jim, "is we need to pick the winner."

December 13, 1913
Sweetheart:

    Three days of fighting have passed and both the rebels and federals occupy more or less the same position as when the trouble started.

    The building is full of refugees and there is not one chance in a thousand of any one being hurt. I am sick and tired of the whole business.

    No one in the city has been hurt though fighting is going on across that wide plain between Dona Cecilia and the mill.

    Sweetheart, I am absolutely heart sore and weary. I should be with you and I know it. Instead, I am loafing around here and can't do a thing unless it is to die of lonesomeness. You are my sweetest heart and we are going to live together if I have to get a job teaching school.

    All of the English and Americans here are at swords points though it doesn't show on the surface.

    Baby dear, we are more than fortunate that you are not here and that I am safe and no possible danger.

Every Mexican in town is on the Kronprinzen Ceciele with the exception of those that are in the Aguila building.

The gunboat Bravo is still banging away. They have shot for three days and most of the nights.

Sweet baby girl, I am a thousand times sad because I haven't seen you for so long. It makes all of the difference in the world.

I hope and pray, my only sweetheart, that everything will come through all right and that we will be together very, very soon.

With all love, I am Your boy,

Everette

Now with nearly two hundred fifty foreign refugees in the Aguila building, the inhabitants were put under a loose martial law. More than twenty men were recruited, a captain was chosen, along with one lieutenant and three sergeants. Patrols were set up for both day and night. Offices on the first floor were converted to a kitchen. Other offices became dormitory rooms. Showers were rigged in the bathrooms from hoses connected to the sinks. Food was served cafeteria style three times daily. Early on the fourth day, De asked, "Jim, what is all that smoke?"

"The *federales* accidentally shelled three oil barges," replied Jim. "A nearby tank and warehouse caught fire. The Mexican workers took charge and put the fire out before it spread. My *mexicano* friends tell me General Aguilar now has four thousand troops across the river. Huerta has only fifteen hundred here in Tampico."

Later that day, the fourth day of the siege, the rebels unexpectedly retreated. The silence was eerie. Pending validation of the withdrawal, everyone decided to remain one more night in the El Aguila building.

"It's true," Jim told Will Buckley the next day. Will had stayed in his office during the siege. "The fighting has stopped. The rebels retired to Altamira. Rumors are they'll burn down the Waters-Pierce refinery. No one knows when they'll attack again, but the *federales* here in town are celebrating. They'll stay drunk for two days."

"The *carrancistas* control the roads, the railroads, the rivers, the telegraph, the entire transportation and communication systems, and the *federales* are celebrating," mused Will. "Certainly the rebels will attack again."

"I crossed the river this morning and watched them burn stacks of bodies," Jim said. "What a stench. I don't know how many on each side were killed, but Huerta isn't sending reinforcements, and the rebel ranks keep growing."

"Is your English company preparing for another regime?" asked Will.

"One regime at a time is our motto. Since Britain officially recognized Huerta, we can't switch sides until he resigns. Our field operations have nearly come to a halt."

"What does your friend Manuel Pelaez say?"

"When I saw him last month he still supported Huerta," replied Jim. "His tune will change if the *huertistas* lose."

Will nodded in agreement. "Everywhere you look, Huerta is under siege. There's no way he can survive, and there's no way any of the rebel leaders will support whoever claims the presidency."

"So who wins?"

"Whoever Wilson chooses to recognize. I hope he has sense enough not to choose Villa. Huerta is a barbarian. Villa is a common brigand."

"Who *should* he support?" asked Jim.

"Carranza is the only one of the bunch who can read and write. How's that for qualifications?" said Buckley. "He loves the Germans even more than Huerta, which is another reason President Wilson must intervene. The President may not soil his hands with concerns for American property and American lives in Mexico, but even he and his pacifist Secretary of State Bryan surely would not allow a German satrapy on our southern border."

"What do your *mexicano* friends think?" asked Jim. "Do they want the U.S. to intervene?"

"It depends who you talk to. Mexicans who want the bloodshed to end would vote for intervention. Others enjoy the prosperity that breeds from anarchy."

"*My* Mexican friends think intervention is *loco* crazy," said Jim. "You and I run with different crowds."

"I'm sure we do. Jim, have you noticed the number of war correspondents? I've never seen so many newspaper men."

"When the bullets start flying, the whores raise the rent, the foreigners take to their fortresses, the *federales* go on a binge, and the war correspondents surface like long lost heirs," replied Jim. "I swear it's more amusing than a family reunion. Did you ever hear from your friend, Mr. House?"

"Not a word," answered Will. "Our government has turned its back on hundreds of millions of American investment and thousands of its citizens. We who stay must remain by our own wits and resources. Expect no help from Uncle Sam."

"You always look at the bright side, don't you, Will? Are you thinking of pulling out, then?"

"Until the rebels or the federals resolve who controls Tampico, I'm staying put," replied Buckley.

"Just like those old mule deer in West Texas. When in doubt, stay put and don't move. It may not be a bad defense."

"Hall, you're prescient."

"Prescient, what does that word mean?" asked Jim and he took out a piece of paper from his shirt pocket. When Will explained the meaning, Jim wrote down the definition.

"What are you doing?" asked Will.

"I may turn into a war correspondent," Jim said with a smile.

"Improving your vocabulary, are you?" Will Buckley was amused.

"Running with you educated types whetted my appetite," replied Jim. "It doesn't take a genius to see what an education can do for you. The way those newspaper boys drink, journalists must have better expense accounts than oil field scouts."

December 27, 1913

Sweetheart Lady:

I am absolutely frantic about you. There are no telegrams and from the only letters I receive from you, I know you are not getting my letters and I absolutely do not know what is to be done.

I am quite sure that we will not be again separated, dearest. Life is too short to have all of the trouble and worry which has been coming along.

Everything in Tampico is as dead as a door nail. In fact I just have two things to do. One is to worry about you and the other is to work.

I am rather sorry that you have decided not to go to the hospital. I know you will probably be all right but I do know that when one wants a hospital, they want it ever so badly. Sweetheart beaner, if anything should happen to you, I don't know what I'll do. You are this whole world and all of the light in it and you are all I have (so far as I know there may be two of you now).

I do so hope that you get this letter, little lover heart, because I love you and think of you, and write to you all of the time.

You are my sweet baby queen and when I have you I'll be the very happiest person in this whole wide world.

Beaner, telegraph me every day whatever happens.

You are the best and dearest and sweetest woman alive and I send you thousands and millions of kisses.
Your lover and husband,
Everette

"Mr. De, you're walking the floor like a pacing horse. You've lit two cigars while I've been standing here," said Jim. "Worrying never fixed a thing."

"It's been almost a month since I heard from Nell. The baby was due last week. Lord, if anything happened to my Nellie…"

"She's in good hands. Everything will be all right. No news doesn't mean a thing in Tampico."

December 30, 1913

Snoozer Bean:
I got your father's telegram this morning about nine o'clock and I have been insanely happy all day to know that both you and the baby have come through nicely. I wish that I could see you right now for I feel very, very proud of you but Mrs. Hodgson says that she wishes I could see the baby before it was old enough to look decent because she is sure it would take some of the conceit out of me but I replied that I am sure she is bigger than Rosa Hayes or Betty Barnhart and twice as smart. Beaner, don't you think it would be nice to call her Eleanor

Virginia DeGolyer or Eleanor Goodrich DeGolyer and then we could call her Nell.

I am expecting more news about such a wonderful thing as this new baby just as soon as its mamma is well enough to write. But the most important thing than the baby is the mamma herself. I am comforted with the telegram that you are "doing fine" but after all, that was only fifty minutes after the baby's birth and I am awaiting another telegram today.

Beaner, I am trying to ascertain when you and the baby can travel. It is entirely probable that we will return to Mexico via Cuba which will break the journey up into easy stages and bring us on a ship with a good doctor in order that there will be no risk in case of possible illness on the part of the junior member of the firm. Bean, when I see that baby, I'll realize that there are three of us but at present we still seem to be two and a possibility.

All day I have been trying to realize that you are a mother and I a father but it is too much. I started to telegraph congratulations but that doesn't seem just proper so I am still trying to think what to telegraph. I suppose that it will come to me before long. Everybody I have seen has sent their love or respects as the case seemed to demand to you.

To talk about anything else seems rather silly after talking about babies and mothers especially when the first is your own daughter and the second your own wife, doesn't it dear?

Sweetheart mother, I really do feel an added responsibility. I guess you feel it firsthand however so I can't tell very much about it. I am wild to know more about my daughter. Mrs. Hodgson is sending you the copy of a poem "My Daughter, oh, My Daughter" which someone sent to Dr.'s mother upon the occasion of the birth of his elder sister. The poem was in turn sent to Mrs. H. upon the birth of Florence. Incidentally, Mrs. H. is writing volumes of instructions and is writing to the baby. She says that she hasn't anything to say to you at all but that there is a lot to be said to the baby. She probably wants to tell the baby about its parents so you had better read the letter first.

Sweetheart wife, I am hoping and praying that everything will come along safely and nicely and I congratulate you on choosing a baby girl. I hope she will grow to be a woman just like her dearest mother. With love to both of you.

Her father,
Everette

Two weeks later, De finally received a letter from the States dated New Year's Eve. Telegraph communications had been severed again and again. Mail by packet from the U.S. ships was the only reliable connection to the outside world and the mail packet arrived at best once a week. The letter was from Nell's mother.

December 31, 1913
Dear De:

I want to tell you about your family and I know you will hurry home to see them. Nell was taken sick Sunday night about 11 o'clock but had been having pains for three days before. She was sick all day Monday, but real hard pain until 7:30pm Monday. Had about one hour of hard labor. Dr. said she could have had it sooner but he kept it back with a little chloroform so she would not be lacerated. It came without the use of instruments and is a nice fat Papa girl. Looks like you and Pearl. She weighs 9 pounds. Is good and sleeps nearly all the time except when the nurse washes her, she then blinks at this old world. Nell is doing just fine. Is hungry and looks well and thinks her baby is the thing. I am so glad Nell is here instead of the hospital. I can help to see after her and at a saving of all of $100 to you in expense. Robert wants to see the baby every 5 min. He goes in and peeps under her little pink and blue covers at her while she sleeps. We have Mrs. Butler for her nurse. She is good and has had lots of experience.

I am so glad she is doing so nicely and hope it will continue. The baby grabs hold and nurses like she understands it. The first time she got a good hold and began in earnest Nell said what is she doing Mama, "I am no all day sucker." Hope you can come soon but don't take her back to Mexico too soon.

We will take good care of them for you. But come when you can. Love from your wife and daughter to its papa.

Lovingly,
Mother Goodrich

P.S from your wife: Sweetheart, her ears are just as flat as can be – I wish I could have you see her. I will write soon. Love Nell

The news of his daughter filled De with a deep happiness he had not known, and an anxiety. He should have been with Nell for their daughter's birth.

Could he not have simply taken French leave like he did when he returned to marry Nell? Back then, though, El Aguila's exploration program wasn't on his shoulders. Given the siege and his responsibilities, the thought of catching the next ship to the States led nowhere except to a formless guilt. How much longer before he saw Nell and his daughter?

De filled his days pouring over geological maps and well reports. He sent Jim to the field weekly to bring in news. The two field geologists, Ben Belt and Charlie Hamilton, both reported that rebels constantly visited the Potrero and Naranjos camps and took food or whatever caught their eye. Hamilton reported that the rebels were courteous to him, but he nevertheless hid his horse in the monte when he camped alone at night.

De tore open the letter. It was the first he had received from Nell since before the baby was born.

> *Sunday*
> *January 18, 1914*
>
> *My Own Husband – Lover:*
>   *I have waited and waited to write to you thinking that you were on the road to me and that you would not receive the letters. I hadn't had a telegram for ten days and no letters have come for two weeks. But on the 16ᵗʰ a telegram came saying you would leave for Norman early in February and suggesting that the baby girl be called Eleanor Virginia. It made me sick at heart to have to wire back to you that her announcements were already out. But lover, I was so sure that you wanted her named Nell Virginia that I didn't even think of wiring to ask you about it. I loved the little message you sent us about both of us being your "Snoozer, and bean and everything." It was doubly nice because that was your very own little code for your beaux. Of course I am dreadfully disappointed as I know we are not to see you until February and for you not to have seen the li'l baby. But before I begin to tell you what a darling she is I shall have to confess to being flat on*

my back with a nurse in attendance. I don't want you to be worried because it is nothing more serious than trouble with my breasts, but I have been very sick with them. I have had daily chills for a week and then the highest sort of fever afterwards and we feared having to lance one of them.

It is what mamma used to have and is called 'weed in the breast' or 'caked breast'. When the milk ducts once act right the nurse says I'll be all well and good but I have to lie still and not make myself take cold. Lover, I have cried for you every day since the baby came. I nerved myself for the endless months until the baby should come. I nerved myself for the arrival itself, without your sweet self to help. But it didn't occur to me that there was anything on earth or in Mexico that could keep us apart after the baby came. I, surely, with you have learned patience don't you think so, dearest? The very longest time we have ever been apart before lacked a few days of being four months, and this lacks only a month being nine months. Well, anyhow I've begun to count to myself that if you should come the first week of February it will be only three weeks. For otherwise I should go raving mad to see you while I am so lonely for you and want you to see our daughter so.

Sweetest heart, it makes me sick to think you are losing all of our daughters 'new-baby' look. She is developing so fast that by the time you come you will never be able to realize what a mite she has been. She is the prettiest, whitest, best darling you can imagine, lover, and promises to be everything we could want in a baby girl. She is absolutely perfectly formed – the prettiest little hands with long tapering fingers, dainty little ears, a cupid's bow mouth and our deepest wish – red-gold hair that is going to curl. She is perfectly well, eats like a pig despite my poor breasts. I often think of our rose kisses – how sweet they were and they are a great help now in bearing my pain and inconvenience because I remember that I am bearing it all for the same sweetheart and for his baby sweetheart.

Precious, please try to get another letter or so through. I awoke crying last night because I hadn't had a letter from you for two weeks.

I love you, husband mine and I do hope to be able to write you that I am well in another few days. Wire me and write me.

I kiss Nell Virginia for you.

Your Truest Wife, Nell

De re-read the letter three times. His heart ached to see Nell and the baby. He didn't have the heart to write Nell and tell her. Nor did he wish to tell her about the epidemic of smallpox. Hundreds of Mexican workers were reported sick and dying. Vaccinations had been given to the foreigners, but the natives were left to their own devices. With the anxiety of another rebel attack and now this even worse and silent killer, social order was breaking down. Still, he couldn't leave Tampico, couldn't simply quit after all he was contributing to El Aguila's success.

Jim Hall reported more atrocities by the rebels. General Aguilar's Santa Marian troops sacked and burned the villages of Tancoco, Amatlan, San Antonio, and Chinampa. Once again they attacked the small federal garrison in Tuxpan, and this time, with the aid of artillery, the garrison fell. General Aguilar immediately moved his troops into Tuxpan and demanded custom duties from all merchants who traded in the area. De asked Jim to find what he could about General Aguilar's movements. On his way out of Tampico, Jim dropped by Will Buckley's office.

"Will, good to see you. What have you been doing with yourself?" said Jim after a short greeting.

"I have something that might interest you." Buckley handed Jim a two-page typed letter.

Telegram February 22, 1914
Confidential for the Secretary of State

Referring to my promise in the latter part of my telegram No. 777 CAPPY, I have the honor to report that General Huerta asked me to sit down alone with him and proceeded to talk to me regarding political matters for a long time. I beg to herewith submit a synopsis as near as possible of what he said to me at Chapultepec Castle on the evening of February 18th. I report

this to you, for while I do not think that it was
intended as an official communication, it was,
nevertheless, I believe, desired by him that it
be brought to your attention. I have no comment
to make but send it for your information.

Jim stopped reading and looked at Will. "Where in the world did you get this?"

Will turned his palms up. "You're not the only with access to information."

Jim stared at him for a second and kept reading.

He said that the relations between himself
and the United States were a matter of regret and
concern to him not only on account of the great
harm that the same were doing to Mexico but also
on account of himself. He pointed out that all
the representations that I have made personally
to him in favor of Americans had always been
carried out and that, at my suggestion, he
had ordered the entire Federal army to give
special attention to Americans within the
various districts under their command; that he
recognized that the attitude of the President
of the United States with regard to the non-
recognition of Governments which arose by coup
d'etats was the right one and that he did not
desire to criticize but rather to say to me
that, in his opinion, the present policy of the
United States towards Mexico, if it defeats him
in pacifying the country, will force the United
States to assume the difficult and unthankful
task of armed intervention in the affairs of
Mexico.

Jim stopped reading again and looked at the signature. "Who is O'Shaughnessy?"

"The American Chargé de Affairs in Mexico City."

He said that in looking at the Mexican
situation one must not lose sight of the fact

224

that Mexico is an Indian country. He referred
to the difficulties we have had with our pure
Indians; that this Indian population has been
successively oppressed by the Spaniards and by
the land-owning classes for centuries; that
during the regime of Porfirio Díaz this same
Indian population conceived the desire for
material betterment but were given no education;
and that under the regime of President Madero the
habit of revolutions became general as the more
adventurous spirits of the Indian population
continued to rise in arms because promises had
not been fulfilled which could not have been
materially fulfilled.

Jim looked up. "Does he think the revolution is a revolt of the Indians against the Spanish?" asked Jim.

"Huerta is an Indian, a *huichol*. He looks at the world through the eyes of an Indian," said Will.

He said that he realized that the existence
of any government in Mexico without the goodwill
of the United States must be most difficult,
if not impossible, and that he felt personally
distressed that he had been so misjudged in the
United States and the difficulties of so many
kinds under which he has been laboring had not
been taken into account. He did not mention the
question of recognition and the interview was
more in the character of a discourse on his part
than of a conversation with me. I told him that
I could not discuss the policy of my Government
but its stand had been made very clear.
He was very insistent that the Indian has
never had a chance to develop and the Mexican
situation can never be settled by placing the
Indian of the soil in a subordinate position to
people of other and more progressive races. He
said that the present task in Mexico which must be
before any Government is not one of establishing
democracy but of establishing order, and that

before civil peace can be arranged in Mexico there must be a general reconstruction of the system of Government as opposed to that established by Porfirio Díaz, whose Government, however, was a necessity of the times and circumstances. He did not criticize the rebels of the north but said they would never, in the event of their triumph, be able to establish a Government in Mexico and that one of their first acts, if they ever did triumph, would be to turn upon the United States whom they are now praising.

Huerta said many other things which I will not report as they are neither pertinent nor relevant. Huerta did not impress me as bitter but as rather weary of pushing the rock uphill and having it roll down again. From the many interviews which I have had with him of late, I am of the opinion that he is leading a much more regular and orderly life.

Nelson O'Shaughnessy

"Where *did* you get this?" Jim asked again.

"I don't ask for your sources. Don't ask for mine," replied Will.

"I thought *I* was a good scout," said Jim. "You're breaking the government's code. That's harder than keeping track of Doheny."

"We all have our talents, don't we?" responded Will. "How is the siege affecting the oil patch?"

"We're at a standstill. Until one side wins, the oil patch is on the sidelines," said Jim. "Mr. De and I are headed to the field tomorrow."

"Why would you go the field," asked Will, "if everything's at a standstill?"

"Mr. De wants to check a couple of outcrops. He says he's close to breaking the geologic code."

When the company launch with De and Jim landed at Tamiahua, Hippolito was there to meet him.

"Hippolito, ¿cómo está?" asked De as the boat bumped the dock.

"Como la tamalera," the Indian replied without expression, grabbing the line that De threw to him..

"Still selling tamales," De said in English. In Spanish, he continued, "Good to hear it, Hippolito. Let's saddle up and ride. We'll drop by Zacamixtle."

They rode through Tamiahua to the small village of Zacamixtle. Before reaching the village, De directed Hippolito to take them to a stream bed he had mapped two years before. When they rode to its edge, De looked around for landmarks, consulted a map from his vest, took his bearings, and told Hippolito to follow the dry watercourse. At a high bank, De told them to stop and tie the horses. He scrambled down into the stream bed, walked a short distance and found the layered bedding of a marl. He took his Brunton compass, calculated the strike and dip, nodded with satisfaction, and climbed out of the depression.

"Did you find what you're looking for, jefe?" asked Jim.

"I found a jackrabbit," De said smiling. "Let's go on to Los Naranjos."

De was surprised at the change in the country. He hadn't been to this area in more than a year. Most of the villages they passed had been pillaged. The trails between villages were overgrown and in even worse condition than when he last visited. Hippolito often had to step off his horse and clear a path with his machete. Most small ranches had been ransacked and abandoned. The livestock had been confiscated by the rebels or hidden from the marauding bands that now swept the region.

At Los Naranjos camp De was pleased to learn that No. 8 had made a good well. He and Jim spent the night in a half-empty dormitory, and Hippolito stayed with the horses. They left shortly after dawn to make Tierra Amarilla before dark. Twice they were stopped by rebels, but his official papers and Jim's explanation of their activities allowed them to proceed.

Just after sunset in the graying twilight, De, Jim, and Hippolito recognized the familiar outline of *Cerro Pelon*. Since the camp had been abandoned, no rigs were running. Several rebels from one of the camp buildings shouted for them to halt. After examining his papers, which Jim knew they couldn't read, and hearing his explanation that General Aguilar had sent him, the rebels allowed them to pass.

Darkness had fallen when they arrived at the Pelaez headquarters. This time no escorts met them on the trail. When they rode up to the front gate, the house was unlit but Jim saw a lantern in the barn. A voice from the darkness directed them to bring their horses. They rode to the barn where a young worker took their horses, put them in stalls, and poured feed into the wooden troughs.

Hippolito spread his blanket in a stall. Jim and De walked to the house, opened the gate and called if anyone was home. A kerosene lantern flickered inside the house, and a soft voice directed him to enter. When they stepped inside the door, a servant carrying the kerosene lantern led him to the library. Manuel Pelaez was sitting in a chair lit by a kerosene lantern, and rose to greet them.

"Come in, *Señor* Hall. *Señor* DeGolyer, it has been a long time." Manuel shook hands, and gestured for them to be seated.

"Yes, yes it has been several months. Thank you for your hospitality," said De.

"How have you been, *Señor* DeGolyer?"

"My wife had a baby in December, a daughter. I have been blessed."

"A daughter. You are a lucky man. What brings you to Tierra Amarilla?"

"Lord Cowdray again seeks your opinion."

"What difference is my opinion to Lord Cowdray?"

"Lord Cowdray recognizes your leadership in this area. He values your assessment of the situation here in the *huasteca*."

"My assessment? Did he mention my rental payment? It is due this month, on March 24, ten thousands pesos."

"I am certain it will be paid," said De. "I prepared you this report on the wells of Tierra Amarilla." De handed Manuel the report. A quick perusal showed the best well making 125 barrels. Most made 20-35 barrels per day. "I regret that the field has not turned out as he had hoped."

"Yes, my cousins from Potrero and Alazan have become wealthy. Does your company still fight the lawsuit on Cerro Viejo?"

"Yes, it is in the courts. However we believe Mr. Doheny pays the judges to delay the proceedings. Their production from Cerro Viejo is now more than twenty thousand barrels per day and we still have no trial date."

Looking at Jim, Manuel said, "You once asked me about possession in Mexico, do you remember?"

"Yes," replied Jim. "You told me in Mexico possession is one hundred percent of the law." Jim detected a slight smile under Manuel's mustache.

"Lord Cowdray wishes to know your opinion of the *constitutionalistas*. General Aguilar has had great success in fighting the *federales*. Huerta now only controls Tampico."

"And the oil taxes, which keep his government alive."

"Barely alive."

"As you know, I support President Huerta. Carranza and his son-in-law General Aguilar are untrustworthy."

"You told me the last time we met that Madero was too weak to govern. Now it appears that Huerta is, too."

"You speak like a diplomat, *Señor* DeGolyer."

"Oil companies cannot afford to choose the wrong side."

"I understand your company is paying General Aguilar taxes. Is that not choosing sides?"

"El Aguila does not pay him taxes on the petroleum. We pay him for protection from the rebels."

"It is General Aguilar's own troops that are committing outrages," said Manuel. "His soldiers have looted every landowner of our food and livestock. My workers have fled the hacienda to avoid the depravations of his *indios*."

"Have your cattle been confiscated?"

"All except what we have dispensed to the *monte*. The General's men, who call themselves soldiers, must be fed. They hand us worthless papers to pay for the expropriated cattle."

"Haciendas in other parts of Mexico have been confiscated."

"Worse than confiscated. They have been pillaged, the legitimate owners shot or hanged, the productive ranch land turned into a wasteland by *peones*. Villa expropriated Luis Terrazas' seven million hectares in Chihuahua, he says for the people. It is for himself, and not for the people."

"Perhaps the *indios* fight because they have nothing to lose," suggested Jim.

"They have everything to lose. Hundreds of thousands have been killed."

"I thought you did not care about the *indios*," said Jim. De looked at Jim with surprise.

"Then you misunderstood me, *Señor* Hall," said Manuel. "*Los indios* in Mexico are powerless and live in poverty. Instead of pitting them against each other, our country must provide schools. They must learn reading and writing and the cultivation of the land, and honest work in different industries. Only then will the conditions of life of the Indian population be improved. Their conditions are made worse every day by their self-styled redeemers."

"Is now a time to speak of schools?" asked De.

"Only by the establishment of schools can the new generation be educated to the fulfillment of its duties, which fulfillment is the best means of enforcing respect for its civil and political rights."

De wondered to himself if this was Manuel Pelaez's real conviction. After all, he was a *hacendando*, and a *criollo*.

"One day the bloodshed will end," continued Manuel, "and the condition of the Indian will improve, but only with education. Today the blood of our citizens sows the seed of Mexico's future. Did you come here to talk about *los indios?*"

"No sir, Lord Cowdray wants your opinion of the political shifts in power."

"What do you mean?"

"In the past you have supported Díaz until overthrown by Madero. You supported Madero until he was overthrown by Huerta. Am I wrong?" De was not certain how this kind of straight talk would be accepted by his host, but he was only stating the known.

"Loyalty must be conditioned upon reality," responded Manuel without smiling, but without acrimony.

"Even though the rebels did not take Tampico in December, do you think they will make another attempt?" asked De.

"Yes, of course. With Tampico, they gain the petroleum taxes."

"Will you support the *carrancistas* if they remove Huerta?"

"Since the *carrancistas* have arrived in the *huasteca* our homes, ranches, and haciendas have not been safe," explained Manuel. "They are strangers to our country. They burn villages, confiscate food and horses, crops and livestock. They disregard property rights as guaranteed by the constitution, and all in the name of freedom. 'Viva Carranza,' he said with disdain.

"They call themselves *constitutionalistas*."

"It is a most unfitting description," observed Manuel.

"What shall I tell Lord Cowdray?"

"Tell your Lord Cowdray I and other landowners will do what is necessary to protect our properties. We will not allow our *hacendados* to be pillaged by brigands claiming they are the representatives of the people. Many citizens in this area have asked me to defend the banner of law and order against treacherous aggressions of false revolutionaries whose proceedings and ends have been limited to destruction, murder, and personal gain."

"Are the *huertistas* not brutal? At any occasion and for little reason they hang hundreds of peasants."

"Huerta is no Madero. He fights brutality with brutality."

"In this area the *carrancistas* effectively control the oil fields. If they remove Huerta's control of Tampico, Huerta may fall."

"If your government would recognize Huerta, it would stabilize the country. By not recognizing the government, and by allowing the sale of arms and ammunition to the rebels, your government is encouraging Carranza, Villa, Zapata, Obregon and all the others to rebel. Without your arms and without your recognition, no Mexican government can survive."

"And if Huerta falls, what will you do?"

"Survive, Señor DeGolyer. Have no doubt. I will survive."

When De returned to Tampico, he pulled the regional map from the wall behind his desk, laid it on the draft table, overlaid a thin onion skin paper, and started coloring the best wells in gold. Although large gaps were present, the wells could be connected by a narrow trend, a trend unrelated to the north-south orientation of the sierras and the subsurface anticlines. The answer to his search for predictability in the Tamasopo was there on the onion skin, staring him in the face. But what geologic model could explain a trend of excellent reservoir rock unrelated to structure?

He thought back to the field trip to the sierras, to the rudist colony, and to its relation to the subsurface. Was the exposed reef in the sierras the continental shelf-edge? How could another reef be present downdip from the shelf-edge?

It suddenly struck him. "Sierra del Abra," he said out loud. His thoughts raced with the possibility that El Aguila had been drilling a buried reef complex on the edge of a carbonate plateau exactly like Sierra del Abra, where he and Jim and Hippolito had first camped, where the springs gushed clear-flowing water in quantities as vast as…as Potrero No. 4 and Casiano No. 7 and Los Naranjos No. 1.

"*Jefe*, you're staring off to the stars and blowing smoke like it was green wood out a chimney. Am I interrupting?" Jim had stuck his head into De's office.

"Come on in, Jim." De put down his cigar. "No, no, you're not interrupting. I was thinking about the Tamasopo."

"There you go again, chasing jackrabbits."

De laughed. Hippolito's *dicho* had become a joke between them.

"I was wondering what you think he meant by 'I will survive'?"

De picked up the onion skin and put it into the desk drawer. "Are you talking about Manuel Pelaez?"

"Sí, jefe. Things look bad for Huerta. Manuel doesn't trust Carranza or Aguilar. I hear he has plans if the Constitionalists win."

"It's only a matter of time before General Aguilar and his *constitutionalistas* attack Tampico again. Breaking up the haciendas would be their next order of business."

"Yep, which explains why Manuel Pelaez and the other landowners are raising their own army to resist the *carrancistas*."

"How do you know that?" De was surprised.

"*Señor* Pelaez is no friend of Carranza. He said he will survive."

"If his security force starts fighting the *carrancistas*, the anarchy of the revolution could reach the *huasteca*."

"Unless Manuel can prevent it. What's that on your desk?"

De looked from the draft table to his desk, which was covered with papers and books.

"I've been researching the history of the petroleum industry in Mexico," replied De. "Tomorrow night I'm presenting a paper to the Mexican Oil Association at the Imperial Hotel."

Jim walked to the desk and picked up the hand-written essay. "Would you mind if I attend?" he asked.

"Not at all, Jim. You're more than welcome," said De. "You continue to surprise me."

"You've rubbed off on me, Mr. De," Jim said. "I mean it. When Manuel Pelaez was telling us how the peasants need an education, I looked in the mirror. I didn't finish the fourth grade. Reading and writing hasn't been my long suit. I need to go back to school."

"When we first met," De recalled, "you were a South Texas cowboy looking for fame and fortune. Now you're an oilman looking to become a scholar."

"I ain't that far gone, *jefe*," Jim said. "You wanted a college degree. I'm thinking I need a high school degree."

"Well, you're more than welcome to attend the lecture, Jim. It starts at seven."

"One more thing, Mr. De" Jim said. "Would you mind if I borrowed a Brunton compass?"

"A Brunton compass? Do you want to become a geologist, too?" De shuffled through his desk and handed over a Brunton. "Do you know how to use it?"

"Sure I know how. I waded through half the arroyos in Tamaulipas watching *you* use it. Maybe I'll find a strike and dip that you missed." Jim laughed. "I'll see you tomorrow at your lecture."

Chapter Eighteen

March — April 1914

"Mr. De, what do you think of the fighting?" asked Jim. "So far the *federales* are hanging on."

"The *carrancista* rebels are poorly coordinated, but they have a superiority of numbers. It's a mess, isn't it?" said De.

"It ain't no way to run a country," concurred Jim.

"What do your Mexican friends say?"

"The say if General Zaragoza's *federales* can keep the rebels across the river, it will be a replay of last December. But most of my Mexicans friends are paying good money to be evacuated."

De could understand why people were leaving. He wanted to go himself, but he felt as though he was on the verge of solving the geological riddle that had bedeviled him for nearly five years.

On April 9 Jim was standing at a wharf on the river when a boat from the *USS Dolphin* landed. The Navy paymaster aboard asked Jim for directions to the office. Jim pointed to the back of the warehouse,

"How are you Navy boys holding out?" Jim asked the two sailors who remained in the boat.

"We're low on fuel and short of women," replied one. "Captain Earle sent the paymaster to buy the fuel from the German. Could you help us out with the women?"

"The town is full of *señoritas*," replied Jim. "But the price for love has gone up like the price of fuel oil. Maybe the *señoritas* are in cahoots with the rebels. Lob a few shells into town and guess what goes sky high? It ain't just their skirts." The sailors laughed.

As Jim was chatting, a contingent of *federales* under the command of a nervous young officer arrived at the wharf. The troops walked directly to the boat, disregarding Jim. The young officer demanded to see the person in charge. None of the American sailors spoke Spanish, so Jim interpreted for them. One of the sailors pointed to the warehouse and the Mexican officer marched to its entrance and unholstered his pistol.

Jim was curious what he wanted and moved toward the warehouse to get a better look. He had only walked a few steps when the paymaster came out of the warehouse, his hands high in the air, in front of the young officer whose pistol was at his back. The young officer ordered the soldiers to arrest the sailors in the boat.

"Wait a minute, *capitan*," interrupted Jim. "Do you see these are Americans?" Jim pointed to the U.S. flag flying on the taffrail pole.

His words were met with silence.

Jim spoke again to the Mexican officer. "There must be a mistake here. These are Americans sailors. The United States is not at war with Mexico."

"I have been ordered to arrest any American sailor who sets foot on this wharf. It is a secure area."

"I am sure you are mistaken. Our sailors and other country's sailors have been coming ashore at this dock for the past two years."

The officer ordered the American sailors to leave the boat. They both looked to Jim. Jim raised his palms upward and told them what the Mexican officer said. "I'm sure it's a mistake," Jim continued in English, "but I'd have a tendency to comply with a man holding a gun on me."

The American sailors climbed out of the boat and stood on the wharf. The federal soldiers indicated with their rifles for the sailors to raise their hands.

Jim stood in silence as they marched off. He rushed back to El Aguila's office and reported the incident to De. De thought it would soon be rectified. Jim returned to the wharf to ask the German what the paymaster had done to prompt such a reaction. While he was talking to him, in barely an hour from the time they had been arrested, the U.S. sailors were brought back to their boat, this time without rifles pointed at them, and accompanied by a captain in the federal army. The captain asked Jim to apologize to the sailors on behalf of General Zaragoza, head of the military in Tampico. Even though everyone understood his gestures, Jim nevertheless interpreted. "He apologizes for any inconvenience. The captain says it was a mistake made by a young fool. When General Zaragoza heard of the arrest, he immediately ordered your release."

The Navy paymaster, angry and still somewhat shaken, completed the purchase of fuel oil from the German, ordered the sailors back in their launch, and returned to the *Dolphin*. Jim reported to De that all had been resolved. In a city under siege, he said, mistakes happen. Later that day, Jim returned to El Aguila's office with more news.

"There may be a Mexican stand-off over the arrest of our sailors this morning."

"What are you talking about?" asked De.

"A friend at the consulate tells me Admiral Mayo has demanded an official apology for arresting American sailors, and has required that General Zaragoza fire a twenty-one gun salute to the American flag."

"You can't believe half what you hear," said De.

"It sounds crazy," responded Jim. "Anyway, I thought you'd like to know the latest."

The latest turned out to be correct. Cables had passed between the naval commanders at Tampico and Veracruz. Word had reached President Wilson of the incident through a young naval assistant secretary, Franklin D. Roosevelt. The President dispatched six more battleships to Tampico, awaiting the response from the Mexican government.

"What in the world is happening?" De asked Jim the next afternoon. "Have you heard any news?"

"General Zaragoza said he could not render the salute nor the apology without the authority of President Huerta, and that owing to the interruption of the telegraph service he had no means of receiving such instructions to meet the ultimatum from Admiral Mayo."

"What does your friend in the consulate say?"

"Huerta has refused the President's demand for an apology," answered Jim.

"That's all we need," said De. "Rebels fighting across the river, the rigs and oil camps shut down, and now this."

"My friend at the consulate said that if Huerta reconsiders his decision, details of the salute with Admiral Mayo can be arranged. If on the contrary he sticks to the position he has taken, the consul is to send a telegram at once to the representatives of the foreign powers and to all the U.S. consulates in Mexico, who are to advise U.S. citizens to withdraw from Mexico until order is restored."

"The Mexicans will be up in arms against us *gringos*, won't they? It will arouse their national pride."

Jim agreed. "Consul Miller has sent word to all Americans to be prepared to move to the hotels."

"There are two thousand Americans in and around Tampico," said De. "Contacting all of them is a big order. Mr. Body sent word that in case of intervention by the U.S., El Aguila will not be a party to the undertaking. The unstated message is that Americans can't take refuge in our building like last December."

"Can a riled up *peon* with a rifle tell the difference between an Englishman and an American?" retorted Jim. "Maybe the English should make preparations as well."

Three days later Jim walked into De's office, closed the door, and handed him a paper.

De glanced at the heading on the crumbled and torn paper. "How in the world did you come by this report?"

"My friend at the consulate carries out the trash. Did I tell you never to leave anything important in a trash can?"

De shook his head, and read the cablegram:

April 12, 1914
SecNav

Mayo reports from Tampico. Code word Abeam. Acknowledge two dash C and four dash C. Have consulted with Consul and will communicate with both sides as soon as practicable; eight hundred reinforcements for Federals arrived last night on San Luis line same force which went out last Monday. Bravo arrived with some troops; town quiet; general opinion seems to be that the Federals now too strong for successful attack of rebels unless latter receive artillery and strong reinforcements; however, from best obtainable information they do not seem to have retired. Anti-American feeling in town extremely strong; Des Moines off Arbol Grande; will use Huasteca's yacht Wakiva to send out further refugees. In accordance instructions have delivered notes reference destruction foreign property and received reply from Constitutionalists signed Caballeros who states his forces respect foreigners and their interests and will guarantee them also. Property loss due to military necessity will be indemnified at proper time. Received message from Zaragosa substance being that he

is ordered to await instructions as to action
in arrest matter. Have voluntarily informed him
that I will not report my failure to obtain
promise of reparation until noon Sunday. Do not
expect compliance with my demands and consider
it desirable that Department's instructions as
to further procedure reach me promptly. 10pm
Saturday. Rebels have not retreated. Desultory
firing during day. Carlos sailed Veracruz 3pm.
Mayo.

"He's right about anti-American feeling," said De. "I've heard shouts for the *gringos* to go home. Thank goodness our gunboats are in the river. Jim, did the consulate spread the word to assemble in the hotels if things turn sour?"

"Yes, the word is spreading. General Zaragoza is now saying the sailors were arrested by the Comandancia de Policia, not by his troops and that they were never incarcerated. He's trying to save face."

"I hope it's not too late."

The stand-off between the Constitutionalists and the *federales*, and between the Americans and the Mexicans over saluting the flag, dragged on for a week. Business went on as usual. Sanborn's Pharmacy next to the Southern Hotel did a lively afternoon business at the soda fountains. Talk at the bars and cantinas was of the fighting. Conversations were rife with opinions about the successes or failures of the factions. Shooting on the outskirts of town between the *federales* and the *constitutionalistas* could be heard night and day.

In spite of the fighting Dr. Hayes arrived in town from Havana. He had scheduled a review and assessment with De of all El Aguila producing properties. The two spent hours pouring over geological maps and reviewed each well file. De had prepared charts on every producing well showing pressure, barrels/day production, salt water production, and temperatures. Most wells exhibited some depletion after the first flush production. Salt water encroachment was erratic, not correlative to a producing rate or whether a well was higher or lower on an anticline's flank. De showed Dr. Hayes a schematic for his idea of saltwater breakthrough.

He was convinced salt water from beneath the oil column displaced oil from the adjacent reservoir rock, a process he called 'coning'. The Potrero No. 4 and Alazan No. 4 still held steady at 37,000 barrels per day and 14,000 barrels per day respectively, with no pressure declines and no salt water. Los Naranjos wells held steady at 40,000 barrels per day.

After they completed the review of every well, De said, "Doctor Hayes, look at this," and pointed to his 1:100,000 regional map that he kept on the wall behind his desk. "I have made an overlay and highlighted only the best wells." De placed the thin onion paper on top of the regional map.

The gold-colored arch covered a forty-mile swath from Cerro Azul to Dos Bocas.

"Gold represents the best wells. Note how they line up in a narrow band extending from field to field."

"You're right, De, it's clearly a trend."

"I call it *faja de oro*, or the Golden Lane. Since I first joined El Aguila, I have puzzled at the Tamasopo's variability. Wells often exhibit different characteristics from an adjacent well, sometimes strikingly so, which certainly is indicative of heterogeneity in the Tamasopo over very short distances. Some entire fields, like Tierra Amarilla, exhibit little or poor porosity development. Yet the really good wells are confined to only a few fields in the Cerro Viejo, Potrero, and Alazan trend, extending to Los Naranjos and as far as Casiano. Within those fields are poor producers, yet a trend of good reservoir rock is clearly evident. The trend is an arcuate shape." He pointed to his overlay. The band looked like a narrow golden arch.

"The lineament doesn't correlate to structure. Why not?" asked Dr. Hayes.

"Geologists will probably be discussing that for the next hundred years," replied De. "Observe that structural alignment occurs on a regional scale, mirroring the alignment of the sierras. The Sierra Madre Oriental trends north-south and the subsurface anticlines trend north-south, which tells me they were formed by the same compressional forces, and probably contemporaneously with the mountains. But the trend of good wells is in an arc and indicates a stratigraphic and not a structural lineament."

"I agree. Go on, Mr. DeGolyer." De could tell Dr. Hayes was intrigued with his theory.

"The arc of good wells follows an ancient rudist reef at the edge of a carbonate plateau, a plateau exactly like Sierra del Abra," continued De. "The reef is highly porous dolomite and was not cemented like the one I observed in the sierras. At the same time the reef was formed, limestone was deposited in slightly deeper water adjacent to the reef. The adjacent limestone represents a stratigraphic change. Move away from the dolomitic reef, sometimes only a short distance, and you encounter much less porous limestone. The reef was leached out, forming cave systems. Wells like Potrero No. 4 are located within a cave system of extraordinary magnitude, like the caves at the base of the Sierra del Abra. Deformation of the limestone into anticlines occurred later, after deposition of the limestone and following exposure to the surface and re-burial. Thus the present alignment of anticlines occurred as a separate event, disassociated with the arc of good reservoir rock. So the lineament of good reservoir rock, this trend," he said, pointing to his overlay, "follows the ancient reef track and is thus stratigraphic...and predictable."[2]

De's enthusiasm for his theory was evident. Dr. Hayes kept nodding as De's explanation sunk in. "We've known for a long time that simply drilling anticlines is not the key," said Dr. Hayes.

"I'm also convinced," continued De, "anticlines are not the only kinds of trap. There will be traps other than anticlines. A loss of porosity stops oil from migrating updip just as well as a buried anticline."

"We'll save that discussion for another day," replied Dr. Hayes. "Tell me more about your Golden Lane."

"Predicting where the best wells will be has been our biggest challenge. We finally have a geologic model that explains how to find the best rocks. When they're located on anticlines, the flow rates can be enormous."

Dr. Hayes took out his pipe, and went through the deliberate ritual of lighting it. Finally he said, "De, your regional view has paid off. Are there lease opportunities on this trend?"

"Cerro Azul has great potential." De pointed to an anticline within the golden arc. "Unfortunately Doheny has it leased."

"Yes, yes. I see that," observed Dr. Hayes.

"Hippolito's village of Zacamixtle sits smack dab in the trend." De pointed to the village on the map. "I've instructed Jim to gather mineral ownership information along the entire trend," he said, pointing all along the gold-colored band. "Hacienda Alamo looks favorable. It, too, is leased. The opportunities that remain seem to be in areas where ownership is in small *rancheros* or even in small village lots."

"De, this is exciting!" exclaimed Dr. Hayes. "If we are to parlay our successes, El Aguila needs to change land strategies and start leasing smaller tracts throughout your trend."

"My recommendation exactly, Dr. Hayes."

"Good work, De. Your analytical thoroughness, gathering data, swapping logs, exchanging our information for others has paid off. Putting the subsurface data into a coherent geological model is what we have hoped for. It takes a lot of creative thinking and a healthy dose of curiosity."

De was pleased with Dr. Haye's reaction. He had pored over the maps for months, trying to piece the puzzle together. Now it seemed so simple, so

[2]see Appendix Two

obvious.

"For the first couple of years," De said, "I had more curiosity than data. Now I'm flooded with data. I worry that too much data will obscure loose thinking. If we focus only on making the foot fit the shoe, we'll miss the next play. But certainly I'm convinced that oil occurs in trends, and that if you desire predictability, playing the trends based on an understanding of the geology makes the best exploration sense."

"I can't agree more. This is exciting, Mr. DeGolyer. El Aguila's annual meeting is in London in July. I want you to present this in person to Lord Cowdray."

"In London!" repeated De. "Nell will like that."

"The turmoil and chaos has slowed our exploration program. Eventually the fighting must stop, but in the meantime, we need more landmen to buy leases on your trend."

De didn't respond. He had learned that his superiors made the policy decisions.

"It's late, Mr. DeGoloyer," continued Dr. Hayes. "Shall we have a drink? Let's walk to the Imperial," said Dr. Hayes, standing up. "Excellent work, young man, excellent work! Lord Cowdray will be pleased."

The Imperial Bar, like all the bars and cantinas in Tampico, was packed with a mixed crowd of expatriates, now predominantly American, who drank, conversed, and laughed as if no rebel army was within a thousand miles. Looking for a table in the crowded bar, De wondered how an impending threat of destruction could energize people in a city under siege.

"Isn't this fighting a mess?" said Dr. Hayes as they squeezed into a table.

"Isn't it, though?" agreed De. "No telling when I'll make it to Oklahoma to see my new baby daughter."

"I'm so pleased to hear she and Nell are in good health. Thank goodness they are not here in Tampico."

"Yes, Dr. Hayes. I miss Nell terribly and I haven't even seen Baby Virginia, but Tampico is no place for either."

"I wouldn't want my wife or child to be in Tampico," agreed Dr. Hayes.

De nodded. He desperately wanted to ask for permission to leave, but he didn't want to abandon Tampico and his responsibilities during turbulent times.

On Sunday April 19 De was in the office when Dr. Hayes told him the latest. "Fred Stork, a friend of mine who works for East Coast, was aboard the *Dolphin* when Admiral Mayo received a long code telegram. Afterward a major of the marines asked Stork if the Aguila Building could be held thirty hours if attacked."

"What does that mean?" asked De.

"The Constitutionalistas have received more reinforcements. The final siege will begin soon."

"Our English co-workers think associating with an American makes them a target. When I walked to the Plaza this morning, friendliness toward Americans by the natives was conspicuous by its marked absence."

"Mr. DeGolyer, a ship leaves for Galveston tomorrow," said Dr. Hayes." I want you be on it. If the siege is protracted, you could be stuck in Tampico for months. You should be in Norman with Mrs. DeGolyer and the new baby."

De flushed and started to protest. Dr. Hayes continued, "Charlie Hamilton will accompany you. Jim and a few other Americans will remain in Tampico. I leave for Mexico City on Tuesday for a meeting with Mr. Body."

De thought of Nell and Baby Virginia. "Dr. Hayes, what a wonderful offer! I can't tell you what this means to me. I haven't seen Nell since September and Baby Virginia is already four months old." He felt a catch in his throat when he spoke the baby's name.

The next day, De left Dr. Hayes office and walked the halls of the building, bidding his Scotch and English co-workers goodbye. He sensed they wished they were leaving with him. In mid-morning he boarded the *Antillian*. The ship had been fumigated and smelled of disinfectant. At noon Jim came aboard to say goodbye and to report that news had been posted in the American consulate to the effect that Huerta had refused absolutely to salute the American flag and that President Wilson had referred the entire matter to Congress.

"Can you believe this, Mr. De?" commented Jim. "Why won't Huerta simply salute the flag?"

"What does your friend Buckley say?"

"He says it's the best thing that could happen. It offers Huerta a diversion from his domestic troubles and the Americans are handed an excuse to intervene."

"What about the Americans here in Tampico?"

"Our gunboats are in the harbor. The *Chester, Dolphin,* and *Desmoine* are cleared for action and are prepared to evacuate us."

"The captain of this ship told us it had just been taken over by the British Admiralty to become a refuge ship if needed. I may not be leaving Tampico after all," said De.

"Well if you do, here's hoping all goes well." Jim shook De's hand. "And if you don't, I'll hold a seat for you at the Imperial bar."

De laughed. "If I don't, I'll take you up on it."

By four o'clock the Admiralty had not commandeered the ship, so the captain of the *Antillian* ordered it to weigh anchor and get underway. As they passed the three U.S. gunboats in the river, De saw they were stripped for action. Sacks of coal and sandbags were piled on the decks for defense from small arms fire. When they passed the Mexican gunboat *Bravo,* no one waved.

As the ship traversed the Panuco River to La Barra and on into the Gulf of Mexico, De thought about the last four and a half years. So much had happened. He lit a cigar and blew smoke at the ship's wake. Unlocking the geologic puzzle was deeply satisfying, but now that he was a father, living in Mexico was not desirable. Family responsibilities had to be balanced with his career, even if that meant quitting El Aguila. Would Lord Cowdray accommodate the balance, or would he quit El Aguila and start his own business? He knew his understanding of the Tamasopo would be highly marketable. Yet Lord Cowdray had been so generous with him. He preferred remaining within Lord Cowdray's empire, but if it meant living in Mexico, the decision was clear. What did the future hold? *¿Quien sabe?* Who knows? It was the first phrase in Spanish he had learned. *¿Quien sabe?*

Chapter Nineteen

April 1914

After seeing De off, Jim walked back to the Aguila building. The whole workforce was glued to the teletype. President Wilson was to deliver a special message in a joint session of Congress. The teletype spit the message and as it came from the machine, one of the Brits read it aloud.

> Gentlemen of the Congress:
>
> It is my duty to call your attention to a situation which has arisen in our dealings with General Victoriano Huerta at Mexico City which calls for action and to ask your advice and co-operation.
>
> On April 9 a paymaster of the USS Dolphin landed at Iturbide Bridge Landing at Tampico with a whale boat and boat's crew to take off certain supplies for his ship, and while engaged in loading, the boat was arrested by an officer and squad of men of the Army of General Huerta. Neither the paymaster nor any of the crew was armed. Two of the men were in the boat when the arrest was made, and were obliged to leave it and submit to be taken into custody, notwithstanding that the boat carried, both at her bow and her stern, the flag of the United States.

Jim thought it odd. The incident had seemed so trivial and now the President of the United States was explaining it to Congress.

> The release was followed by apologies from the commander, and also by an expression of regret by General Huerta himself.

Jim thought of what Will Buckley said about Huerta using the incident to distract attention from his military reversals.

> Admiral Mayo regarded the arrest as so serious an affront that he was not satisfied with the apologies offered, but demanded that the flag of the United States be saluted with special ceremony by the military commander of the port.
>
> The incident cannot be regarded as a trivial one, especially as two of the men arrested were taken from the boat itself - that is to say, from the territory of the United States; but had it stood by itself, it might have been attributed to the ignorance or arrogance of a single officer.
>
> Unfortunately, it was not an isolated case.

The Brit reading the teletype coughed. Jim looked at the El Aguila employees. Now there were enough to fill a five-story building. Only a few Americans remained.

> As far as I can learn, such wrongs and annoyances have been suffered to occur only against representatives of the United States. I have heard of no complaints from other governments of similar treatment.

Several people disputed the President's statement. Rebels had killed British citizens as well as American. Mexican courts were notoriously anti-foreign.

> I, therefore, felt it my duty to sustain Admiral Mayo in the whole of his demand and to insist that the flag of the United States should be saluted in such a way as to indicate a new spirit and attitude on the part of the Huertistas.
>
> Such a salute General Huerta has refused, and I have come to ask your approval and support in the course I now propose to pursue.

What in the world was President Wilson asking Congress to approve? Jim moved closer to hear better.

> But I earnestly hope that war is not now in
> question. I believe that I speak for the American
> people when I say that we do not desire to
> control in any degree the affairs of our sister
> republic. Our feeling for the people of Mexico
> is one of deep and genuine friendship, and
> everything that we have so far done or refrained
> from doing has proceeded from our desire to help
> them, not to hinder or embarrass them. We would
> not wish even to exercise the good offices of
> friendship without their welcome and consent."

Just as these words were spoken, the electricity went out. Since the rebels had attacked in earnest, electricity had become unreliable. A groan rose from those listening to the narrator. Kerosene lanterns were lit. Everyone questioned what the President's request to Congress had been. That evening in the bars, speculation was rife. What approval had President Wilson asked Congress for?

April 21 dawned gray and overcast. Jim rose, dressed, and walked to the Plaza Independencia. There the talk was the same: intervention or diplomacy? The mood among Americans was angry and apprehensive. Those whose property had been destroyed were outraged that their government would not hold the Mexicans accountable. Jim bought a copy of the *Tampico Tribune* and perused the front page. The paper reported President Wilson's address to the joint houses of congress, but provided nothing about its conclusion. He stepped across the plaza to the Southern Hotel. Its owner, Mr. Fouts, told him the rumor was that President Wilson had received approval from Congress to use all necessary action to insure the safety of Americans and to uphold the integrity of the flag.

"What do you think he intends to do?" asked Jim.

"I have no idea, but I hope he shows some backbone. If this tinhorn, two-bit

Mexican government can mistreat Americans at will, our property and lives are not safe."

Jim nodded in agreement. When he stepped across the street and looked out at the harbor, he saw that the three American gunboats were moving toward La Barra on their way to the Gulf. He wondered why they were leaving. The plaza was strangely quiet. All the vendors' sheds were closed. He decided to ask Will Buckley what he thought of the President' speech, and walked to the Campana Building. When he passed a group of Mexicans, one looked at him sullenly and spit. Will Buckley was in his office, his feet on his desk. He was reading the *Nationale*.

"Come in, Jim," Will said, folding his paper and standing up to shake hands. "What brings you downtown?"

"Did you read the President's speech last night?"

"All but the punch line. I understand that Congress gave him approval to act."

"Which means?"

"We'll find out. Bryan or Lind will probably come down and wring their hands and politely ask Huerta to be a nice old Indian and to hand over the government so democracy can reign. You can never trust an idealist."

"I just saw our three gunboats pull out of the river. What are they up to?"

"Really?" Will frowned. "They're the only thing between us and the natives. Have you ever experienced such sullen resentment? I've been in Mexico since 1908 and have never seen anything like this. Mexicans are blaming America for all their miseries."

"Casting blame on someone else removes it from their own shoulders," observed Jim.

"Yes, well, casting blame is one thing. Shooting innocent people is another. What is the latest rumor?" asked Will.

"My contacts tell me the U.S. has a contingency plan to take over the oil fields."

"I'd bet the Dutch, the Germans, and the English have similar plans," said Will. "They don't need battleships to evacuate citizens."

"What do you intend to do if it occurs?" asked Jim.

"Me? I'll ride it out," said Will. "One way or another, the oil will keep flowing,"

"The question is, will the oil keep flowing with me in Tampico, or with me somewhere else," said Jim with a smile.

"I've been in Mexico for nearly six years and it's always been in a turmoil," replied Will Buckley. "I'm staying put."

When Jim walked into the El Aguila building, he could sense the apprehension. "What's up?" he asked.

"Have you heard? Your Consul Miller announced that all Americans should be prepared to evacuate."

"Evacuate?" groaned Jim. "The last time we evacuated we were stuck on the ships for three days with nothing to eat and drink except ship's gruel and English tea." Jim heard a muffled roar, like the growl of a primal beast, coming from the street. He cracked open the front door. An angry mob of Mexicans wielding clubs and carrying stones passed in front of the building. "Maybe this time is different," he mumbled and opened the door wider. He saw more groups of Mexicans gathering in the streets. He slammed the heavy door, slid a bolt in place, turned and spoke to one of the Englishmen. "Barricade this door when I leave," he ordered, and left the building, moving across the street toward the plaza.

When another angry group of natives passed he ducked into a doorway. At the Plaza Independencia a collection of Mexicans armed with clubs had gathered around a man hammering a poster on a pole. Jim ducked into another doorway, ran out the back of the building, and made his way to the Southern Hotel. In the hotel lobby an assemblage of American women and children were being herded upstairs. Men were shouting at them to leave all their possessions with the bellboy. Some of the children were crying. Jim spotted Edward Lynton and pushed his way through the crowd toward his friend.

"Edward, are we being evacuated?"

"Have you seen the mobs? Since the invasion, Americans have been ordered to evacuate."

"Invasion? What invasion? I don't see any marines."

"Of Veracruz. They say our battleships are bombarding Veracruz."

"What?" Jim was astonished. The President's message had only been delivered the night before. American ships must have already been on station offshore Veracruz when the president's message was delivered to Congress. "Where are our gunboats? I saw them leave the harbor this morning. How can we be evacuated without them?"

"Apparently the gunboats left without a faretheewell. Two thousand Americans in town waiting to be evacuated and as many Mexicans howling for our blood. It could get ugly."

Jim stopped for a moment to gather his thoughts. More and more people were filling the hotel lobby. Mr. Fouts was shouting at the women to move upstairs and to remain in the hallways, away from the windows. Jim pushed his way to the side door connected to Sanborn's Drug Store and exited on a side street. He tried to dodge Mexican men running toward the two plazas. One spotted and shouted, "*muerte el gringo!*" but Jim kept moving and none followed him. He pushed through to another street beyond the plaza and spotted Americans running toward the hotels. Some carried rifles. He asked what was happening. One man shouted over his shoulder that the posters announced the invasion and were rallying the natives to kill all Americans.

By alternately dodging into doorways and sprinting from block to block, Jim made his way to the American consulate. Marine guards at the gates waved for him to enter. Inside the consulate he elbowed his way toward the central reception area where Consul Miller was imploring the crowd to remain calm, to leave all their belongings, and to congregate immediately into a group that would make its way to the Southern, Imperial, and Victoria hotels.

"Don't take anything with you," the consul shouted to the crowded room. "Our marine guards will lead the way. Make haste. We'll evacuate as soon as our gunboats arrive."

Voices from the crowd were derisive. "Where are our gunboats? They've abandoned us! They left the harbor this morning!"

Consul Miller tried to calm the apprehension. "I've sent Mr. Layton to Her Majesty's ship *Hermione* to endeavor to communicate with Admiral Mayo and to inform him of the incendiary notices which are being posted. Don't panic," he implored. "We'll all be safe if we keep our heads. Women and children, keep to the center. Now, follow the guard," and he directed the assembled to fall in and move forward behind the marine guard. He then ordered several men to proceed to the outlying districts to bring anyone left behind.

As he left the building, Jim overheard Consul Miller saying he had known nothing about the invasion, that it was a complete surprise to him, and that if it was true, Americans would reap the hatred and vengeance of all Mexicans.

Having confirmed that the consul knew nothing, Jim started retracing his way back to the Southern. He rounded a street corner and saw another mob of Mexicans. A ringleader was working the crowd into hysteria. A man Jim knew from the camps recognized Jim, ran to him and asked if it was true America had invaded Mexico. In a loud voice so that others could hear, Jim said he did not believe the rumor, that he heard a sailor on the *Carlos V* and an American sailor had started a row in Veracruz and a group of our marines had been put ashore to break up the fight and preserve order, and that by tomorrow we would receive full reports and that the rumor of invasion would be dispelled. He could see the uncertainty rise in some of the Mexicans.

Jim turned and jogged to the El Aguila building, pounded on the door and shouted to open it. From the other side a voice called they could not open the door. Jim looked over his shoulder, saw no one, moved hurriedly to a side door, shouted his name again, and demanded they open the door. The door cracked opened. A pair of British marines blocked his entry. Breathless, Jim asked, "Any news? Have you heard any news?"

Tom Ryder, who was now in control of the Tampico office, stepped in front of the marines and replied, "We received a wireless from the ranking officer of *HMS Hermione* that stated the United States and Mexico are at war and that England, being a neutral country, was not to interfere."

"What are you saying?" asked Jim incredulously. "Our gunboats must have been ordered to Veracruz. Americans have no way to get to our ships. Our women and children are in the hotels."

"I am only stating what the officer of the *Hermione* wired. Since England is a neutral country and not at war with Mexico, all Americans are forbidden to enter these premises."

"What? Ryder. Are you telling me I can't enter the Aguila Building?"

"You should report to your consulate."

Jim did not tell him he had just come from the consulate. "Where is Dr. Hayes?" he asked.

"The Doctor and the other American employees have moved to the Imperial."

Jim couldn't believe the Englishmen had forced the Americans to leave the premises. "Your English skin is as white as mine," Jim said to Ryder dismissively. "If the mob turns violent, they won't ask for your passport."

"The captain of the Ward Line *Guantanemo* is sending marines to escort us to his ship. It flies the Cuban flag."

Jim thought for a second. Night was falling. Crowds of roaming Mexicans could still be heard shouting "kill the gringos". Shots rang out in the early evening air. "I'll remember this, Ryder. Don't think you can boot Americans to the mob and not pay a price."

The two guards pushed Jim into the street and bolted the door behind him. Determined to make his way back to the Southern, he figured the approaching darkness would conceal his return. Nightfall also raised the anxiety that the Mexicans would turn to violence.

Jim moved stealthily from street to street, avoiding the mobs. He entered Sanborn's drug store, scurried to the small entrance between Sanborn's and the hotel lobby, pounded on the door and shouted his name. The door cracked opened and he was allowed to enter. A great din of voices rose from within. The lobby was filled to standing room by Americans who had been streaming in from all over Tampico. The men who let him in immediately bolted back the door and pushed furniture against the entrance.

"Is everyone in the hotels?" Jim gasped.

"We don't know."

He looked around the lobby and recognized several men. Many held rifles and pistols. All the women and children had moved upstairs. He saw Consul Miller, whose demeanor was still calm and controlled. He pushed his way to the consul and asked if arrangements were made for American gunboats to evacuate them.

Consul Miller did not answer directly, but replied that he had sealed the doors of the consulate and placed a written notice that all affairs of the American Consulate had been temporarily placed in the hands of the English Consul Wilson, and that any and all Americans were to proceed to the Custom House and embark on either English or German craft. Then the consul turned to a man next to him and asked, "What about vice-consul Bevins, have we heard from him? He and his family were at La Vara. Any news from the Americans marooned at the Pierce Oil Company tank farm? And Butler, in jail for smuggling arms, how can we spring him out?"

Jim moved out of the crowded lobby and made his way to the mezzanine. He could do no more. He wished again he had his forty-fours. In Mexico, in a revolution, surrounded by a mob who wanted to kill gringos was no place to be without your own weapons. Relying for his own protection, even relying on the

U.S. Navy, had proven naive.

By ten o'clock the size of the mob outside the hotel had grown to several hundred and the clamor had reached a fevered pitch. The glass storefront of Sanborn's shattered and looters could be heard ripping everything from the shelves. At the same time Mexicans began battering the front door of the hotel with the butt end of hand tools, rakes, and clubs amidst more shouting to kill the Americans and to burn the American flag flying from the roof. Rocks broke out the windows of the hotel, including the upper stories. Inside the lobby, men with loaded rifles and pistols grimly waited, knowing their smaller number would not hold the mob long at bay, but the barricaded doors held. Squinting out from a shattered mezzanine window, Jim guessed at least six hundred Mexicans surrounded their hotel. Torches lit their faces, contorted with a mindless mob anger. Jim knew it was only a matter of time before the hotel door gave way. Where it would end he refused to speculate, but he opened his pocket knife and wished again for his own pistol.

Rain began falling, first only a light drizzle and then heavier drops fell, turning into a drenching downpour. Still the crowd stayed, shouting and brandishing whatever weapons they carried. Those battering the front door temporarily abandoned the task, probably to look for a more effective ram.

Near midnight, from the direction of the plaza Jim heard a great upwelling roar. Peering out through the broken window, he saw Mexican troops in uniform led by officers on horseback forcing their way through the crowd. The crowd parted as they rode to the doorsteps of the Southern. The men on horseback turned their horses to face the crowd and spread out along the length of the hotel. A crescendo of angry voices rose as the crowd expressed its disapproval. They demanded blood. Two German officers and a Mexican officer dismounted and walked up the hotel steps. Jim couldn't see or hear what happened next, but in short order the door opened and men in the lobby were commanding the Americans to line up, to holster their pistols and lower their rifles. The women and children were ordered into the hotel lobby. The message was clear: the Mexican army had come to remove the Americans from the hotel.

Jim joined the crowd in lobby. When the hotel door swung open, a tumultuous howl arose. Mexican soldiers pushed through the crowd, clearing a passageway to hold the mob in check. The Americans filed out the hotel, led by the two German officers. When they walked through the angry mob, Mexicans spat on them and shouted obscenities. A few Americans were hit with clubs. In the pouring rain everyone was soon soaked. Jim was relieved to see they were being marched in the direction of the docks. He didn't want to be saved from a howling rabble only to be imprisoned by the *federales*.

When they reached the wharf, another group of Americans from the Imperial Hotel joined their ranks. At the dock, German officers and sailors in full uniform from the German cruiser *Dresden* directed them to embark in the ship's boats. Groups of twenty were put into each launch and were shuttled to the German cruiser. Jim waited to leave the wharf until the last boat. As he left Mexican soil, he pondered what could have happened had the army waited a few more hours, or done nothing to rescue them. He didn't understand why Germans had directed the evacuation. Where was the American navy?

Onboard the cruiser, German sailors showed the Americans to the crews' galley, where they handed out dry towels and offered hot tea. A man told Jim that when the German commander of the *Dresden* realized that no American ships would evacuate their own countrymen, he and another German officer marched to General Zaragoza's headquarters and demanded that the Mexican army escort the Americans to the docks where his ships would evacuate them. Failing that, the German commander promised to bring his own sailors and marines ashore to disperse the mob.

The remainder of the night, the American yacht *Wild Duck* and Huasteca Oil Company's yacht *Wakiva*, both now flying the British flag, shuttled Americans from the German cruiser to the American battleships in the Gulf. By mid-morning the evacuation was completed. The Americans were not told why their own gunboats had left the harbor the previous morning, leaving them to the mercy of a howling mob of angry Mexicans. Though indignant at their own government's failure, they were nevertheless relieved to be safely removed from Tampico.

Chapter Twenty

April 21, 1914

De spent an uneventful April 21 at sea. His great concern was whether their ship would be quarantined. Before entering Galveston Bay, the ship's wireless operator asked if war had been declared. The answer was "no", which spread disappointment among the Americans. The English, Mexican, Spanish, and Japanese passengers did not express regret. At noon a pilot boarded to navigate the ship to its berth. He informed the *Antillian's* captain that they would be quarantined, and handed the captain a notification that stated "American marines have taken Vera Cruz". A great shout erupted when this was read over the ship's intercom.

At the quarantine station onboard the ship De was able to wire Nell that he was safe and in quarantine in Galveston Bay, and to please come as soon as she could and bring the baby.

Time passed slowly the following two days at anchor in Galveston Bay. Speculation centered on the invasion. The captain reported that a message from Carranza demanded the Americans withdraw. While in quarantine, Commander Mori sent off countless wireless messages, to whom De had no idea.

Late in the afternoon of April 24 the destroyers *USS Reid, Flusser,* and *Preston* passed in file down the bay and out to sea. De felt a deep sense of pride seeing their great high bows, four funnels, and low, sleek outlines. An Army transport, the *Sumner* followed the destroyers. Her decks were covered with men and she was accompanied by numerous tugs and launches. As she passed De's ship, the shore batteries gave forth a twenty-one gun salute. Next came the cruisers *USS McClellan* and *USS Kilpatrick*, which flew the commander's red flag with a single white star at her foremast. More transports followed, all being convoyed by the destroyers to reinforce the Army's Fifth Brigade in Vera Cruz. Tears welled up in De's eyes when he witnessed this show of American naval force. He glanced at the Mexicans aboard and saw tears in their eyes as well, but he surmised their tears were for a different reason. As each of the transports passed by, his ship gave three whistle blasts, and received whistle blasts in reply.

Finally, after what seemed an interminable delay, the *Antillian* was cleared from quarantine. With the other passengers, De crowded to the deck, waiting anxiously to proceed down the gangway. When he passed the captain, De shook his hand and thanked him for bringing them safely to the United States. As he walked down the gangplank, De kept craning his neck over the crowd, tiptoeing for a better view, looking for Nell, hoping she would be there. At the bottom of the ship's ladder, just before stepping onto U.S. soil, he spotted his beautiful Beaner, golden-haired, blue-eyed, smiling brightly, and holding a tiny pink-faced cherub.

The End

Photo courtesy of Peter Flagg Maxson

EPILOGUE

After the invasion of Veracruz, the reader may be interested in knowing what happened to the historical events, to the oil activities, and to most of the characters.

The historic events

The U.S. invasion of Mexico on April 21, 1914, caused a great outpouring of anti-Americanism throughout Mexico. Riots broke out, American flags were desecrated, consulates and businesses were stoned, non-American, foreign-speaking whites wore identifying flags on their lapels to distinguish them from Americans. Of the more than two thousand American citizens who were evacuated from Tampico, the great majority carried with them neither belongings nor money, and were incensed that they had been treated so rawly by their own government.

No official explanation was made why American gunboats departed Tampico harbor the day before the Veracruz invasion, leaving the Americans with no means to evacuate to ships in the Gulf of Mexico. Some suggested Secretary of the Navy Josephus Daniels did not know that Tampico was several miles up the river from the Gulf. It was not determined whether the German naval officers came to the aid of the Americans for humanitarian reasons, or to prevent an American take-over of the oil fields in case American citizens were massacred by Mexican mobs.

The invasion of Veracruz was a bloodier action than anticipated. More than 3,100 U.S. troops fought in combat. Nineteen were killed and forty-seven were wounded. An estimated four hundred Mexicans were killed or wounded. In November 1914, the Americans withdrew from Veracruz and the occupation was terminated.

Tampico fell to the Constitutionalists in May 1914. Within thirty days after the invasion, Americans began returning to Tampico and the oil fields.

In July 1914 General Huerta's government collapsed and Huerta fled to the German cruiser *Dresden*, eventually making his way to Spain. In April 1915 Huerta arrived in New York and negotiated with Franz von Rintelen of German Naval Intelligence to purchase weapons and arrange U-Boat landings to start a war against the United States with $30 million in German funding. American intelligence agents uncovered the plot and captured Huerta and Pascual Orozco on a train in New Mexico. Orozco was killed after he tried to escape. Huerta was held in a prison in El Paso, where he died of cirrhosis of the liver in 1916.

On August 15, 1914, Obregon, who supported Carranza, entered Mexico City and a few days later declared Carranza as president. Civil war immediately broke out among the Constitutionalists. In December 1914 Villa and Zapata occupied the capital and were photographed at the Palacio Nacional in the president's and vice-president's chair. In 1917 Carranza was officially recognized as President, and a new constitution, largely written by Obregon, was approved. Article 27 of the new constitution provided that all minerals belonged to the federal government, negating the private ownership of minerals. In 1920 Carranza did not back his ally, Obregon, for president. Other generals supported Obregon, forcing Carranza to flee. He was caught in the *huasteca* and murdered, allegedly at the direction of Manuel Pelaez.

Obregon became president in December 1920. During his presidency Mexico was recognized by the United States in 1923. Obregon was assassinated in 1928.

On August 1, 1914, World War I broke out. By then the combatants' navies depended on foreign oil. During World War I only eight sources supplied the growing world dependency on petroleum. The Allies supply came from the United States, Mexico, and Persia. Germany depended on its supplies from Russia, Rumania, and Poland. The remaining supplies from the Dutch East Indies and India were too far and tankers too scarce to affect the conflict. Since then reliance on foreign crude has become vital to relations among nations.

During the Mexican Revolution, Germany intrigued to hinder the flow of oil to the Allies. In 1917 the U.S. entered World War I on the side of the Allies. Two events triggered the U.S. entry: Germany's lifting the ban on unrestricted submarine warfare against ships of neutral nations, and the Zimmerman Telegram. British agents decoded a telegram sent from German Foreign Secretary Zimmerman to the German ambassador to Mexico, proposing that Mexico enter the war on Germany's side. In return for German support, Mexico would regain her lost territories of Texas, New Mexico, and Arizona.

The Mexican Revolution lasted from 1910 when Díaz resigned until 1920 when Obregon took power. It is estimated more than a million Mexicans died in the Revolution.

The oil activity:

The Golden Lane rapidly propelled Mexico into one of the world's largest oil-producing nations and was the backbone of the Mexican oil industry throughout WWI and into the 1920s. It produced more than 1.5 billion barrels of oil from mid-Cretaceous (Albian to lower Cenomanian) rudistid reefs. The reefs were formed as atolls rimming an ancient carbonate platform. The best oil production is in an arcuate trend that follows the western rim of the platform.

After 1914 new oil discoveries continued to be made in the Southern Zone in the Golden Lane. In 1916 Cerro Azul No. 4 was brought in by Doheny. It blew out at an estimated rate of 260,000 barrels per day and produced an estimated 87 million barrels. Zacamixtle became a major producing field. Leases for four-acre tracts were bought for as much as $100,000 dollars and 25% royalty.

The lawsuit between El Aguila and Doheny over title issues in Cerro Viejo was settled in 1918. Doheny was allowed to keep all the oil he had produced until then ("possession is one hundred percent of the law"), and afterward the production was split equally with El Aguila.

In August 1914, El Aguila's Potrero No. 4 again blew out and caught fire. After four months the well was once again brought under control without apparent damage to the reservoir. The well continued to flow 35,000 barrels per day until 1918 when salt water began encroaching. Its total production was estimated to be more than 130 million barrels, making it still today one of the world's greatest oil wells.

The minor characters:

Geoffrey Jeffreys (1885-1953) went to Mexico in 1904 as assistant field geologist to S. Pearson & Son, Ltd., predecessor to El Aguila Company of Mexico. He rode jungle trails through Mexico and Venezuela, mapping oil seeps and surface geology. He left El Aguila of his own volition, spent his career as a consulting geologist, and died in Jackson, Mississippi.

Chester Washburne worked as a geological consultant and in the 1920s was hired as a geologist for Felmont Corporation, one of the DeGolyer companies. He was released from work due to alcohol-related problems. Thereafter Chester remained a geological consultant.

Ben Belt (1889-1962) graduated in 1910 from the University of Oklahoma with a degree in geology. He worked for El Aguila in Mexico until 1914 when he went to work for Mexican-Gulf Oil. In 1917 he became chief geologist for Gulf Oil Corporation. He retired from Gulf in 1955 as vice president and managing executive.

Charles W. Hamilton worked for the Oklahoma Geological Survey under Charles Gould. He met Everette DeGolyer in Norman in 1911 when De returned to complete his degree. Hamilton spent forty-five years in the oil business, capping his career as a vice-president for Gulf Oil Corporation.

J.B. Body (1867-1940) was educated at City of London College and at age

23 started work for S. Pearson and Son, Ltd., Lord Cowdray's company. He worked twenty-five years in Mexico, overseeing construction of the Grand Canal, Veracruz Harbor, and the railroad across the Isthmus of Tehuantepec, as well as El Aguila's oil activities. He returned to England in 1915 and remained with the company another twenty-five years until his death.

Amon Robertson (1899-1972) was shanghaied to the Tampico oil fields when he was fourteen years old. He was married in Tijuana, had two daughters, and eventually became a Church of Christ preacher.

Ludwig Witzke left Germany in 1912 at age 24, became involved in German intrigues in Mexico, and was arrested in 1918 in Nogales, Arizona.

Reverend William Bayard Hale worked on President Wilson's 1912 election campaign and was dispatched by the President as an undercover agent to report on the Mexican situation. He conspired to take U.S. Ambassador Henry Lane Wilson's place. He was later exposed to be a German spy.

Edward Lynton worked for the Consolidated Copper Company in Cananea, Sonora. Following a bloody strike, the mines were closed and he migrated to the oil boom in Tampico. Lynton briefly worked for El Aguila in 1919-1920, and eventually became a geologist for the Standard Oil Company of California.

The major characters:

Manuel Pelaez (1885-1964) was one of the more enduring figures of the Revolution. When political power shifted, he changed allegiance. In December 1916 he returned from exile and formed his own well-paid army in the Huasteca to protect the owners of haciendas and smaller ranches. To pay for his army, Pelaez charged each of the larger oil companies 30,000 pesos per month. Probably as a result of his army, the Huasteca region suffered less depravation than other areas of Mexico. During the revolution, oil continued to flow with few interruptions. Manuel Pelaez died of natural causes at age 79.

William F. Buckley Sr. (1881-1958) received a law degree from the University of Texas in 1905, and in 1908 with two brothers opened law offices in Mexico. In 1913 he founded the Pantepec Oil Company in Tampico. In 1915 he gave up his law practice to speculate in oil leases. In 1921 he was expelled from Mexico for his activities against provisions of the 1917 Constitution. He became wealthy from oil interests in Venezuela and other international holdings, moved his family to London, Paris, and eventually to Connecticut. One son, James L. Buckley, became a U.S. Senator. Another son, William F. Buckley, Jr., founded the *National Review* and became a well-known spokesman for American conservatives. One of his grandsons, Christopher Buckley, is a well-known author.

Edward L. Doheny (1856-1935), with Charles A. Canfield, discovered oil by digging a mine shaft near Patton and State streets in Los Angeles in 1895, setting off an oil boom in southern California. Due to his success in Mexico, Edward Doheny became one of the richest men in the world. In the 1920s he and Harry Sinclair were accused of offering a bribe to Secretary of Interior Albert Fall, which became known as the Teapot Dome Affair. Doheny fought civil and criminal suits for ten years. He was acquitted of offering a $100,000 bribe to Fall, even though Fall was convicted of accepting a bribe from Doheny. During the trials his only son, Ned, and Hugh Plunkett, a family friend and employee, died of gunshot wounds in a murder-suicide. In 1925 he sold his oil interests to Pan American Petroleum Company. He and his second wife, Carrie, became philanthropists and funded the construction of churches and libraries in southern California. Today the Doheny Eye Institute is a world leader in vision research. The movie *There Will Be Blood* was loosely based on Doheny's life.

Weetman Dickinson Pearson ...(1856-1927) was awarded a baronetcy in 1894, making him Sir Weetman Pearson, and in 1910 became Lord Cowdray, taking the title from the ancient Cowdray estate in Sussex which he had acquired. In 1917 he was honored as Viscount Cowdray. Under his direction the company founded by his grandfather, S. Pearson & Son, grew into one of the world's greatest engineering firms. In Mexico during the Porfiriat his firm undertook projects that included the Grand Canal, the railroad across the Isthmus of Tehauntepec, and the modern harbor in Veracruz. As a result of the Spindletop discovery, Lord Cowdray became seriously interested in oil, hired Anthony Lucas and several English geologists to prospect on his lands in the Isthmus of Tehuantepec and later near Tampico. Under the direction of Dr. Williard Hayes and Everette DeGolyer, his oil company, El Aguila, became one of the world's largest producers from its discoveries in the Golden Lane. El Aguila was sold to Shell Oil in 1919, shortly after Potrero No. 4 started making salt water. Everette DeGolyer kept a life-size portrait of Lord Cowdray above his desk.

Dr. Willard Hayes (1858-1916) received an appointment to the United States Geological Survey in 1887 and left its employment in 1911 to become Vice President of Mexican El Aguila Oil Company. After evacuation from Tampico on April 23, 1914, Dr. Hayes returned to Washington D.C., where he underwent an operation. He never regained his health and died on February 10, 1916, at age fifty-eight.

Ed Hopkins (1882-1940) resigned from El Aguila in 1914 and became manager of International Petroleum Company in Tampico. In 1916 he became a geologic consultant and lived in Washington, Houston, New York, and Dallas. He was a director of Santa Fe Corporation, Petroleum Finance Corporation, and Drilling and Exploration Corporation. He served as a board member of the Dallas Symphony Society, the Dallas Museum of Fine Arts, and as trustee for the Dallas Public Library. He and De remained life-long friends. In his memorial, Everette DeGolyer said of Hop "to know him was to like him and to know him, even for a short time, was to be his friend. He was one of my life's best friends. Theoretical problems interested him but little."

Hippolito was De's *mozo*, or personal guide and servant, who accompanied him on geological field trips. Nothing is known about what happened to Hippolito. The incident of his striking the manager of Los Horcones Hacienda with his machete was true. De loved and collected *dichos*.

James H. Hall returned to Mexico after the Tampico Incident but relations with the British remained strained. On October 20, 1914, he wrote to De that "I was molted from the festive plumage of the Aguila…the high honour of being the detachor is mine." In 1915 Jim moved to Norman, Oklahoma, where he completed his high school education. He led a successful career in the oil business, working ten years for The Texas Company (Texaco) and later for the Barber Asphalt Company in New York City. During World War II, De hired Jim as an assistant in the Petroleum War Department. Jim and De shared correspondence for forty years, and maintained a lasting, sometimes feisty relationship. Jim addressed letters to De as "Dear Mr. DeGolyer." De addressed letters to Jim as "Dear Hall" and later as "Dear Jim". A fine sense of humor and a large vocabulary pervade Jim's correspondence. In a letter to De written in 1926, Jim wrote, "on the surface we most viciously criticize trivialities where the life flux of the subject is broader, swifter, clearer than the turgid waters of the critic." Jim Hall was interviewed by Everette DeGolyer's biographer, Lon Tinkle, in 1971. Tinkle described him as "a man of far-ranging mind and prodigious memory".

Nell Goodrich DeGolyer (1886-1972) was born in New Florence, Missouri. Her parents moved the family to Norman, Oklahoma, so that the children would have access to higher education. She graduated from the University of Oklahoma in 1906 with a degree in piano. After graduation she taught piano and German at the University. She purportedly met De when she graded his German paper. She moved with De to Mexico immediately after their marriage on June 10, 1910. Their first child died following birth in Tampico. Their next child, Virginia Nell, was born in Oklahoma in 1913. In 1916, the DeGolyers moved to Montclaire, New Jersey, while De worked in New York City. Three more children were born in New Jersey: Dorothy Margaret (1916), Cecilia

Jeanne (1919), and Everette Lee, Jr. (1923). In 1936 the DeGolyers moved to Dallas. In 1939 they built Rancho Encinal near White Rock Lake. Nell was involved in many civic activities. She was a founding member of the Dallas Planned Parenthood and the Dallas League of Women Voters. One of Nell's passions was gardening. After her death their house was given to SMU and then sold to the City of Dallas and is today the home of the Dallas Arboretum and Botanical Garden. Nell Goodrich DeGolyer died May 3, 1972, at the age of 85.

Everette Lee DeGolyer (1886-1956) was born October 9, 1886, in a sod hut in Greensburg, Kansas. Throughout his career, DeGolyer was instrumental in the organization of several major corporations. After the Tampico Incident and invasion of Veracruz, he continued to work for and later became a consultant to El Aguila, and in 1919, with the financial backing of Lord Cowdray, organized the Amerada Petroleum Corporation, remaining as president and chairman of the board until 1932. In 1925 he organized Geophysical Research Corporation, one of the first companies to provide seismograph service for the oil industry. In 1936 he organized DeGolyer and McNaughton, a world-wide reservoir engineering firm that still exists. During World War II DeGolyer was a deputy administrator for the Office of Defense and Petroleum Administration for War, and as chief of mission to the Middle East was one of the first to recognize its vast oil reserves, and the geopolitical implications. Early in his career DeGolyer developed an interest in book collecting and built extensive collections in the areas of English literature, the history of science, and the history of the Southwest. He was the principal financial backer for the *Saturday Review* magazine, and was a lecturer at MIT, Princeton, and the University of Texas.

Everette DeGolyer's curiosity and his determination to obtain reliable subsurface data marked him as one of the first pioneers of the oil industry to explore for oil using scientific methods. His work and success advanced the sciences of petroleum geology, geophysics, and reservoir engineering. DeGolyer spent his career striving to understand and visualize the subsurface, and in sharing technology. He was one of the founding members of the American Association of Petroleum Geologists (AAPG) and was its president in 1925-26.

The DeGolyer Collection is housed at Southern Methodist University. On December 14, 1956, at age 70 after a lengthy illness, Everette DeGolyer took his own life. Everette Degolyer was only five feet six inches tall, but he stands as one of the giants of the oil industry.

APPENDIX ONE

The Crude Oil Industry of the Tampico Region, Mexico
March 8, 1912
E. DeGolyer, Chief Geologist, Cia. Mex. De Petroleo
"El Aguila" S.A.

Introduction:

Of the newly developing oil regions of the world, that of Tampico, Mexico bids fair to be the greatest. Development here during the past year has progressed to such an extent that the position of Mexico has changed from that of an importer of approximately one million barrels of crude and refined oils during the year 1910 to that of an exporter of more than seven hundred thousand barrels of crude oil during 1911 and at the rate established to date, an exporter of more than four million barrels of crude oil for the current year. Such material progress in the oil industry in conjunction with the widespread evidences of fields yet undeveloped and the knowledge that the Mexican oil industry is yet in its infancy give evidence to the future greatness of the fields of this region.

No comprehensive report on the oil industry in the Tampico Region has been made public at any recent date. The only detailed information which is kept at the present time is that kept by the individual operating and marketing companies and such material is naturally regarded as confidential. Bearing such conditions in mind, the author takes pleasure in rendering this report to the British Consul in Tampico with the understanding that the report will be used only by the Government which he represents and will, in every respect, be considered confidential.

Area

The area of the Tampico Oil Region can only be estimated roughly since development has progressed so little. The area over which seepages occur is that part of the coastal plain between the Rio Soto la Marina and the vicinity of Jalap. This area is roughly triangular in shape, being bounded on the east by the Gulf of Mexico and on the southwest and northwest by the front of the great central plateau. It comprises roughly an area about 17,000 square miles. Tampico is the most central point of any importance in this district and on account of its harbor, railways, and position with regard to inland waterways, is the distributing point for the oil region. The name of Tampico is also used to describe the oil regions and was adopted because of the importance of the town in the development of the various fields.

Surface Indications of Petroleum

Throughout the region under discussion, there are numerous exudations of petroleum or liquid asphalt. These vary in size from small seepages a few inches in diameter to asphalt lakes a hundred or more feet in diameter such as those occurring at Solis, Chijol, Cerro Viejo or Cerro Azul. The asphalt varies in consistency from a nearby oil (15 degree Be) to various hard veins and in certain parts of the same region, there are seepages of a paraffin base light oil. I myself have personally visited more than a thousand of these seepages and it is quite probable that there are several thousand in existence. These seepages undoubtedly denote the existence of certain amounts of oil in the subsoil near the points where they occur and it has been quite as clearly demonstrated that oil occurs in localities where there are no seepages. The Topila field is an example of an oil occurrence where there are no seepages.

History

The surface deposits of asphalt and liquid oils must have been known to the early Indian inhabitants of the country and it seems quite probable that they made some use of the bitumen in their arts. This is evidenced by the common occurrence of Indian mounds in the vicinity of various seepages and by the existence of a walled up seepage in the vicinity of the present Furbero Field at the time of its discovery by a certain Dr. Autrey in 1868. I have never made complete examination of any of the mounds referred to above, but partial examination shows them to contain broken pottery, burned sandstones and shales, obsidian chips, and broken obsidian implements: the whole probably the remains of the pottery workings of a primitive people. Indian tradition has it that this part of the coast was settled about the seventh century and the various oil springs must have been know to the Indian inhabitants since very little later than that early date.

During the second period of the attempted utilization of bituminous deposits of the surface and the subsoil, various companies were organized and concessions granted in order to explore the various subsoil deposits and to attempt to exploit the surface deposits. These attempts were generally unsuccessful.

The Memoria de Fomento of 1865 states that in 1864 permission was given to a certain Don Idefonso Lopez to exploit "deposits of petroliferous substances in the hacienda de Los Rusias, jurisdiction of Soto de la Marina". This is probably one of the first acts recognizing in any way the possible value of the oil deposits, since it occurred only five years after the drilling of the world's first oil well: the Drake well in Titusville, Pennsylvania.

In 1869 a company of wealthy Mexicans, known as "Companie Explotadora de Petroleo del Golfo Mexicano" was formed with the object of developing and working the oil deposits of Cougas, now know as Furbero. This company drilled one shallow well and drove a tunnel into one of the oil springs, but failed because of mismanagement.

In 1873 the asphalt vein at El Christo on the Rio Tempoal was being exploited, the work probably being the first of a long series of mistakes in thinking that the asphalt was a coal. This work was soon abandoned.

In 1878 certain periodicals of Veracruz and "El Miniero Mexicano" published notices relative to oil seepages in the Canton of Tuxpan. In the same year, a very complete list of seepages in northern Veracruz was published in the "Exposition de la Secretaria de Hacienda".

In 1879 the Dr. Autrey who originally discovered the oil springs of Cougas denounced them and erected a still at Papantla and refined some 4,000 gallons of kerosene from the crude oil. In 1880 he attempted to sell his interest in this property, but the deal was never finished and in 1885 the mining law vesting the title to oil deposits in the subsoil to the owner of the surface was passed and the property passed from Autrey's possession.

Between 1880 and 1885 two wells were drilled at Chapopotal in the Hacienda Cerro Viejo, but there was so much fraud connected with this work that the operations were abandoned.

In 1889 various shallow wells were drilled in San Jose de las Rusias and in the vicinity of Soto la Marina by a certain Manuel Flores.

Various local "coal" companies flourished between 1890 and 1900, but since they worked on the views of asphalt instead of coal, there were doomed to failure.

The third and present period, which is the period real exploration might be said to begin, with the work of the Mexican Petroleum and Liquid Fuel Company, Ltd (English) and that of the Mexican Petroleum Company, Ltd. (American) in 1901. This period is marked by the earnest and effective work of foreign capital. The operations of the Mexican Petroleum & Liquid Fuel Co., Ltd were unsuccessful and in 1902 this company abandoned their operations in the Papantla region. The operations of the Mexican Petroleum Co. were more successful and by 1904 they had practically developed the Ebano Field which still produces oil. About this time various asphalt companies (Barber and Pan-American) secured leases on the various fields. Working the surface deposits proved unprofitable on account of lack of transportation facilities, however, and the leases were sold to various oil companies.

In 1906 the Oil Fields of Mexico Company (English) brought in the Furbero Field and on July 4th, 1908, the Pennsylvania Oil Co. (English-American, Pearsons-Rathbone) brought in the world famous Dos Bocas well. This well caught fire immediately and burned for fifty-seven days. At the end of that time, the salt water extinguished the fire and had ruined the field. No oil was saved, though the well is generally supposed to have been the world's largest well.

In February 1910, the Cia.a Mex. De Petroleo "E; Aguila" S.A. (Pearsons) brought in the Tanhuijo and Potrero del Llano Fields. During 1909 the Huasteca Petroleum

Company (American) had brought in the Juan Cassiano Field and was building an eight inch pipeline from the field to the tidewater at Tampico. Just as the line was completed in September 1910, and when the production of the field had dwindled to about 200 bbls daily, the Huasteca Co. brought in their Cassiano Nos. 6 and 7. The first well was good for about 18,000 barrels and the second for about 30,000 barrels daily.

In the meantime, the El Aguila Company had been building their Potrero del Llano-Tanhuijo line to Tancochin and a line from Bustos to tidewater at Tampico. Just as this line was nearing completion, the now famous Potrero del Llano Well No. 4 came in. This well flowed about sixty days before it was closed probably wasting six or eight million barrels of oil. It was finally turned into an immense earthern reservoir and afterwards completely closed until production facilities were completed. In March 1911, the East Coast Oil Company S.S. (American-Southern Pacific) brought in their Topila Well No. 2 and during the same time the Aguila Company in their Tierra Amarilla field.

At the present time exploration or exploitation is going on at thirty different places in the Tampico Region, about seventy companies or individuals being actively operating either in the actual drilling or in leasing lands.

Production

It seems probable that in 1912 production of Mexico will go to twenty or thirty million barrels, thus bringing Mexico from the position of seventh in the world's production of petroleum up that of third in importance.

At the present time there are nine fields in the Tampico Region which are producing oil, or are capable of production. They are Furbero, Potrero del Llano, Tierra Amarilla, and Tanhuijo, whose outputs are controlled by the Compania El Aguila; Ebano, Chijol, and Juan Cassiano, controlled by Mexican Petroleum Company, Ltd of Delaware (Doheny); and the Topila and Panuco fields, the greater part of whose production is controlled by the East Coast Company. These nine fields have a potential production of at least 175,000 barrels per day, of which 58% is controlled by the Aguila

Company. The actual production at present is about 80,000 barrels. Of the actual production which is being marketed at the present time, about 60% is being handled by the Huasteca Company (a subsidiary of the Mexican Petroleum Company Ltd of Delaware). Production at the present time is controlled by transportation facilities, or rather curtailed by a lack of them.

Storage

A year and a half ago there was little or almost no storage in the Tampico fields. At the present time there is, roughly speaking, about twelve million barrels of steel and concrete storage, either built or building, and about five million barrels of oil stored in earthern tanks or reservoirs.

Land Conditions

The lands of the Tampico Oil Region are usually owned in large blocks and on this account, single subsoil leases often cover thousands of acres.

This handling of the lands in large blocks, together with transportation difficulties, favors the large companies. There are, however, numerous subdivided properties where blocks as small as a few acres may be taken up.

By far the largest holder of lands in the oil regions of Mexico is the Aguila Company. The Mexican Petroleum Company (Huasteca Petroleum Company) and International Petroleum Company are also large holders of lands.

Future Of Oil Industry in Tampico Regions

To say that the Tampico Oil Region bids fair to be one of the world's greatest oil fields is only to repeat that which has been said at the beginning. At present, the oil produced is quite heavy and particularly adapted to use as fuel. Other fields are being developed at the present time where oils are of the same quality as the best Pennsylvania grades. It is as a probable source of fuel oil however, that the Tampico fields will become most prominent and within the next few years. If transportation facilities at the present time were such that Mexican wells could be opened to their widest capacity, an amount equal to at least a third of the fuel oil used at the present time could be produced.

E. DeGolyer (signed)

APPENDIX TWO

An over-simplified summary of the geological processes that formed The Golden Lane follows, as the author understands them today:

Picture the earth a quarter billion years ago. All the continents have amalgamated into a single super-continent called Pangea. During the Triassic (248 mya to 206 mya) the super-continent starts to fragment by stages into the modern continents. Plates of the North American hemisphere break away from Eurasian plates at about the rate a fingernail grows, an inch and a half a year, twenty-three miles or so every million years. Prolonged periods of rifting, which involves both crustal extension and a spreading center, form the proto-Atlantic Ocean and Gulf of Mexico.

During the Jurassic (206 mya to 144 mya), rifting along the western edge of the Gulf of Mexico causes the formation of valleys (grabens) and basement uplifts or ridges (horsts) at the plate boundary. The future Golden Lane will develop over a horst block.

During the Cretaceous (144 mya to 65 mya) global temperatures rise by as much as 25 F degrees warmer than today, melting the polar ice caps, and raising sea levels by as much as a thousand feet. Carbonates (limestone, calcite, aragonite) are deposited in the warm tropical water over the horst block. and are primarily composed of the skeletal remains of microscopic single-cell life forms. During the mid-Cretaceous, as sea levels continue to rise, rapid upward growth of frame-building marine species on top the horst block form a carbonate platform or atoll. Deposition of the Tamasopo (El Abra) carbonates over the horst block thicken to as much as three thousand feet (1000 m) with slopes as steep as 45 degrees to the surrounding ocean floor. Rudists, specialized bivalve mollusks that become extinct at the end of the Cretaceous, build reefs along the atoll's outer boundaries. Shallow lagoons line its interior.

Sea levels rise and fall, occasionally exposing the top of the atoll. Erosion along the platform margin sheds reefal debris, the Tamabra Formation, onto the deeper ocean floor. When sea levels are low, the limestone topography is karsted. Acidic rainwater seeps through fractures into the reef. Some of the limestone is altered to dolomite. Rainwater dissolves the dolomite, forming cavities in the rock matrix. As rainwater and then underground streams move through the buried reef, more dolomite is dissolved and caves form, following the ancient reef track.

Sea levels fall and for a time no sedimentation is deposited over the western part of the exposed atoll. The missing sediments represent an unconformity, or a gap in the depositional record. A rapid world-wide transgression or sea level rise during the late or Upper Cretaceous drowns the reef.

Plate movement in the late Cretaceous shoves the western boundary of the North American Plate into the eastern boundary of the adjacent Pacific plate, forming the Rocky Mountains and the Sierra Madre Oriental, a compressional process known as the Laramide Orogeny that lasts 40 million years (80 mya to 40 mya). The compression forms anticlines in the subsurface parallel to and east of the mountain front and tilts the buried atoll down to the east.

As subsurface temperatures increase with deeper burial, oil is generated in organic Cretaceous shales or Jurassic limestones. Oil migrates through sediments into the cavernous porosity within the buried reef and is trapped where the ancient reef track crosses an anticline.

During the Tertiary (65 mya to present) clastics, mainly sandstones and shales, cover the area east of the sierras. During the Oligocene (33 mya to 24 mya), hot basaltic material from the mantle moves up through the weakened crust to the surface, forming low-lying hills on the coastal plain. Oil seeps to the surface through fractures near the igneous plugs.

Changes in the Tamasopo (El Abra) Limestone vertically or laterally are called stratigraphic changes and explain why one anticline can be highly productive and another is not, and why one excellent well on an anticline can be next to a poor producer. The excellent well would be drilled into the highly porous buried reef, and the poor well would be drilled into dense limestone deposited in the adjacent lagoon.

The book cover depicts the oil fields of the "Golden Lane Atoll" superimposed on the present-day coastline south of Tampico. The western rim of the atoll that follows the ancient buried reef is known as The Golden Lane.

GLOSSARY

anticline A fold in rock that resembles an elongated dome; the fold is convex upward, the youngest rocks are on top, and the oldest rocks are on bottom. In the early days of oil exploration, anticlines were recognized as reservoirs holding oil in their upper part if porous rocks within the anticline were capped by an impermeable trap, often a shale. See trap.

atoll A circular coral reef that surrounds a lagoon and is bounded on the outside by the deep water of the open sea.

basalt A dark-colored, very fine-grained, mafic, igneous rock composed of about half calcium-rich plagioclase feldspar and half pyroxene.

bedding Layering that develops as sediment is deposited. Beds of rock are rock units that can be mapped. When deposited, older rocks are overlain by successfully younger rocks.

breached seal An impermeable seal that has been broken, allowing the oil or gas to leak out of an anticline or other trap.

brecciated Rock that has been broken into angular fragments. When a buried cave collapses, the cavern fills with brecciated fragments of the roof and other overburden materials.

Brunton compass A type of compass patented in 1894 by a geologist named David W. Brunton that is used for calculating dip and strike of bedding. The user looks down into a mirror and lines up the target, needle, and guide line on the mirror. Strike is measured by leveling the compass along the bedding being measured. Dip is taken by laying the side of the compass perpendicular to the strike.

buried fault See fault.

cap rock An impermeable rock, usually shale, that prevents oil or gas from escaping upward from a reservoir.

carbonate rocks Rocks such as limestone and dolomite made up primarily of carbonate materials.

cavern An underground cavity or series of chambers created when ground water dissolves large amounts of rock, usually limestone.

cementation The process by which clastic sediment is lithified by precipitation of a mineral cement among the grains of the sediment, usually occluding permeability.

científicos A circle of technocrat advisors to President Porfirio Díaz.

compaction A process whereby the weight of overlying sediment compresses deeper sediment, decreasing pore space.

compressive stress Stress that acts to shorten an object or body by squeezing it.

continental shelf edge A shallow area of continental crust covered by sedimentary rocks or reefs that is submerged below sea level at the edge of a continent.

criollo Mexicans of pure Spanish decent

curanderas Women who use local plants and materials for curing ailments.

deposition The laying down of sediment, usually by wind (eolian), rivers (fluvial and deltaic), lacustrine (lakes), or marine (oceanic).

dip The angle of inclination of bedding measured from the horizontal. Downdip is the direction away from the crest. Updip is the direction toward the crest.

dissolution The process by which soluble rocks and minerals dissolve in water or water solutions.

dolomite A carbonate rock similar to limestone CaMg(CO3)2.

extrusive rock An igneous rock formed from material that has flowed molten from onto the surface of the earth.

fault A fracture in rock along which one rock is moved relative to rock on the other side.

fold A bend in rock or in bedding.

four-way dip The dip away from the crest in all directions, thus indicative of an anticline.

gravity A measure of how heavy or light oil is compared to water. Lower API gravity indicates oil is heavier.

igneous plug A body of igneous rock that penetrates through sedimentary rock from the mantle. If extruded to the surface, it can form a hill or mound.

intrusive rock An igneous rock formed when magma solidifies within bodies of the preexisting rock.

karst A type of topography formed over limestone or other soluble rock and characterized by caverns, sinkholes, and underground drainage.

laccolith A mass of intrusive igneous rock that has been injected into sedimentary rock and solidified by cooling slowly, allowing time for larger crystals to form.

leaching The dissolution and downward movement of soluble components of rock and soil by percolating water.

limestone A sedimentary rock consisting chiefly of calcium carbonate CACO3, and formed either by skeletal fragments from marine or lacustrine organisms or by the chemical precipitation of calcite or aragonite.

magma Molten rock generated within the earth.

mala mujer The local name of a thistle which is painful to touch, translated literally as 'bad woman'.

metamorphic rock A rock formed when igneous, sedimentary, or other metamorphic rocks recrystalize in response to elevated temperature, increased pressure, chemical change, and/or deformation.

oil trap see trap

permeability A measure of the ease with which fluid can travel through a porous material.

plateau A large elevated area of comparatively flat land.

pore space The open space between grains in rock.

porosity The proportion of the volume of a material that consists of open spaces. Porosity determines the amount of oil within a given volume of rock. The higher the porosity, the more oil in place within the rock matrix.

quien sabe (Spanish) Who knows?

sediment Rock or mineral fragments transported and deposited by wind, gravity, water, or ice, precipitated by chemical reactions, or secreted by organisms, and that accumulate as layers.

shale A fine-grained, finely-layered clastic sedimentary rock composed predominantly of clay minerals. Often a source of hydrocarbons when introduced to heat and pressure. Also often an impermeable layer that traps the migration of oil or gas.

stratigraphy The variation in rock type vertically or laterally reflecting changing environments of deposition.

strike The compass direction of the line produced by the intersection of tilted bedding with a horizontal plane. Structural strike is perpendicular to dip.

talus slope An accumulation of loose angular rocks at the base of a cliff that has fallen from above.

trap Any barrier that accumulates oil or gas by preventing its upward movement. Oil and gas are lighter than water and migrate updip, or toward the surface, through porous and permeable rock until restricted by a barrier or trap.

unconformity   A gap in the geological record; an interruption of deposition of sediments.

wildcat   The first well drilled on an unproven prospect

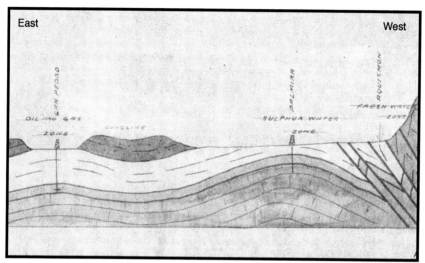

East

West

DeGolyer's subsurface cross-section in 1911.

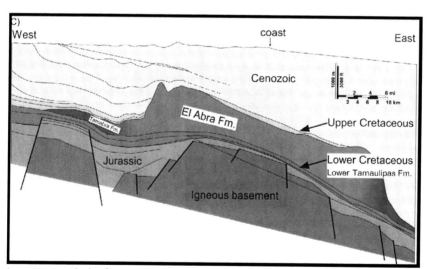

Jason, Kerans etal subsurface cross-section in 2011. Courtesy of American Association of Petroleum Geologists, Bulletin v. 95, No. 1 (January 2011), pg 108.
The Tamasopo Limestone is today known as El Abra Formation.

About the author:

Sam L. Pfiester was born and grew up in Ft. Stockton, Texas. He graduated from the University of Texas with a degree in Plan II. In 1968 he joined the U.S. Navy and served two tours in the Vietnam War. On his second tour, he was the senior advisor to a Vietnamese river patrol group, and later wrote *The Perfect War* about his experiences. In 1971 he was hired as a landman by Clayton W. Williams, Jr. an independent oil operator. He worked for Clayton Williams ten years, eventually becoming exploration manager. Since 1982 he has operated his own exploration company, Pfiester Oil and Gas. He and his wife Rebecca have three grown children, and reside in Georgetown, Texas.

CPSIA information can be obtained at www.ICGtesting.com
Printed in the USA
LVOW07s1021231015

459482LV00033B/1615/P